ISBN: 979830047250

Imprint: Independently published

No Time for Goodbye

BY

LIAM FLOOD

Chapter 1

July 1995:

Drazen Itsakovic stirred in his sleep. He made to turn over on to his side; surely it couldn't be time to get up already? He felt like he had only been in bed for a few moments. As he tried to move, he felt the pressure on his chest and realized Sonja must have fallen asleep cradled in his arms again. He sighed and realized that all was right with his world. He wouldn't disturb her but would lie quietly until she stirred. He slipped back again into a satisfied slumber but awoke as the pressure seemed to intensify on his chest. Maybe Sonja would have to lose a little weight! He smiled as he thought; I won't be the one to tell her.

He could feel a slight throbbing in his head and realized in his half waking and half sleeping state where the headache had originated. Yesterday had been his Grandfather Mirko's seventy fifth birthday and they had partied long into the night. Toasts had been made; songs had been sung; the food had been superb and he realized he had drunk far too much slivovitz. He would pay for it today in the fields. He realized that it was high summer and knew that would only make it worse. Still, maybe it was worth it. He loved the old man dearly and his wife, Drazen's Grandmother. They all still lived together in the small country house: Old Mirko and Edita, Drazen and Sonja and their two children Zoran, who was thirteen and little Diana, who was eight. Drazen's parents lived in the city but Drazen himself had always loved the land and the countryside and he had spent all his summers with his Grandparents. When they had gotten too old to tend to their land, Drazen had offered to come and live with them permanently. He had been scoffed at by many of his friends in the city but he had never had any doubts. From his earliest days, he knew that this was what he had wanted.

Life wasn't easy on their small land holding but Drazen was a hard worker and his Grandparents had helped when and where they could. He had known Sonja from the local village for as long as he could remember. She had given him his first kiss behind a haystack when they were both twelve and they had later experienced all the joys of young love together as they progressed thru their teens. Neither of them had ever been interested in meeting anyone else and they had been married when they were both nineteen. Again, some people had shaken their heads and said that they were too young but that had been fifteen years ago and their love had only grown stronger. They still made love most nights and invariably fell asleep in each other's arms.

He felt Sonja stir a little and prayed that it wasn't too early and that he'd be allowed just a few more minutes of sleep. He knew that whether or not she woke, his Grandmother would soon rouse him. Today was going to be a busy day on their farm. His friend Elvir who owned both a tractor and a cutting machine was calling to cut the wheat that Drazen had planted last spring. It had been a beautiful hot summer and they were assured of a bumper harvest. Most of the grain he would sell to the flour millers in the city but he would keep enough to grind flour for themselves so as to ensure they had a plentiful supply of bread throughout the harsh winter months. That reminded him; the butcher from the village was due to call too at the end of the week. He would kill one of Drazen's fat pigs, half of which he would purchase for sale in his shop and the other half, Drazen would salt and keep for the winter. There was always something to do and there never seemed to be enough time but it was what he had always wanted; to be his own boss and to produce his own food for his family.

He felt what seemed like dust catch in his chest and he coughed to clear it. That was another thing Sonja would be on to him about; he needed to quit smoking. Ach, but he was only thirty four; he could enjoy them for a few more years yet. All the men in the village smoked and it was almost like a ritual when they met in the evenings to chat and have a cigarette. He coughed again and found difficulty breathing; of course Sonja was still pressed against his chest but perhaps he would try to cut down on the cigarettes; yes, he resolved to try.

He half opened his eyes but drifted off again. It must be earlier than he thought as it was still dark. He had detected a flash of brilliant sunshine out of the corner of his eye but that was surely the dawn and the sun rose at what time these mornings? Was it five am? Yes! That gave him another two hours before Grandmother Edita would call him for his early morning cup of coffee. He smiled and closed his eyes tightly. Ah, life wasn't so bad after all.

When he woke the next time, it again seemed like he had only slept for minutes but it must have been more because this time he heard the steady throb of the diesel engine away in the distance. That would be Elvir arriving for his day's work. Ah damn it, Grandmother would make him welcome and give him coffee. They were the best of friends and Elvir would not begrudge him an extra few minutes in bed. He wasn't sure if it was the alcohol from the night before or whether he had been working too hard lately but he had to admit that he felt very tired. The drone of the diesel grew louder as it approached the farm gate; it seemed to hover for a moment but then faded away into the distance. Perhaps it wasn't Elvir at all but another man heading to work on a nearby farm. Ah bliss, he could grab a few more moments of sleep.

A few minutes later, the diesel engine was back. Perhaps Elvir had gone on an errand or maybe it had been a different tractor but for some reason the engine sounded the same. Ah but didn't all diesel engines sound similar? The machine kept moving and again the sound faded. Maybe there were lots of people on the move this morning; and why not? It was the beginning of harvest time. The back of his head felt wet and he realized that he was sweating; another side effect of drinking too many shots of slivovitz which no doubt Sonja would remind him of when she was changing the bed clothes.

My, she was sleeping soundly this morning; not a peek or a movement out of her. Perhaps she had had more to drink last night than her usual few glasses of wine? She was normally up ahead of Drazen although no one ever managed to make it ahead of his Grandmother. He thought again of how lucky he was. There was friction in so many families with in-laws but not in his. Sonja loved his Grandparents as much as **he** did and they loved her dearly. It helped that they had known her since she was a little girl but still; sharing a home was never easy and he was proud to say that he had never heard a cross word between his wife and his Grandmother in the fifteen years that they had been under one roof.

The diesel engine had faded but now came closer again. Poor Elvir he thought, perhaps he had started already? But no, the wheat wasn't that near the house so he wouldn't have been able to hear him. Ah, perhaps Grandmother had asked him to do some other task. The diesel grew louder and he felt the dust in his throat again and had to cough, this time more strongly. He tried to turn on his side so as not to disturb Sonja with his spluttering but he found he couldn't. He was still very tired but he forced his eyes fully open and tried to rub the sleep from them. It had grown darker and the sun was only barely visible now. How could that be? The sun should have grown brighter; ah, unless his Grandmother had drawn the drapes to allow him sleep. But no, he would get up now anyway. He tried to rise but still could not. He adjusted his eyes to the semi darkness and saw a grey shape on his chest. Sonja didn't wear grey. What was this?

The sound of the diesel grew louder still and a shower of dust descended, causing him to cough violently and this time temporarily blinding him. He rubbed his eyes again and eventually the horrible realization dawned. No, this couldn't be, but it was; Sonja wasn't lying across his chest but a man was and on top of him was another man. To his right and left he could see arms and legs and bodies and blood and brains and gore. He almost screamed but at the last moment, self preservation kicked in and he kept silent. But it was hopeless; he was trapped beneath a pile of bodies with just a tiny chink of light visible. He struggled to free even one of his arms. He prayed; he had never been a regular at Church but he prayed now; he prayed like he never had before. His legs also seemed to be frozen in place but he kicked and he detected some movement.

The diesel now became frighteningly noisy as it made another pass. Yet more dusty yellow clay was dumped into the open grave where Drazen lay trapped. He had no idea how large the grave was. Slowly things began to come back to him. He had been in the fields with Elvir and Zoran and Mirko. The soldiers had come from the village and rounded everyone up. They had initially been friendly and said they just had to take a census of all the men and boys. But Drazen was suspicious; he was reluctantly separated from his beloved Sonja and Zoran and Diana. He remembered how the soldiers had initially wanted to bring Zoran also but had left him as he had appeared to be no more than a child. But other fathers and children had not been so lucky and all had been brought to this freshly mown meadow where the earth mover had excavated an enormous hole. People were in such shock that they went almost silently to the edge and stood while the soldiers shot them in the back of the head. Dozens, hundreds, thousands of his countrymen had perished; it was like a bad dream. They had known the war was on and that ethnic tensions were heightened but it had never been a problem in their little village so they had assumed that the controversy would pass them by.

But then the soldiers had come and there had been no escape. He felt the side of his head again and realized that the wetness was a mixture of sweat and blood. The bullet to the back of his head which they had intended to kill him with had obviously glanced off his skull and had just put a dent in it; but it had stunned him and knocked him out cold and he had fallen into the pit. He had no idea how long he had lain here or how many more poor souls had met their end after he had fallen.

He again struggled to free himself. He fought the urge to scream but he was beginning to panic. Every pass the earthmover made now, the diesel engine seemed to get louder; nearer; lessening his time; reducing his chances to escape. He marshalled all his strength and managed to free his right leg. But it was frozen from inaction and he couldn't get it to move. Openly panicking now, he heaved against the body on his right and managed to free his right arm. The smell of blood and sweat and fecal matter and rapidly decaying bodies filled his nostrils and assaulted his olfactory senses. The stench was overpowering; but the will to live, to survive - is man's greatest and strongest motivation. He vigorously rubbed his right leg and managed to restore circulation to it. His left arm was next. He again gave an almighty heave and managed to move the body to his left just a fraction. He now had both arms free but his left leg was hopelessly trapped.

The earthmover made another pass; its closest yet and a huge quantity of earth spilled down on the occupants of the pit, almost burying Drazen in the process. This was it he thought; the next pass will finish me. If I don't get out before then, I'm finished. He fought to control his panic again. He rocked back and forth and from side to side, building momentum. He pushed and heaved only to fall back again, tears streaming down his cheeks. He thought one last time of his beloved Sonja and his little Diana and his fine boy Zoran and he heaved until he thought his heart would burst – he freed his left leg. It was frozen stiff and useless but he could drag it. He started upwards, towards the tiny crack of light which was all that was visible now. The day had seemed to become darker somehow. He made a metre, then two, then the diesel engine throbbed and whined and came so close as to be almost on top of him. He anticipated the massive mound of earth falling into the pit and held his breath. He was almost buried and the place where he had just come from had disappeared beneath the earth. He coughed and spluttered again and, now covered completely in earth, he crawled towards the surface. As he agonizingly dragged himself centimeter by centimeter, he became aware of the import of what had happened; of the vastness of the tragedy that had transpired. He gazed at the bodies all around him. All of them were dead; there was no point looking for survivors. This was appalling but he had to try to distance himself; he had to concentrate on getting out of here. As he neared the surface, he thought he recognised a flash of colour to his left; glancing at it quickly, he recoiled in horror. It was a shirt his friend Elvir had bought in the market some weeks before. Elvir had worn it today and the poor man was still wearing it. Drazen fought the urge to scream and to go seeking revenge there and then.

He slowly dragged himself to the edge of the massive pit and quickly realized that the day hadn't gotten dark after all. There was still a bright sun in the sky. He glanced at the amount of earth that had been disturbed and gasped. It seemed to stretch for about two hundred metres, twice the length of the football field which had been here and where he had played in his youth. He could only guess at the amount of bodies that had been buried. This was a massacre; this was genocide; this couldn't happen nowadays, could it? Had he been transformed backwards in history? The imminent return of the diesel engine quickly reminded him that he had not. This had happened here today, now, in the last decade of the Twentieth Century. He lay flat on the earth camouflaging himself as best he could. As far as he could see from his prone position, there was no one about now. The soldiers had departed and everyone else seemed to be dead. The only other person present seemed to be the driver of the excavator.

He waited until the digger moved as far as he reckoned it was going to go and then crawled rapidly away from the pit. He was so covered in dirt and earth that he was unlikely to be seen anyway but he wasn't taking any chances. He managed to reach the safety of a hedgerow.

He kept his eyes sharply focused on the man who was driving the machine. He was shocked as he realized it was Goran, a resident of his small village. He wasn't a close friend but he was part of the circle of men with whom Drazen enjoyed an occasional glass of beer or a shot of slivovitz or a cigarette with. But why? Goran had never seemed like someone who had problems with his neighbours; he wasn't a bigot or a racist. Had he been stirred up by the extremists who wanted to pull the people apart or had he been forced to do this task? Drazen couldn't afford to stay around to find out; he needed to find his wife and family and to flee this hell hole, this terrible place, this killing field. This day, which had started out so well, would change his life. The innocent boy who had played all his life in the fields and had never wanted to do anything but be a farmer had died that day and was gone forever. He cautiously made his way back along the track. Tears flowed freely down his face as he thought of the tragedy that had befallen his village; he thought of his polite neighbours and his warm kind friends and his colleagues; all gone, all massacred by fanatics. He decided not to risk the roadway lest there be stray patrols. Instead, he would try to return to his home through the forest. He prayed that there would be someone waiting for him as he turned off the road at the sign post for Srebrenica.

Chapter 2

After several minutes hurrying through the forest, he realised that he had no idea as to where he was headed. He had lost all sense of direction. The forest, with which he had been familiar for most of his life, was now a stranger to him. He sank to his knees to allow himself a brief respite. He noticed that he was shaking violently and realised that he must be in deep shock. His head began to spin; all he could see was the green of the forest floor and the bright sunshine seemingly burning down through the treetops. He thought he heard a noise and dived for cover in the undergrowth. After he had lain still for a while, he figured it must just have been a small animal. His senses were so heightened and his heart was beating at a fantastic rate. He tried to take some deep breaths as if he kept on like this, he'd have a heart attack and be of no use to anyone. He would also accomplish what the death squad had failed to do and he would never see his family again. He fought his panic and his grief and forced himself to lie still.

Eventually the shaking subsided and he took stock of where he was. He hadn't walked in this forest since he was a boy but surely he would figure it out. It was not as easy as people might have thought though, particularly in a dense forest. When he thought he had calmed enough, he ventured back on to the path. He checked the position of the sun and guessed at the time so as to make his way back in the direction of his home. He felt that he knew the area well and he thought that he was no more than five or six kilometres from his home. This was nothing to a fit man walking in the forest on a normal day, but this was about as far removed from normal as you could get. Only God knew what patrols he would meet on his way. Could he trust any of his neighbours? Could he trust any of the townsfolk? He decided not to speak to anyone or even make contact with anyone. He'd wait; he'd have to wait until the light faded, even though it would be agonizing. What would he find when he reached home? The thought caused him to again momentarily tremble but he cast it from his mind. He needed to be strong. Surely his family would be safe; the death squad only took men and boys. He thought again about his boy and it almost broke his heart. Zoran was thirteen but looked younger, that was probably why they had left him. But who was to say they hadn't come back and made another sweep. He knew his poor Grandfather was dead. He had seen the man fall. The memory now was almost surreal; it was almost as if the whole scene had been a dream. One minute they had been working in the fields; the next they were loaded on to the trucks at gunpoint.

But it had happened and it was all too real. People would have to hear of this atrocity; someone would have to tell the authorities. He sobbed as he thought of it; what authorities? This land was locked in an evil conflict; a war of hate and bitterness. But someone had to be told; this was an enormous crime; the world would have to be told. But first, there was his family. Drazen didn't harbour any thoughts of revenge. He was a peace loving man; just a simple farmer. Anyway, what could he do against the might of an army? And yet, the sense of injustice, the wrong, the waste and the sheer madness of it all burned inside him.

He eventually found what he assumed was the right track. It would lead him deep into the forest where hopefully no one would be lurking. It would bring him back out into a little clearing high above his land holding. He would be able to see his house from there and he could wait until dusk. He fought the urge to run; care was of the utmost importance now. He'd be of no use to anyone dead and if he was found by a Serbian patrol, that would undoubtedly be his fate.

After two hours of cautious progress and several detours, he reached the little clearing. Having checked painstakingly in every direction, he slowly crept from the forest and made his way to the edge of the clearing where it overlooked the village of Konjevic Polje. In the distance, he could see the larger town of Cerska and the Cerska River. From the angle of the sun, he reckoned that it was about seven in the evening. He lay flat on the edge of the promontory and scanned the area spread out beneath him. It was eerily quiet; there wasn't a single soul moving. There were cows in the fields but there was no one bringing them home to be milked. And yet the scene looked unperturbed. Dwelling houses and outside farm buildings were untouched. Barns abound, some filled with food already harvested, others yet to be replenished for the harsh winter ahead. No one was working; no one was in sight. It was as if he was watching a live video feed but someone had pushed the pause button. That word from earlier in the day resurfaced; surreal.

He now focused again on his own home. He saw the neat little flower garden in the front which his Grandmother tended and which was her pride and joy. At high summer, it was resplendent in a mad riot of colour. He saw the tidy little farmhouse which had been in the family for three generations; he and his Grandfather had repainted it last month and it shone brightly now, the bright white paint glistening and accentuated by the still strong sun. Likewise, his stone barn was in good order. They had also kept its galvanized steel roof well maintained, unlike many of the others in the vicinity where the ravages of winter had turned the shining steel to rust in many cases. His pigs were nosing about in the field behind their pig sty. But where was his family? He again fought back the despair and the urge to make a mad dash down the hill. It would make sense for them to stay inside after what had happened. They would surely have heard the gunshots and feared the worst. Sonja would have wanted to protect the children at all costs and even though she herself would be highly distressed, she would hold it together for the children. His eyes filled with tears again as he thought of seeing them and despite all that had happened, he thanked God that he would soon again hold his wife and children.

But he would have to wait. Even though he could see no one or couldn't hear a sound, he didn't move. There would be patrols; of that he was certain. The blood thirsty militias might be sated for the day but he wasn't going to take the chance. The bones of a plan began to form in his mind but he wasn't at all certain that it would work. He would wait until dusk and then quietly return to his farmhouse. Then he and his family would slip away into the night. They could not stay here, not now, not after what had happened.

His wife and children were young and strong and they would understand. He thought of his poor Grandmother; she wouldn't leave of course. She had spent all of her life here. But what would become of her. She couldn't stay there alone; he would have to insist she come too. He would not leave her. He almost broke down as he thought of the many kindnesses she had shown them all over the years. But old Edita would understand; she would know that they could not stay here now; if Drazen was discovered, it would mean certain death, probably for all of them, if the militias found that he had been hidden.

He had never thought things would come to this. There had been stories and rumours of villages being attacked and atrocities committed in other towns and villages of Bosnia. Some said that the Serbs wanted to drive all the Bosniaks out of the region but surely this wouldn't happen. He knew that there were many refugees living in and around Srebrenica who had left their own villages. People had said that they were living in appalling conditions without enough food or clean water. Others had said that they were being preyed on by Serb militias and killed indiscriminately. There were also stories of women and girls being raped. Drazen had also been aware of the previous conflicts in Croatia and Slovenia and the stories of the horrors that had reputedly happened. There had been rumours of people being displaced there too but he had never thought it would happen here. There was no ethnic tension in Konjevic Polje. There had been Serbs and Bosniaks here for generations; there were even some Croats. All had lived together in harmony as far as Drazen ever knew. He had continued in his naivete to work his farm. Now he knew that he probably should have fled before things had come to this. But to where would he have fled? His parents had an apartment in Sarajevo but he had not visited them there for months.

Since the old Yugoslavia to which they had all belonged had begun to break up around 1991, things had changed and some of the old ethnic divisions had been fanned and stirred up again. The entire country had been held in an iron grip by Tito from after the Second World War until his death in 1980 and the structure that he bequeathed had lived on for a further eleven years until communism started to crumble right across Eastern Europe. Tito had been a war hero and had been immensely popular, even at one stage opposing Stalin and getting away with it. His willingness to allow a degree of flexibility in his communist beliefs and his fostering of enterprise had allowed Yugoslavia to develop at a much faster pace than the Soviet influenced Warsaw Pact nations. Yugoslavia had enjoyed an economic boom of sorts in the 1960's and 70's as a result. Internally, Tito had been clever enough to know that there really was no such country as Yugoslavia and that he was really presiding over six different nationalities. No one had ever managed to maintain peace in the Balkans for as long as he but he had done it by the suppression of nationalist sentiment. He had constantly stressed that there was strength in brotherhood and unity and he was strong enough to be able to keep the nation free of ethnic strife during his lifetime and for a period thereafter. But what is suppressed will inevitably resurface and tensions between the Yugoslav republics gradually emerged. Slovenia and Croatia had seceded and now the conflict had spread to Bosnia.

But Drazen never thought it would come here or even if it did, that he would see his friends and neighbours shot and killed indisriminately, for no reason other than that they were Bosnian Muslims. This type of thing had happened during the Second World War but that had been fifty years ago. No one had thought it would happen again. This was Europe in the last decade of the Twentieth Century. He reminisced now about some of the old stories he had heard his Grandfather relate about injustices and unfairness in some of the towns and villages. His Grandfather had been a fair man and would always give both sides of the argument. He would carefully lay out the story in a logical manner and would work out a solution. Drazen often joked to him in later life that he would have made an excellent politician or a mediator but the old man would laugh. Drazen also remembered that the old man would always finish his stories by saying that they should all be grateful that they had none of those problems in their village. Unfortunately we have now, Drazen thought and again his heart quaked as he thought of old Mirko. He could see him now, up in heaven, for he was sure the man was there, speaking philosophically and saying he was lucky that at least God had spared him until he had reached his seventy fifth birthday. If only all men were as intelligent and as reasonable, he thought.

Dusk began to fall. He had lain here now for well over two hours and he had not seen a single person move. This did not make sense he felt. The militias had come for the Bosniaks but why weren't his Serb neighbours or the Croat family on the far side of the village moving about. He thought it through again; now that he analyzed it closely, he realized that none of them kept cows, so there would be no need for them to bring them in for milking. But no, surely there was work to be done on a bright July evening. What he didn't want to admit was that all of his neighbours, regardless of nationality, were probably in deep shock and preferred to remain indoors. His own three cows were still grazing happily in the field directly behind his cowshed. What would become of them now, he thought. But he had to cast the thought from his mind; there had been too much bloodshed here today. The animals would have to fend for themselves; he would have to safeguard the people.

He came back to his plan. He intended to flee but to where? Surely there would be patrols everywhere and document checks. If they were stopped in Serb held territory and identified as Bosniaks, they would be finished. On the other hand, if they could locate some Bosnian troops, but he realised he wouldn't know one from the other or wouldn't even know where to begin to look. There were militias roaming the countryside and no one knew to whom they were loyal. There was supposed to be a Dutch U.N. contingent too so if they could get to where they were stationed, perhaps they could be safe. But then he remembered stories that the U.N. people were merely observers and allowed the militias to do what they liked.

He thought it was now dark enough for him not to be detected. If there were soldiers or militia stationed anywhere in the valley, they appeared to be very quiet. He hadn't detected a single movement now in over two and a half hours. No, if there were any soldiers about, they had probably repaired to the bars in Kravica and Cerska to celebrate their act of genocide. It was time to move. He slowly made his way down the side of the hill, seeking cover in the shadows where he could. He moved relatively quickly and covered the two kilometres to his home in under half an hour. He first checked the barn and out buildings but there was no one there. His pigs had appeared to have gorged themselves on whatever food they could unearth in their enclosure and seemed to be sleeping.

His heartbeat quickened as he approached the farmhouse. He was completely unarmed so if there was someone holding his family, he had only his bare hands with which to defend himself. He doubled back to his cow parlour and retrieved a hefty stick which he used to guide his cows home in the evenings. He had never had occasion to actually use it on any of the animals.

He took a tight grip of the stick now in his right hand as he approached his front door. He listened intently for voices but heard none. All was quiet. Perhaps the children had already gone to bed; surely not? Perhaps all were still in shock. Tears blinded him again as he tried the door handle. It was unlocked and gave to his gentle push. Inside, all was in darkness. The panic rose up again as he entered. He couldn't bear the tension, "Sonja," he called out but it sounded more like a sob. "Sonja," he called out again. "Zoran! Diana! Grandmother!" But there was no reply. He tore thru the house and out into the kitchen. No one. He ran upstairs and hit each bedroom in turn, calling out each of their names over and over again in ever increasing despair. But there was no one home; no one at all. The house was as quiet as the grave.

Chapter 3

He knew then. The panic which had almost overcome him completely at several stages during that long afternoon and evening was gone. He now knew with absolute clarity what he needed to do. It was almost as if his life had moved on to a different level. Yes of course he was still concerned, heartbroken in fact, for his family, but panic and despair would not bring them back, if indeed any of them were still alive. The militias had only come for the men – that was what he had thought. But he had only assumed that; the bastards had probably come back later for the women and children.

He realised that he hadn't eaten since breakfast. Although it took him an enormous effort of will, he forced himself to open the pantry where Sonja kept their food. Everything was still there, untouched, all carefully arranged and preserved. He had heard stories of families being burned out of their homes and villages but they were now being cleverer about it he thought. They wouldn't burn Drazen's home; why would they when it was neat and clean and abundant with food and provisions and well equipped with livestock. No, they would give it to a Serb or perhaps even a Serb family who would either move there voluntarily or be forced to move from another area in order to increase the population and ultimately justify their Bosnian Serb Republic. Drazen was not a bitter man and right then, he felt that if he could locate his family, he'd be glad to leave his farm – the Serbs were welcome to it. If they could not live together in peace, then he would prefer not to live there at all.

He drank some of the water which Sonja had pumped fresh from their well that morning. He then forced himself to eat some bread and sausage from the pantry. He would need his strength where he was going, that was if he could survive. The army had called two weeks previously, accompanied by some of the U.N. personnel on the pretext of 'keeping the area safe'. They had asked all the locals to hand over their weapons if they had any. Drazen and his Grandfather were peaceful men and gladly handed over their old hunting rifle. The leader of the soldiers had been friendly about it. He had even given them a receipt and had assured them that it would be returned when hostilities ceased and when 'all this mess was cleared up and things had quieted down'. Drazen and his family had taken this as a positive sign, again in pure naiveté. He now realized that all the Bosnian Serb army had wanted was to ensure that when the raiding militias came, the people would not be able to defend themselves and they would be able to quickly and efficiently expel the Bosniaks.

But old Mirko had been cautious. His army service revolver was still in the attic and while it was old, he had oiled it regularly and it was serviceable. Drazen retrieved it now and removed it from its sackcloth cover. He checked and loaded the weapon, satisfying himself that it would be more than useful in an emergency. His Grandfather had kept plenty of ammunition for the gun and he placed this in a back pack which was also kept in the attic. He and his son had used the pack on occasional mountain climbing treks in the beautiful scenic areas of this part of Bosnia. But that part of his life was now a distant memory and was from another time, possibly even another person's life. He calmly returned downstairs where he placed as much food as he could into the pack. He figured he would need to be mobile so he took the absolute minimum in terms of weight. He took the three sharpest knives from the rack in the kitchen, placing two of them carefully inside the pack but keeping one on his belt, where he had also secreted the revolver. He found a torch and spare batteries in a closet. Holding back tears, he fetched his favourite photographs of his wife and children and of his Grandparents from the drawer in the kitchen where they were kept. He wrapped them in plastic and put them inside a small leather pouch which he placed inside his shirt. He then took his warmest jacket and cap; it was still very warm here but it would be cold in the mountains, particularly at night. He took nothing else. He sipped a last drink of the sweet fresh water from his own well and then cautiously exited through the back door. He did not take the time to look round his house and when he crossed the field towards the village, he did not look back.

His life in this village, in this farmhouse, was over – forever. It was now quite dark but there was a bright moon to see by and he moved slowly until his eyesight adjusted and he found his night vision. He made his way carefully in the direction of the town. He did not use the road but walked in the shadows parallel to it. All was still eerily quiet. He found that the apprehension which had seized him earlier had now gone completely and he felt strong and determined. He had cleaned the cut on the side of his head and it had been, as he had suspected, just a flesh wound. The bleeding had stopped and it would heal fully in a day or two. He was young and he was fit and he was determined. Gone was the docile farmer who had submitted far too easily to the militia that afternoon. He had of course hoped that it would only be a routine search and that they would all be returned to their homes but the look in Sonja's eyes as he and Mirko boarded the truck should have told him; he should have known; but what could he have done? Realistically, very little; he would probably have been shot on the spot and would now be dead for sure. There was no point beating himself up about it anyway. He needed all his energy and he needed to focus. His first priority was to ensure he was not caught again; if he was, they wouldn't miss the second time. If he was killed, all would be lost. After that, he had to find his family. To do this, he had to believe; no, he had to be absolutely certain that his family were alive. He could not give in to a single negative thought about this; he had to be firm. He mumbled a quick prayer that he was right and continued towards the village.

Colonel Sefer Milanovic had also had a trying day. He was a tall, handsome man with darkish blonde hair who had spent most of career in the military. He had been born in Belgrade and was a Colonel in the regular Serbian armed forces but he had been on assignment in Bosnia for over a year now. The Chiefs in Belgrade officially took no part in what was happening elsewhere in the Balkans. Sefer and the people on the ground knew differently. Let's say, Belgrade had a strategic interest in 'getting the job done' in Bosnia but couldn't admit this for fear of even worse international criticism than they were already receiving. But they had made it quite clear to the Colonel as to what was required. How it was achieved was up to the Bosnian Serbs and their militias. Colonel Milanovic was not a cruel or a violent man but he had seen enough violence and sheer naked racist hatred in the past twelve months to last a lifetime. He had taken no part in the killing himself nor had he indulged in the sick games that many of his compatriots had and had often invited him to partake in. But he was, after all, a soldier and soldiers followed orders. On the face of it, the order indirectly given to him was simple – all he and the Bosnian Serb Militias had to do was to clear all Bosniaks out of the predominantly Bosniak area of Central Podrinje. In reality, it was incredibly difficult.

They had started with the removal of the Bosniaks from the ethnic territories in Eastern Bosnia and Central Podrinje. The Colonel very quickly realized that he was not advising a professional well drilled army. No, the Bosnian Serb Militias were a raggle taggle band of tough, battle hardened men who had seen action in many parts of the former Yugoslavia. They were reasonably well disciplined in terms of following orders from their own superiors but they generally ignored the tall Colonel. They knew who and what he was.

What all of them had in common, and this was what drove the whole campaign out of control, was a fierce hatred of anyone who was not a pure Serb. He had grown up with an awareness of racial and ethnic tensions but no more than most of his fellows, he had not realized how deep seated and how vicious these tensions and feelings ran. He had seen things in the past year that he wanted to forget. What memories these people had or what had been instilled into them he could only speculate. He was having difficulty sleeping and his consumption of alcohol and tobacco had increased at least five fold. It was one thing capturing small towns and villages in a disciplined military fashion. The problem was that once the areas were securely in their hands, the Serb forces – the military, the police, the paramilitaries and, sometimes, even Serb villagers – applied the same pattern: Muslim houses and apartments were systematically ransacked or burnt down; Muslim villagers were rounded up or captured, and sometimes beaten or killed in the process. Men and women were separated. Women and young girls were raped indiscriminately. While some of the men were detained in the prison with a view to eventually repatriating them to a different part of Bosnia, Sefer doubted it would ever happen. These militias had a blood lust and the more they killed, the more they wanted to kill. He felt it wouldn't end until the entire country was ethnically cleansed. But he was only an adviser on military matters; he wasn't in charge so he was effectively powerless to prevent it. He could call Belgrade but he knew it would be pointless; they wouldn't want to know.

The current offensive on the Srebrenica area had begun in earnest over a week earlier. In the following days, the five

U.N. observation posts in the southern part of the enclave had fallen one by one in the face of the Serb forces advance. Some of the Dutch soldiers had retreated into the enclave after their posts were attacked, but the crews of the other observation posts surrendered into Serb custody. It was too easy really. The Dutch 'peacekeepers' had no idea what they had let themselves in for; had no idea of the type of people they were dealing with. There were some token defending Bosnian forces but they also fell easily. The problem in fact was how little resistance the militias encountered. The leadership had been emboldened by the reports of these successes and the pathetic resistance from largely demilitarised Bosniaks, who had sheepishly given up their weapons a few weeks before. As there had also been an absence of any significant reaction from the international community, Karadžić had issued a new order authorising the Drina Militia Corps to capture the town of Srebrenica and to liquidate the outlying villages.

Sefer knew this would be a disaster. While up to this, the killing had been vicious, it had at least been sporadic and most of the Bosniaks had either been moved or had fled voluntarily in the face of the Serb attacks. But he knew that they had not gone far and most had fled primarily to Srebrenica. This was the last safe enclave and of course the U.N. had 'guaranteed' it, hadn't they? Sefer knew different; he knew that the U.N. were and would be powerless to defend the place. Without the support of a massive international force, the Serb Militias would be able to do as they pleased. In fact, there was strong evidence to suggest that the Dutch U.N. Commander was, if not exactly complicit with the militias, he certainly did nothing to stop them. He felt a sense of impending catastrophe and that morning in the office, he had sent an urgent message to his superior officer in Belgrade which read:

" My Dear General Halidovic –
I continue to serve as instructed and I can confirm that the operations we discussed have proceeded as planned, at times with astonishing speed. However, I fear that we have now reached a crux. Many of the people whom you wish to remove from this region are now effectively surrounded and trapped. Even if the militias wanted to remove them peacefully (and I can categorically assure you that this is not the case), it would be impossible due to the sheer numbers and the logistics involved in this. People cannot simply be moved about in vast numbers as you would move pieces on a chess board. The U.N. have now completely capitulated and have left the militias to do as they please. There is no way that I can guarantee that we can arrange for only Serbs to stay in this part of the country while removing all others elsewhere without incurring enormous bloodshed. I beg your forbearance with me on this if I am to suggest that perhaps this is what our ultimate masters intend anyway. But I digress. This is not for you or me to speculate on. We are mere soldiers doing what we were trained to do. I would however caution you that what is likely to happen here over the next days will live long in the collective memory. What we are facing here sir is genocide, on a phenomenal scale. I do not wish to sound in any way alarmist but please advise our superiors that unless the militias and the Srpska Republic army are ordered to stand down at this point, genocide will happen. It will be the task of our superiors and, I fear, their

successors to explain that to the world. I can do no more than that. Please advise.
Sincerely, Milanovic."

He had received a brief reply:
"Your comments have been noted and conveyed to higher authorities. There has been no change to your orders."

He now downed his sixth shot of slivovitz of the evening and followed it with a beer. His worst fears had come to pass. It had begun. Thousands had been murdered today and this would only be the start. Now that the militias had been given a real taste of bloodshed, there would be no stopping. They would scour every town, every village, every enclave in the Bosnian Serb Republic until every last Bosniak was eliminated. He was a loyal soldier but this was not why he had joined up. He loved his country as much as the next man but these people whom he was advising weren't soldiers. He would not have likened their behaviour to that of animals because animals only killed for food or for protection. These people killed and plundered and laid waste for pleasure and the more they killed, the more they seemed to enjoy it. And it wasn't just the ordinary soldiers. He scanned the bar now and he could feel the sheer joy and elation of the officers as well. Most of them were drunk and they were toasting each other continuously. Stories of how many each had killed were tossed around like the bottles of beer that they swilled from. He had heard more and more gruesome tales as the evening wore on. The alcohol removed all inhibitions and officers boasted freely of how many they had raped, of how they had slit throats; how they had slain the women and children of the Bosniak pigs.

The early morning had been tense. Astonishingly to Milanovic, residents had crowded the streets. It was almost as if they were lining up to be taken potshots at. They obviously hadn't realized the danger that existed. They still felt the U.N. would deliver on its 'guarantee' to protect them. When the Serb militias had advanced, the so called protecting U.N. force had fired a few token warning shots over the attacking Serbs' heads and their mortars fired flares but they had not fired directly on any Serb units. They had been afraid to.

To be fair, he had heard that the U.N. Commander had sent many urgent requests for air support to defend the town, but no assistance had been forthcoming. He had heard that while air strikes had been planned, they were abandoned following the Bosnian Serb Army's threats to kill Dutch troops and some French pilots who had previously been taken hostage. With nothing to hold them back, the militias had systematically taken over the town and shot anyone who had offered even token resistance. They had then rounded up the Bosniak men from the surrounding streets and fields and villages and had executed them summarily. Mass graves had been dug and filled with bodies. Anyone who escaped the first surge was later rounded up or just shot and killed where they stood. Late in the afternoon, he had seen Mladić, accompanied by Živanović, Krstić and other senior Bosnian Serb Army officers taking a triumphant walk through the empty streets of Srebrenica town. The remnants of that group were still toasting and celebrating with their colleagues.

The Colonel was sick at heart and wanted to be any other place but here. He had grown to disrespect and now despise most of the men he was paid to advise. He spoke merely of military matters and had long since stopped advising them to treat the prisoners and the civilian population with dignity.

"Hey Sefer," one of the militia Colonel's called to him from across the room, "Don't drink alone, tonight we must celebrate. Come and join us my friend."

He didn't wish to antagonise them any more than he already had. These were people who had come for a bloodfest and while he was in no immediate danger from them as a fellow Serb, who knew what could happen when they were roaring drunk? He ordered another shot and took it, together with his beer and joined them.

Chapter 4

There were ditches on either side of the road but Drazen chose to keep close to the trees so he could take cover if required. At one point, the tree cover came right up to the ditch and he was forced to walk along its edge. He thought he spied a shadow in the hollow and immediately threw himself to the ground, drawing the revolver for protection. He scanned all round but again all was quiet. He strained his eyes on the ditch and then he recoiled as he caught the smell again; decaying flesh. He gradually discerned the outline of a body at the bottom of the trench. Taking another brief look round, he slid down and risked turning on his torch. The body was lying face down and was quite dead. He turned it over to see if he could identify the person and immediately regretted it. The man had had both his eyes gouged out and had had a cross deeply etched on to his forehead. Drazan did not recognise him but there was little left to recognise. So they were defiling bodies as well as killing them.

He made his way slowly along thru the hollow. It was wide and deep and quite firm as it was summer time so he found it allowed him to move easily without being detected. The problem was that he couldn't see what was on the road so if there happened to be a passing patrol and they shone a light, he'd be a sitting duck. He calculated the risk and on balance, decided to continue. It would get him to where he was going faster and he doubted there was anyone about. The more progress he made, the more convinced he became. Every hundred metres or so, he found another body. Practically all had been mutilated. Many were missing eyes, noses, ears and lips. These bastards knew what they were doing. As he drew closer to the town, the reflected light made it even clearer and the numbers of bodies increased. He even came across one poor man who was still alive, barely. The man was unconscious and was slowly bleeding to death so Drazen could do nothing for him. There were no emergency services here; no hospitals; no ambulances to call. It was every man for himself.

About one hundred metres from the town's outskirts, the ditch ended abruptly. He slowly crawled up out of it and lay flat on the ground. He waited for five minutes, scanning all round him to ensure there were no patrols before he resumed. The absence of patrols; in fact the absence of anybody at all confirmed for him what he had suspected. There were no patrols because there was no one to patrol any more; the militias had assumed that they had killed them all. But where were the women and children? He steadied himself as the pictures of his family flashed before him again. He told himself again, panic will not get them back. Bravery and cunning and stealth might. He made his way through the town, stopping every twenty metres to check he was alone. But all was quiet apart from the sounds of the night. Drazen prided himself that he knew all of these as he had spent most of his life in the countryside. If a strange sound intruded, he'd know it.

He detected vague sounds in the distance. They were coming from the direction in which he wanted to go so he initially decided to circle them. On second thought, he might learn something. He made his way slowly along the street, hiding in the shadows. Many of the street lights were broken and those that were operating offered only a dim illumination anyway. As he drew closer to the sounds, he realized it was some sort of party or celebration. Only one group of people could be having a party in this town tonight he thought. He crept ever closer. The sounds of singing and shouting and the clink of glasses was coming from a bar in the Serb part of town, one that he had occasionally frequented and had never encountered any trouble in. Not tonight though, he thought; all is changed now. He ducked into the alley which ran beside the bar and made his way to the rear entrance.

The bar was crowded. There was a large group of people standing at the bar and a big group of Serbian Army officers seated at a table towards the rear. Everyone seemed to be outrageously drunk. Although he understood the language perfectly, he could only make out snatches of conversation and slurred words. These were the people who had tried to kill him; who had thought they **had** killed him this afternoon. Yet he felt strangely detached and unemotional. The bar was brightly lit and he had an uninterrupted view through the open rear window. To anyone inside, he would be practically invisible. The man at the head of the table of army officers got unsteadily to his feet and commenced to make a toast; something about a glorious victory over the heathen pigs or something. Drazen's emotional detachment vanished instantly and he thought: what wouldn't I give for a hand grenade; or better still, a sub-machine gun? But the moment passed and he realised that even if he had had both, he would only have gotten himself killed. The toast was concluded and all rose to touch their glasses to the leader's and several whooped loudly. Not only do they kill us in cold blood, Drazen thought, but then they drink toasts to celebrate it. He noticed that one man seemed unenthusiastic. He sat with the group and had joined the toast but while he sat with them, his body language showed he was detached and would have preferred to be elsewhere. Perhaps he was from a different regiment. His uniform was different but there was such a variety of dress and Drazen wasn't familiar with army battle dress anyway. He noticed that the man whom he wished to see was drinking shots of slivovitz at the bar and showed no sign of departing for home any time soon. That was fine; He could wait. For a moment, the army officer who seemed detached from the group and downright depressed seemed to look directly at him thru the window and met his gaze. The man did not react and it was only a momentary thing but Drazen did not waste any time. He moved swiftly down the alley and away from the bar. He took cover behind an old shed and watched but no one emerged. The man whom he sought lived alone so he decided he would go to his house and wait for him.

He gained access to the small house easily enough. The man had left his back door unlocked. Although Drazen didn't expect anyone else to be there, he took no chances and checked out every part of the place before he settled down to wait in the man's bedroom. The house was still, the silence only interrupted by the loud ticking of the old grandfather clock downstairs. He had often admired the clock in the past and the man had proudly spoken of how his own grandfather had brought it back from Germany after the first Great War and that it had been in the same spot ever since, reliable as only German clocks would be. The sound of the tick-tock rhythm was hypnotic and it again brought him back to how things had been before; before all of this and before this day of all days. He forced himself to forget the past; his previous visits to this house could have been a million years before or in a different galaxy, such were the changes that had been wrought in the meantime. He was now a man on a mission and he needed to concentrate.

He tuned out the ticking of the clock and listened intently for the slightest sound. He need not have bothered as his target announced his arrival long in advance. Drazen heard the singing coming up the street from at least a hundred metres away. The man had a rich deep voice and he was sure it was him. The singing was done in drunken snatches and was interspersed with laughter and loud belching. This was where things got complicated; the man was not alone. This wasn't an immediate problem as Drazen assumed they would part at the man's door. But he wasn't so lucky. His man insisted that the friend come in for one final shot of slivovitz and they both arrived noisily downstairs. Still no great problem as Drazen was upstairs out of sight. However, one shot became two and then more singing started. Drazen had never been one for physical violence and while he was young and fit, there were two men below so he forced himself to wait and to go with his original plan.

Eventually, he heard the sound of loud snoring. This was followed by a half hearted attempt by his man to rouse his companion but this was unsuccessful. Judging by the state that both seemed to be in, Drazen felt the visitor might sleep until morning. His man belched loudly again and started up the stairs. He hit the wall switch and the landing was flooded with light. Drazen was seated in darkness beside the man's bed but he calculated he would not be seen even if the man switched on the bedroom light as there was an ancient heavy wardrobe which masked him. He need not have worried. The man stumbled across the landing and practically fell into the bedroom. He had obviously taken off his jacket downstairs and didn't bother shedding any further clothing. He collapsed on to the bed and drew his feet up after him.

Drazen moved as quickly and as stealthily as a cat to the bedside. He jammed the dish towel he had taken from downstairs into the man's mouth and stuck the sharp knife to his throat. The man had not fully gone to sleep and was wide awake instantly.
"Move a muscle and you die," Drazen said. The man tried to take in his surroundings, blinked his eyes several times but looked mystified.
"Now Goran, I'm going to take the gag from your mouth to ask you a question. I will only ask you once. If you call out, I will slit your throat. If you refuse to answer, I will do likewise. Do you understand?"
The man nodded blindly and Drazen removed the gag but still kept the point of the knife pressed firmly against the man's jugular. Drazen's night vision was strong and he could see the man quite clearly. As Goran's eyes began to

adjust, he could see the horror accompanied by something like sheer terror cross the man's face.

"But, but, but Drazen," he said. "You're dead. I saw you fall. Jesus, God."

"Well now I'm back from the dead Goran so don't mess with me. Where is my family?"

"I, I, I don't know. Drazen, you must believe me. These people, you have no idea. They're inhuman; they're evil; they forced me to fill in the grave. I'm so sorry. I would have been shot if I refused. Please, you must believe me."

Drazen forced the point of the blade further upwards and drew blood.

"Wrong answer Goran; I'm asking you for the last time, where is my family?"

"Sorry Drazen, taken away, in buses, fleets of buses, all of them. I don't know to where, maybe Tuzla, maybe Sarajevo. I swear I don't know where for sure."

The sound of loud snoring came from downstairs as Drazen considered.

"Who drove the buses? Who organized the evacuation?"

"Drazen, I swear I don't know. Look, my friend, you must understand. This is ethnic cleansing they call it. They want to kill all the Bosniak men so as there won't be a next generation. It's all done by the militias, nothing to do with us townspeople. You must believe me. The word we hear is that they have agreed to spare the women and children if they agree to move out of the region, but I swear I don't know where they have been taken to."

"And you were forced to fill in the graves yes?"

"Yes, of course. Look, we are friends, yes? We have always lived together in peace. These militias forced me because I am the only man in town with an earth moving machine. I was as shocked as everyone else at what they did."

"Yes, you were so shocked that you had to spend half the night with these thugs drinking and singing songs."

"What could I do? If I refused I was afraid they would shoot me."

"OK Goran, I believe you even though I shouldn't but we were friends before. Who would know where the women and children have been taken?"

"Possibly the Bosnian Serb Commander but I'm not even sure of that. No one in the bar spoke of where they may have been taken."

"And where would I find this Commander?"

"Right now, I believe he is still in the bar but I have no idea where he stays."

"OK Goran, I will leave now. I want you to consider carefully what I am going to say. I am not a violent man but I almost died today and my family is missing so I will kill you without a second thought if you disobey me, you understand?"

Goran nodded violently.

"Right, I will leave now. You didn't see me tonight. I wasn't here. I died today along with all the rest. There are no Bosniaks left in the area, right? If you tell anyone you saw me or that I am at large, I will kill you."

"Yes, yes of course my good friend and thank you. Good luck Drazen my friend and may God go with you on your journey."

As Drazen rose to leave, two things happened simultaneously. He caught something in Goran's eyes. It was only a slight movement but in the same instant he realized that the snoring had stopped. He whirled round

just in time to avoid the blow from the heavy poker that the man from downstairs carried and was bearing down on him with. He was momentarily shocked that it was another of his erstwhile smoking colleagues that he had known all his life. The man missed with the poker and stumbled. As he fell, Drazen kicked him viciously in the ribs and he doubled over a fell in a heap. The man hit his head on the ground and lay quite still. Goran rose to protest:
"Sorry Drazen, he must have thought it was a burglar. Forgive him, he's totally pissed anyway. Forgive us both."
"I'm leaving now Goran", Drazen said. "Remember what I told you and tell your friend the same goes for him if he opens his mouth later."

He slowly made his way downstairs and left through the back door. He had never struck a man in anger but he would have killed tonight, of that he had no doubt. The town was now almost completely still. He glanced at his watch and saw it was after three am. He had no idea where he would sleep tonight or when and if he would sleep at all. But that was the least of his problems. He decided to wait to see if Goran would do as he had been instructed. He knew the man did not have a phone in his house so he would have to leave to raise the alarm. He fervently hoped the man would have sense and go to sleep but he was disappointed. Not ten minutes later, the door opened quietly and Goran looked left and right, checking that the street was clear. He turned left and headed back towards the centre of town in the direction of the bar and unfortunately, the police station. Drazen jumped silently from the shadows at the side of the house. He saw the look of guilt and terror in Goran's eyes and he did not hesitate.

"Taking a walk Goran? I thought you'd be sleeping it off by now?"
"No Drazen, sorry, it's not what you think, I was just….."
Drazen pounced, grabbed the man in a vice like grip and slit his throat from ear to ear in one swift movement. He had never killed a man before but he had assisted the butcher to kill a pig every winter.
"Yeah, you were just heading to the police station to tell them about me. I'm sorry my friend but you had your warning."

The blood had spurted everywhere, great fountains of it and there was an awful lot of it on Drazen's clothes. He seemed impervious to it though. He had seen a lot of bloodshed that day and was now almost immune. He quickly and silently dragged Goran's body backwards through the door and let it slide to the ground. There was a trail of blood but he doubted it would raise an eyebrow as there was blood everywhere. He had seen blood splashes all over town where people had been shot, presumably as they tried to flee the death squads. The road out of the town was dark with it. He knew now that he would have to eliminate the man upstairs also. He didn't know if the man had seen his face but it wasn't a chance he was prepared to take. It had been a mistake to leave them in the first place. He knew that now and he would learn from it. This country had gone to hell; it was kill or be killed. That was the only way he would survive. He listened but heard no sound. He quickly checked the street but there was no one about. He locked the doors and crept upstairs.

The other man was still lying where he had fallen, to the left of Goran's bed but he seemed distorted somehow.

Drazen didn't dare to turn on the light switch but he risked his torch. He was again shocked beyond belief as he saw that the man's head was battered out of all recognition and he was as dead as the man downstairs. How many more shocks, he thought. How much lower can this country descend but then he saw it. Goran was on his way to tell the police or the militias that his house had been raided by a Bosniak. The intruder had beaten his friend to death with a poker. He had managed to hold him off and the man had fled. But why; why did he need a cover story; why did he need to kill his friend? The militias would kill any Bosniak they set eyes on. Did Goran have a grudge against the man? Some other ancient feud not for once rooted in ethnicity? It was crazy he felt; what had become of his country when men went drinking and got drunk together and then came home and one had beaten the other to death. Had the other man recovered and had they quarrelled? No, there wouldn't have been time and he would surely have heard. He hadn't heard the impact of the blows with the poker but he wouldn't; blows to soft tissue make little sound. He sighed out of pure disgust and went downstairs.

The reason why Goran had killed his erstwhile friend still lingered in his thoughts and he began to grow suspicious. Was it connected with money? Goran's dead friend had his own small haulage business and was reputed to be wealthy. Drazen went through Goran's pockets. He found his internal passport and other identity papers. He put these in his pack as they might be useful. Both he and Goran were both of medium height and dark skinned. They didn't really look alike but he might pass for him if the inspection of the documents was hurried. Yes, the documents could be valuable. They identified Goran as an ethnic Serb. But then, Goran would be eventually found dead with his documents missing and his name might be placed on a list. It could be difficult. He did not have his own identity papers as they had been confiscated when the militias had taken them away. In any event, they would be useless to him in this area. He'd worry about what to do when he got to territory held by his own people if he got that far.

He went through the rest of Goran's pockets. He felt a large bulge. What was this; a large wad of cash and in U.S. dollars. Now he knew why Goran had murdered his friend. There must have been five thousand dollars in the bundle. Goran had obviously gone through the man's pockets and saw a chance to get rich quick while at the same time reporting a renegade Bosniak. It was the perfect set-up. He would have been believed because they'd want to believe him and it would redouble their hatred of the Bosniaks that one of them had killed a colleague who had been drinking with them only an hour beforehand. Goran might have been drunk but he was clever and a cold blooded bastard to boot. Drazen had no qualms about pocketing the cash. He would need all the help he could get. He checked the man's pockets upstairs and of course they were empty. That confirmed the entire set-up. He did a quick search of Goran's house and discovered about another five hundred dollars and some local currency which was effectively worthless.. He then calmly went to the man's kitchen and made himself something to eat. After he had sated himself, he went to the man's closet and took a pair of jeans and a warm shirt, a jacket and a cap and scarf. In a drawer he found a pair of strong gloves which might be useful in the mountains at night. In another drawer he found an old pair of binoculars. He didn't wish to carry any more weight than necessary but these might be useful. Goran's clothes fitted him reasonably well; at least they were bigger than his own so if he used a belt, the jeans would fit fine. Goran's clothes were better quality than his own. He placed his old blood-soaked clothes in a pile beside the fireplace. He realized that he was now doing things that twenty four hours previously he would have considered abhorrent but this was a different scenario; this was life and death; there could be no room for sentiment. He would have to make the best of every situation. He needed to remain strong and he would keep his own food and provisions for later.

He had realised what he now needed to do and he calmly went about his task. He decided that if Goran and his friend were found dead and documents were missing, there would be suspicion and there might be an intensive search. The fact that they were killing every Bosniak they found anyway possibly reduced that threat but he wasn't taking any chances. The last thing he needed was a search party heading after him. Better that everyone thought he was dead.

He moved quickly now to complete his plan and ensure he gave himself a decent head start. Goran and his friend had been drinking all evening and had been seen leaving the bar drunk. They had returned to Goran's house for more slivovitz. Both men smoked and drank too much. He heaved the man's body downstairs and seated both him and Goran in armchairs. He then lit cigarettes and placed them in both men's mouths. It would be unlikely to be noticed but he did it anyway. Then he fetched two bottles of slivovitz from the kitchen and spread them liberally around the room. He put on his back pack and opened the rear door. His last act in the house was to throw a lighted match and close the door. He heard the whoosh as the alcohol lit instantly. Before he had cleared the rear wall of Goran's garden, the flames had engulfed the downstairs. Before anyone was awake in the town, Goran and his friend would be toast.

As he made his way back along the roadside, he realised that dawn was breaking. Back in the direction from which he had come, he could see the smoke and flames but no one else had apparently noticed them yet. About three hundred metres south of town, he turned off the main road and headed down a track. His only option now was the mountains. He was utterly exhausted but he forced himself to go on. He could not sleep until he reached a safe place high above the valley that he had known since he was a child. If he had paused for even a moment to contemplate all the empty houses which he passed and of the people who had lived in them and whom he would never see again, he might have broken down completely. But he didn't look; he just kept going straight ahead. This was Bosniak territory and he knew he would not be disturbed because there was no one here any more. He would reach the mountains and then he would rest. He tried to calculate his chances and he figured he had two advantages. First, he knew the area extremely well and the militias didn't as they were strangers to the place and second, everyone thought he was dead, so no one would be looking for him. As far as the death squads knew, this whole area had been ethnically cleansed.

Chapter 5

But he had reckoned without Sefer Milanovic. The Colonel knew that there was at least one Bosniak who had escaped the massacre. He had seen the man looking intensely through the window of the bar and he knew him instinctively as a Bosniak. He had returned the man's gaze and the man had fled. Sefer took no action as he had seen enough bloodshed for one day. If the man had managed to escape the militias, good luck to him. Colonel Milanovic had no quarrel with him. In any event, he thought it highly unlikely that the poor devil would survive the following day anyway. The militias would move on to the next town and more genocide but if they missed a few, the villagers were more than capable of either pointing them out or doing the job themselves.

As he took his morning coffee in the local hotel, he pondered the situation. If the man had escaped, why had he come back? Surely he would have known that to enter the town was highly dangerous. But then everyone was drunk so perhaps it wasn't. The man was obviously looking for someone but in a Serb bar? Maybe he was intent on revenge. One man though; surely it was highly unlikely? The Colonel thought of how vulnerable they all had been. If the man had had a machine gun or a grenade, he could have taken out a hell of a lot of officers, him included. He would have to advise against any future similar gatherings, or maybe not, as he might just be wasting his breath. Fuck these people he thought; most of them are sub-human and not worth saving. As a loyal honest Serb, they disgusted him to his core. Today the militias were moving on to Potocari, where the whole killing spree would start again.

After yesterday's breakthrough, there would now be no one to stop the militias or to cry halt to the madness. The word would eventually filter out in all its horror to the international community and there would be condemnation and wringing of hands. But it would be too late; far too late. These bastards had their programme worked out for the next week or more and it consisted entirely of killing innocent civilians. He was probably the most highly trained soldier in the area and he was powerless to prevent it. He sighed deeply and lit a cigarette. It was still early and the killers would be sleeping off their hangovers. Even though he knew he shouldn't, he asked the waitress for a shot of slivovitz with his coffee.

He gazed through the large picture windows of the upstairs dining room at the picturesque scene that lay before him. That was what was so tragic about the entire episode. This was a beautiful country and people had lived together here in peace for generations now. The landscape was pretty and the soil was rich; the food and drink were divine. But now all that was put on hold. The countryside was pock marked with burnt out houses and barns, holes caused by shelling and of course the tell-tale mounds of yellow soil that were the mass graves of the dispossessed and the disposed of. At least around here they hadn't yet started burning the place down or had they? He noticed a house a little way off on the edge of town which appeared to be burnt out. He couldn't recall any burnings here the day before but who knew what the villagers had gotten up to when they were unleashed and allowed to vent their venom on their erstwhile neighbours. He again thought of the man he had seen the night before and imagined him as the solitary Bosniak left, forever wandering the country in search of his friends and family but never to find them. Have you already been killed, my brave fellow, or have you sought refuge in the mountains, he asked aloud. The waitress looked at him curiously but he ignored her. He gazed at the rising sun peeping over the tops of the peaks in the far distance and raised the shot of slivovitz to the man in a mock toast. He downed the liquor in one, lit a cigarette and then rose wearily to go meet his 'colleagues' for one more day of madness.

Drazen was indeed in the mountains. He had arrived, only minutes beforehand, at the little cave in the upper reaches of the Brestovik peak, twelve hundred metres above the valley. He and his school friends used to take shelter from the scorching sun there after a mad dash up the mountain during their summer holidays. They would exhaust themselves in their striving to be the first to reach the cave. Drazen had never been the strongest climber and had usually arrived in the middle of the pack. But he was a careful climber and unlike some of his fellows, he had never had a mishap. Those days now seemed to be from a different world but the little cave was still there and he knew there were parts in it where he would find sanctuary. He had checked around the edges of the cave for any signs of recent occupation but had found none. The area at the mouth of the cave was actually overgrown and he had to disturb the foliage as he ducked inside, taking care to replace the grasses and leaves and to leave the entrance looking exactly as it had been. He very quickly found the secret area at the rear of the cave. He needed to remove some of the stones and then squeeze thru the opening he had created into a smaller chamber. It wasn't as easy as when he was a teenager but thankfully his farm work had kept him fit so he hadn't gained too much weight. He then replaced the stones, placed his backpack on the ground and lay down. Within seconds, he fell into an exhausted, deep, dreamless sleep.

The by now occupying force were due to rendezvous at the police station at 08.00 to plan the day's advance on Potocari. Colonel Milanovic was not looking forward to it but he would do his duty. Needless to say, he was the only one present at eight o'clock. The Duty Sergeant eyed him suspiciously but nodded him thru to the meeting room. Milanovic enquired as to how the man was and asked after his family and the attitude softened somewhat. After a few moments, he came back with a pitcher of coffee and offered to pour some for the Colonel.
"All quiet now I suppose Sergeant," Milanovic commented.
"Yeah, nothing much happening here, apart from that idiot Durkovic."
Incredible, thought Milanovic. God only knew how many murders had been committed here the day before. Thousands of people had died. Possibly one of the worst and most cold blooded massacres in history had been carried out and yet the town's policeman was reporting that 'nothing was happening' and that he had nothing to do. But of course he was a Serb policeman and no Serbs had been murdered; only Bosniaks and they were considered sub-human. The fact that the streets and roads of the town were stained with blood and the ditches along

the country lanes were strewn with bodies made no impact. The only thing the Sergeant wanted to talk about was some local Serb who had done something stupid. He decided to play the man's game.

"And who, may I ask, is Durkovic and what has he done?"
The Sergeant smirked:
"Oh, nothing for a man of your rank to worry about Colonel; but you'd remember Durkovic. He drove the earth mover yesterday that filled in the graves. Remember he was boasting and singing about it last night in the bar; claiming it was his glorious victory over the Bosniak scum? Idiot did nothing apart from drive the digger and he had to be threatened to do that, but then when it was all over, he wanted to claim the credit."
"Yes, indeed I do remember the man; quite a loud mouthed oaf as I recall."
"That's him but, well….."
The Sergeant was so amused that he had to pause again, almost doubled over and then laughed loudly.
"He only went home last night pissed drunk and set fire to himself and his mate."
"You mean he did it deliberately or it was an accident?"
"No, no, of course it was an accident. Both of them were paralytic drunk leaving the bar and they went to Goran's house for more. The bloody idiots fell asleep and one of their cigarettes set fire to the place. I'd say they were so drunk that they passed out and didn't even realize they were burning their arses."
With that, the Sergeant bent over and laughed uproariously again. This place really has lost all vestiges of humanity, Sefer thought. The Police Sergeant's amusement at the death of anyone and his refusal to take the matter seriously

would be disquieting in any event. These were not normal times but the man who had died had been a fellow Serb. The Sergeant had obviously had no time for the man when he was alive. Sefer was still the only occupant of the meeting room so he decided to continue in conversation with the policeman. Anyway, he might learn some useful intelligence.

"So, how do you know it was an accident?"

The man seemed taken aback and his eyes narrowed.

"What else could it be? He hardly topped himself deliberately. When we found him this morning, after a neighbour had seen the fire, the place was practically razed to the ground but Goran and his mate Luka were still sitting in the armchairs with glasses of slivovitz, or at least their skeletons were. Ah you should have seen them; it was like a scene from a movie."

At this, the man dissolved completely with laughter. The Colonel just shrugged.

Three other men in uniform entered the room at this point, all looking distinctly hung over. The Sergeant hurried to straighten himself and saluted:

"Good morning Major, ah, Lieutenant, Colonel."

The men threw vague salutes in response. The man whom the Sergeant had addressed as Major said:

"Ah you can relax Sergeant, no need for formalities this morning. What's so funny anyway? Are you still celebrating yesterday?"

"No sir," the Sergeant replied and then proceeded to tell the story of how the idiot digger driver from the day before had burned the arse off himself and his friend the night before. The three officers seemed to have a similar sense of humour to the Sergeant and all three broke into loud fits of laughter. It became infectious and the next people to come into the room immediately joined in the laughter, some even unaware of what it was they were laughing at. When some of the earlier arrivals calmed down enough to draw breath and relate the full story to the newcomers, the whole scenario started again. Colonel Milanovic found himself alone once more; the only man in the room who did not see the joke. But he would forgive them this black humour; he was intelligent enough to know that it was merely a release from the tension caused by the mass killings of the previous day. Surely these men were human, or at least some of them were; and surely they were capable of feelings. He suddenly found his attitude changing or softening slightly. After all, these men were also following orders. Maybe they were trying to make the best of a bad situation? Was he beginning to empathise with them? Was it because of his constant exposure to them or had the two shots of slivovitz he had had for breakfast distorted his brain?

When the laughter eventually subsided, everyone took a mug of coffee and sat around the long oak table in the meeting room on the second floor. Colonel Bogdan Mistakovic of the Bosnian Serb Army chaired the meeting. As Sefer was of equal rank, he sat to the Colonel's immediate right. Mistakovic opened the meeting by congratulating everyone on the previous day's 'victory'. He was proud to report that none of the Serbian forces had been killed or indeed none had even been wounded. Sefer wondered what the locals could have wounded them with. No mention was made of how many Bosniaks hadn't made it. The Chairman proposed that they now concentrate on the next task in the master plan; the movement of their forces to Potocari and the further displacement of any non-Serbs found in the area. Milanovic noted that there was no direct reference to 'killing' or 'liquidating' the Bosniaks. The operation was couched in more polite language like 'displacement' or 'removal'. All at the table nodded agreement at Colonel Mistakovic's proposal and he immediately spread out a large scale map of the region to plot their strategy. As men were rising to group together to view the map placed in front of the Colonel, Milanovic remained seated but asked for the floor. Mistakovic shrugged and nodded for him to proceed. The other officers resumed their seats but the body language said this was an unnecessary interruption.

"Colonel and colleagues," he began. "You are aware that I am not authorized to take any active part in this campaign. I am here merely as an adviser. So that is precisely what I am going to do, advise. Firstly, I can find no fault with your military strategy in the region. It is well planned and well thought through. It has led to swift and decisive victories up to now and you and your men are to be complimented on its effectiveness and I will be mentioning this in my report to Belgrade. What I must caution about however is how you treat the civilian population when you capture a town or a city or even a village. I fully understand that you are following orders from your superiors but if I am not mistaken, I think those orders say to 'capture and secure the area and clear the entire region of Bosniaks'. I agree that the order is not specific as to how this task should be carried out but I am certain that it does not state that they should all be killed or liquidated."

He paused at this point and glanced round the table. There were a few gazes of hostility but most had their heads down or had neutral expressions.
"My dear colleagues," Sefer recommenced, "It is my opinion that what happened here yesterday will live long in the collective memory. Let me remind you that the Germans are still reviled for what they did to the Jews over forty years ago. I, like all of you, am a proud Serb. I love my country and I want to see it grow and prosper. I **do not wish** to see its name tarnished for generations to come. And believe you me, if we continue in this vein, it will be. As I said, what happened yesterday alone is probably enough to damn people's opinions of us but if we pull back, even now, even at this late stage, perhaps yesterday's carnage can be explained away by the excuse of a renegade militia group or a misunderstanding of orders by over zealous recruits. But I guarantee you, if we go on to Potocari and do the same and afterwards to every other part of this enclave and systematically exterminate the Bosniaks in the same manner, then our name will be reviled for a long time. Gentlemen, this is not 1942, this is 1995. There are T.V. crews and reporters and cameramen everywhere. The world will hear of this and the world will firmly place the blame on Serbs everywhere."

He paused for breath and sipped some of his coffee. A Lieutenant at the end of the table called out:
"There are no reporters here; they all fled; afraid of their shadows; too tough for them. No one took photos here Colonel. No one knows but us."
"And what about the families that left on buses? Will they not report us as murderers when none of their men are ever seen again?"

"But who will believe them? They're just Muslim gypsy scum."

Mistakovic intervened:

"Perhaps you are right Ivan, but I think the Colonel's point is that the operation has gotten too big to hide completely. Am I correct Colonel?"

Sefer nodded. Mistakovic took a sip from his coffee and offered:

"Then what would the good Colonel recommend us to do? You do realize we have been given a most difficult order."

"Yes I do Bogdan, but there has to be another way. I realize that speed is of the essence in any military operation but surely you can mobilize enough buses to transport the men as well as the women and children out of the territory."

The hawkish Lieutenant and the end of the table laughed cynically and raised his hand to speak again. Mistakovic nodded to him.

"And what would you have us do then Colonel when the scum would re-arm themselves and attack us and our families in our beds at night. You know what these people are like. You cannot give them a second chance. We have to be rid of them and their ilk once and for all."

"That's strange Lieutenant, I was under the impression that most of them were simple peasants or farmers. From what I've seen, none of them took up arms until we started our offensive."

The Lieutenant coloured and replied angrily:

"That's typical of the attitude of someone who grew up privileged in Belgrade. You ***don't know*** these people. I was born here and ***I do*** because I've lived with the scum all my life. Who are you to tell us what to do in our own country?"

"Ivan, Ivan, enough," Mistakovic countered. "There is no need for that. The good Colonel is one of us. He has, I believe, our best interests and those of the wider Serbian population at heart and I believe he also takes what you would call a 'world view' and that is very important also."

He paused and then addressed himself directly to Sefer: "I can see your point Colonel Milanovic but please understand that these are difficult orders that we have been given. We cannot just move people about in an orderly fashion. We are not organising games or sending children to a summer camp. It is not possible to send people where they do not wish to go. Without a threat of violence, believe me, they won't leave. Apart from that, if we don't move swiftly and decisively, we could get bogged down here for months. Also, as you well know, some of the villagers are more than capable of eliminating the population for us."

Sefer felt compelled to interrupt:

"I am sorry to interrupt Colonel. I understand the difficulties of carrying out the order and I do appreciate the logistical problems. I am also aware of the capabilities of the local population. But if they commit crimes, there is a police force to deal with them. If that force is incapable of acting, so be it but I will not be a party to a disciplined military unit undertaking genocide."

Mistakovic touched him gently on the shoulder and said softly:

"But I fear, Sefer, there may not be any other way. We both know that what we are doing is really what Karadzic wants, even if he won't admit to it publicly. If you are truthful to yourself, you know in your heart that it is also what Milosevic in Belgrade wants."

He then announced to the table:
"Colonel Milanovic is a dear and valued colleague who has provided us with much valuable advice and assistance and I wish to take formal note that his advice to us here this morning has been duly noted."
He nodded to the junior officer who was taking notes and continued:
"We will endeavour to carry out the Colonel's advice where possible. Now, can we return to the plans for our troops?"
Sefer announced that he was aware of the military tactics for the day and that he approved of them; he had seen the plan and almost knew it by heart, and he asked to be excused. Colonel Mistakovic readily agreed.

Sefer knew in his heart that his advice would again go unheeded. When those militias smelt blood, they would go on another killing spree. The Bosnian Serb commanders knew this too and used it to their advantage. In fact, if anything it would get worse. They would continue until there were no more Bosniaks left to kill. After that, if they were not sated, they might even start to fight with each other. He went downstairs and checked with the desk Sergeant as to the location of the burnt out house. The Sergeant confirmed that it was as he thought, the burnt out shell he had seen earlier from the dining room window. He left the station and set off in the direction of the house, pausing to light what must already be his tenth cigarette that morning. He reached the burned out house in less than ten minutes. As far as he could see, the police hadn't bothered to cordon it off or to even conduct a cursory examination of the scene.

The whole building, which had been made entirely of wood, was reduced to ashes. As it was mid summer, the timbers would have been as dry as tinder and it was likely that they would have been engulfed in minutes if not seconds. There was an admixture of smells including burnt timber and plastic and rubber but above all, Sefer detected the pungent smell of burnt flesh. However many killings he had seen, the smell always got to him. The area was still very hot although the fire had burnt out by now. The two skeletons were there as the Sergeant had reported, seated on the springs of what had presumably been armchairs of some sort. He wandered into the ruins and examined the positions of each. The fire must have burned fiercely as there was practically no flesh left on either skeleton. The bone matter had disintegrated in places also. The Colonel knew nothing about fires or combustion; neither was he a trained policeman or a forensic scientist but the scene seemed too perfect to him, almost as if it had been staged. Then again, maybe not; perhaps he was just curious and was imagining things? A minivan drew up alongside him and a man got out and headed for the ruins.
"Excuse me", Sefer said, "but I think the police may not be finished with the examination of the fire as yet".
"But the Sergeant told me to go ahead and remove the bodies", the man said. "I'm Joakim, the undertaker".
Sefer shrugged and mumbled:
"You must be a busy man this morning"
"What was that?" said the man.
"Nothing", replied Sefer. "Go ahead with your work".

He sighed and lit another cigarette. He took a last glance at the ruins, turned and once more cast his gaze towards the mountains. Have you already commenced taking your revenge my friend, he thought.

Chapter 6

In fact, revenge was the last thing on Drazen's mind. Survival was his first priority; thereafter, the struggle to reach a safe haven, if one could be found in this war-torn hatred-ridden country. But the ultimate goal was to see his family again. He allowed himself now to think about his two beautiful children again and of course his beloved Sonja. He made a deal with himself that he would allow a few moments each day for reflection about them but only if he was secure. The rest of the time, he would try to cast them from his mind, concentrating fully on where he was and where he needed to go. He had woken in his cave at mid morning. He had initially lain quite still, listening for any sound but there had been none, save for the distant twittering of the birds, seemingly the only inhabitants of this high sanctuary.

He drank some water and ate a small piece of bread. He now had a decision to make, several decisions in fact. Goran had said that the women and children had been taken away in buses and he had believed him. The man was a coward and he had been terrified when he had been interrogated. But he hadn't known exactly where the buses had gone to. Tuzla & Sarajevo were more or less equidistant, maybe sixty kilometres; easy on a paved road, horrendously difficult through high mountain terrain during high summer. He made his way to the front entrance of the cave and gingerly felt his way back into the sunshine. It was going to be another scorching day. He had to seek shade as the sun was relentless, particularly at this level where the air was thinner. This would no doubt slow his progress too. Still, he was by nature an optimist; at least it wasn't mid winter. Without heat, he knew he wouldn't survive up here. He wouldn't last for more than a day or two if he was still here when the snows came.

He figured he had brought enough food to last him a week, maybe a bit more if he spared it. That was if he could stay alive for a week. He thought of how fickle life can be; yesterday morning he was planning a normal day on his little farm. His mind was on the harvest and what he hoped would be a bumper crop. His chief concern would have been how much to sell to the millers and how much to keep to see his family through the winter. But before the day was even half over, he was surely within seconds of death in that hell hole. Then later in the same day, he had had to kill a man. Today he was planning his survival in the most hostile environment he could imagine. But people are resilient and can adapt to even the worst conditions. Since the dawn of time, man has been challenged. He was sure many of his countrymen had faced even worse horrors in the past and had survived. He wondered how much more of this he could take without breaking down but he quickly banished the thought; he wouldn't let his countrymen down; he ***couldn't*** let his family down. He suddenly found himself imbued with a fierce determination; a strength of will that he had no idea he possessed. And perhaps he hadn't before; but by God he did now and he knew that he would never go quietly again. He would fight to the death; more to the point, he'd try to make sure he wasn't put in a position where he'd have to.

Having repacked his bag and bade farewell to his hiding place, a last reminder of his youth, he set about assessing his options. He knew in which direction Sarajevo and Tuzla were but getting there was another thing entirely. He knew the area in the immediate vicinity of his village and he knew the mountains from his climbing days in his teens but he had no experience of navigation or of how to survive in hostile terrain. The last thing he needed was to wander around in circles using up his precious supplies of food and water. But he convinced himself that this would not happen. He knew he possessed a good sense of direction and he had a fair idea of what the mountain range looked like all the way to Sarajevo. And he could always use the sun, if he was allowed the luxury of travelling by day. He had only been to Tuzla once and he really had no idea of what the terrain was like in that direction. That more or less settled it; he would head for Sarajevo.

Before he set out, he decided he would use Goran's binoculars to carry out a more comprehensive check in all directions. He found a secluded spot and trained the powerful glasses on the valley far below. As he wasn't at the very top of the mountain, he could only see to one side but at this height, he was allowed a fine broad vista. He could see for up to thirty kilometers and his view covered most of the villages and towns in the Srebrenica enclave. He could see his own village of Konjević Polje and the road from it to Bratunac. He saw the River Cerska snaking its way peacefully thru the valley and the town of Cerska in the distance. He could see the field at Sandići, where some of the men had been taken and the agricultural warehouses at Kravica. He looked at the vacant school in Konjević Polje and finally he forced himself to look at the football field in Nova Kasaba. The mound of yellow earth was clearly visible, a great ugly stain on the countryside covering the bodies of his friends and neighbours; covering the sins of the militias and covering the beautiful green grass where they had all played together when they were younger. He swept the glasses further out and saw the lovely little village of Lolići and the village school of Luke. They were all silent and deserted. Back to the east in the direction of the Serbian border, there was little activity but he could at least see some people. He could see some burned out buildings and numerous abandoned homesteads. There were also many holdings where men and women still worked in the fields and which had been left virtually unscathed. These would no doubt be the lands and houses owned by the Serbs. He thought, ruefully, that if he had had the time to come up here a few days beforehand and see the devastation that had been wrought by the advancing Bosnian Serb Forces and their associated militias, he might have taken the decision to flee with his family before it was too late. But there was no point in speculating now on what might have been.

At the outer edge of his vision, he saw a large group of military vehicles heading north in the direction of Tuzla. These were led by tanks and armored personnel carriers with some jeeps and standard troop transports in the middle and more A.P.C.'s bringing up the rear. He had already decided that he was heading for Sarajevo but the sight of so much military might heading in the opposite direction made it definite. He could only hope his family had been sent to the capital. He swung the glasses back towards the west and south. There was military activity there too but to a lesser extent. He put away the binoculars and started downwards. He could make progress at the top level but it would be gruelling and extremely slow, not to speak of being dangerous. No one travelled up this high except the few signs of life he had seen; the sheep and goats. If he descended to about nine hundred metres, there was a little used but serviceable path. That risked exposure but he had little choice in the matter. There was another much more comfortable and well used track a further five hundred metres down but that was too close to the valley for comfort. There would no doubt be patrols and while they may not be looking for him, if he was identified as a Bosniak, he believed he would be summarily executed.

The Serbian Armed Forces command centre in Belgrade was not a happy place to be that morning either. Milanovic had filed his report the previous evening and while he had been matter-of-fact and had reported strictly in military terms, the message had been clear. The militias were finally out of control. The fact that they were probably carrying out the deep seated wishes of their ultimate leaders was immaterial. General Branislav Jankovic was the head of a professional fighting force that, although they had no direct involvement in this dirty war, were mandated to provide advice and funding. Well, they had been ordered to but their sympathies would have allowed it in any event. But now, a conflict that had initially been an inter-necine conflict fought between professionally equipped warring armies had degenerated into wholesale slaughter. There was so much mud and dirt thrown up by the militias that some of it was bound to reach Belgrade and some of it was bound to stick. General Jankovic was keen to ensure that none of it would adhere to him. He arrived in his office in a foul mood; the Defence Minister had called him at six and not alone had he ruined his sleep, by effectively blaming him for the carnage of the previous day, he had effectively ruined this one on him also. He could have told the Minister that he and his Cabinet colleagues were fucking hypocrites but he had a feeling that mightn't have been too well received. He sat heavily into his swivel chair behind the large oak paneled desk. "Get me Milanovic, wherever he is," he shouted at his subordinate. The man scurried away to attempt to trace the Colonel and Jankovic sat back and lit a Marlboro cigarette.

Milanovic hadn't said 'I told you so' in his report, not in so many words, but the implication was clear. He had made reference to 'previous advices' and 'earlier reports'. What the fuck had he expected Jankovic to do; tell the Government Ministers that things were getting too hot? That would have gotten him a one way ticket to early retirement or worse, redeployment to some vague outpost. He wished this bloody war would finish one way or the other. There were rumors that if the Bosnian Serbs continued their campaign, Belgrade might suffer air strikes. That was a double edged sword for the politicians. People might rally behind the national flag but at the same time, they weren't stupid. They'd know that it was the support their politicians provided to the militias that was bringing ever increasing opprobium on the Serbian capital and if people were killed in the strikes, it could rebound badly for Milosevic and his cronies. For now, they wanted a really tight lid placed on whatever was going on in and around Srebrenica. In his heart of hearts, he knew that this was impossible. It was like asking him to pour the champagne back into the bottle after the cork had popped; in fact it was worse; the bottle was smashed in pieces on the floor. Milanovic was right; this was going to be a P.R. disaster. The Colonel was a good man; shrewd tactically and a highly professional soldier. It was his bad luck to be posted to Bosnia when things went bad but he might recover. The man was still young. Jankovic himself wasn't and if and when this went pear shaped, they'd be looking for bodies in more places than Bosnia. Records could be destroyed; reports deleted. But it wouldn't work. There'd be more than enough evidence to prove that Belgrade was in this up to its collective neck. With this in mind, the General had decided to set about saving his own.

The junior officer rushed back into the room to tell him that he had finally made contact with the Colonel. Reception wouldn't be good as he was mobile and on a field radio. Jankovic decided on a conciliatory approach, initially anyway. The officer indicated the connection was made and he lifted the receiver:
"My dear Sefer."
"Hello, is that you General Jankovic? I'm afraid I can't hear very well."
"Yes, it's me Colonel. I believe you had a trying day yesterday."

There was a pause on the other end followed by a hiss.
"I'm sorry General, can you repeat please?"
Jankovic was beginning to lose patience. He now shouted down the line:
"Colonel, can you not find a land line phone that's working? This line is terrible and I have important orders for you."
"Negative General. We are in the field and continuing the operation. As far as I know, there are no working land lines in this area."
"Ah, that's somewhat better," the General said as the line seemed to improve.
"Tell me, are the local commanders with you?"
"No, but they are nearby."
"Right, Sefer, listen to me now and listen carefully. Forget all this 'we are only advisers crap'. We have to start telling these bastards what to do or else we'll be destroyed. You were correct in your assessment yesterday I fear."
"Thank you General; I have tried again this morning to impart the potential consequences of their actions to the local commanders but I fear my words will not be heeded. We are now on the way to Potocari. It is ostensibly a military operation but I fear for what will happen when they try to implement the 'relocation' part of their orders."
"Yes, yes, yes, but don't worry about that for now. Didn't you say that the majority of the Bosniaks in the region had already been liquidated?"
"Well I cannot be sure General but yes, a large number of them had relocated to this region in addition to the locals and yet more were brought in from outlying villages but there are sure to be others still situated in isolated pockets."

"Yes, but don't worry about them. Have all Bosniaks been eliminated from around the Srebrenica enclave?"
"I believe not General; we have heard that many of them may be hiding in the mountains and there are sure to be some who escaped yesterdays exercise."
"That's what I'm getting at Sefer. Tell me: were there reporters or cameras there yesterday? Were there people who saw what happened and escaped?"
"My understanding is that all reporters and cameramen were escorted outside the enclave before the operation commenced. I didn't see any personally but I'm afraid I cannot give a definitive answer. On your second question, I believe it is very likely that there were people who witnessed the operation who escaped."
"Fuck it, that's what I thought. Those inefficient bastards; you have to hand it to the Germans; when they eliminated people, they didn't leave any films or witnesses behind. I might have known. Now Sefer, listen to me and listen carefully and this is a direct order. I know you are a professional soldier and you will do your duty. It is absolutely imperative that no witnesses to this 'operation' are left alive. Forget about Potocari and Tuzla for now. I want you to tell these bastards that they better get their house in order in Srebrenica or Belgrade will cut off their supplies of both armaments and funding; and Sefer, this is not from me, this comes directly from the Minister of Defence himself."
Colonel Milanovic sighed deeply.
"That is understood General, I will try to convene a meeting of the leaders immediately and I will pass on the order. I will keep you informed."

"Good man Sefer; remember this may be a dirty job but it is ultimately for the good of Serbia and for all of our futures."

He thanked the Colonel again and cut the connection. Jankovic instantly felt better. He had anticipated some trouble with Milanovic. The man had a dislike for killing, particularly the unnecessary kind. But he was a disciplined soldier and he would do his duty. He opened the bottom drawer of his desk and extracted a bottle of Johnny Walker Black Label he kept there. He took the water glass on his desk and poured himself two fingers. He downed it in one and lit another Marlboro. Maybe the thing could be salvaged after all. He decided to phone Ivanecivic and bring him to lunch.

Chapter 7

Drazen slowly made his way down the side of Mount Brestovik. He travelled in a zigzag fashion, constantly changing direction, taking cover and stopping to check carefully that he was safe and not under observation. His progress was painfully slow but it was better to be safe than sorry. He took cover where he could but was very much aware that it was a bright sunny day and visibility was excellent. Anyone with a decent set of field glasses in the valley scanning the hills for signs of movement at this level would probably detect him. What he hoped for was that they wouldn't suspect anyone would be moving at this level. When he got to the lower level, he knew there would be cover from the tree line which would provide some respite and allow him to make faster progress. However, the downside was that navigation would be more difficult and his own ability to scan for patrols would be reduced.

After an hour he stopped to take a break. He found excellent cover on a little shelf which protruded slightly outwards over the valley. He was protected by the overhang of a larger rock just above his position. He was also grateful for the respite from the heat as the flagstone he lay on had not been directly exposed to the sunlight and was still cool to the touch. When he looked around, he was pleased that he had made significant progress; not just vertically but also laterally along the side of the mountain. He was fit but at the same time, he wasn't used to this type of activity and with the hot sun, he was sweating profusely. He removed his cap and found it was drenched. This wouldn't do. He needed to preserve his energy for the long journey ahead of him. At this rate, he'd be exhausted by mid afternoon. He also realized his heart was beating quite fast. He resolved to calm himself; he took some deep breaths and his heart rate slowed.

He again scanned the valley below. Worryingly, the military activity seemed to have increased and unlike earlier, it didn't seem to be heading out of the area. In fact, the more he looked at it, the troop carriers seemed to be conducting a coordinated grid search of the valley. This was not good news; still, he was relatively safe in his lofty perch, for now anyway. The heavy artillery couldn't operate at this level. They could send patrols but even if they did, he felt they wouldn't come this high but would concentrate on the lower reaches of the foothills where people would be more likely to seek shelter; definitely below the tree line. If the military were searching in the valley, they would be sure to be scanning the mountains for any sign of activity also so he resolved to be even more careful. In fact, he considered waiting right there until darkness fell and he could move more freely but he quickly discarded the thought. He did not know the hills as well as he thought and the last thing he needed was to go wandering around in the dark, possibly taking a fall and breaking something. If he broke a leg up here he'd be finished. Even worse, he might stumble into a Serb patrol. No, he'd make best use of the light; it would be bright until ten thirty anyway and he would make what progress he could.

He took another drink of his precious water and started off again. After a while the terrain got rougher and the path seemingly ended completely at times only to reappear after a brief detour usually involving a steep climb or a descent. The plus side was that the cover was better and he could move with near certainty that he could not be seen from below. As if to dampen his spirits, he heard the drone of an aircraft in the distance. It sounded like a small plane so he was taking no chances. He gauged the direction from which the plane was travelling and took cover behind the largest rock he could find. The aircraft passed overhead flying at relatively low altitude and confirmed his suspicions that it was a spotter plane. He stayed where he was, waiting to see if it made another pass but it continued in the same direction and eventually the sound faded completely.

He had been walking for perhaps another twenty minutes when he came to a relatively flat open area with an overhanging promontory. He reckoned it would afford him almost as good a view of the entire valley as he had had from the peak so he assessed where he could gain the maximum amount of cover; then crept to its outer edge and once again raised the binoculars to scan below. The sight which was unveiled before him made him gasp. Well below, perhaps a further two hundred metres down the mountain was a large column of people, slowly wending their way along the wider flatter path which he had resolved to avoid, other than at night. There must have been hundreds, no, possibly thousands of people in the column. He scanned them with the binoculars and recognised them as Bosniaks. His heart jumped. He wasn't the only one left after all; not by a long shot. His immediate thoughts were to rush down the mountain and join the group and to seek some news of his family. But he had long since forced himself not to give in to impulse so he was cautious and held back.

His first thought was that the plane which had flown overhead would surely have spied parts of the column. They were moving relatively quietly but the group was so large that surely they couldn't all have taken cover. The column snaked backwards in a long seemingly never ending line. He could see where it started way ahead of his own position but he could not see where it ended and he was scanning at least twelve kilometres of mountainside. The column was led by armed men in uniform, presumably regular Bosnian Army troops sent to escort the group to safety. The long line of the column seemed to be mostly Bosnian Muslim men but there was also an occasional soldier. The men seemed to be in poor condition and were badly clothed. Most had no caps to protect them from the hot sun and some seemed to be close to exhaustion, possibly from dehydration. He had no idea how long they had been on the march. He did not recognise anyone and he quickly realized that this column hadn't come from Srebrenica yesterday; this group must have been on the move for some time. The head of the column was now about three kilometres north of his position and he was even beginning to lose sight of some of it. Yet there seemed to be no end to it. He then saw some women and older people and even some children. But he still saw no one he recognised. His heart went out to these poor souls; they were his own people. Hopefully they would reach safety but he feared for them. He very quickly put the thing together. In his naïveté, he had wondered if the patrols below were looking for him; he need not have flattered himself. It was obvious now who they were looking for. Where this huge number of people had come from, he could only speculate. Obviously displaced persons driven from their homes, just like he had been, but the sheer scale of it took his breath away.

It is said that there is safety in numbers but Drazen felt a lot more secure in his high eyrie than the people he was looking down at. Much as it pained him, he decided to stay where he was; for now anyway. There were simply too many of them and they were bound to be seen by some of the military units. How they had gotten this far undetected he wasn't sure. The fact that they were spread out over a huge distance was both a weakness and a strength; they would be difficult to attack and isolate but also, it would be impossible for the troops at the head of the column to defend anyone in the middle of it or realistically even those that were only a few hundred metres away. In reality, it was naivety in the extreme. Did those at the head of the column think the Serbs would politely attack them where they were strongest? But on reflection, he supposed what else could they do? They were trying to escort a large group, thousands of people, to safety along a narrow path over rough terrain. There was probably nothing in the army service manual about this; it was unprecedented so you made it up as you went along.

Almost as if to validate his decision not to go down to join his fellow countrymen, a massive shell exploded two hundred metres below. Drazan was far enough away not to be affected directly by the blast but he did feel the after shock as the super heated air from the explosion rushed upwards. All he could see below was a huge pall of smoke. As it cleared, he realized that the shell hadn't scored a direct hit on the column but had struck a ridge just above their position and had dislodged a huge amount of earth and stones, effectively blocking part of the trail. Whoever the targeting soldier was, he wasn't far off and he scored a direct hit on the column with his second shell. After that, all hell broke loose. Drazen pulled back and hunkered down as tightly as he could to the large rock he was lying on. There was little else he could do. Below him, blast after blast exploded, pounding the column all along its length. The artillery operators were relentless. He saw huge showers of wood, stone, green foliage and earth thrown high into the air and spread over a wide area. He heard agonizing screams which chilled him to his very core. This was a different form of terror to what he had experienced the day before; now that seemed like a dream; it was all done so quickly and efficiently and in an organised fashion. What he was watching below was sheer carnage; this was war in all its raw horror. The noise was deafening and he had to cover his ears tightly to prevent them from being damaged; and *he* was two hundred metres above the battle.

What battle, he thought as he pounded the earth in frustration; this was just slaughter, not pure and not very simple. His fellow Bosniaks were utterly powerless to defend themselves; some were armed with ancient looking rifles and some had hand guns but against the howitzers of the Bosnian Serbs, they might just as well have been armed with sticks. The shelling continued unceasingly and was aimed all along the column. Drazen had no idea if people had managed to flee or if all had been lost. He couldn't afford to move either to attempt to find out. Suddenly the shelling stopped abruptly. He had to shake his head several times and rub his ears to get his hearing back to normal. The adjustment was stunning; disorienting. So this was what war was like, he thought. His hearing eventually returned to some kind or normality and then other sounds started to filter in; horrendous sounds; men screaming in pain; calling to God or to anyone who might help them. As the smoke cleared, he realized he had a direct view of hell. Tears stung his eyes as he saw the dead bodies and parts of bodies strewn in all directions. The mountainside had been pounded into dust and was unrecognizable. There was blood on the earth and blood on the trees and plants and shrubs; the blood of his people;

incredibly, there was almost as much red visible in places as green. The path where the column had been walking did not exist any more. Most of it had been blasted to rubble and driven down the mountainside. Some of it still hung on, protruding at crazy angles. No one could have survived that he thought. And yet, people had as he could see some men attempting to minister to the badly wounded. But it was a hopeless task. If you were wounded up here, you would die up here.

He knew what was coming next and he scanned down the mountain to find it. The Serbs hadn't stopped the bombardment because they had run out of ammunition. No, they had stopped so as not to hit their own troops who were now making their way covertly up the hillsides. They were generally in groups of four and were in full battledress and armed to the teeth. Drazen had a perfect view and he would have loved to take a shot at them but he knew it was utterly pointless from that range with an old revolver. What would have been worse would have been to draw attention to himself. He suspected the Serbs didn't think anyone was moving at his level. He watched below as the 'clean up' squads systematically searched along the route taken by the column. Occasionally he heard screams or brief volleys of gun fire. These bastards weren't taking any prisoners. They weren't even affording their enemies a chance of a decent burial; people were just shot where they lay or where they were discovered. He occasionally saw some people make a run for it but they never stood a chance and were summarily gunned down. He continued to watch, almost as if he were transfixed. Or perhaps he felt that someone ***should*** watch; someone had to bear witness to what was happening here. The truth would have to be told somewhere. Right now, *he* looked like the best bet to do that.

None of the soldiers seemed to venture any higher on the mountain; it was as if they knew exactly where the column of refugees had been and had set out to efficiently eliminate them. Then it struck him; the column had surely contained several thousand people over its length. It could well have been infiltrated. He still figured he was safe and risked moving from his position to try to get a better overall view of the scene. Off to the north, he could see that a good sized portion of the head of the column had actually survived and had sought higher ground. But between it and him, there was devastation. He could not detect any signs of human life save for the occasional glimpse of a Serb patrol. There was still an occasional gun shot as yet another straggler was caught. Back to the South and East, parts of the column had survived also and as far as he could see, they were holed up and preparing to fight. Some of them had found a particularly good spot protected by an overhanging rock so it could not be attacked from above. But surely if the Serbs started shelling from below again, their position was hopeless. Or perhaps they were out of range and the heavy artillery was repositioning itself.

Drazen was no expert on warfare. In fact, until today, he hadn't known the first thing about it but he was learning fast. The more he scanned the positions taken by the heavy guns below, the more he realized that they probably were just out of range of the area occupied by the tail of the column. The vehicles could move over rough terrain but they could not climb a mountain. The Serbs had tanks also but he could see none of them in evidence with this unit.

The Serb artillery units and their foot patrols all seemed to withdraw back down into the valley and for a time there was almost complete silence. He contemplated moving on but thought better of it. There was no way he was risking exposure with thousands of Serb forces directly below him. He'd wait until dark and then either try to link up with the head of the column or go it alone. Beneath him, he again detected movement. A number of additional trucks and troop carriers came into view. He immediately recognised them as being from the United Nations as they were all painted white, except one ambulance which had a Red Cross on its side. Perhaps there was some respite for his people after all.

A white Land Rover jeep then made its way across open ground in the direction of where the tail of the column was holed up. It climbed the first part of the foothills and eventually came to a halt on the brow of a small hill. A soldier dressed in a blue uniform emerged from the front of the jeep carrying a white flag of truce. He climbed on to the hood of the jeep and he had a loud hailer in his right hand. He waved the white flag with his left and raised the megaphone.

"My Bosnian friends," he began, in halting Bosnian. "I am Colonel Ruud Van Dort of the United Nations Protection Force for Bosnia. We very much regret what has happened here today. Please understand that there are very few of us and we are limited as to what we can do to help you. But I have good news; peace talks have been underway to attempt to resolve this terrible conflict. Agreement has been reached this afternoon to allow me to escort you to safety behind Bosnian Army lines. Please come with me and my colleagues. We promise you protection and safe transportation towards Tuzla under UNPROFOR and Red Cross supervision. You can see both of us are here in the open ready to escort you. You are already in a very difficult position and if you do not submit to our escort, I cannot be responsible for what might transpire with the remaining Serb militias. As you can see, they have now withdrawn to a discreet distance. For your own protection, please come down from the mountain and we will escort you to safety."

With that, he dismounted from the front of the jeep, sat in, and it turned round and went back down across the slight rise, over the rough track and on to the main road. After a brief hesitation, the members of the column began to trek wearily down the mountain. They were a sad, tired looking lot, some carrying comrades who had either been wounded earlier or in today's attack. They looked gaunt and drawn. Most were poorly dressed with their clothes in many instances reduced to little more than rags. Most had probably had to leave their homes in a hurry and presumably had brought nothing with them except the clothes on their backs. Drazen stole a brief glance back to the north. The head part of the column could now no longer be seen at all and had obviously sought deep cover. Or perhaps they were too far below him and were merely on a part of the mountain that wasn't visible from his perch. He drew his eyes back to the descending group which had formerly been the rear of the column. He was again surprised at how many there were. There must have already been almost a hundred seated by the roadside with the U.N. troops but the line still went all the way back up the mountain. He realized then that he had never seen where the column actually ended so there may well be many more.

He watched, fascinated, as so many of his countrymen filed down the mountainside to safety. Why were so many on the move? He supposed it was obvious. What had Goran called it? Yes, ethnic cleansing; the removal of all Bosniaks either forcibly or voluntarily. This group had decided to go before they were pushed. At one stage he was tempted to join them but he was conscious that the Serbs were still in the area and would no doubt be scanning everyone who came off the mountain. He was already a dead man and he wasn't going to risk recognition by someone who thought he had already been sent on his way, escort or no escort. And then there had been last night. If the Serb police suspected foul play in Goran's death, they may be seeking him. He wasn't sure if that Serb officer had gotten a good view of him but he was sure their eyes had locked. Eventually the crowd thinned and became a trickle and about an hour and a half after the U.N. officer had stood on his jeep, the remnants of the column were all assembled by the roadside. Drazan reckoned there was well over a thousand people, perhaps as many as fifteen hundred. The overwhelming majority were men. He couldn't be absolutely certain from this distance but he was sure he had counted no more than five women.

The Bosniaks appeared to have a proxy leader who was involved in conversation with one of the U.N. Commanders. Drazen tried to fine tune the binoculars to zoom in on what was happening. The men appeared to be in animated conversation and the Bosniak leader appeared distressed. Drazen began to get an uneasy feeling about the situation. He scanned left and right and deeper into the valley. He could still see the Serb units but they were resting on the main road from Konjevic Polje to Nova Kasaba. So the column was safe for now, or was it? Something pulled at his insides; there was something wrong with this picture, but what? He moved the glasses back in the direction of the U.N. Commander again. By now, several Bosniak men were arguing with him and some seemed to be arguing with each other; but the vast majority of the men just sat quietly by the roadside. Then it struck him: the U.N. Commander had promised them 'protection and safe transportation'. There was no transport; no buses; no trucks; not even the most basic form of transport. Did the U.N. expect the column to walk to Tuzla? Quite possibly, as that was essentially what they had been doing up to now anyway. But no, how could a dozen U.N. soldiers escort and protect this number of what were effectively refugees? The argument persisted. Another U.N. truck arrived seemingly loaded with water. Ah, perhaps that had been what the argument had been about. Slowly, one by one at first and then in little groups, the column of men took some water to drink.

The U.N. Commander got back into his jeep and headed north in the direction of Tuzla. He was followed by the Red Cross ambulance and a U.N. troop carrier. When they had advanced about two kilometres they halted and waited for the long column to follow. The group rose and trudged along after them, with the other U.N. troop carrier bringing up the rear. None of the U.N. soldiers were planning to walk, Drazen thought, and why hadn't the Red Cross ambulance rendered assistance to the wounded? No, perhaps it had. He had been watching the others so intently he may not have seen it. He decided he'd wait until the column was well clear and then check to see where the Serbs moved to. Whatever direction they headed, he resolved to go in the opposite one, provided it wasn't backwards. The column had spread out a little now and the front runners were already a kilometre ahead of the stragglers. Good luck to you my friends, he said to himself.

He was about to shift his position to try to recheck on the front part of the earlier column when a movement in the grass below him caught his eye. The meadow to the west side of the road had been mowed and the hay was almost ready to be gathered in. It had been turned to dry in the sun and lay in broad golden wisps throughout the field. But suddenly the hay wasn't golden any more, it was green again and it was as if the entire meadow seemed to move. He momentarily squinted and adjusted the glasses but his eyesight was not deceiving him. The meadow hadn't moved; the stacks of hay had, revealing green clad Bosnian Serb soldiers in full battle dress. There must have been at least a hundred of them, spread all along the length of the road. It was over in about a minute. The Serbs just opened fire and the Bosniaks had nowhere to go; they were just ruthlessly mown down; cut to ribbons by the heavy machine gun and automatic rifle fire. As some tried to flee, they only made the job of the Serbs easier. They ran to the other side of the road where there was a large ditch. There they fell and died, not even putting the soldiers to the trouble of clearing them off the road.

Drazen pounded the ground again. For the third time in less than twenty four hours, he had just witnessed cold blooded mass murder. A trap, he should have known it was a trap. But they were U.N. weren't they? Or were they? And what could he have done. Tears again freely flowed down his cheeks as his countrymen were slaughtered like cattle. The Red Cross ambulance was reversed to where the carnage had taken place and the back doors opened. Two men inside were roughly pulled out and thrown on top of their colleagues in the ditch. He could just barely hear their cries of pain and protest. One of the soldiers who had emerged from the meadow and taken part in the slaughter seemed to say something to his commander who calmly turned round and shot the two wounded men, almost as an afterthought.

Drazen had seen enough. He couldn't stay. He needed to get away from there. What he had always remembered as a beautiful place now offered no more than a bleak landscape viewed on a road to nowhere. He began to run; whereas before he had moved with stealth, he now ran with no idea of where he was going; all caution was abandoned. This was his mountain, his countryside, his special place. This was all he had ever wanted. But it had been ruined. It was now a killing zone, a place that had been damaged, defiled, brutalized, dehumanized. Where beforehand, it had been full of wonderful childhood memories, days spent playing innocently and endlessly in the fields, those same fields were now littered with the rotting corpses of the friends he had played and laughed with. He ran in the direction of the first part of the column but with only a vague notion of direction. The impact of the brutality of the two days hit home fully and he was almost delirious with stress and grief. He never even saw the foot that sent him sprawling along the path. He hadn't even realized he had been tripped as he fell heavily on to his right shoulder. As he tried to rise, he cursed as he remembered that in his haste to get away, he had forgotten his back pack. He was quickly brought back to reality and realized he had bigger problems by the cold steel of the rifle barrel pressed against his forehead.

Chapter 8

Colonel Milanovic was now thoroughly depressed. He was on his third pack of cigarettes of the day and although it was only four thirty in the afternoon, he had already downed three shots of slivovitz. He was back in the little bar where he had encountered the Bosniak the previous evening. His colleagues had begun celebrating again with what was for them, good reason; what his excuse was, he wasn't sure. Yesterday and today he would carry with him to his grave, he knew. He could have dismissed it as war or collateral damage but Sefer Milanovic did not think like that. He was a professional soldier and he would fight to the death, having no hesitation about killing if the need arose; that was what he had been trained to do. But what these people were doing was something else entirely. Realistically though, who was he fooling? He had known it would be like this, ever since he had been asked by Belgrade to assist and advise 'our Bosnian Serb colleagues'. He had obeyed without question of course. Foolishly, he had thought that his status and his role as 'adviser' would assure that the conflict took place with a degree of humanity. But he was only kidding himself. Like all advisers, he was simply that. Advice could be heeded or ignored. He was not in charge; hell, it wasn't even his army so he had the worst of all possible worlds. He was, in effect, a highly paid, totally unheeded figurehead. To Belgrade, he fulfilled their obligations and kept them informed of what was happening. To the Bosnian Serb Commanders, he was at best someone they occasionally sounded ideas off or at worst an irritation. He was ineffective, neutered, silenced, kept at arms length and felt totally useless and was now close to despair.

The supreme irony of it was that much of today had inadvertently been *his* fault. The request from Belgrade to search for stragglers and to ensure the entire operation was sewn up tight with no recriminations going back to the capital before proceeding with further operations had been conveyed by Sefer. It had initially led to a blazing row between him and half of the officers who were leading their divisions onwards to Potocari. Their reaction, when he had requested a field conference to advise them to cover their tracks, had been utterly hostile. Even junior officers were openly critical of him, one even suggesting he had lost his nerve and should get the hell out of their way. It seemed to Milanovic that they were saying that he was cheating them out of their daily ration of blood lust. They were eager to advance to Potocari and to continue the slaughter. Eventually, he refused to listen to such scathing criticism and what was effectively insubordination and he sought a conference with Colonel Mistakovic. He advised the Colonel in no uncertain terms of what Belgrade had effectively ordered. As much as Mistakovic did not like it, his wiser side prevailed and he ordered most of the units to turn back and to spread out into individual patrols. Two of the most vociferous commanders were allowed to bring their troops forward to Potocari but the majority of fighting men stayed put.

Mistakovic had assured Sefer that his men would no doubt have a fruitless and probably utterly frustrating day, chasing shadows and men who were long since dead. The Bosnian Serb Colonel's attitude had changed considerably after the spotter plane had detected the column. After that, the pattern had begun all over again.

Milanovic's depression was interrupted momentarily by the mention of his name in the background. Colonel Mistakovic was in the throes of making yet another toast. "Sefer, my good friend, we are talking about you. Come and have a drink with us." "We wish to thank you," said a Major with a large bushy moustache and heavy jowels, who was waving around his beer glass and liberally spilling the liquid in all directions. Milanovic glanced in the direction of the group. All were now standing and facing in his direction. He reluctantly wandered over to the group. Mistakovic drew himself up to his full height and started:

"It is not good luck to make apologies as part of a toast and yet I wish to say to our friend here from Belgrade that we were not as polite to him as we should have been this morning. Gentlemen, the good Colonel is first and foremost a fellow Serb and he is committed to our cause." There were nods of agreement all round.

"Secondly, Colonel Milanovic is a wise man and he possesses the ability to view this war strategically, a facility which we, in our euphoria, do not always have. Today and yesterday have been resounding successes. But we should not forget that but for heeding the Colonel's advice this morning, many hundreds, if not thousands of the enemy would have escaped. People say war is hell and war is certainly chaotic but I am glad that at least one man is thinking clearly and I want to thank him, on behalf of all of us for his invaluable advice today. And I also want to assure all of you, that from now on, if the Colonel advises something, I want people to listen. Gentlemen, we are winning this war but we need order and discipline. I want no more running off in all directions just because we achieve an initial victory."

Again, there were nods and grunts of agreement. The Colonel raised his glass:

"Gentlemen, the toast is to Colonel Sefer Milanovic and I would ask all of you to drain your glasses."

The bar was filled mainly with Bosnian Serb military officers but there were also a few locals. All joined lustily in the toast, draining either their glasses of slivovitz or tankards of beer. Although the last thing he felt like was celebrating, Sefer nodded his thanks and acknowledged the toast from Mistakovic and the enthusiastic response from his fellow officers. At least he was grateful that they hadn't asked him to reply. Proposing a toast to what was effectively cold blooded murder would have been beyond him. He sat down again and fished in his pocket for his pack of cigarettes. He found it empty and shrugged. He made his way to the bar and purchased another. As he opened his fourth pack of the day, he wondered whether the cigarettes or the alcohol would kill him first because as sure as hell there was no chance that he'd die in this war. This wasn't a conflict where there was a chance he might get killed. There was only one side in a position to win this and only one side in a position to hurt the opposition and they seemed hell bent on continuing to do it until they had literally cleansed the land of anyone who remotely resembled someone not of their own persuasion. He drew deeply on his cigarette, ordered a half litre of the local beer and took both outside on to the veranda. Toast or not, he had no wish to stay in this company any longer.

"You've got about thirty seconds to state who you are and what the fuck you're doing up here."
Despite the heat of the day, Drazen felt the cold steel of the rifle pressed against his forehead. Through frightened eyes, he stared up at the man who was standing over him. The man was tall and dark haired but hadn't shaved for days. His hair was bushy and his eyes were so dark brown as to be almost coal black He was in uniform and it definitely wasn't the same as the one that the Serbian soldiers he had watched had been wearing. Nonetheless, it was so tattered that it was difficult to ascertain where it had come from.

Was the man with one of the militias? Drazen thought he recognised the insignia of the regular Bosnian Army. But people said the army was fragmented; that the Serbs had seceded and some of the Croats too, so which side was this man on? Drazen felt he didn't have a choice; the man he was staring at looked like a Bosniak but he wasn't sure. One thing he was sure of was that the man would soon kill him if he did not identify himself so he had to go for it:
"I am Drazen Istakovic from Konjevic Polje, just down at the bottom of this mountain. Please, I am running from the Serbs. You are Bosnian Army, yes?"
The man eased the pressure of the rifle but only marginally. He moved his eyes to his right side and indicated with his chin to a colleague who was out of sight. The second man, who was in the same uniform, strolled over.

"So you are a Bosniak, are you? Do you have identification?"
"No, please, you must believe me. I was part of the group who were shot yesterday afternoon. The Serbs took all of our I.D. The bullet only grazed my head and I managed to escape. I have been hiding out up here since".
The soldier finally eased the pressure and relaxed. He sat down on a rock, extracted a cigarette from a pack and offered Drazen one.
"Pleased to meet you Drazen, the name's Raif, you're a lucky man you stumbled into our patrol and not a Serb one because if you had, you'd now be as dead as those poor bastards down in that ditch."
Drazen inhaled deeply on the cigarette and apologized:
"I'm sorry Raif, pleased to meet you."
His eyes filled up with tears again.

"You're the first person I've spoken to since yesterday. Then this afternoon, the slaughter of those poor people just put me over the limit. I couldn't bear to watch any more and I ran. I didn't think there was anyone at this level."
"There wasn't," Raif replied. "We decided to seek higher ground when our charges left us. We were part of the column which was attacked at lunchtime. We were escorting the people at the rear of the column. We didn't fancy our chances with the U.N. 'protection force'. Looks like we were correct although our initial reluctance to go with them was because we were clearly identifiable as soldiers and we might have constituted a legitimate target for the Serbs."
"But they are killing everyone," Drazen said. "And it now appears that even the U.N. is helping them."
"For all it matters, I don't think those were U.N. personnel you saw this afternoon. I suspect it was just equipment the militias either stole or confiscated. These bastards are clever. We told the people in the column not to go but most of them were so exhausted, they didn't seem to care. Anyway, what are your plans?"

Before Drazen could answer, one of Raif's colleagues came rushing over and placed a finger to his lips. Raif introduced him as Hamdi. Like Raif, the man was also tall and had a dark, swarthy complexion. Both men were considerably taller and broader than Drazen and looked like they worked out a lot. Hamdi's uniform was also torn and frayed and the man's eyes were deeply sunken. Drazen reckoned these men hadn't slept much in perhaps days.
"Good to meet you my friend," Hamdi said, shaking Drazen's hand with a smirk. "You're a lucky man you

didn't get your throat cut. You should move more carefully."

Drazen was about to tell the man that he usually did when the man hushed him again and whispered:

"There was a Serb militia patrol on the path directly below here. We thought they'd stay on that level but now thanks to your careless bounding around up here, they may loop back and will probably come higher."

"I'm sorry," Drazen whispered in reply, "but I was in shock at the massacre below."

"We're in shock too," said Hamdi, "we saw it also, but not only that, we foretold it. Did Raif tell you? We had been in the rear of the column protecting the citizens. I thought those soldiers were not U.N. and I advised our people not to go with them but as we weren't sure if it was a trap, they decided to take a chance. You know, perhaps they *were* U.N. soldiers but we have seen enough of the weakness of those people these last few months. They are totally useless where protection of Bosnians from Serbs is concerned. They've allowed themselves to be bullied and over ruled time and time again."

Suddenly Raif and Hamdi became fully alert. They pushed Drazen down beneath the undergrowth on the side of the trail and signalled for complete silence. Both took cover in neighboring thick foliage. Now that the shelling had long ceased and the noise of the machine gun fire had faded, all sounds seemed magnified somehow. A barely audible sound came from the right side of the path. It could have been someone stepping on a twig or kicking a small stone out of the way. There was no further sound that he could detect. The slight noise was enough to put the Bosnian soldiers on high alert. Their senses seemed to be magnified. Raif looked across and once again put a finger to his lips and Drazen was pushed down deeper into the undergrowth and signalled to stay precisely where he was and not to move a muscle. For another few minutes, nothing at all happened and he began to wonder if the previous sound had been his imagination. Then he detected movement; the Serb patrol came slowly, in single file; four men in full battledress, with automatic rifles at the ready, all with fixed bayonets. They were still perhaps twenty metres away. Drazen lay transfixed, staring at them through the thick foliage. He was careful not to make a sound but he eased the old revolver from his pocket. When he turned to look, he instantly felt a sense of panic. Raif and Hamdi and their men had disappeared, as silently as they had come. What was he to do now? He certainly wasn't taking on four heavily armed men. He tried to sink even deeper, willing himself to be invisible.

The patrol was spread out over a distance of perhaps twenty metres, with each man five metres apart. The point man scanned the surrounding area and indicated to his colleagues to follow. The second man kept his eyes to the right and the third man exclusively scanned the left side of the mountain. The man in the rear merely watched his colleagues. As they passed Drazen's lair, the point man raised his left hand briefly and the other three men all halted in unison. The point man drove his bayonet deep into the thicket of mountain furze about a metre from where Drazen was lying. He then shrugged, continued walking and signalled his colleagues to follow. They began to move away and he risked a breath. He only then realized that he hadn't dared to take one since the patrol had stopped. All four men passed his hiding place and as the

terrain up ahead began to open out and the thick brush began to fade, the point man began to move a little faster. Drazen's senses were still on ultra high alert and he suddenly heard what sounded like a crash up ahead; something like the sound of a falling tree or something landing in the brush. The point man raised his arm again and his colleagues stopped as he went to investigate. Suddenly, in a blur of motion which Drazen barely detected, four other men emerged from the brush, each of them less than a metre behind the individual soldiers in the patrol. The movement happened so swiftly that none of the patrol members had the time to call out to the other. In the space of about a second and a half, four sharp knives were inserted in four throats. Blood flew in every direction in great fountains but the four men of the patrol were instantly silenced. Within a further two seconds, the soldiers had hidden the bodies in the undergrowth. Raif returned to where Drazen was hiding, beckoned him up and said one word:
"Follow."

Chapter 9

The group, now five in number, moved swiftly along the path with Drazen in the middle. He felt they were moving very fast, yet the four Bosnian soldiers seemed to be on high alert and very careful. He couldn't help thinking that if a Serb patrol happened to be hiding in a similar manner to the way the Bosnians had been earlier, then they were all sitting ducks. But the more he thought about it, the more he realized it was unlikely. The Serbs were on a seek and destroy mission against civilians. Probably the last thing they had expected to encounter up here was a highly trained army unit. No, the Serb patrols would be in the open; they'd be looking for stragglers; refugees from the conflict who had either been separated from the column or for people like himself, who had just escaped from genocide.

They travelled for about an hour, putting a good five kilometres between themselves and the sight of the ambush. Drazen found it tough going as they were still at a high altitude and the terrain was very primitive in parts. Eventually they stopped to rest when the mountainside opened out again and where there was very little cover. He assumed they would wait here and only try to make further progress under cover of darkness. The men had very little food with them but were more than willing to share. Drazen cursed his folly at forgetting his back pack which had contained his food and drink. At least he still had the money and the documents hidden in his clothing and the binoculars around his neck. The soldiers readily accepted him and he could see their bond growing firmer. When they had eaten and drank, Raif introduced the small, quiet man who had said nothing up to now as their Commander, Mehmed Pasic. Drazen was surprised that this small, wiry man was their boss. Like the others, he had not shaved for days and his uniform was ragged. His face was round and unlined and youthful and Drazen figured the man was possibly still in his late twenties or early thirties. When he looked into his eyes, he saw immediately why he was the commander. Mehmed Pasic had light brown eyes that showed kindness but also intelligence and a grim determination. It was as if he was saying, I'll respect you and leave you alone if you respect me but if you don't, I'll stand up for myself and you'll suffer the consequences.

"So Drazen," he said, "we get to speak at last, nice to meet you. Forgive me for ignoring you back there but I had other things on my mind. I understand you survived yesterday's sad event at the football field."

Drazen nodded soberly and related his full story to the man, who listened intently.

"Indeed, your story is similar to that of many," Pasic said. "Our countrymen have taken a terrible toll over these past few months and particularly these last few days. I can only speculate as to where it will all end. May I ask what are your plans, apart of course from trying to find your family?" Drazen nodded. "When I saw the massacre this afternoon, I think I panicked and I was torn between running for my own safety and trying to make contact with the head of your column and warning them not to heed U.N. promises if they were offered them. I saw the head of the column seeking shelter on higher ground earlier."

"Did you indeed," said Mehmed thoughtfully. "A sensible course of action in the circumstances. It is our plan to attempt to join them by this evening if we can locate them but it shouldn't be too difficult."

"I watched the column this morning for a long time," said Drazen. "How many people were in it initially?" Mehmed considered: "Oh, we didn't know the exact number but I'm sure there were more than five thousand. There were less than one hundred of us soldiers assigned to guard the column, partially because our army had become fragmented, both physically and philosophically." Drazen raised his eyebrows. "Oh yes," Mehmed continued, "all the Serbian soldiers have either joined the regular Bosnian Serb Army or one of the militias. The Croats are either unwilling to fight with us or want to form their own group to join with Croatia. While some colleagues have remained loyal, I'm afraid the vast majority of those of us who are left are Bosniaks. We had very little chance of guarding the column as we had to go through the most dangerous part of eastern Bosnia which is mainly held by the Serb militias. Yet, all of us volunteered; I guess someone had to. Unfortunately we failed. I have no idea how many escaped at the front of the column but I fear that most of the people who started out were slain."

"How long have you been traveling," Drazen asked. "Surprisingly enough, only five days," said Pasic. "You see, when we started out, people were optimistic. Our column consisted mainly of men, whose women folk had escaped earlier by public transport of some sort. These poor people thought they would just have to walk for a couple of days and felt because it was summer that it wouldn't be a problem. However, they had not realized that their trek entailed crossing extremely hilly terrain in the height of the summer heat. Most individuals started out with enough rations for only two days; by the third day, people were beginning to eat leaves and slugs. Finding suitable drinking water was a major problem and dehydration set in quite early on."

"Yes, I noticed that the people who came down from the hills this afternoon were in a poor state", said Drazen. "Indeed," Mehmed continued, "and of course we tried to move at night so they were also suffering from lack of sleep and physical exhaustion. If you factor in that many had already been subject to harassment and may have been exhausted even before setting out, it made their journey even harder. Unfortunately, it was extremely difficult to engender a spirit into the group and I'm afraid there was little cohesion or sense of common purpose. Dear God, it seemed to me that many of them grew almost delirious and were just waiting for it all to end. I am sorry we failed them but I fear it was an impossible task from the outset."

"No, I'm sure you haven't failed them," Drazen said. "I was watching the column from above you this morning and it looked suicidal to me to attempt to cross where you did with so many people." "I agree," Mehmed replied, "but what else could we do? If we had stayed where we were, the militias would have slaughtered all of us days ago. The only chance for this nightmare to end is for us to effectively give them what they want; to vacate the land and get to safety behind official Bosnian Army lines." "

But they don't appear to want to allow you", Drazen protested. "I mean, your column *was* vacating the area quietly and without protest and they cut you down indiscriminately."

"Yes, I fear the extremist elements have taken full control of all the Serb units. They are afraid that we will return to our houses and our lands when there is peace so they want to make absolutely sure that there will never again be

Bosniak people in these parts. It's like the Nazi's attitude to the Jews – they want a final solution."

They spent the next few hours under cover and weren't disturbed by any more patrols. It appeared that the Serbs had given up for the night. The Bosnian soldiers were almost certain that the missing patrol hadn't been discovered. For a start, it was significantly higher up the mountain than those of its colleagues; then there was the fact that the bodies had been well hidden. There was lots of blood but they had done their best to cover it over with sand and gravel and foliage from the mountainside. Mehmed reckoned that even if another patrol had discovered the bodies, they would be in no mood to chase down the perpetrators, not after the wholesale slaughter that their side had been responsible for today. No, if there were any reprisals, they were likely to be from shells and mortars from the Bosnian Serb military in the morning. The patrols were by now likely to be in the bars and small taverns toasting another day of slaughter. The sun gradually sank behind the mountains towards Sarajevo creating a brilliant kaleidoscope of pinks and purples and oranges gradually fading to dark blues and greys. Eventually it was dusk and time to set off again.

Mehmed ordered Drazen to stay well back towards the rear of their little patrol. In fact, he walked with and chatted to Raif, who was now bringing up the rear. Although they were unlikely to encounter any patrols, it was dark and potentially twenty times more dangerous than travelling in daytime. They made very slow progress as the ground was uneven and treacherous in parts. There was a three quarter moon but in the areas where the forest thickened, it was almost impossible to make out where they were going. Drazen's night vision was fully focused but without any reflected light to guide them, it was useless. At times, the sky seemed to close in on them and the trees seemed to cast crazy sinister dark shadows. To men who were unsure of where they were heading and unsure of what they might find around the next bend, it was a nightmare. He found himself realizing how exhausted the people in the column must have been and how any offer, no matter how dubious, might have sounded like salvation. At times, the man at the back of the patrol could not even see the man next to them, not to speak of Mehmed on point. Raif and Drazen suddenly bumped into the soldier directly in front of them. The man had seen Mehmed's signal to halt and had stopped dead in his tracks. Murmured apologies were stifled as the soldier signalled for complete silence. Mehmed came back to them and the little group huddled together. "Can any of you smell anything?" Mehmet asked. All shook their heads. Drazen couldn't hear a sound apart from the nightime hiss from the woods. The only things he could smell were leaves and plants and timber and wild flowers. "Someone is cooking up ahead," Mehmed said. "I'm sure it is our colleagues but let us approach with extreme caution lest it isn't." The group became even more tight knitted and slowed their pace considerably. Mehmed led the way but picked each step with great care. They all moved soundlessly, not even cracking a twig or rustling a piece of grass. Drazen followed their path. These guys are good, he thought. By now, he had detected the aroma that Mehmed had picked up earlier; if he wasn't mistaken, it appeared to be roasting meat.

Then Mehmed raised his arm and signalled for the group to halt and to take cover. Again, the patrol just seemed to melt into the trees on either side of the path with Drazen following Raif. "We wait here," the man said with a smile. "It's Mehmed's turn to play scout tonight". They waited for no more than ten minutes when Mehmed came back along the path accompanied by another man. The patrol emerged from the shadows and embraced the new man, who was introduced to Drazen as the overall commander of the column, Hasan Munic. "Thanks be to God some of you survived," Munic said, "we feared everyone else in the column was lost to us; welcome," he said to Drazen, embracing him also. "Join us in our camp. We have some mountain goats which were victims of the Bosnian shelling earlier today but we will take what we can get as supplies have been scarce. Please share with us. We can guarantee you safety for tonight at least as our camp is well guarded. As to what tomorrow will bring, only God knows."

Drazen thanked the man profusely and made his way into the camp with the rest of the patrol. A camp fire had been lit and the meat was being roasted over it. The aroma was delicious despite the harrowing circumstances. He looked around and could make out only men although he had seen some women and children at the head of the column that morning. Still, the fire had been lit behind some rocks where its light could not be seen from the valley and the people sitting around were in deep shadow. Some of the men rose up when they saw the patrol arrive and embraced their colleagues but most people just sat on the ground seemingly in a stupor or lost in their own private hell. Food and fresh water was distributed by others in the group. Visibility was limited but Drazen reckoned there was no more than one hundred people in the camp, perhaps twenty more if all the unseen look-outs guarding the camp were included. Maybe an outer limit of one hundred and fifty. Yet that morning, he was sure he had seen thousands of people spread out over ten or twelve kilometres. He felt sure that there were more people hidden but he was afraid he might intrude on these people's grief if he asked.

He was handed a plate of food by a passing soldier and as he sat down to eat, he was joined by Mehmed and Hasan, the commander, who was anxious to hear Drazen's story and to glean whatever intelligence he could from him. Drazen retold the story of his narrow escape and subsequent flight and his plans to try to locate his family in Sarajevo and the men listened in silence. Hasan and Mehmed exchanged glances when he was finished.

"What is it?" Drazen said, "Do you know something about my family?" Hasan sighed deeply. He was a tall, loose limbed man and he was sitting with his long legs crossed and his plate resting on his knees. He had a strong square face with almost sculpted features. He looked more Germanic than Slavic with his fair hair turned golden by the sunshine, his blue eyes and his perfect white teeth. He eyed Drazen with sympathy and said: "you are a brave man to have made it this far but I fear you may have to retrace many of your steps if you are to succeed. You see, we cannot get to Sarajevo; it is impossible, all the mountain passes are blocked by Serb forces. To attempt to cross would be suicidal. Our only chance and yours too my friend is to try to reach Tuzla. There is a corridor still open but we plan to avoid that as we are sure it will be targeted by the Serbs sooner rather than later. There is another way but it entails leaving the cover of the mountainside and recrossing the valley from whence you came." "But, but," Drazen protested, "we can't make our way in the dark and during the day, the valley is crawling with Serb forces."

"You are correct my friend," Hasan said. "There is no doubt it will not be easy but I believe it is preferable to going over that mountain to our left. Of course you are free to go. We will not detain you and we will wish you luck but I would beg you to reconsider before you start. We sent out patrols earlier this evening to check and there is just no way past. The area on the other side of that rise is fully secured by the enemy. They have heavy artillery which I am afraid would cut us to pieces." "But they know we're up *here*," Drazen said. "All they have to do is close up around us tomorrow morning in a pincer movement and we're all dead men." "And women", said Mehmed quietly. Drazen raised his eyebrows. "Yes, there are fifteen women in our column Drazen and ten children. They are sleeping now and are well guarded. But I fear they are weak from the last few days and the weeks of hardship so we have very little choice left."

"So are we just going to go down into the valley in the morning and fight them?" Drazen asked. Hasan shook his head. "No my friend, we are going to go down there **tonight** after everyone has eaten and gotten some rest. As I say, it is your choice as to whether to join us but as you say, the Serbs know that some of us have survived up here and there is no doubt they will come looking at first light. What we propose to do is to go down the side of the mountain which wasn't shelled and which still has cover from the woods. We have to emerge into the open when we reach the valley but if we do it at the darkest and quietest part of the night, we may succeed. There are less than one thousand of us now and if we can cross the asphalt road from Konjevic Polje to Nova Kasaba without being detected, we may confuse the enemy. Before they send any patrols in the morning, they will commence shelling. They may think that they have gotten all of us, therefore allowing us to head for Tuzla or Zepa. In fact, I feel we should split the column if we do manage to cross the asphalt road. It will increase the chances that at least some of us will make it. There is excellent cover in the woods on the other side of the valley and if we can make headway before the Serbs know we are gone, we may have a chance."

Drazen considered the man's words. So there were more than one hundred; thank God for that he thought. The plan sounded good. What had he to lose? He could stay up here alone but if he tried to cross the mountain pass, he was likely to be apprehended, in other words, shot on sight. If he retraced his steps, he could possibly hide in the highest part of the mountain indefinitely but what would he live on? Plus he wouldn't make any progress in tracking down his family. He decided to take the chance. He nodded at the commander. "Your plan is courageous and it just might work. I'd be proud to be allowed to travel with you but I must warn of one thing. Many of the houses you will pass in the valley are occupied by Serbs and we have no way of knowing if they will report us if they see us passing in the middle of the night. My guess is most of them would."

Hasan smiled at him, showing his perfect white teeth. "Ah, we are aware of that Drazen," he said. "In fact, that is where you come in. This is your village, your home territory, right?" Drazen nodded. "And you know which houses are occupied by Serbs so which ones to avoid, right?" Drazen smiled and nodded again. The commander had planned it all. He realized now that it was **he** who would be at the head of the column as it made its way stealthily thru the night.

By now, everyone in the bar was out-of-their-minds drunk and the talk was just meaningless babble. Milanovic lit another cigarette; he had long since lost count of how many he had smoked. He took his beer out on to the veranda. He smelt the cool night air and listened to the silence. All was quiet now but in the morning the guns would start up again, relentless in their pursuit of the Bosniaks and it was he that was now encouraging them. He longed for it to be over and to be back in his little flat in Belgrade with Irena and little Ana. But he feared this would be a long, dirty, messy war and that at the end of it, no one would want to know anyone who was in any way associated with it. What would his family and his friends think of him? Surely they knew he was a good officer, just following orders? But what would happen when the news of the atrocities filtered out and it **would** come out despite their attempts to squash it. Would his friends forgive him? Would Irena forgive him? He found himself thinking back to the previous evening and the Bosniak he had seen thru the bar window. Did you survive today my friend, he wondered. Probably not, unless you were clever enough to stay high and out of range or managed to escape in some other direction. Highly unlikely too, as all the angles were covered and you are a civilian. No, on balance, he figured the man would have been lucky to survive the carnage of the day. He dragged deeply on his cigarette and raised his glass of beer. Then he swallowed what remained of it in one and staggered back to the small hotel to his bed, hoping to avoid encountering yet more nightmares.

Chapter 10

Through the night they came, with the utmost stealth. They were barely perceptible to each other and totally invisible to anyone else who didn't know they were there. They had left at 02.00, having listened acutely to any sounds emanating from the valley for over an hour beforehand. When the last shout had died away, when the last engine had died and when the last noise had faded and the valley was stilled, they had set out. They moved slowly and uncertainly at first, as they descended the rocky path, always keeping to the tree cover and always mindful for any sound. Then as the men in front acquired a rhythm and began to move a little faster, the column acquired momentum. They had, probably for the first night in some time, eaten and drank well, and even though they were far fewer in number than previously, they moved with a purpose, even a confidence. That this was born out of sheer desperation was something that Drazen tried not to dwell on. He was now leading the column with Hasan; Raif was no more than an arm's length behind them. They had asked Drazen to lead them not just because he knew the houses in the valley but because it was his territory and he was the obvious choice to guide them on the uncertain path. Not wanting to dim their optimism, he hadn't told them that it was many years since he had trodden this particular path but as he seemed to negotiate it reasonably well, they hadn't noticed. Perhaps the tide had turned and the group was finally having some luck. Maybe their God had not deserted them after all, although Drazen had his doubts.

At 03.30, they crossed the asphalt road. This was where they were likely to be most exposed but despite waiting in the trees for fifteen minutes and painstakingly scanning in every direction, there did not seem to be a soul awake in the valley apart from themselves. In the time they waited, not a single vehicle used the road nor did they hear the sound of one in this valley or in the next. All was still; it was just a beautiful calm mid-summer's night; at one time, wonderful to behold, reminding Drazen of his days courting his beloved Sonja. How many nights had they sat by the banks of the Cerska River, drinking their few beers and smoking their cigarettes? The Serbs had been there too and the Croats; all had lived in harmony. At least, no one had ever bothered *them*. Summers were special to him because he had usually spent his winters with his parents in Sarajevo, longing for the onset of spring and then the long summer days working on his Grandparent's farm and his nights of bliss with Sonja. But that was now from a different world; from a place he no longer inhabited or could ever inhabit again. His entire world had been shattered inside a few hours. A nudge from Hasan followed by a nod told him they were ready to commence crossing the road. No words were spoken; no sound made. Drazen had brought them to the part of the valley that was least populated as most of the houses had been lived in by Bosniaks and surely hadn't yet been re-allocated or reoccupied by Serbs. They crossed in small groups and having safely traversed the road, immediately took refuge in the thick woods to the north. All had crossed by 03.45.

Hasan estimated that first light would dawn around 04.30. They would be moving through dense forest in the opposite direction to the Serb military units and as it was unlikely that anyone would be up and about before 06.00, he decided it would be best to get as much distance covered as possible, away from this once beautiful valley, now forever consigned into their collective memory as bringing only terror and suffering. The area north of the road was more familiar to Drazen and the path, being at ground level was more navigable so they made good progress, all the while ensuring that they were not observed and maintaining absolute silence. He couldn't help but admire the discipline of the women and children who uttered not a whisper or a word of complaint despite the discomfort of their situation. At 05.30, it was fully bright but they still had the cover of the trees. Drazen, despite his exhaustion, advised the column commander to try to continue if people were able, as he knew of a place a little further on where they could conceal themselves reasonably well. Soon they began to climb again and by 07.00, they emerged above the treeline on the opposite side of the valley. They could again see the entire enclave laid out before them but this time, all the artillery units appeared to be facing in the opposite direction.

At Hasan's instruction, they all stayed low until he and his men had fully scanned the area and deemed it safe. Drazen then showed him why he had advised them to try to reach this spot. Undetectable from the ground, the hillside turned in on itself in a series of folds, each providing perfect cover from everywhere except overhead. They could only hope that the spotter plane employed the previous day had been moved on. The group spread themselves throughout the first two folds in the hillside and collapsed, exhausted. Sentries who had slept earlier in the night were posted and Drazen, after a brief drink, lay down with the remainder of the group. He barely had time to realize that he had only slept for three hours out of the previous forty eight before he was comatose.

At the same time, Colonel Milanovic was beginning another day in hell. He had sent a message to Belgrade the previous evening while in a drunken stupor, asking to be relieved of his duties in Bosnia. He thought that his reasoning at the time had sounded plausible. He had reported on the 'successful' round up of Bosniaks and the fact that practically all of eastern Bosnia was now secure in Bosnian Serb hands. Yes, the militias would still be doing some more 'tidying up' but there was no further work for or need for a military strategist. The response was immediate and unequivocal; the Colonel was to stay exactly where he was until advised otherwise by Belgrade. He now perused both messages as he tried to eat his breakfast. He dreaded to read the message he had sent while drunk but to his surprise it was fine. Damn it, it even made sense. What the hell did Belgrade want him to stay on here for? If he was discovered, it would cause them further embarrassment and he was serving no useful purpose, or was he?

As he sipped his coffee, the officer who had disagreed so violently with him at the previous morning's meeting arrived in the dining room and nodded briefly. The Lieutenant had been one of the officers who had continued to Potocari when most of the divisions had remained in Srebrenica. He had returned later in the evening in a foul mood. Seemingly there had been many thousands of Bosniaks in Potocari or thereabouts but the Serb militias had failed to find them. Surely it was rather difficult to lose a few thousand people in such a small area, Sefer thought, and he even allowed himself a small smile as he contemplated the Lieutenant's situation, whether it was either misfortune or incompetence. Whichever, he found himself hoping that the extra day's head start that the Bosniaks had been allowed would be enough to get them to safety. He hadn't the slightest qualm about being disloyal; to him, war was war and he was as brave as the next man but indiscriminate killing of innocent civilians had no place in any war. Yes of course he knew that in every war there were civilian casualties and he also knew that this type of killing had occurred in every war since the dawn of time. To him, that still did not make it right. He wasn't of a political bent but he was prepared to acknowledge the Bosnian Serbs right to self determination in their enclave in eastern Bosnia or even their ultimate subsuming into Serbia itself. But this was a task that could have been achieved militarily with a proper army and that was what had actually happened. The subsequent slaughter had just been an aberration and unconnected to the military operation.

Yeah sure, he thought, as he took his coffee on to the terrace as usual and lit his first cigarette of the day. He gazed at the mountains again. All was quiet up there now. There might still be the odd person hiding out but he doubted it. The entire area seemed to radiate an eerie sense of emptiness. The only sounds were of birdsong, cows being brought to be milked and an odd cock, one of the few brave enough to continue to announce the onset of the new day. He hoped, for the sake of the fowl, that it was a Serbian cock as if it was of any other ethnicity, its optimism would soon be shattered. He pondered the morning briefing meeting and what hare brained ideas would be aired today. He had already more or less decided to remain silent, unless something was being proposed which might be very embarrassing to Belgrade. Considering what had already transpired this week, he very much doubted that would happen.

In the event, the meeting was a relatively routine one. The Lieutenant, possibly emboldened either by drink or by his fellow officers ignorance of what had happened in Potocari, reported that 'many' Bosniaks actually **had** been discovered in Potocari and had been liquidated. Whether or not this was true made no difference to Colonel Milanovic; both scenarios depressed him. The consensus was that any remaining Bosniaks in the enclave would head for Tuzla. All other routes were now impassable. It was agreed that all Bosniak civilians were fleeing the region as rapidly as possible. But rather than let them go and then secure the area for the longer term, the plan for the day was to follow and liquidate as many of them as possible. Milanovic spoke not one word but pushed his chair back from the table and walked away.

Chapter 11

The folds of the hillside not only provided the safety of cover from all sides but the slight overhang gave protection from the strong midsummer sunshine. It was well into the afternoon when Drazen awoke. He was shocked when he realized he had slept for seven hours. But all was well; new sentries were at their posts, having relieved those from the previous night. Even though they now appeared to be relatively safe, extreme caution was still the norm and people spoke barely above a whisper. A woman offered him some bread and fresh water from a mountain spring which he gratefully accepted. A small child, Drazen thought it was a boy but could not be certain, clung to the woman and appeared traumatized. Drazen motioned for the woman to wait; then he dug into his pack, which he had recovered untouched on the return journey and produced a hunk of cheese. He cut off a piece and ate it with the bread and offered the remainder to the woman who gratefully nodded her acceptance. He again dug into the bag and found a chocolate bar, some of the booty he had relieved Durkovic of and handed it to the child. The boy's eyes widened but he did not accept the chocolate until the woman nodded to him. Drazen produced two more bars and handed them to the boy. It was as if a sense of normality had returned to his life; after all the misery and suffering they had endured on their long trek, the chocolate seemed to break the spell and lift the sense of gloom which had been the boy's demeanour beforehand. The woman whispered to him that he might like to share the chocolate with the other children. All cares forgotten now, he broke from her and ran to his friends with the precious treasure.

As he watched the boy depart, the enormity of the situation hit him again and he thought of his own son. He hadn't seen Zoran for what, three days at this stage. He calmed himself; it was only three days, yet it felt like half a lifetime. So much had happened; so much had changed; their lives had become irrevocably altered; shattered, torn up at the roots and cast in different directions. He then thought of Sonja and Diana and he had to catch himself. But they would meet again; he would find them all. They were all alive and well, somewhere in this war torn country. To contemplate anything less was to enter a place even more horrible than he now found himself in and would have been unbearable mental torture. It did intrude upon his thoughts for a split second but he dismissed it out of hand. He told himself that the Serbs were only interested in Bosniak men; women and children were being spared; there was some humanity to be found, even in this place where his God had appeared to desert and where life had been devalued to the point of almost worthlessness.

He pulled himself out of his reverie and invited the woman to stay for a while. She sat with him on a fallen tree trunk which had probably fallen victim to the high winds that had raked the area the previous winter. He quickly learned

that the woman was called Tatjana and that she was the wife of Hasan. The small boy was their son, Salim. Hasan was still asleep as he had stayed awake well into mid morning to ensure all were safe and secure. He had also tried to contact some of his fellow Bosnian Army colleagues by radio but to no avail. Tatjana bowed her head when she said this; both of them had the same thought but no words were spoken; it would have been too painful to contemplate so silence was the best option. Drazen told her of his narrow escape two days before and of his search for his family. Tatjana was optimistic:
"We heard that the women and children evacuated usually reach Sarajevo or Tuzla or some of the other Bosnian towns. It seems that the Serbs are only interested in eliminating the men. I pray that you will find your wife and children when we get to Tuzla."
Drazen nodded and thanked her sincerely but there must have been something in his expression, perhaps a shadow over his eyes which caused her mood to darken. "You don't think we will make it, do you?" she said, deep lines furrowing her brow. She was an attractive woman, probably no more than thirty, with sallow skin, light brown hair tied back with a scarf and deep dark brown eyes like pools a man could drown in if he spent too much time looking into them. But she was worried now and much of the colour had been drawn from her face and her eyes grew misty. Drazen considered his reply:
"I'm sorry if I gave that impression Tatjana but I think we all stand an excellent chance of reaching Tuzla. Perhaps it was my worry for the fate of my family which made me seem pessimistic. Believe me, I am not; I have never in my life wanted something so badly. I so want to believe we will make it; that we will all be reunited with our families

and that this nightmare will end. I won't lie to you. I fear we have more perils to encounter before we reach safety but your husband is the man to lead us. I personally feel much safer now than when I was trying to make progress on my own; in fact were it not for your column, I might well be dead already."

"No, don't say that," she said, touching his arm. "You are a very brave man. Hasan has told me some of your story and you will be fine; you are a survivor; I know it. You will not rest until you see your family again. But it is a tragedy nonetheless; so many people slain; so many young lives wiped out. Yesterday morning, we must have numbered at least seven thousand when we set out. How many are we now; just a few hundred; and why? Why do they do this to us? Why do they hate us so much? What did we ever do to them?"

Drazen shrugged and nodded his sympathy.

"I'm not sure anyone can say for certain," he replied. "I have always lived in this country in peace. My father also lived without conflict. But I know our country and the broader region has many nationalities and that there are deep lying conflicts which have been there for centuries. I was never imbued with these by my parents when I was growing up and I had truly believed that they were long since gone and that I would live in peace throughout my lifetime. Sadly, that wasn't to be and it appears that many other parents didn't take the line that my father and mother did and passed on the old conflicts and prejudices to their children. I am still shocked when I think of my Serbian neighbour. It is frightening to think that you can know a man all your life and yet not know him at all. I always thought Durkovic was a decent person; hard working and a good neighbour. What did it matter that he was a Serb and we were Bosniaks? It never did or at least that was what I had thought. He may have harboured some well hidden prejudice or perhaps not; maybe we will give him the benefit of the doubt. It may have been the arrival of the Serb militias that persuaded him to change his attitude. He may have felt it was his ticket to survival."

He suddenly noticed that Tatjana was watching him intently, her eyes firm, focused and unwavering.

"You know," she said. "In many ways you remind me of my husband. You are strong willed, determined and brave. But yet you possess something more. Maybe it is a deep sense of humanity. Despite what you have been through, you are prepared to forgive your Serb neighbour, even though he almost buried you alive. You are a fine man, Drazen Itsakovic and I so hope you are successful. But be careful. You trust too easily. There many infiltrators; people who will befriend you and tell you they are your friends but who will betray you in an instant. Be very careful with whom you tell your story to and don't speak to anyone at all unless you have to. It is a shame but that is what our country has come to."

He thanked her for her kind words and for the food and drink. He apologized for keeping her from her son but she waved him off. She then excused herself and set off to join the children. He rose and went to join the sentries, resolving to check out what was happening in the valley. He had barely moved a few steps when the silence was shattered by a loud explosion. The Serbs had re-commenced their shelling but they were well off the mark, the shell exploding harmlessly about half a kilometre away. Hasan was awake instantly and was up organizing the group into as deep cover as they could find. Drazen and Hasan crept towards the edge of the promontory which afforded a view of the broad valley below. As they focused on trying to assess the Serb forces in the lowlands, another shell exploded, closer this time but still off target. It appeared the Serbs were getting lazy and just systematically shelling the hills. There would be no patrols, at least not for the moment as even the Serbs would be careful not to target their own men. Another shell exploded, this time further away than the first explosion.

"Looks like either an attempt to make the woods impassable or a lazy way of trying to eliminate us," said Hasan.

"If we stay behind the rocks, we should surely be safe," Drazen said, "unless they change the angle of fire and start shelling the higher ground."

"I don't think they can; I think that is the limit of their range. Remember we are very high here and their heavy guns can't climb very far".

With that, another shell ripped through the forest, a lot closer this time, sending shattered wood and foliage and earth in every direction and opening a deep crater just below their position. Perhaps Hasan was correct. The ground beneath them, which they had traversed the night before, was becoming increasingly close to impassable.

"Let us take cover my friend," said Hasan. "We should be safe until nightfall."

In the valley, the Bosnian Serb Lieutenant Ivan was gone beyond frustration. Having played a key role in the blood-letting on the first day, he had missed out on the second day's slaughter by his decision to go to Potocari. As far as he was aware, all exits from the valley were blocked so there must be, had to be, several thousand Bosniaks still hiding out somewhere. Yet his patrols had failed to find a single one. They had discovered the remains of their own ill fated patrol from the previous day, which had been made short work of by Raif and Hamdi and the Bosniak soldiers, but the culprits were long gone. Because there was precious little left to do and on the off chance they might hit the Bosniaks he believed were hiding out, he ordered the systematic shelling of the hills on all sides. Huge areas were already torn up by yesterday's shelling and the Lieutenant had enough ammunition to make sure the entire area would be impassable by nightfall.

Milanovic was in his usual role, merely observing. He was beginning to wonder why he even bothered to accompany the armored division today. It would have been far more interesting to sit on the terrace and smoke cigarettes. Still, he was a professional. The more he saw of the Lieutenant, the more he felt the remaining Bosniaks were probably safer if he said nothing and did not intervene. Lieutenant Ivan did not seem to be the brightest and would be able to balls it up all by himself. From Milanovic's viewpoint, indiscriminate shelling was just a waste of ammunition. Mind you, he thought, they did have a lot of it, all provided by ***his*** Government. He covered his ears as yet another shell blasted away from the ground artillery. He received a brief tap on the shoulder and turned around to see a junior officer. When the noise wave abated, the officer said: "Telephone call for you Colonel sir."
Milanovic strode towards the radio truck and entered through the rear doors. A radio officer saluted and handed

him a set of head phones. The man then discreetly exited the truck leaving Sefer alone.

"Colonel Sefer Milanovic," he intoned.

"My dear Sefer, how are you on this beautiful afternoon?" It was Jankovic and by the sound of things, he had had a liquid lunch.

"I am fine General Jankovic sir", Milanovic replied.

"Good news, good news, my dear Sefer. I have today spoken to our dear Minister of Defence and you are to return to Belgrade immediately. Tell those Bosnian idiots to provide you with an escort to the border. It is, I understand, firmly in Serb hands so there should be no trouble. One of our staff cars will meet you there this evening at 18.00. Is that clear?"

"Very clear sir, I will return to base immediately and set out for the border. I should make 18.00 without difficulty."

"Very good my dear Colonel; the staff car will escort you straight to my office immediately for debriefing; that will be all for now. I wish you a pleasant journey." Milanovic's initial elation at being called home was dimmed somewhat; straight to old Jankovic's office at nine pm at night? The man was always gone home by four in the afternoon. Still, it was war time. He removed the head phones and exited the truck. His intention was to find a transport; a safe means to return to base. But with all this shelling, who knew what one of these mad bastards might hit. No, the hell with it, it was time to flex his muscles. He was leaving anyway so why not. With a new found confidence, he marched over to the Lieutenant's vehicle and demanded to see him. After a moment, the Lieutenant emerged.

"You wished to see me Colonel?"

"Yes I did," said Milanovic. "I have just received urgent instructions from Belgrade. I am ordering you to cease this ridiculous shell fire and return to base immediately."

"But, but, Colonel, we haven't cleared the hillside and…" The Lieutenant took one look into Milanovic's unblinking piercingly clear blue eyes and hesitated. He now saw steel where he hadn't expected to find it. In a flash, he immediately regretted his earlier comments and indiscretions. Here was a man who received orders from Belgrade. He did not finish his sentence but returned to the truck and immediately gave the order to return to base.

Chapter 12

The sun went down in a blaze of glory but the light quickly faded and the area became overcast. Drazen suspected they would soon see a thunderstorm and presumably heavy rains. Good, he thought. It will keep the Serbs indoors and give us some cover to move. Also, the rain would be refreshing after days of baking in the extreme heat. Some of the men who had done the day watch were still catching a few hours sleep so the column was quiet, with conversation barely above a whisper. Although it was only 9.30 in the evening, it was almost full dark. Hasan was anxious to move but not until everything was checked. The sentries who had been posted on all sides reported the all clear. In fact, any Serb patrols they had seen all day were either in the valley or concentrating on the other side of the hill where yesterday's massacre had occurred. It appeared that their enemy had not realized they had made it through the valley the night before and that they were now on the Tuzla side of the hill. But Hasan was still sceptical. So was Drazen, who feared a possible trap. They sat, drinking coffee which Tatjana had made.
"Perhaps," said Tatjana, "the Serbs have forgotten about us or think we are all dead. After all, there were almost ten thousand of us yesterday morning and now we are only what, just under one thousand."

The men dropped their heads and Tatjana coloured when she realized the enormity of what she had said. Hasan reached out to touch her hand.

"Don't fret, my little Tanuchka, you are correct," he said. "We grieve for our fallen colleagues and there are very few of us left now but that means we must try even harder. Apart from our own survival, someone must live to tell what barbarity happened here. Someone must survive to tell our fellow countrymen and the rest of the world of the savagery we have witnessed."

Two of the sentries which Hasan had sent along the trail to scout then returned and came to the group.

"The trail appears to be safe sir," said one of the men, "although we cannot be sure about the higher passes"

"Thank you Murat," said Hasan. "So, my dear friends, shall we set out?"

They all rose and went to take their positions.

"Before we leave, let us all say a private prayer for the success of our flight and pray that our God travels with us this night," said Tatjana.

Milanovic had packed his few belongings in record time and having said a brief farewell to the Bosnian Serbs, had set out for the border. He was collected as agreed and comfortably reached Jankovic's office by 8.30 pm. The car was cleared straight through the entrance to the complex and traversed the courtyard at high speed to the main office building. It was an imposing nine storey red brick building and there appeared to be much more activity than there would normally be at this time of night. The car park was almost full and the lights were on in many of the offices. The Serbian Army car dropped him to the front door. He walked through the corridor, took the lift to the eighth floor and walked the few strides to the familiarity of Jankovic's office. He had been fastidious during his assignment and he had recorded each stage in fine detail. He had already made copious notes during the months he had spent in Bosnia, detailing each incident and his role in it, if any. He had sent almost daily reports to his superiors. He had spent the journey updating his notes on the activities of the past few days as he was sure Jankovic would want a full report. He had no idea how wrong he was.

General Jankovic's personal assistant was an attractive sergeant called Kristina. She greeted Sefer warmly, kissing him on both cheeks and giving him a brief embrace. He could hear several voices from the next room so he assumed the General was busy.
"I've arrived early Kristina but as the General doesn't wish to see me until 21.00, could you be a dear and get me some of that wonderful coffee you make?"
"My dear Sefer, I'll be delighted to bring you coffee but there is no need to wait. The General has company but he left instructions that you are to go straight in as soon as you arrive." She winked at him as she mentioned the word 'company' but Sefer had no idea what she meant.

He knocked briefly and entered the General's office. The first thing that hit him was the cloud of smoke. The air was thick with a mixture of the aromas of Cuban cigars and fine cognac. Perhaps his request for coffee had been premature. The General rose from his chair and greeted him warmly with a bear hug.

"My dear Colonel, you must be tired from your journey, have a seat; join us. The group was seated at the General's long conference table. There were seven men including the General. Sefer took the only remaining chair on the extreme right of the group. The General and two other men were in full uniform. Four other men were in civilian clothing, expensive suits by the look of them. No introductions were made and the men largely ignored him. While this might have appeared unusual in many societies, Sefer wasn't unduly surprised. It wasn't the first time that he hadn't been introduced. Some people felt themselves to be so important that they didn't even wish to be *introduced* to mere mortals, never mind to speak to them. Even though he was a full Colonel, he obviously didn't rate with these men but it didn't bother him. He recognised one of the men as the Minister of Defence. Who the others were was a mystery but from their demeanour and the way the General appeared to defer to them, these were very big fish indeed.

The General took a crystal glass from a side cabinet, poured a generous measure of cognac from a large bottle and handed it to Milanovic. He also proceeded to refill the glasses of his other guests. Hmm, Sefer thought, Hennessy X.O. Nothing wrong with my sense of smell anyway; very expensive so we are obviously dealing with heavy hitters. The General offered him a cigar which he declined. He asked if he could light one of his cigarettes and the General told him to go ahead. Most of the guests were chatting quietly among themselves but it wasn't possible to discern any one conversation. When the General had finished replenishing the cognac and cigars, he cleared his throat and there was silence.

"Colonel Milanovic," the General began. "Some of us in this room you know. Some you don't but that is of no consequence. Rest assured that I can guarantee the bona fides of each of these gentlemen and I can assure you that each is a true Serb who has nothing but the interests and the future of Serbia at heart."

He paused but Milanovic said nothing, merely nodded for the General to continue.

"My dear Colonel," Jankovic continued: "I and my colleagues are indebted to you. You have done a fine job in that hell hole that is Bosnia and you have protected the interests of our Motherland. We have many advisers in Bosnia at present but can you confirm for me that you were the only one assigned to the Bosnian Serb military in the region of Srebrenica, Banja Luka and Tuzla?"

Milanovic knew that the General knew this to be true so he wondered where all this was headed.

"To the best of my knowledge Comrade General, that is true."

"Ah good; splendid Colonel".

Sefer noticed that the General was sweating profusely. He supposed it was a hot evening and the man had been drinking cognac but still, he appeared nervous. The man to the right of the Defence Minister now spoke for the first time. He was tall and angular, with jet black hair, a thin face and a bushy moustache. He wore a dark suit, with a white shirt and a dark tie and he reminded Sefer of an undertaker. Plenty of work for him in Bosnia, he mused. The man spoke:

"It must have been very difficult for you Colonel, what with all those bandits."

"I am a Serbian Army Officer, I do my duty," Milanovic replied.

"Quite," the man said, "and we appreciate your valour and your devotion to duty but nonetheless, it can't have been easy. You see, General Jankovic here showed us copies of your reports."

Sefer was mildly surprised. Still, this man was presumably an adviser to the Minister for Defence and would be entitled to see the reports. For all Sefer knew, the man might even be the Minister's superior.

"Yes indeed," the man in the black suit continued, now donning a pair of half moon spectacles, "very comprehensive reports and very well written and neatly typed, if I may say so. You possess an excellent command of the language Colonel."

Milanovic wondered where this was going but said nothing. The man continued:

"Now Colonel, I'm sure you will want to rest up for a day or two, perhaps see your parents and family before you return to Bosnia but if you can see your way to helping us with these reports, we would be very grateful."

Milanovic was in a spin. Return to Bosnia? He thought he was finished in that God forsaken place. But the General had said, what was it that the General had said? Yes, only to report to Belgrade immediately. Sefer had confused the order with his request of the previous night that he be allowed to return home. A few days, see his parents, back to Bosnia, ah fuck this. He realized he had made no reply. He cleared his throat.

"But of course sir, General, if there are some points in the reports you need explained or some detail clarified? I'd be glad to oblige."

The man in the dark suit smiled thinly but it was for the briefest time and the smile never reached his eyes, which were like his suit, his tie and his demeanour, cold and dark. "Oh no Colonel, you must forgive me. Perhaps I haven't explained myself very well. There is nothing that needs clarification. In fact, as I say, the reports are very clear, indeed, perhaps even a little too clear for the interests of Serbia. Do you follow me at all Colonel?"

Sefer followed the bastard alright. Now he knew why they had called him and why all the top brass were here. The reports he had filed over the previous days were potentially dynamite if they leaked out. He had actively tried to halt the butchery, he had killed no one nor had he taken any hand, act or part in the slaughter. But the fact that he had been there would allow the rest of the world to scream that Serbia was complicit in a massacre. Given his adviser status, they might even assume that he had directed it. He made eye contact with the General but the man merely rolled his eyes and gave a small shake of his head. The message was clear; don't mess with these people. The dark man continued:
"You see, it is just a question of words really, words that could be misinterpreted. For example, I'm sure our Bosnian Serb brothers engaged in battle with the regular Bosnian armed forces. Oh there may have been the odd civilian involved but I am sure, as indeed I'm sure you are Colonel, that these men were bandits; hardened, violent criminals; cruel, blood-sucking devils who live in the hills in those parts and would cut your throat for a few dinars."
Sefer was disgusted but he was powerless to do anything. He took a large gulp of cognac and lit another cigarette. The General rushed to replenish his glass and discreetly

squeezed his shoulder as he passed. The message was clear; don't let me down; don't let the army down; don't let Serbia down. The man spoke again.

"We are all friends here Colonel, friends of Serbia. I'm sure you will see it is of the utmost importance to our nation."

Sefer took his time answering, eventually selecting the reply he was sure the man required. What could he do? The man had been extremely polite but they always were when they were threatening you. He had even mentioned that he knew Sefer was married. He knew his wife and his children and his parents and his brother and sister were here in Belgrade too. Just a mention was enough.

"I suppose it might be easier for all concerned if you just removed whatever words require adjustment, re-type the report yourself and I'll sign it for you."

"A splendid idea Colonel; indeed, I hope you will forgive me but I have already taken the liberty of doing so and I have asked Kristina to type them up. Believe me, I was acting in all of our best interests. Rest assured Colonel that there will be no sanctions on you in this matter. You are a fine Serbian officer who did his duty to the letter and your country appreciates you for it."

Who the fuck was this slime ball and what gave him the right to speak on behalf of Serbia? Sefer was not a violent man as he seethed inside, he fought to keep his emotions in check. He swore that if the exchange had happened in a bar, he would have decked the dark man, who continued to drone on:

"So, if you would be so kind as to sign the revised reports on your way out, it would be greatly appreciated. Colonel, you are an intelligent and clever man and I can see that we are similar men, of one mind, we both think alike."

An appropriate retort occurred to Milanovic but he said nothing. The thin man was smiling broadly now, as were his colleagues around the table. The deed had been done; the evidence destroyed and the butchery of a nation forgotten about at the stroke of a pen. Milanovic locked eyes with the man and gave him a look that would burn through cold steel. He then downed the cognac in one, nodded to the rest of the gathering, saluted the General and walked out. Kristina shrugged and placed the reports in front of him. He didn't read a word; a soldier obeys orders; does what he is told; no matter how distasteful. He signed each report and returned them to the girl.

He gave Kristina a brief hug, left the office and turned right into the gent's toilet. Perhaps it was the cognac on an empty stomach but more likely the bile came from his sheer disgust at his superior's willingness to draw a line through the deaths of thousands of innocent people. Whichever, he retched and threw up until there was no longer anything left in his stomach. He then went downstairs and instructed the driver to take him straight back to Bosnia. His emotions in a mess, he was no longer sure what purpose he served and whether life was worth proceeding with. He certainly could not see his family at this time. He was so sickened that in a perverse sort of way, he was glad to be going back. The only small satisfaction he took with him was that when he had eyeballed the undertaker leaving the meeting, he could have sworn the man had flinched.

Tuzla was the only option so the column proceeded, slowly at first, then with a little more confidence as they met with no resistance, no patrols and no checkpoints. It was as if the Bosnian Serbs hadn't contemplated them getting this far or even into this sector and had apparently left the uphills totally unguarded. The night was cooler but the air was still heavy and most were sweating profusely, either from the atmosphere or the tension or most probably a combination of both. Just before midnight, the storm hit. A huge vertical lightning strike rent the sky in half and momentarily lit up the countryside as bright as day. It was accompanied instantly by a series of massive thunderclaps, seemingly so close overhead that they were almost more frightening than the shelling that the group had become familiar with. Within minutes, vast sheets of rain swept down, instantly soaking all they touched and virtually obliterating vision. After a brief consultation, Hasan decided further progress was pointless and they decided to wait out the storm. They took cover where they could, huddling beneath trees and beside any rocks they could find. Everyone was drenched but that was the least of their worries. Hasan hoped their reconnaissance group, which was operating at intervals up to five kilometres ahead of the main group, had taken the same decision.

The storm lasted no longer than fifteen minutes but in that period dumped millions of tons of water on the landscape. As the rain faded, night vision slowly returned; the air felt lighter; the atmosphere was fresher and even though everyone was soaking wet, a sense of optimism seized the group and they started to make better progress. The path was treacherous but Hasan was well organized. He had six heavily armed scouts patrolling ahead. When the point man came across a particularly dangerous stretch, he waited for the next colleague, guiding him and eventually the remaining five men through the hazard and then waiting for the main column, before hurrying ahead and becoming the final scout. The second man now became the point man until he found a dangerous stretch and so on. Drazen was now fully absorbed into the group and although he was not a soldier and had no military training, his knowledge of the terrain and his natural survival instincts made him almost an equal with the troops in terms of tracking. He and Hasan were leading the main column and making excellent progress; Drazen reckoned they had covered about fifteen kilometres and it was still only 02.00 am. At this rate, they would be almost half way to Tuzla by morning. He chatted amiably with Hasan and his men, exchanging stories of their families, what their lives were like before this dreadful war and what their hopes and plans were when the terror was over. He was struck by the unquenchable optimism of the human spirit. These men had been through hell and back, yet they dared to hope, even as they again risked their lives to escort the column to safety.

Even as they chatted, all were on full alert and all seemed to spot it simultaneously. About one hundred metres ahead, two of the reconnaissance group were gathered. Either there was a particularly dangerous stretch or something was wrong. As they crept closer to the two men, the other four scouts emerged silently from the trees until the full column was reunited. The faces of the men were downcast, seemingly resigned to some new calamity. "Why have you stopped," Hasan asked. Raif spoke up:

"The storm may have been a sign from God. I was operating on point at the time and the bright lightning flashes allowed me to see the enemy up ahead. There is a pass which is not physically blocked but there are soldiers, presumably Serb militia, guarding it, just waiting to ambush us. Thank God for the lightning as I fear I would have stumbled straight into them. I have no idea how many there are but I would estimate at least a hundred. They are hidden in the trees and behind outcrops but the lightning allowed me to see clearly. I climbed that high tree after the first strike and I could pick out soldiers up to five kilometres away. There may be an entire division up there; it is impossible to guess."

The optimism which had infected the group after the storm dissipated instantly as the news of the latest hold-up spread.
"Is there any way some of you can get any closer without being detected," Hasan asked, almost in a whisper.
"Not without the danger of getting blown to pieces, no," said Hamdi. "When Raif saw the Serbs up ahead, he also noticed that a lot of the ground had been disturbed. I crept forward a few metres to check and there are land mines planted up there. We might be able to get through in day time, assuming the Serbs move on, but at night it would be lethal. Plus, if we set one of those things off, we would alert them and we might be trapped."
Drazen asked if he might ask a question and Hasan waved him on.
"Of course Drazen, our friend, you are a part of us now so please do."
"Raif, I know this place. It is called Kamenica hill. I think there is more than one exit. Did you notice if the Serbs are

gathered closely or spread out along the hillside?" Raif thought briefly.

"It was just flashes, you understand, but very bright flashes. I think most of them are concentrated around the main pass but I can't be sure. But I didn't see any other way to get through. Are you sure?"

"Yes, it will mean retracing our path and going downhill to the next level on the other side, the Sarajevo side of the hill. The path is narrow but I'm sure we can get through, that is if the Serbs haven't blocked that way also."

Hasan quickly analyzed the situation:

"OK, so the options are to go around the hill, guided by Drazen or to stumble through that minefield and make a stand here. We would probably be able to see off a hundred Serbs at nighttime, but who knows how many of them there are and what armaments they have. I suspect they won't have been able to bring any heavy artillery up here but if we do engage, we will just put the entire Serb militia on alert and we are bound to lose some of our men. Remember, they may not know we are up here so I think stealth is our best option. All agreed?"

There were nods of assent from everyone and the word was passed quickly.

"Drazen, my good friend," said Hasan, "I know you've been through much and you are not a trained soldier, but can I ask you to help us once again? We need someone to guide us around this hill. The scouts could do it but if you already know the terrain, it might help to speed us up."

"Of course," Drazen replied. "I was just about to suggest it."

"Thank you and be careful," said Hasan. "Tread slowly and if you feel any soft earth beneath your feet, stop immediately. I doubt the Serbs have mined the entire hillside but we can't afford to take the chance."

The men then embraced, Drazen went to the front and the column set off again, more wearily this time, now that their primary hopes of escape had again been dashed.

Chapter 13

Colonel Milanovic was back in Srebrenica by 2.00 am. His erstwhile colleagues had all retired for the night and the bar was empty. He knew sleep would be impossible so he once again sought refuge in alcohol. He eventually found the night porter and demanded a cognac. The porter gave him a brief glance, decided that this was not a man to be argued with, despite the lateness of the hour, and furnished him with a bottle of Remy Martin. Milanovic took it to the balcony, poured himself a generous measure and downed it in one. He lit a cigarette and inhaled deeply.

He was furious; professionalism was and always had been his forte. Now these bastards in Belgrade wanted him to participate in a blatant cover-up. He ruminated on the saying that the first casualty of war is always truth. This wasn't his bloody war but he had tried to serve his country as professionally as he could. But a cover-up on a grand scale like this was impossible. Surely they knew that? What had happened here would leak out; he was certain.

His country would be forever tainted with it and unless he could do something and fast, he would be personally blamed for it too. He could see a promising career going down the toilet. He could see it all clearly: First would come the denials. These would become more vehement as the accusations grew ever stronger. Eventually, some concession would be made but it would be passed off as a dreadful mistake. The Belgrade Government would deny that they had any direct involvement and he and his colleagues would be quietly repatriated. But there would be no glorious homecoming for them. He would probably spend the rest of his days stamping forms in some remote outpost, that was if he survived at all. Those people in Jankovic's office this evening wouldn't think twice about liquidating anyone who had an involvement; they might even throw a few people to the wolves, blaming them and denying any direct involvement or even knowledge of the massacre.

He needed to protect himself and he needed to do it fast. He was getting steadily drunk and he noticed that half the bottle of Remy was already empty. He could already begin to detect some light on the far horizon. He resolved to attend the morning's briefing meeting. He had been to Belgrade and the Bosnian Serbs wouldn't know what his orders were. In fact, they probably thought they had seen the last of him. He'd show them, but he needed to be alert and fresh. He replaced the cork in the bottle of Remy and brought it back to the bar, leaving some notes for the night porter. A quick shower to freshen himself up and maybe even an hour of sleep if he was lucky. He needed to assert himself with these bastards. Maybe it was already too late but he wasn't giving up yet. He checked his watch; it was

05.00 am. The place was absolutely still. In the deepest recesses of his mind, a plan began to form.

On Kamenica Hill, self doubt had begun to plague Drazen again. The forced detour was risky as they would now be below the Serb forces whom the patrol had seen lying in wait and for the first time since he started his flight, he would be vulnerable to attack from above. He began to wonder if he wouldn't be better off on his own. Was he being selfish? Probably, but he could not lose sight of his primary goal. He would help these people as much as he possibly could but his overriding mission had to be to find his family. His mind had been assailed with so many horrors in the preceding days that he knew he wouldn't, couldn't be thinking as clearly as he would under other circumstances. There were still almost one thousand people in the column; the odds of all of them evading the Serb patrols was surely lengthy. Were the odds of one man alone any better? Perhaps, but he would stay with the group for now.

While they had to move slowly and carefully anyway, he could detect the demotivation cut through the column again. Men and women were trudging where only recently before they had walked briskly. These people were weary; they were lucky to have had something to eat and drink but that might not last much longer and they would then be forced to forage for food. They had been exposed to dangers hitherto unimaginable and had been in the open, often under the burning sun, for days. Looking at their eyes, even in the pale light of dawn, he thought he detected early signs of delirium in some of them. This was dangerous as if any of them were to crack, they might reveal their location and it could be dangerous to the entire group. He had been drifting through them, checking on people, ensuring progress was being made during a broad flat stretch of countryside. Now, as he knew the path was about to become treacherous, he made his way to the front again and discreetly sought out Hasan.

The column leader was aware of the decreasing levels of morale and had similar concerns to Drazen. They spoke briefly and considered their options. It would be bright daylight soon and they had no way of knowing what awaited them on the other side of the hill. Drazen wasn't entirely sure of the area but he thought there was cover up ahead, although it would entail moving even further downhill. Stopping right now wasn't an option. They were exposed up here and as soon as dawn fully broke, they would be visible from the valley on the Sarajevo side. If there were Serb patrols or armoury down there, it would be suicide. They couldn't go back as the Serbs they had seen during the night would be alerted and could come round after them in a pincer movement. The next mountain pass was just visible now from their standpoint. Hasan passed the word back along the column that they would be stopping briefly soon.

They crept slowly around the protruding rocks and scanned the landscape through binoculars. The dark shadows of night were just giving way to shafts of watery sunlight. From their vantage point, they imagined they could almost see as far as Tuzla but it was an illusion. Their pace had slowed and the detour had cost them valuable progress. From here, it was probably at least another forty five kilometres. If they managed to find a safe hiding place for the daytime and if they managed to give the Serbs the slip, it was still reachable in two days. But would Tuzla be in Bosnian hands or would they be walking into a trap? No time to think that far ahead for now. Both agreed that their path seemed to be clear. No movement could be detected apart from the odd mountain sheep grazing easily in the morning light. They could see the tree line below them and to their left. It was no more than four kilometres distant. They both nodded to each other; the signal was given; they were on the move again.

"I am sick and tired of this relentless stream of invective and innuendo, not to speak of what you say when my back is turned. These morning conferences are a farce; I've never heard one intelligent conversation about military strategy. Call yourselves professional soldiers? You're not fooling me so don't try to fool yourselves. What you are is a killing machine; you waste valuable resources to sate your blood lust and satisfy your petty prejudices. I've seen enough of it. From now on, I want to see a disciplined, professional force who will engage the enemy in battle whenever they encounter the enemy, that is if there are any enemy soldiers left. If you encounter civilians, you will treat them like civilians; that is, you will allow them to get on with their business; these people have no quarrel with a professional military force; do I make myself clear?"
"As crystal Colonel Milanovic," Mistakovic replied, with an icy calm, "but may I respectfully remind you that while you are a very valued colleague, that your role here is in an

advisory capacity. As far as I am aware, I am still the commander of this division."

"Yes indeed you are, but may I remind you Colonel," Sefer replied, "last evening I was called to Belgrade for urgent instructions. These came from the very highest levels of Government. I am to inform you that the only people killed in this area over the past few days have been soldiers and a few bandits. Bosnian Serb militias have not fired on civilians and have had no hand, act or part in what is being called in the west, ethnic cleansing. Belgrade is aware that there is a war on and earnestly supports its fellow Serbs in this struggle. However, Belgrade would be horrified to learn that the conflict was anything but a military one and would under no circumstances condone the murder of civilians. Were such actions to be brought to their attention, they would have no option to but to immediately cease all armaments support and sever any links with Bosnian Serb forces. Do I now make myself clear?"

No one said a word but you could cut the tension with a knife. Some of the commanders shrugged or feigned indifference. Others, including the Lieutenant, almost levitated with hatred burning from their eyes. Sefer was pushing it but he felt he had them. They had no way of knowing what he had been told in Belgrade; he had gilded the lily but so what? He was damned if he would write incorrect reports. From here on, his reports would be, as they had always been, factual but this time, if he could help it, there would be no need for Belgrade to doctor them.

"Very well Colonel," Mistakovic replied calmly. "We will pass Belgrade's instructions along the chain of command, starting with this room. Gentlemen, you have all heard what the good Colonel said. I intend to take it seriously. If you engage the enemy, you may use whatever force is necessary to defeat him. If you encounter civilians, you may only use force if you are subjected to attack. Given the few remaining Bosniaks in the region, I consider such an event unlikely. Is that OK with you Colonel Milanovic?"

"Perfectly so," Sefer replied, "and may I thank you for your cooperation. We are all Serbs and we have common cause but that is no excuse for savagery, but I have said enough for now."

There was silence in the room once more. Mikstakovic asked if all commanders were clear about their new instructions. The Lieutenant, barely able to supress his anger, raised a hand.

"Colonel, Sir, we have received intelligence reports that the shell attack two days ago on the column of Bosnian militia, accompanied I might add, by hardened and violent criminals, was not entirely conclusive. We know that the column contained many thousands of men and while our attack was successful, we believe that a section of this column escaped and is still in the area."

Sefer probably should have kept his counsel but a combination of frustration, rage and alcohol made him comment:

"Yes, and despite blowing half the valley apart yesterday with valuable ordinance, you failed to locate even one of them, am I correct?"

The Lieutenant ignored him and continued:

"Sir, we now have reason to believe that these men may have crossed the main road between Konjević Polje and Nova Kasaba in an effort to reach Tuzla and may be hiding out in the hills. Sir, these are not civilians, these are Bosniak militia and your permission is sought to continue to hunt them down and engage them. Sir, there are also, we fully believe, dangerous criminal elements travelling with this group whom we believe are legitimate targets. They pose a serious hazard to our troops as evidenced by the brutal massacre of our patrol two days ago."

Mistakovic sighed and looked at Sefer, then nodded, indicating he should address them again. He's making sure this will be down to me, Sefer thought. Well, to hell, he wasn't giving in now.

"I will be more than pleased to accompany you on your search Lieutenant," Sefer replied. "Should we encounter these dangerous elements and come under attack, you will have no option but to defend yourself. However, if there is no attack, I suggest you either leave them to go on their way or, if they are as you say, dangerous criminals, take them into custody and we will soon see if they are."

"Excellent idea Colonel Milanovic, thank you," Mistakovic replied. "So, let us depart gentlemen. I wish you all another successful day."

Chapter 14

Sonja wasn't sure how much more of this she could stand. Over the past few days, her husband had been taken; presumed shot dead and she and her children had been transported around the country in buses. Her son had been spared in the initial cull of Bosniak men but when they had been taken off the buses in Potocari, her son was separated

from her and little Diana. She screamed frantically at the Serbs to leave him be, that he was only a child but she was answered with a rough swipe from a Serb backhand which sent her sprawling. Zoran was ordered away at gunpoint along with some boys of similar age. She was helped to her feet by Drazen's Grandmother, Edita. Frantic, she tried to chase after the Serbs and her son. Edita stopped her with a plea that she would get them all killed.
"Apparently, they are taking the boys to another camp," Edita said. "They are just segregating the men from the women."
Sonja was distraught but helpless. Bitter tears ran down her cheeks and she was convinced she would never see her son or any of her men folk again. To make matters worse, she was separated from Edita at the next checkpoint when another group of Serb militia decided to reorganize the groups differently again.

She was put back on the bus, less crowded now and apparently headed for Sarajevo. But she had no way of knowing; it was pure speculation and the Serb guards would not tell them. They travelled no more than thirty or forty kilometres and turned into what appeared to be a military camp of sorts. It wasn't all that large, perhaps a square kilometre and was surrounded by high barbed wire fencing. All of the buildings were a drab olive green and camouflaged so that there was little difference between them and the surrounding trees. The bus drove through a checkpoint and headed for the rear of the installation to a long row of single storey huts. There, the women were ordered to take their few belongings and march to one of the huts where they were informed that they would stay the night. Sonja was still frantic about being separated from

Zoran but was trying desperately to maintain the front for Diana that he was fine and would join them later. The women hurriedly left the bus to barked Serb orders to vacate. As Sonja was exiting, one of the guards made a mumbled remark about fresh meat and grabbed her breasts. Sonja recoiled, screamed and shouted an oath but the guard just laughed loudly, saying to a colleague, "we've got a right little screamer here, she'll be great fun later on."

The hut was stifling, with no ventilation and it stank of stale sweat and urine. The outside temperature was at least thirty so Sonja reckoned it must be close to forty in here. There were about sixty beds, all arranged in bunk format, three high. Each had a thin strip of some form of material but it was of such a flimsy nature that it couldn't reasonably be called a mattress. The doors were locked as soon as the women entered and the windows were all heavily barred. This was no dormitory; this was effectively a prison. Immediately, Sonja's hopes were dashed. She hugged her daughter tightly to her so that she would not see her tears. There were about forty women already in the hut, most of them lying on the bunks, staring, not moving. Some sat on the lower beds, chatting quietly to each other and some were smoking. All were dressed in the flimsiest night attire, presumably because of the stifling heat. The smoke seemed to hang in the air and made the atmosphere even worse so Sonja tried to steer Diana to a place with clearer air but it seemed impossible; one part of the hut was as bad as the next. Their fellow travelers looked around tentatively, seeking places to put their few belongings and make their own. No one spoke and most of the women avoided eye contact. No one needed to speak; Sonja knew what this was. She had heard about their uses in the Croatian war and there had been rumours that all sides were involved in this obscene practice. This was, in polite terms, a female detention centre; in reality, one of the so called 'rape camps'. She was suddenly almost overcome with an overwhelming sense of despair.

She found a vacant space near a window that was partially open and allowed the merest hint of fresh air from outside. One of the women motioned for her to sit on the bed. Gradually, the new arrivals found places all over the hut and eventually someone broke the silence.
"Welcome to Vilina Vlas girls, or hell as we call it," this from a woman lying on a top bunk, seemingly chain-smoking. The woman could have been any age from twenty to forty but was probably only in her early twenties. She looked like she had been there longer than anyone but who knew? She had long dark hair which looked like it hadn't seen shampoo for some time; she had a round face with sallow skin and high cheekbones. You could say that she had once been beautiful; perhaps she still was but there was something missing, something lost, epitomized in the emptiness of her hard staring eyes.

Suddenly everyone began talking at once and the tension, which had already been high, seemed to explode. The cries of women and young girls echoed throughout the hut as they learned what was to be their fate. Bouts of hysterics broke out all over the hut.
"Oh for fuck's sake girls, keep it down please," said the woman on the top bunk. No one seemed to take any heed and after a while, she swung her legs down and surveyed the group. She noticed that Sonja and Diana never took their eyes off her.

She lit another cigarette and cleared her throat. Gradually, silence filled the room. If there was a leader in here, this girl appeared to be it.
"Girls, ladies," she started, "I assume all of you want to survive? Well we won't get through any of this if we all get hysterical. I don't like this any more than you do. It's fucking disgusting but I aim to survive it. I'm no different to any of you girls. I was brought here over a year ago. I have no idea where my husband is or whether he'd dead or alive but that's not your concern. What you've all got to do in here is stand together to survive – remember that's the key word – that's all we can reasonably do. We are all in it together and we will all try to survive it together. We owe it to ourselves and to each other. I know, you can say it's easy for me, I've been here a year but it isn't, believe me. I hate every stinking moment I spend in this place. I would cut the throats of every one of those fucking Serb bastards that run this place if I got the chance. I would cut their balls off and feed them to the pigs. I, I would do a lot worse but let's just say you know where I stand. I guess you all know by now what this place is; it's a Serb rape camp."

Gasps echoed around the hut but everyone stayed rapt, apparently in awe of this strong woman. She continued: "In other words, it is a leisure facility for those bastards who brought you here and are trying to exterminate us in our own country. But politics is of no concern in here. Girls, please steel yourselves for me: you are all going to be raped, sexually assaulted, violated, call it what you will, repeatedly, continuously. Did you not notice that you are all fairly young and all of you are pretty? No? You didn't notice that they shipped all the older women off elsewhere? Neither did we at first but we sure do now." One girl started to cry softly and Sonja thought she noticed the older woman's mask slip slightly, but it was only momentarily. The woman continued.

"We are all the same here girls; we will all support and help each other. We will see each other through the worst of this because we are going to survive it. I know this may sound horrendous to you new girls but believe me, this is the only way to last in here. These people are merciless; they are cold, cruel and heartless. I won't call them animals because they are worse than that. They will sometimes come as a group and have us right here in full view, just to humiliate us more. Other times we will be brought to their private quarters. I know what I am now going to say will sound disgusting and contrary to every screaming impulse in your bodies but please, please, for your own sake, don't resist; it only makes it worse. If you resist, they will force you anyway and they will beat the shit out of you. Girls have been beaten to death in here, believe me. I don't expect you to like these people or to even be civil to them but please, I can't say it often enough, don't resist. Try to meditate – take yourself out of the thing mentally – do whatever works for you but protect yourselves. Some of these men are pure sadists and are prone to beat the girls anyway so for God's sake don't give them an excuse. Just remember throughout, you are not alone. We will be here for you, just keep that in your mind and you'll get through it. If you're good, they might even give you a drink or a packet of cigarettes. If you give them a blow job without any fuss, you can get several packs of cigarettes."

There was a brief snigger from one of the girls but this was instantly cut short by a baleful stare from the woman who had been speaking.
"As I say, it's about surviving, do it and don't think about it. Try to imagine you are far away from here. And they do feed us, the cuisine isn't great but at least we get food and water. Oh, and by the way, my name is Selma."

Sonja was frantic and immediately spoke up:
"Selma, I'm Sonja, my little girl is only eight and she appears to be the only young girl here. Surely she's too young for this place?"
Selma looked over at Diana, took another drag from her cigarette and seemed to think deeply for a moment.
"They've never brought in a girl this young before. Our youngest is little Fadil over there who's twelve whom we try to protect as much as we can. They usually bring single girls or married girls with no children. It seems to be more convenient for them. But they may have made an exception with you Sonja. I don't wish to unnerve you any more than you are already but do you realise that you are stunningly beautiful? You will be most attractive to them you know. Perhaps they wanted you and didn't want to separate you from the child. On the other hand, they just might have a paedophile or they might have someone who likes a Mother and daughter combination."
Everyone heard the shriek like gasp from Sonja. The way Selma had just mentioned it casually seemed cold, offhand, but Sonja knew it wasn't. The woman was deadly serious but just trying to protect them. Selma continued:
"I hope to God for both your sakes they haven't but they change all the time so it is a possibility. Remember these people are sub-human. They have absolutely no morals

and no compassion. They even seem to take extra pleasure in the amount of abuse they give us because we are Bosniaks. What you have to realize ladies, is that these people hate us. Their hatred is not rational but it is raw and visceral."

Selma stubbed out her cigarette and lit another. All the women seemed to start talking at once. Sonja sat with her arms wrapped so tightly around Diana, she might have caused her difficulty breathing. But Diana did not complain. The little girl hadn't said anything for some time now and Sonja was worried that she might be traumatized. She rocked her back and forth telling her over and over that her Mummy would take care of her. She hoped to God she could keep her promise.

Selma then spoke again:
"Oh, something I forgot. These fuckers think they are funny or maybe they try to scare us psychologically. You'll know when they are coming for us when you hear the 'March on the Drina' played over the loudspeakers. That's the signal for the boys to come out to play. Oh, and I also forgot, it isn't just the bastards who run the place who can use us. All Serb militia, soldiers, policemen, anyone in any sort of authority has a free pass to come here. I know; it gets worse; some of them are filthy. But don't forget, no matter how bad it is, we will be here for you when you return and we will stand or fall together".

Sonja now realised that Selma was far from the indifferent girl she had seemed at first. In fact, she seemed to be incredibly brave. Sonja felt inspired by her talk and her encouragement and almost felt as if she could survive this hell but then she realized she was different; she had Diana. She couldn't afford to take a chance on her little girl being abused; the thought terrified her. She waited until everything quieted down and sought out Selma privately. They had a brief conversation and Selma nodded but looked worried.

Some time after eight o'clock that evening, when the shift changed, they heard the drone of the fighting song from the loudspeakers. Several of the new girls began to shiver and many were crying openly. Other women tried to help and put their arms around them. The sliding of the bolt in the door was deliberately loud and sounded almost like the crack of a rifle shot signalling loudly that this was it, there was no escape; they were trapped. Sonja recognised the brute who had manhandled her earlier. There were five other men, three dressed in soldier's battle fatigues, one in a militia uniform and one in plain clothes. The soldier who had escorted them to this hell hole seemed to be the chief organizer. He called out a list of about twenty girl's names and then merely pointed to the newer girls who had not yet been recorded. Sonja almost fainted as he pointed a fat, filthy finger at her:
"You, come here."
A few moments earlier, Sonja had herself convinced that she would get through this but at the sight of her pursuer, all her previous conviction evaporated instantly. She grew weak and dizzy and her stomach heaved. Selma was beside her and squeezed her hand.
"Go ahead honey," she said. "Don't worry, they don't want me tonight, I'll take care of Diana. We'll play a nice game and Mummy will be back soon."

Sonja stepped forward. The man grabbed her roughly and pushed her into the middle of the group. They were then marched across the compound at gunpoint. These guys were not taking any chances. Girls were dropped off at rooms and barracks and private quarters and offices, pushed inside to waiting men, all utterly terrified. The number of girls was diminishing ever further and Sonja still hadn't been assigned. If that pig came near her, she'd be sick, she wouldn't be able to help herself. Eventually, there were only two girls remaining, Sonja and one of the girls who had already been there for some months. The soldier knocked on a door and a tall heavy-set man emerged.
"Here she is sir," said the soldier, laughing. He then turned to Sonja and prodded her with his rifle.
"What a pity for you bitch, you don't get to fuck me on your first night. The camp commander here has taken a fancy to you. But don't you worry my little sweet, there will be plenty of other night's for old Milos here to introduce you to his cock. You can ask Nina here later, she'll tell you it's a huge one."
"That will be all; thank you Milos," the camp commander said, with a frown.

Sonja turned away from the soldier in disgust and came face-to-face with the camp commander. He was short and squat and ugly and overweight but at least he seemed to be clean. She realized that she was clinging to anything she could hold on to, even the smallest hope. But terrified as she was, she had the presence of mind to realise this was the camp commander. This changed the game completely if she could use it to her advantage. But as he came closer, she was trembling so hard she was afraid she would keel over.

"Come with me," he said, gruffly, to Sonja.

"Please, this is my first evening here, I am so nervous, may I sit down," she said.

"Of course," he replied, "would you like a glass of wine?" Sonja automatically said no and the commander chuckled.

"Don't worry; I won't try to poison you. I need you for far more important matters."

Sonja shivered and felt sick again. She reached out and took the wine he had poured for her, drank it down and it steadied her nerve a little. She grabbed the bottle and rapidly poured another one and drank it a little more slowly.

"Feeling better then, that's it. Now, you are Miss Sonja I believe? Yes, very nice."

He placed his hand on her shoulder as he stood over her. Sonja shivered again despite the heat in the room. The man fixed her with a cold look and continued:

"I'm sure that dirty old Milos and most of the camp, not to speak of most of the town would like to get their dicks into you Miss and that's where I come in. You see, if you are a good girl and play ball, I might see my way to protecting you from the worst excesses of the men and believe you me, Sonja, can I call you Sonja, you do not want to see that. Oh, I could tell you some stories. They've had competitions you know for how many can fuck one girl. Oh I've seen it. I think we reached sixty once before we ran out of men and then we had to start again."

He laughed loudly.

"But of course I don't get involved in anything like that. No, if you will be a good girl, you will only have to service me. Now I do have particular tastes but more about that

later. You need another glass of wine?" he said, refilling her glass.
"But of course I also forgot, you have a little girl too. Yes, very, very pretty I believe. Now you won't be aware of this but old Obrad from the militia is a paedophile."
Sonya's eyes went wide.
"Yes, indeed, now he doesn't know I know but I can't be around all the time to keep an eye on him so I think it's really crucial for you to make sure he doesn't get a chance to get near the little one, eh?"

Sonja took another long drink of wine and cleared her throat. She breathed deeply.
"Yes sir, I think we understand each other."
She forced a smile and the commander returned it, squeezing her arm.
"Good, great, I knew you'd see the sense of it girl. So, shall we go to the bedroom then," he said, pointing to the door in the far corner.
"You may shower of course."
He followed her into the room and allowed her no privacy. He undressed fully and lay on the bed.
"In case you were wondering, I showered earlier my dear," he said.
Sonja very quickly undressed and dived into the shower. She scrubbed as much of the grubbiness of this shit hole of a camp as she could off her body and luxuriated in the hot water and perfumed soap. She then wrapped a towel around herself and emerged, quietly and demurely from the bathroom.
"Mmmm, splendid," said the commander.

"Drop the towel please, when you are sufficiently dry. Now, as you are new and I am tired, I will go easy on you tonight. Sort of 'break you in' as they say."
He laughed heartily.
"So, whenever you are ready, just a body massage and some oral relief should be perfect to start with."

Sonja dropped the towel and tried to banish everything from her mind; the traumas upon traumas that had already happened to her that day. Even the thought of what had transpired made her dizzy. She noticed that the camp commander was already erect and it took every ounce of her willpower not to throw up. She got on the bed and started to massage him. She felt his rough hands on her breasts and on her body and the excitement building in him. He had a new toy to play with and it was all his. She massaged his stomach, chest and shoulders and he moaned with pleasure. She then asked him to turn over and she sat astride him, massaging his shoulders and down to his lower back.

"Oh that's good Sonja, fantastic," he moaned.
Sonja thought back to earlier that day, when the soldiers had come. She had been preparing vegetables for their dinner and had had to abandon them. But she hadn't abandoned the sharp cutting knife that she had been using and had slipped it inside her dress. No one had bothered to search her at any point. She had been killing pigs on her Father's farm since she was sixteen; one more wasn't going to bother her. She slipped the knife from between her cheeks and quick as lightning, sat on his back, grabbed hold of his hair and slit the commander's throat from ear-to-ear.

Chapter 15

When Sonja had killed pigs, they had been controlled and tied down. Receptacles had been provided to catch the valuable blood to make the puddings, so nothing had prepared her for this. There were oceans of blood, fountains of it, on the walls, the ceiling, the bed, the floor, the door and of course, on Sonja. The commander had coughed and spluttered for but an instant and then died. What an efficient little assassin I've become, she thought.

Her next actions were to try to calm herself; she had been through so much that day alone. Don't panic, she told herself. No one is going to disturb the camp commander on his first night with his new woman. She slipped off the bed and returned to the shower. The blood washed off easily but she showered as she had never showered before. It wasn't the blood, it was the smell and the touch and the taste of that man that had invaded all of her senses. She scrubbed until her skin was red, then she thought of little Diana and quickly dried herself again. She thanked God that she hadn't had to go any further; she couldn't even contemplate it and though the room was still hot, she again shivered involuntarily. She then thought of all the other girls in all the other rooms who were not as lucky as she and who were at present undergoing untold obscenities. She felt selfish and thanked her God she had survived this so far.

After the initial adrenalin rush subsided, she realized how quickly she had been transformed from innocent housewife to cold blooded killer. She felt no regrets though. He had defiled her, abused her, treated her like a piece of meat and most importantly, he had threatened her child. He might not have been the worst in the camp but he was its leader, so ultimately it was he who allowed this type of subhuman behaviour to flourish. No, he had gotten what he had deserved and so would anyone else who dared to abuse her or any member of her family. She found inner strength she never knew she had. She thought briefly of Drazen and Zoran but it was too painful so she put them to the back of her mind.

She dressed quickly and hurried out to the living room. All was quiet. She risked a brief glance through the window and could see no one about. Then it struck her; there wouldn't be anyone about because the men were taking their pleasure with her fellow inmates. Oh, to have another twenty or thirty knives or even guns, she thought. But she couldn't worry about that. Her first priority had to be to get Diana and herself out of here and as far away as possible from this hell. The gatehouse would be guarded, of that she was certain, but apart from that, the compound would be relatively quiet. She saw the commander's tunic thrown over a chair and searched it – nothing. She gritted her teeth and returned to the bedroom. Ignoring the corpse on the bed, she grabbed his trousers. She found a wad of cash, a packet of Marlboro cigarettes and a lighter. She took all three – she didn't smoke but other people did. Back in the living room, she searched his desk; papers, photographs, pens, the usual mish mash but nothing of value. To the left was a small cabinet which opened upright. She lifted the lid but it was locked. Not even knowing precisely what she was looking for, she returned to the desk. Less cautious now, she began emptying out drawers. When they discovered the base commander was dead, there would be one almighty stink so no one would be worried about overturned furniture. It looked like the commander wasn't a man who took too many chances with his personal belongings. Unfortunately for him, he had taken one chance too many with his personal security. Probably being used to getting his way and being able to bully whoever the newest girl his men had seized had made him careless. Apart from the sheer arrogance and brutality of his behaviour, Sonja hadn't believed his promise of protection for an instant. She knew that when he grew tired of her or as soon as another young beauty was brought to the camp, she would be discarded like old clothes and passed down the line to his men to have their way with her. The thought again made her heave.

In the last drawer of the desk, she found a small key. She tried it in the cabinet; there was an audible click and the top sprung open. She had hit the jackpot. There was a large pile of cash, mainly U.S. dollars, two pistols, boxes of ammunition and a bunch of keys including the ignition key and a remote control for a VW vehicle. She dumped all of the contents into a satchel she had found beside the desk and made her way to the exit. She opened the door as quietly as possible and checked her surroundings. There was still no sound; to all intents and purposes, the camp could have been asleep. But she wasn't fooled; she knew what terrible deeds were being perpetrated behind these walls. She could only hope that no one was outside because if she was spotted, she was done for. She removed one of the pistols from the satchel, cocked it and set off gingerly. A pistol shot would immediately alert the entire camp but what choice did she have? She still had her knife but doubted she'd get as close again as she had got to the commander to allow her to use it. It was full dark now, the camp illuminated but only in places with pale lighting. There seemed to be many gaps where lights were either absent or not working. This suited her fine. Even though it was painstaking, she stopped at each corner to check, forcing herself to be calm and thorough. As she passed one doorway where one of the other girls who had travelled with her on the bus had been delivered to, she heard a girl sobbing; at another door, she heard a group of men laughing loudly and lustily. Her first instinct was to kick in the door and blow all of them to kingdom come but she forced herself to pass and tried not to think of what was transpiring mere feet from where she stood.

After what seemed like half an hour but was probably only five minutes, she reached the door of the hut where the girls were housed. She again looked all around her but saw no one. She tried the heavy bolt on the door and slid it back silently. She pulled the handle – nothing, damn it, there was a mortice lock as well as the heavy bolt. She fumbled in the satchel for the bunch of keys and tried each one in turn. None fitted – she tried again, frantic now. Diana was behind that door and if she had to claw at it with her bare hands, she was getting her out of there. Tears returned to her cheeks as again, none of the keys worked despite her forcing them to turn. She should have known; the commander wouldn't have the key to the hut; he let his men do the menial task of selecting the girls for him. She was about to despair when she thought she heard something; a noise, faint. She dropped on all fours and again checked around her, straining her ears to identify the sound. After a moment, she realized it was coming from the hut. A barely audible voice was saying: "Sonja, Sonja, is that you?"
Relief flooded through her.
"Yes, yes, it's me, Selma?"
"Yes, go to the gardening shed around the back of the hut. There are tools there that might force the lock."
She dashed blindly around the side of the hut. It was black dark here and she didn't notice the step downwards. She tripped and fell heavily, momentarily winded. The satchel had flown ahead of her but she quickly recovered it and

continued, more slowly now, partially through caution and partially because her ankle hurt like hell.

She reached the small shed at the back and felt for the door. There was a bolt which slid back and the door opened inwards. Thank God it was unlocked. It was as black as ink inside and she stumbled about, feeling for something, anything she could use. A spade, no, that wouldn't be strong enough. She tripped over a wheelbarrow and fell against something hard and cold. Even though she had hurt her jaw and felt blood on her cheek, she quickly forgot her pain when she felt what she had fallen on: a pickaxe – perfect. She retraced her steps from memory and made it back without further incident. She whispered as loudly as she dared:
"OK Selma, stand back, I'm gonna try to break the lock." She had to check around her again. This would probably make a loud noise and a loud noise could bring men running from everywhere but she had to take that risk. She raised the pick and smashed it into the lock. The impact of steel on steel seemed to her like the explosion of a shell in the quiet. She tried the door; the lock hadn't budged, not a centimeter. Still, no one came running. She raised the pick again, hitting the lock harder this time. It refused to move; this was hopeless. She needed to calm herself as she was becoming frantic again. She forced herself to think, is there a better way? She doubted she'd possess the strength to prize the door open but maybe; if the blows had weakened the lock. She forced the sharp end of the pick into a tiny gap between the door and the jamb, and then worked it back and forth to try to gain a little extra purchase. Satisfied with the grip, she pulled with all the strength her small frame could muster. There was a groaning of wood

and metal. She jammed the top of the pick still further into the gap and pulled again, this time until every muscle ached. There was a loud crack, the lock burst and the door flew inward. Sonja fell backwards and dropped the pick, adding to the din. As if by some miracle, still no one came running. Perhaps the men had grown careless, never expecting resistance from a group of women.

Sonja rushed inside and embraced Diana who was waiting with Selma. She quickly turned to the group and said softly:
"Don't ask questions, I was brought to the camp commander's rooms just like Selma thought would happen. I found a bunch of keys including these for a VW. Do any of you know if it's on the base?"
"They're the keys of that bastard's Passat. It's kept in a garage behind his office but he rarely takes it out."
"OK, let's hope he keeps petrol in it. Selma, how do we get out of here and who else is coming with us?"
"The easiest way is to drive through the front gate."
"But how do we get past the guards?"
Selma smiled wickedly.
"It will be our pleasure to take care of them for you; just give us two minutes. As to who else is coming, we all are but take Aida and the three youngest girls with you in the car. We will take our chances in the countryside. The only pity is that we can't take the other girls with us."
"But there'll be patrols; you'll be recaptured."
"Maybe, but not necessarily; I know this area, you don't, so get as far away from here as you can. Head for Sarajevo. There'll be fewer patrols and checkpoints that way. The Serbs think everyone wants out of the capital so they'll be looking in the other direction. When you get

close to the city, ditch the car. Other than that, I don't know what to advise you."

"OK, Selma, thank you so much. Good luck and I hope we meet again."

"Take care dear Sonja and Diana."

They embraced briefly; Sonja gave the second pistol to one of the other women and her sharp knife to Selma. She distributed the money between all of them. Then the women filed silently out of the hut and crept, unseen, towards the gatehouse to the front.

Sonja and Diana and the three teenagers hurried to the garage behind the commander's hut. Sonja breathed another sigh of relief when she realized this shed was unlocked also. She pressed the remote control and the doors clicked open. They climbed in and waited. Sonja didn't hear a thing but within minutes, Selma emerged at the side of the shed and gave her the thumbs up. She turned the ignition of the Passat, sweat pouring off her, now that she had sat still for a few moments. It started smoothly and she cautiously emerged around the side of the building. Selma kept urging her to hurry, signalling that all was clear. She didn't dare use lights but at this point, her eyes had adjusted to the darkness. She saw the gatehouse and the raised barrier. There wasn't another soul to be seen. The other women were gone, vanished like ghosts into the darkness. Presumably Selma would join them later. Sonja felt a momentary pang of guilt for the women left behind. Who knew what despicable punishments they might endure when the Serbs found they had been outwitted by a group of women. But she couldn't save everyone and the moment passed. She accelerated through the barrier, turned right and the little group tasted freedom, at least a form of freedom, once again.

Selma went back into the gatehouse and lowered the barrier. No point in alerting those bastards any earlier than she had to. They'd know soon enough when they returned the girls to the hut and saw the broken lock. Or would they? If she forced the lock back in place, they might not notice the bolt or they might even think, in their drunken sated state that they had left it like that. These men were sloppy. What about the commander? Perhaps they would assume that he was so pleased with his new love that he had decided to keep her until morning. It was a chance but worth taking. It meant the difference between a one hour start and maybe a seven hour one. She looked with disdain at the two guards who'd just gone the same way as the camp commander. She felt no remorse; both men had abused her and she was glad they had gotten their just desserts. She turned and wearily made her way back to the hut. She fixed up the lock as best she could and pulled the door closed behind her. Then she sat up on her bunk and lit a cigarette. She had thought long and hard about leaving with Sonja and the other girls and every fibre of her being had screamed at her to leave. But without her, she was afraid the other girls would not survive. They were her rock, she knew. With tears streaming down her cheeks, the first tears she had shed in many months, she settled down to wait for the others. They would need her more than ever now.

Chapter 16

The initial exhilaration of freedom rapidly gave way to caution and fear. Sonja had no way of knowing when the break-out would be discovered or when the commander's body would be found. She presumed both events would happen almost simultaneously. If the girls were found to have escaped from the compound, the commander would have to be told, whether or not he had a woman with him in his quarters. If there was no reply from the commander, they would quickly put it together and break in, even though she had locked all the doors securely when she left to give herself as much time as possible. How soon would it be before a heavily armed checkpoint hove into view? The car had a military plate but that would only pass a visual inspection. If she was forced to stop or even slow down, the sight of two women and four girls driving through the night in an official vehicle would immediately sound the alarm. The car did have very dark tinted glass which afforded some privacy. She had taken the commander's cap and tied her hair up but the cap was far too big for her and wouldn't pass even a cursory inspection.

She had no idea where she was headed apart from the rough idea that it was in the direction of Sarajevo. The road was reasonably good and there was very little traffic. But this was war time. All signposts and traffic signs had been removed so she only assumed because of the quality of the road that she was still headed in the proper direction. Aida sat up front with her, also wearing a cap pulled low over her eyes and all four girls were in the rear, little Diana hugged closely by Fadil and her two companions, Zudha and Dzenana. No one had spoken a word since they had escaped from the compound. It was as if all five were collectively holding their breath. Eventually, Aida broke the silence. She was a relatively tall, strongly built woman, who would probably have a better chance of passing muster as a Serb militia man but as she was unable to drive, the task fell to Sonja.

"I am from Sarajevo," she began. "As far as I know, the city is completely blockaded now, but there are ways to get in and out if you contact the right people. Selma gave me the name of a man who lives in a village close to the city who may be able to help us but I am not sure how to find him."

"Do you know the name of the village," Sonja asked.

"Yes I do, but have you noticed that all the signs are missing? It will be difficult. Selma gave me directions and I will try to follow them. Stay on the main road though. There shouldn't be any checkpoints unless they discover we are missing. It is still only eleven o'clock and the guards don't usually send the women back until at least one in the morning. Don't go anywhere near the mountains as the Serbs have installations in them all, dropping shells and mortar fire down on the city constantly. They even have snipers operating up there, picking off innocent people walking in the streets."

"I'm sorry Aida," Sonja said. "I was so naïve. We didn't realize in our little village how bad things had become in the city. Drazen's parents must have been trying to protect us, telling us that everything was fine but to stay away for the moment."

"I understand. I realize you will wish to contact your family but please be aware that it is very dangerous. Even if you enter the city safely, that is no guarantee. The militias attack constantly. I will try to get you in but forgive me if I don't go with you. I got out of the city in 1993 and I have no wish to return until this terror is over."

"We heard that there was some fighting but nothing on the scale you describe."

Aida sat silently for a moment, considering the girls in the back and then shrugged.

"You might as well know. The second half of 1992 and the first half of 1993 were the worst, at the height of the siege. There was initially heavy fighting and the Serb forces outside the city continuously shelled the Bosnian defenders. But the Serbs infiltrated and eventually won control of most of the major military positions. They eased up on the shelling then but their snipers took up positions both outside and in the city, killing innocent civilians at will. You will see signs that the Bosnian's erected signs saying 'beware of snipers' in many places, particularly on Ulica Zmaja od Bosne, the main street which eventually leads to the airport. Have you heard of [Admira Ismić and Boško Brkić](#)?"

Sonja shook her head.

"They were a couple who, as a protest, foolishly tried to cross the lines between the Bosniak and Serb sides and were shot down in cold blood. They are now famous in Sarajevo and have become a symbol of the suffering."

"But didn't the United Nations protect the city? We heard they had put in a security force."

Aida snorted.

"Oh, they did provide safe passage in and out for some people but they didn't protect the city from the militias, no way. We have no idea how many of our people have been killed, except that it is thousands. The situation is chaotic. People have lost their entire families. Women like us have been carried away in their thousands to be defiled by those thugs."

Sonja noticed that Aida had become quite emotional so she let her be. Eventually the woman said:

"The city is in a bad state from all the fighting and shelling. Our soldiers were poorly armed and had to capitulate too easily. Because the Serbs now control most key installations, it is probably easier to move around as they won't fire on their own people. But believe you me, these people will fire on anything if they suspect there are Bosniaks inside. They have shelled practically every building in Sarajevo, including hospitals and medical complexes, not just industrial buildings, government buildings or military facilities. We would bring the wounded to our hospitals and they would shell them again, trying to finish them off. It was relentless. As for our libraries and theatres and cinemas, they're practically bombed to extinction. Cultural life in Sarajevo has almost come to a standstill. In 1993, they even shelled a football game. Can you imagine? Yet people still live and try to work in the city; some people's courage is truly outstanding but I just had to get out. I had seen too much."

Sonja noticed that Aida said nothing of her own family or as to how she had ended up in the camp if she had escaped the city so she respected her privacy and did not ask. They drove in silence for a while, miraculously never encountering a checkpoint. It must surely be after one in the morning now, Sonja thought. They drove through numerous villages, all in total darkness, with no one about. The few vehicles they met seemed to also be military vehicles of some sort who paid them no notice. But how much further would they get in safety?
"Aida," are we anywhere near that village Selma told you about?" she asked.
"I honestly don't know Sonja, I think it might be close but I can't be sure. Selma said to look for a major roundabout

followed by a road overpass and she said it was the third village afterwards. I've seen several roundabouts and overpasses but none together although we must be reasonably close to the city. I can see the outline of the mountains in the moonlight."

After another ten minutes they found the village. It was no more than a hamlet, two dozen houses and something that looked like it might be a shop or a cafe or both. All were in total darkness. They drove through the village slowly and Aida took charge. She told Sonja to hide the car in the thick woods on the outskirts. She would go back into the village and search for the man Selma knew, a Nasser Kovacevic.
"Sonja, these are all Bosniak people, unless they have been infiltrated, but I doubt it. Still, we shouldn't take any chances. Stay with the girls. If I am not back in half an hour, just go, anywhere, hide in the woods but don't go near the city on your own. Don't worry though, I'll be OK, I'm sure."
Sonja did as she was told but she was suddenly afraid again. She was now the guardian to three other girls apart from Diana. All sorts of thoughts rushed through her head. Could she trust Aida? She immediately dismissed the thought and berated herself for even considering it. This was a brave woman, one of many who had already risked their lives for her and Diana. She waited for five minutes, ten minutes; time seemed to crawl. How would they survive in the woods if they had to flee? Surely anything was better than the hell hole they had broken out of? Eventually, fifteen minutes had past. Had something gone wrong? It suddenly struck her; the Serbs were ethnically cleansing Bosnia. Surely in a village this close to Sarajevo,

they would already have driven out the Bosniaks and replaced them with their own people? Should she flee? Sixteen minutes, seventeen. Were they torturing Aida even as she waited? The tension was burning her up, making her sweat profusely, yet at the same time shiver. She got out of the car and walked around, forcing herself to calm down. She looked back at the silhouettes of the houses outlined in the pale moonlight, willing Aida to return. Then a thought struck her: she had heard that the Bosniaks were usually burned out of their homes but this village looked intact, undamaged. She momentarily calmed and sat back in the vehicle.

On twenty five minutes, the passenger door opened a crack and for an instant, Sonja thought her heart had stopped. But it was only Aida. She could have kissed the woman, she felt so relieved. Aida was accompanied by an older man, maybe mid fifties, thin but wiry. He was bald on top but had a dark beard and moustache.
"Girls, this is Nasser," Aida said. "He says he will take us to safety. There is a place in the woods. This is a mixed village and although there hasn't been fighting here, he trusts no one. Thankfully I found him after only knocking on one other door and that house is also owned by a Bosniak."
The girls all got out of the VW and took their few belongings. Nasser nodded at them but did not speak.
"He says we must all go with him," Aida said. "The car is safe here for now as it is dark but he will come back and hide it later."

The little band set off through the woods. Sonja was loath to leave the apparent safety of the car but she knew they had been lucky to get as far as they had. Within a few hours, this would probably be the most hunted vehicle in the Balkans. She trailed the man through the pitch black woods. The thick cover afforded by the trees blotted out all trace of moonlight and it was so dark that they all had to hold hands and travel in single file but the man seemed to know where he was going. Nevertheless, Sonja held on tightly to the pistol concealed in the folds of her skirt. Her other hand was wrapped tightly around Diana's and she had asked Fadil to carry the satchel. The man seemed genuine but she was so consciously aware that for the third time that day, she had had to put her life and the life of her daughter in the trust of a complete stranger.

Chapter 17

Sonja was weary. She had had so much adrenalin pumped through her system this day that she was ready to collapse. Now she thought she knew how prisoners eventually gave up and would admit to anything an interrogator wanted. A brief flash of Zoran being questioned about his family entered her mind and she shuddered. A small voice at her waist said:
"Are you OK Mamichka?"
They were the first words Diana had spoken for some time and they immediately brought her back into the moment.
"Yes darling, Mamichka is fine, just a little tired."
"I'm tired too Mam, can we rest soon."
"Yes of course darling, we haven't far to go."
Sonja hoped she was right and almost as if by magic, a small wooden hut materialized in front of them out of the blackness. Nasser, obviously a man of few words, now spoke for the first time:
"This is an old wood cutter's hut. It's been in my family for years but it is hidden so deep in the woods, very few people even know it is here. You will see in daylight how well hidden it is. You have travelled a long way today and you have all been through terrible things. The facilities here are not great but you will be safe. I am certain of it. Here is some food and drink".
He handed Aida a large bag that he had been carrying. Sonja was so grateful, she wanted to throw her arms around the man but he seemed polite, reserved.
"I will now return and hide that car. Don't worry, where I put it, no one will find it and we may even be able to use it again. We Bosniaks still know a thing or two and we are

not beaten yet. I will return for you tomorrow but I cannot say at what time as I have my work. Rest assured though, I will return. Now eat and drink something and get some rest. I'm sure all of you are exhausted."

The women thanked Nasser but he dismissed it with a shrug.

"You would do the same for me in different circumstances. We have to help our own people. I bid you good night ladies."

It was late, almost dark in fact, when Nasser returned the following day. He apologized profusely for the delay, pleading that he had to show up at work and needed to ensure that none of his Serb neighbours saw him heading for the woods. He assured them that it was for their safety as much as his own and they understood completely. His wife Sanya had come with him and they had brought a veritable feast of food and drink. It was all good, wholesome local food. There were Cevapi, Bosnian kebabs made from sausages, Sarma, meat and rice wrapped in cabbage leaves and also potatoes, tomatoes and lots of pickled vegetables. They also brought fresh milk and water and even some small chocolate bars for the girls. The women couldn't thank them enough and hugged Sanya tightly. These were good people, who were risking their lives to help them and also giving them the best of food from their own table.

After they had eaten, Nasser sat them down to discuss Sarajevo. Aida had changed her mind about returning to the city. During the long day, she and Sonja had discussed their respective families openly. Most of Aida's family, including her parents, grandparents and two of her sisters had been killed when a massive Serb shell had hit their apartment. Aida had been working late that evening; otherwise, she would have been killed also. The shell had devastated the block and over one hundred people had been blown to pieces. Aida had fled the city thereafter. She still had one brother but she had no idea whether he was alive or dead. He had enlisted in the Bosnian armed forces when the conflict had begun in 1992. As far as she knew, he was in the Tuzla area but she could not be certain as she hadn't heard from him in over two years. He had a wife and daughter who had moved to Tuzla with him but she had not heard from them either.

"To think that all this chaos was going on around us and we continued to run our little farm in blissful ignorance," Sonja said.

"Yes," Aida replied, "but you couldn't have known. The conflict obviously hasn't affected everywhere. For instance, this village apparently still has Serbs and Bosniaks living side by side."

"The frightening thing was how suddenly everything changed. One moment, I was preparing dinner and my husband was working in the fields; my children were playing happily. Then in an instant we were just torn away from everything we had known all our lives; the men taken away and shot, the women and children transported; the shock is still with me."

Aida had put a comforting arm around her. Now that they had had the full day to think, Sonja had lost some of the bravado she had acquired the previous evening through a combination of adrenalin and sheer terror. She had time to think about Zoran and contemplate all the horrendous things that could have befallen him in the hands of those thugs. She thought about Edita and where she might be. Zoran was an intelligent and a resourceful boy and she hoped he might some way be safe and find his way to his grandparents. Edita was an old woman and no threat to them so they would surely leave her alone. Sonja was an optimist and she refused to give up. It was only when she thought of her husband and his Grandfather that she almost broke down. In this case, it was pointless to hope, she knew. The Serbs wanted to cleanse the land of Bosniaks so they had shot any able bodied Bosniak man they encountered. Perhaps some day she might return and find her husband's body but for now she had to find safety for Diana; at least she was sure where her little girl was and she would fight to the death to protect her. If all else failed, at least she would have her.

She had reflected on her time at the camp the previous day. Things had happened so quickly and so violently that it seemed almost surreal to her now. She gave thanks that she had had the opportunity to escape from the worst of the tortures inflicted there and she then thought about those marvellous women. It was amazing how they had managed to survive and keep their sanity. Selma was obviously a big factor in keeping them together and giving them support. She supposed it proved that people can survive anything if they are not alone – if they have support. There were so many of them, all suffering horrendous abuse but all supporting each other. When she thought of Selma, she wondered had the woman actually taken the option of escape at all? The women had encountered no checkpoints the previous night; had Selma covered for them and delayed the discovery? She hadn't seemed in any hurry to leave the place when Sonja was driving out the gate. Tears came to her eyes again as she contemplated the woman's bravery.

The long day had only given her time to worry and she was glad when Nasser and his wife Sanya had appeared. Now they could focus on something. The teenage girls had taken Diana away to play a game so it was just her and Aida with Nasser and his wife. The man spoke softly but clearly:
"I know you ladies wish to get to Sarajevo but it will be difficult. The city is fully blockaded. I also need to advise you that even if you do get to the city, it is not safe. People are being killed there every day. It is also not the city you might remember. Practically every building has been damaged in some way and many have been destroyed completely. If you still want to attempt it, I will help you in any way I can. I have to tell you that it might be easier to find you safe passage to Tuzla, even though it is a lot farther away."
"But my husband's parents are in Sarajevo and I don't know anyone in Tuzla," Sonja pleaded. Nasser stole a quick glance at Aida who nodded imperceptibly.
"OK, I will do my best but it will be dangerous for you and the child and bear in mind that Sarajevo is not the city you remember. It is a city at war where danger lurks at every corner, particularly at night and it will be at night that we will attempt to enter it."
Sonja nodded.
"I know and I really appreciate your help. It's just that, I can't stay here waiting for the war to end. I know you have

not said so but we cannot stay here. We will only endanger you and your family if we are caught. The Bosnian Serb militias will be looking for me specifically after we escaped from their camp and I would only endanger everyone if I stay. Someone is bound to notice eventually." Nasser nodded in agreement.

"You are correct Sonja, you cannot stay here indefinitely. You have not been the first people I protected and you will not be the last but yes, it is best if you keep moving. I don't know what you did back at that camp and I don't want to know but perhaps you over estimate the Serb militias. They are in the main a disorganized fragmented bunch; many of them are not trained at all, they are just blood thirsty thugs. So, they probably won't bother looking for you specifically. Any Bosniak will do them."

Sonja shuddered inwardly when she contemplated his words. She hadn't killed just any militia man. She had killed a camp commander. She had also been indirectly responsible for the death of the two gatehouse guards; not to speak of the escape of almost thirty women. They would surely be searching for her. If she was caught here, Nasser & Sanya and the entire village would be put to death, she was certain of it, now that she realized what was happening in this country.

"Nasser," she began again: "My husband's parents are now the only people I know in the world. I have to try to protect my daughter but I also want to get my son back or at least try. My father-in-law is connected. He knows people. He will know what to do. I don't even know where to start. I realize that I may be endangering the girls but what options do I have?"

"Yes, I understand. We too would like to protect them but I fear we could not hide them indefinitely. If Sarajevo is the only option, then we must try. There are only two possible ways to gain entry. It is more difficult to leave the city but that doesn't make it easy to enter it either, believe me. We can try to get around some of the Serb positions in darkness but that is the more dangerous option; if we were caught, we would all die. The other option is the tunnel."
Sonja and Aida's eyes went wide.

"Yes," Nasser continued, "there is a tunnel, of that I am sure. I do not know where it starts or ends but it does exist and has for some time. Very few people know of it; obviously not the Serbs or they would have bombed it out of existence. I have helped some people who have escaped the city through it so I am fairly certain it is still operational. The catch is that as far as I am aware, it is operated by Bosniak criminals; these are hardened men who use the tunnel to smuggle arms, drugs, alcohol and food; anything they can make money from. These men are extremely dangerous and I cannot vouch for them. What I do know is that they will charge significant money and I cannot help you with that as I am a simple farmer."

"That won't be a problem I think," Sonja answered, a little uncertainly. "We do have dollars. Can you find out what they would charge to take the six of us into the city? If we can get there safely, I know my father-in-law will safeguard us."

Nasser sighed deeply. The poor man was torn. He wanted to help them but was afraid he might be leading them into an even more dangerous situation. But was there an option? He knew that sooner or later, one of his nosy Serb neighbours might become suspicious. People watch everything in small villages and there are no secrets. All that needed to happen was for a neighbour to see him or his wife heading into the woods with food and whisper a word in the ear of a local militia man. He wasn't sure they would do it but he wasn't sure they wouldn't. Trust no one was the order of the day.

"OK ladies," he said. "I will make discreet enquiries. We have brought you enough food and drink to last for a few days. I may return tomorrow or it may be later. I will only return when I have definite news. In the meantime, keep a sharp look out. Very few people come this deep into the woods but I can't be certain."

He rose to leave. Sonja and Aida offered to pay him and Sanya for the food but their protests were waved away and both refused to take a cent. They returned to the hut with the girls. It was basic but comfortable. Sonja knew that although she still felt exhausted, sleep would not come easy tonight. On the previous night, she had just collapsed from fatigue. Now her mind was too active weighing up her predicament: would the bandits just take their money and kill them? Would they do worse? Aida had told her that it wasn't just the Serbs who operated rape camps. Sonja was shocked to hear that the Bosnians did it also; and the Croatians. It seemed as if all the peoples of this benighted region wanted to inflict unspeakable suffering on their neighbours. Aida told her that it went back hundreds of years. It had been simmering and building for generations in Tito's Yugoslavia but the lid had been kept on it until now. Sonja had only ever been in her own village and in Sarajevo and while she was aware that she lived in a multi-racial environment, she had never been aware of the tensions or of the sheer naked hatred that could be unleashed once these tensions were allowed come to the surface. She also tried to banish the terrible thoughts that kept intruding on her mind about the fate of Zoran, Drazen and the rest of her family. With all their futures hanging by threads, she settled down for what would be a troubled night's sleep.

Chapter 18

It was two nights later when Nasser returned, this time alone. Sonja had been growing increasingly frantic over the passage of the two days, wondering if the man had been discovered. Would the militias be coming for them; had they been seen by some of the villagers? She pined for her son and grieved for her husband. She knew that it was all pointless and that it was the amount of time she had that was playing tricks on her mind. But she could not rest easy. Aida was a rock, preparing the food, helping the girls when they became fretful or frightened and even playing games with Diana. Sonja shook herself out of her worrisome state when she realized how lucky she was. These three teenagers were all Muslims. There was no doubt that all had been abused many times by the militias in that camp. Yet they were brave, stoic, willing to put on a brave face. What future had they? They would be viewed as defiled and might even be cast out by their own people. The girls had not spoken about their ordeal to her and she had not asked. Aida was acting as a surrogate Mother to them, comforting and helping them. They also loved Diana and the little girl seemed to have rediscovered herself and come back from the trauma she had suffered on the first day. She was laughing and smiling and playing with the girls although they were careful to be quiet and not to wander from the surrounds of the hut. Sonja had no idea how much of what had been happening at that camp Diana had taken in. She prayed it had gone over her head but she daren't ask. She had told Diana that they were on a journey and that all would be reunited eventually. How much the girl believed she didn't know or possibly didn't want to know but she was certain that Diana didn't think they were on holiday.

"We have had some good luck at last ladies," Nasser said. "I have managed to agree with these people to take you into Sarajevo in exchange for the car you drove here. That is ideal as it is of no use to me and I cannot hide it indefinitely. They usually charge about five hundred dollars per person to assist people to leave the city. I don't know what they charge to enter it but either way, they are getting a good deal. But it will be good for you as you can keep your money. There is no doubt you will need it at some point."

"But do they know that it is a Serb vehicle?" Sonja wondered.

"Of course they do," Nasser smiled. "But that is of no consequence to black marketeers. The car is in good condition so it will probably be sent south within days. The plan is that you will have to drive to another village even closer to the city. You will do this tomorrow night. I will give you precise instructions but I cannot travel with you. Apart from the fact that there is not enough room in the car, these men do not wish me to associate with them. I have made the arrangements with an intermediary."

Sonja could feel rising panic again.

"But what if these people just take the car and abandon us," said Aida, "Or worse, take the car and kill us?"

"It is a valid point," Nasser said, "and I appreciate your concern. However, I don't think they will. These men are dangerous without a doubt and are hardened criminals. However, they make a living from smuggling so there is no reason for them to kill you or abandon you. I know it is a secretive operation but if word were to get out that they

did not deliver on their side of the bargain, I can only assume it would be bad for their business. If you don't wish to go through with it, I understand fully and I will try to cancel. It is indeed unfortunate that you have four young girls and that you travel entirely without male company."
"What do you think?" Aida asked.
"I don't know," said Sonja. "Nasser, what nationality are these people?"
"I have never met them but I believe they are Bosniaks. As I say, I can guarantee nothing where criminals are concerned but I don't think they would harm their own people." Sonja made her decision there and then.
"Nasser," she said. "We will go. We will take the chance. What other choice do we have? We owe you so much for taking care of us and we have no wish to place you or your wife's life in danger any longer. All I will ask you is for one more favour."
"Of course," said Nasser, "just name it."
"Pray for our safe journey."
Nasser nodded slowly and made eye contact with both of them.
"So, tomorrow night I will come and lead you back along the path. It will be late, probably not before midnight, but be ready to move at all times. Don't worry. There haven't been any Serb patrols in the village and no one seems to have noticed anything. You travelled a long distance on your first night so if they are looking for you, they probably have no idea what part of the country you are in. I doubt they will abandon their ethnic cleansing plans anyway, just to chase down a few women and girls."
Sonja thought differently but said nothing.

The tunnel was surprisingly comfortable as it was almost one and a half metres high and a metre wide. The women only had to duck their heads slightly and the girls could walk freely. It was dark of course but their guide carried a powerful flashlight to guide them on their way. They had met their first guide close to the village which Nasser had directed them to at one in the morning. The man was masked and did not speak, merely gesturing to the women what they should do. Sonja had to get in the back of the car with the girls and the man drove the VW through the outskirts of the city. The night was pitch black and he drove slowly, without lights. It was as if they were driving completely blind but he steered them unerringly to the entrance of the tunnel. He had stopped on two occasions to check something by radio. When they had reached the mouth of the tunnel, they were handed over to a small, dark haired man, called Samir. The driver merely nodded to them and disappeared with the car. Their new guide spoke quietly and rapidly to them. He first apologized for the fact that they presumably had had to pay the man who disappeared in the car. Aida confirmed that they had but had only given him the car but as they did not need the vehicle, it was fine. The man said:
"Before we go any further, please allow me to tell you to relax. You will come to no harm here. People think that it is criminals who operate the tunnel but it is not. I am not a criminal. I am just trying to save lives by either helping people to escape or to carry food into the city so that those still inside won't starve."
The women sighed with relief and thanked Samir sincerely.

"I am but one of dozens who do this work voluntarily. The man who brought you here is not one of us but that is his business. We deal with him because it is for the good of our people. He charges money but at least he is trustworthy."

"Thank you," Sonja said. "You are a brave man but how have you kept the tunnel a secret all this time?"

The man's teeth flashed as he smiled in the semi-darkness. "Ah ha, that is our little secret but I think you can probably guess. You see there are many tunnels or at least many entrances and exits. They are opened and closed all the time. That is why the man who guided you here tonight did not know until the last minute where to go until we advised him by radio. We feel sure he is to be trusted as we have dealt with him before but he is a criminal so we do not take chances. Tonight the tunnel will leave you in the suburb of Butmir."

"That is not far from where your father-in-law lives," Aida said. "You told me his address is in Stup. It is the opposite side of the city from where I lived but maybe it is safer. I can only hope so."

For the first time in five days and nights, Sonja started to hope again, this time really hope. Papa Istakovic would surely be distressed but he'd also be delighted to see them and he would help, she knew it. The man was like her husband, he would do everything in his power to locate his family. The thought of Drazen darkened her mood again but she resolved to put on a brave face for Diana.

Apart from being comfortable, the tunnel was surprisingly short and after just over a kilometre, they emerged into the basement of a house in the suburb of Butmir. They were the only ones coming into the city but they realized when

they entered the house that there was a large queue of people going the other way. The house was full of men, women and children, all carrying a few hurriedly saved personal possessions in small cases and all manner of carrying bags. The frightened faces of those fleeing immediately informed them that Sarajevo was far from safe, but then they had known that, Sonja thought. Samir brought them upstairs to the kitchen and introduced them to an elderly frail looking woman called Milosk who offered them tea. They graciously accepted.
"Are you tired," the lady asked.
"No, no, not at all," Sonja said. "We haven't travelled very far tonight. We were waiting close by until we got the signal to move."
"Indeed, I see, but you must stay for some time yet anyway so please make yourselves comfortable. You see, we are facilitating many people in this tunnel but we cannot risk drawing attention to our house. We are in an area where practically all of the population is Bosniak but we can't take chances. If someone were to notice crowds of people coming and going at all hours, we would only draw attention to ourselves."
"We understand completely of course, just tell us when it is safe to leave."
Milosk nodded, poured some more tea and sat with her guests.
"Very few people want to re-enter the city these days. I will not ask you your business but I am sure you have been told that Sarajevo is not safe?"
The women agreed but assured Milosk that they needed to search for a relative that could help them.
"Indeed," she continued. "This war has ruined our city. I have been operating this tunnel for over two years now. Oh

there are other entrances but most people have come through here as it is an ideal holding area and it can be approached discreetly. I have seen the population diminish before my eyes. It is a tragedy but I suppose better that they leave for their own safety and peace-of-mind. I don't enter the tunnel myself nor will I as I will not leave Sarajevo. This is my home you see. I was born in this house and I intend to die here."

"We thank you from the bottom of our hearts, you are a brave lady," Aida said.

The old lady waved her away with the ghost of a smile and thought for a moment.

"Brave, is it? No, I'm not brave. I'm just helping people who are in distress. Look at me. I am an old woman. What have I to be afraid of? What can the Serbs do to me if they come calling? No, hopefully this terrible war will soon pass but while there is danger out there and while there is a breath in my body, I'll be here. I hope to live long enough to see the city at peace and become a real city again. I pray that the people who passed through this house will return by a more regular route and I hope some of them will remember me. Do you know that the population of this town was nearly half a million before the war, well, over four hundred and fifty thousand anyway. It was a wonderful joyful thriving growing city. Now what have we? Less than half that. There were eighty thousand children in Sarajevo; now there are probably less than ten thousand; I don't know but a hell of a lot of them have gone through my basement. I don't blame their parents for an instant though. They're young; they are our country's future; they must be protected. Do you know that all of the children who have come through my house were traumatized in some form or other? Some saw their parents or other family members killed. Some have witnessed massacres. Some have been shot at by snipers – yes, little children, shot at by trained cold blooded killers. They've been bombed and shelled and have had to live in underground shelters. I long for this war to end but I also fear terribly for the future. The psychological trauma suffered during the siege will bear heavily on the lives of these children for many, many years to come. I can only hope it doesn't fester into another powder keg of bitterness which will explode in the next generation."

The old lady paused to think but no one intruded on the silence. She had spoken so powerfully and so passionately, yet she had barely raised her voice above a whisper. The women were in awe and deeply touched.
"I plead with you to be careful out there," she continued. "Patrols of militia roam the streets. There are snipers on the roofs of buildings so don't stand in the open. Go about your business quickly and stay indoors as much as you can. The city will not be as you remembered it but don't be frightened. There are still many good people here and I sincerely hope your relative is among them. But please bear in mind too that very many thousands have been killed including hundreds of children. It got so bad at one stage that they had to convert parks, fields and other open space to use as cemeteries. Not all of these were filled by the Serbs either. Some people couldn't leave but couldn't cope so they took their own lives. You see, all the while the Serbs have maintained the blockade. The tunnel now helps us to bring in food but it wasn't always like that and it was too much for some people. Our city is in a sad state right now but I live in hope that some day soon it will be

peaceful again and I will be able to walk in my favourite parks and visit the museums and the libraries and the Oriental Institute, if they are still there. But go ahead. You need to go now. Sorry you had to listen to the ramblings of an old lady. Here, have some more tea before you go and may God go with you. Remember where we are and if you wish to leave the city again, we will facilitate you. But do not come here of your own accord because it may not always be safe. Here, call this number and say you are looking for friends, visiting from the country. The man who operates the phone is in another part of the city. He will contact us and we will get word to you as to when it is safe to come."

The women rose and thanked Milosk profusely, each hugging her gently. They exited through the rear door. It was four thirty am. There was a thick stand of trees behind the house which backed on to a park. They had been told to cross the park and emerge carefully in groups of three at a side entrance which was permanently open. Two women and four young girls travelling together at that time of the morning would only attract attention, Bosniak suburb or not. Milosk had told them that as part of their occupation, the Serbs had thrown many Bosniaks out of their homes and that these were now occupied by Serbian families. It was unlikely that anyone would be awake at this hour but they would move with great caution nonetheless. They headed in the direction of Stup, where Drazen's Father and Mother had their apartment. As they moved closer to the city, the once fine houses they passed gave way to small apartment blocks and eventually, in the distance, she could see the tower blocks which she had remembered visiting. Sonja led the way accompanied by Diana and Fadil, by now almost inseparable. Aida was about five minutes behind with the other girls. Sonja still carried her pistol and she had given Aida the knife but they felt safe for now as there was no one about.

The buildings loomed up ahead. Now, which one was Papa's? From a distance, silhouetted against the first strands of daylight, the tower blocks looked like mighty edifices, like a mini Manhattan, almost a pretty vista. Closer examination told a different story; all were in various states of disrepair and many had parts missing from them where they had been struck by Serb shells. Most were crumbling from neglect anyway. The buildings themselves were dirty and streaked with grime but it wasn't just the buildings. Dirt was everywhere. The sidewalks were cracked and broken and there were large crevices at regular intervals, whether caused by explosions or neglect she couldn't say. The children's play areas looked like no one had played here for a long time. A few bent and twisted swings and an upended see-saw were all that remained of the previously vibrant kiddie's playground where Zoran and Diana had cavorted during their visits. The entire estate looked deserted but it was very early in the morning and on closer examination, signs of life were evident in some of the flats from the pale flickering lights. While this area had seemed to escape the worst of the fighting, the walls of the blocks were still pitted and blackened in many places by gunfire. To be fair, the area had never been pretty. At its best, the estate would have been described as some of the ugliest of Soviet or in this case, Yugoslav 'Architecture'. In its current state, you could gratuitously call it a slum.

She found Papa's building and checked where the names had previously been neatly listed beside the digital bell call. The device had been shattered, wires ripped out, hanging loose in the early morning breeze. It was too early to wake Papa anyway; she would let him sleep. She would wait for Aida. After a few minutes, she saw her friend approaching. There was still no one else visible on the entire estate. In fact, since leaving the house, they had not yet seen another single soul. But Sonja wasn't worried. A sense of relief rushed through her; for days, she had been carrying the burden of responsibility for her entire family. It was weighing her down but now she would have someone to share that burden. Papa might even in time lift it entirely.

She tried the entrance door of the building and it gave with a creak. She beckoned Aida and the girls to follow. They tried the lift; no such luck. Lifts rarely worked in tower blocks; how could they be working in the middle of a war? They trudged up the twenty four flights of stairs to the twelfth floor, stopping several times to draw breath. Papa lived in apartment number 709 on the twelfth floor, that much was imprinted into Sonja's brain. By the time they reached the floor, it was 05.45. Sonja knew Papa rose for work at six so she didn't mind disturbing him fifteen minutes early. She pressed the doorbell. She didn't hear it ring internally but the doors were heavy. She waited; there was no reply. Perhaps he was in a deep sleep. She pushed the button again; no response. She felt her pulse quicken and fear rose bile from her stomach into her throat. She gently tried the door and to her surprise and dismay, it opened inwards easily. Papa always double locked his door at night. She called out gently, "Papa, Mama," but there was no response. She pushed the door fully open and gasped. The pale sickly sunlight was streaming in through broken windows. The flat was empty apart from a few pieces of smashed furniture. At this level, the breeze was quite strong and a chill caught hold of her. A rat skittered across the room causing her and the girls to jump. She dared not show the rising panic which seemed to be trying to possess her entire body. With massive willpower, she held herself together but she felt hot tears on her cheeks. Where were they? Had they too abandoned Sarajevo? Ah, their neighbours would know; she remembered Mr. Buric in 710 and Mrs. Ganic in 711. They shared the twelfth floor with Papa. She dashed out and rang their doorbells also. No response. She tried the doors and found the same scenes; abandoned flats; broken windows; wrecked furniture; filthy floors. This was no longer a place where people lived; this was a ghost building; the entire block was as quiet as a tomb.

Chapter 19

It came seemingly out of nowhere. Drazen was no weather expert and even though they were still at a height of over a thousand metres, he hadn't expected fog on such a bright sunny morning. Still, fog sometimes descended without warning and if it gave them extra cover, so much the better. The strange thing was that it did not appear to be coming from the higher ground they had vacated but was localized over the woods where they had taken refuge. Within minutes, the fog had closed around them but something was wrong. Most of the refugees were asleep, many exhausted from another night of trying to avoid the enemy. Sentries had been posted at all strategic points but would they be able to detect infiltrators in this fog?

Probably not. He ran to the clearing at the edge of the woods to see what visibility was like in that area. But as he ran, he felt his breathing become laboured; he was tired for sure but he was young and fit; this shouldn't be happening.

Then he detected the sweet smell in his nostrils and he realized his mistake. A mixture of dismay and fright coursed through him as he abandoned his journey to the clearing and returned to where Hasan and his wife and child were resting. He shook Hasan and the man was wide awake instantly.

"Hasan, we must leave, we must go now, I thought it was fog, look; but it isn't, it's some form of chemical smoke. If you inhale deeply, you can detect it but be careful; this could be deadly. The Serbs are trying to smoke us out." Hasan had everyone on high alert within about ninety seconds.

"We can't continue towards Tuzla," Drazen said. "They'll be waiting for us for sure. We also cannot go back the way we came. The only option is to go deeper into the woods, as far and as fast as we can. Try to get well beyond the fog."

Hasan agreed and asked Raif and Hamdi to pass the word along to their colleagues.

"At least we will be travelling downhill so progress should be quicker," Hasan said. "God knows what awaits us at the other end."

"These woods are dense and they go for a long way," Drazen said. "If the Serbs are in there, they won't be able to bring their heavy weaponry with them so perhaps they will leave that side unguarded. Maybe they only released the smoke in this area speculatively but they are for sure going to be waiting for us on both sides of the pass. I think this way is our only chance."

On and on they went, coughing and spluttering. The few gas masks they had were given to the women and children. Drazen was correct about the woods; they were unlikely to be detected in there but that was because many areas were all but impassable. The undergrowth was heavy and within minutes, they were cut and bleeding from thorns and brambles. People were muttering and complaining, whether from the underfoot conditions or the chemicals released by the Serbs, Drazen wasn't sure. All were tired; most had been woken hastily from too little sleep; all had suffered huge trauma in recent days; people were at the end of their tether. Discipline began to break down. Whereas before, the Bosnian Army personnel had maintained a guard at the front, rear and perimeter of the group, this began to unravel. Drazen and Raif led the way, trying as best they could to clear a path through the undergrowth but it was a losing battle. Hasan was close behind with his wife and son. Hamdi was assigned to the rear but they had been travelling no more than fifteen minutes when he came racing up to his commander.
"Hasan, we have to stop; it's getting crazy back there; fights have broken out all over the place; people are delirious, some seem to be hallucinating. It must be the effects of that smoke on those who were weaker or maybe suffered greater exposure to it. A lot of people have sat down and have refused to go any further. They say we make our stand here."
"But Hamdi my friend, it would be suicide to make a stand here or indeed anywhere else any more. We cannot match

the Serbs weaponry. Our only chance of survival is to avoid detection and try to out wit and out run them."
"I know that," Hamdi agreed, "but please, can you try to convince the others?"
Hasan nodded and asked Tatjana to stay with Salim. Hamdi automatically took up guard beside his commander's wife.

By now, the vanguard of Drazen, Raif and two other soldiers realized something was amiss and slowed their progress. They had cleared the cloud of smoke so there was no imminent danger but if the Serbs had suspected where they had been, it would only be a very short matter of time before they figured out which way they had fled. All were anxious to continue. Drazen suspected the smoke had been speculative as there were many other areas where they could have hidden. He felt it was just a lucky guess on the Serbs' part. He volunteered to see what was holding up the main column. He made his way back to where Hasan had turned and was briefed by Hamdi. This was disastrous but even as he ran back to help his friend, he knew it was probably a mistake. For sure, perhaps he was being selfish again but his first priority had to be to try to stay alive and find his own family. If these people wanted to give up now, that was their problem surely? Yet he continued, even breaking into a run as he realized how far back the main group was and how little progress they had made.

After another half a kilometre he encountered Hasan, who held up a hand to tell him to halt. The man's eyes were wide with fear. When Drazen looked over his shoulder, he could see why. Dozens of men lay around, either on the ground or propped against tree trunks, their mouths open, nostrils streaming, eyes vacant. A few stragglers were arguing incoherently with each other, making no sense, pushing and trying to punch each other almost as if in a drunken stupor. The further he looked, the depth of the tragedy became even more apparent. Men had either cut their own thoats or had been killed by colleagues. More men hung from tall branches of trees, their lifeless heads lolling to the side. It was like a scene from a Hieronymous Bosch painting of Hades. Drazen felt his stomach heave and he retched violently. He felt his eyes streaming and was unsteady on his feet. Hasan, tears in his eyes, put a comforting arm around him and dragged him back deeper into the woods, their colleagues rapidly following.

"We must flee my friend," Hasan said. "There is nothing we can do for these poor people. It must be the gas or the smoke or whatever chemical agent the Serbs released. I think we probably escaped the worst effects of it as we were in the deeper part of the woods. This is a disaster; it is disaster piled upon disaster but we must go on. I feel for our people as much as anyone but some of us must make it."

Drazen asked for some water to rinse his mouth and steadied himself.

"I'll be fine Hasan," he said. "It was just a reaction to the carnage back there. I'm afraid I just lost it for a moment or two."

They had now made it back to the rest of the group. Hasan looked around him to take stock. Within a few days, his group had been reduced from five thousand to what was now a mere fifty people.

All stopped briefly to rest. Now that Drazen had regained his faculties, he noticed that Hasan looked deeply shaken.

The man lay against a tall tree and for a brief instant Drazen wondered if the hallucinogenic that the Serbs had used had gotten through to him also. Tatjana squeezed his arm to comfort him and he nodded. Drazen felt compelled to do likewise:
"Hasan, whatever you do, don't blame yourself. What happened back there was a tragedy but there was absolutely nothing you could have done about it. You are still the leader and these remaining people need you more than ever. I need you to lead us. There is no shame in this; it is not of our making but of the enemy. You know you have done everything in your power and more to help your people but we have encountered almost insurmountable odds."
Hasan nodded, embraced Tatjana and then Drazen and said:
"But I wasn't prepared for this; to see our own people kill each other and for many to take their own lives. After all they've been through, it is just too distressing."
"Hasan, listen, those people were under extraordinary mental distress. Their nerve endings have been worn red raw over the past few days. They obviously hadn't a chance when that gas was released. It is terrible but we must try to recover from it, for our nation, for our people."
"Thank you," Hasan responded. "My heart is broken but you are correct; we must go on. I must lead this group while there is a breath in my body and a drop of blood left in my veins. If even one of us makes it, it will be worth it."
There were now forty two men, five women and five children. Twenty five of the men were soldiers, including the commander, Hasan. There were seventeen civilians including Drazen. There was no longer any need to pass instructions down the line; everyone was within earshot;

everyone knew the enormity of what had happened and the seemingly impossible task that awaited them but not one refused when Hasan suggested they proceed.

"I believe the briefing stated that these people were, and I quote: "hardened and violent criminals who will stop at nothing to prevent being taken prisoner and to enable their escape into Bosnian territory," the Lieutenant stated. My orders and those of The Drina Corps who have joined us and the various brigades as ordered by the VRS Main Staff was to assign all available manpower to the task of finding any Muslim groups observed, preventing them from crossing into Muslim territory, taking them prisoner and holding them in buildings that could be secured by small forces. Our colleagues from the Drina Corps observed these criminals trying to sneak around their positions late last night."
Milanovic bristled and thundered back:
"Where in your orders did it instruct you to release poison gas over these people? I realize Lieutenant that you are a dedicated officer, if a little over zealous but I did not imagine you to be a complete idiot."
The Lieutenant coloured, unsure of a response.
"The use of chemical weapons is banned by the Geneva Convention and just about every other article of war anywhere," Milanovic said. "What do you suggest we do here Lieutenant, another cover up?"
"I don't see the need for any cover-up of anything Colonel. We are soldiers fighting to establish the Free Republic of Srpska. Things happen in wars but as you can see, many of these people were Bosnian military and the rest look to me

like hardened criminals. In any event, all of them are dead so what's the panic?"
Milanovic shook his head in exasperation.
"And have you counted the bodies Lieutenant? Why are you so sure they are all dead. I would have thought that a cursory examination of the surrounding woodland would show even a simpleton that their colleagues have escaped."
The Lieutenant coloured again.
"Sir, we have dispatched foot patrols. We estimate there are no more then ten men remaining. We feel sure that we will capture them by nightfall."

The Commander of the Drina Corps who had initially detected the Bosniaks, a General, had remained silent throughout the conversation. Sefer now thought he detected a smirk on the man's mouth. He was conscious that he had already made an enemy in the Lieutenant. One was enough, he needed allies and one had potentially hove into view.
"General Svero," he said. "I realize you outrank me so I can only advise you on the situation. However, I bring extreme concern for the situation from Belgrade."
The General nodded and thought for a moment before replying.
"I understand Colonel, and what would Belgrade's advice be on the current situation?"
"It seems relatively obvious to me General. The Bosniaks that have escaped are surrounded. They could not go forward towards Tuzla as your forces had blocked the pass, they could not go back towards Srebrenica as that way is totally in Serb hands. If they loop round through the higher pass and try to reach Kravica, they hit mines and Serb checkpoints. To the east, the mountains provided an

impassable barrier so their only option was to go through the woods. I am no expert on this area but the maps indicate that those woods continue for almost fifteen kilometres towards Potocari. I also understand that they are almost impassable in places. My guess is that these people were already heavily fatigued before they even entered the woods. By the time they make it to the other side, they will be beyond exhaustion. I would suggest that we proceed to Potocari and wait for them. If they are soldiers, I suggest we detain them; they could well provide useful intelligence on the state of the Bosnian military. If there are civilians with them, we may also detain them for questioning. I would not, I repeat not, recommend liquidating any of them."

"Excellent suggestion Colonel, I agree entirely," General Svero said.

"Don't *you* agree Lieutenant?" he smiled.

Sefer didn't know if he was being played but decided to wait it out. He said:

"May I suggest General, that I accompany you to Potocari? Your men did a fine job last night. Were you or me to have arived earlier, we could well have many more Bosniaks to interview."

He said this with a pointed look at the Lieutenant. The General nodded but said nothing.

"Lieutenant," Sefer said: "Will you please take care of the clean-up operation here?"

"But Colonel, I think it appropriate and essential that I accompany you and the General to Potocari."

"I don't," said Svero. "This is your mess Lieutenant, you clean it up."

The Lieutenant coloured again but saluted briskly and withdrew.

"By the way Colonel," Svero added," I would like it to be known in Belgrade and elsewhere that while it was my Drina Corps who detected these Bosniaks, that it was the Lieutenant and his men who seem to have 'mislaid' them. I also want it to be recorded that it was not my men who released poison gas over them."

"Of course General, as you wish," Milanovic said.

What was Svero playing at, Sefer wondered. Trying to grab some of the glory for himself no doubt. He was hardly trying to ally himself with Milanovic. No, if they captured some important Bosniaks and obtained intelligence from them, he would get the kudos. With Lieutenant Ivan absent, he could also claim credit for this morning's battle, omitting any mention of chemical warfare of course. Still, he wasn't stupid so he might well be the ally Sefer needed to dig himself out of Bosnia. He was already wondering how he would explain this morning's 'incident' at Kamenica hill. The Bosnians had self destructed to be sure but if the issue of chemical weapons became known, the consequences would almost be as bad as those for the events earlier in the week. Still, he couldn't carry responsibility for the entire war on his shoulders. He settled back into his troop transport for the short trip to Potocari. Operations in this part of Bosnia were winding down. There were a few other pockets of resistance in parts of the country but the Serbs had captured what they wanted. Sefer Milanovic was an astute man and he felt sure that had he been in charge earlier in this war, he could have avoided much of the unnecessary bloodshed. If they wanted to move people around the country that was fine with him; there was no need to massacre them. He asked his driver how far they were from Potocari and was told twenty kilometres. He pulled down his sunglasses and settled back to relax. This could be over soon he thought. There would be hell to pay for years he knew, but for now there appeared to be an obsession to round up every last Bosniak in the region. Rather than opposing it, he reckoned his best chance of influencing the situation was to play along. He'd concentrate, like the others, on the few remaining Bosniaks that he was sure were at that moment furiously trying to negotiate the thick woods close to Potocari. He rarely made a misjudgement but on this occasion, he was wrong.

Chapter 20

Kamal Redzic was tired, bone tired. He had eaten little in recent days and had only drunk from the nearby stream. He was existing on wild berries that were none too plentiful in the woods where he was hiding out. Most were over ripe and many had rotted in the extreme summer heat. At least he was safe for now. No one would venture this deep into the forest. He had roamed these woods as a child and he knew every hollow in them. It was only with incredible good luck that he had managed to escape the carnage at Potocari. Of the rest of his family, he had no idea if they were dead or alive. His parents had lived in Potocari and he had been on his way to visit them when the Serb militias had attacked. He had seen the armored cars and the cattle trucks that he knew transported men to their deaths and he knew what was happening. He had abandoned the trip to his parent's house and had escaped detection, hiding out in an old henhouse when the other men were rounded up. He had overheard the Serb commander saying that they were being transported to Tuzla, a safe Bosniak enclave, for their own protection; Kamal knew better. He had seen at first hand, the savagery of this war manifested at places like Sijekovac and Mostar.

When the trucks had left, the militia stayed in the town and he fled to the woods. For the first two nights, he had risked raids on some of the farms which adjoined the woods. He scavenged for potatoes and occasionally vegetables but a close encounter with a watchful Serb farmer three nights ago had made him abandon this plan. The man had sneaked up behind him and was about to strike him over the head with a shovel when some sixth sense kicked in and Kamal turned, narrowly avoiding the blow. The farmer had connected with his shoulder. Kamal's instinctive reaction was to throw the plant he had in his hands at the man. The clay had momentarily blinded the farmer allowing Kamal to make his escape pursued by a string of Serbian oaths.

Since then he had existed on berries and spring water. He had only a rough idea of where he was and he felt sure he was going round in circles half the time. He had roamed the woods as a child but he had never tracked in the countryside before. From an initial state of pure fear, he had descended to one of high alert but as he hadn't seen anyone, friend or foe now for two days, he was beginning to relax. He was aware that he carried no weapon which would allow him to defend himself other than his bare hands and he was none too skilled with them. He reckoned that his best chance lay with the fact that the Serb militias didn't know he was there and after all, he was only one man so why should they be worried about him. He had resolved to wait it out and hope that the war eventually ended. How long this would take he wasn't sure but it was the best plan he could come up with for the moment.

This evening, he had found a place to conceal himself within a thick copse of trees and he had just settled down with the few berries he had gleaned on his travels that day and a bottle of water he had saved from the stream. He thought he heard some movement in the trees to the east and he burrowed deeper into the thick grass and scrub. He listened intently but heard nothing, nothing at all, until the rifle was placed at his temple. Kamal almost soiled himself with fright. The man had seemed to materialize out of the air. One moment there was no sound, no movement, the next he was staring down the barrel of a gun. The man with the gun seemed completely relaxed.
"State your name, where you come from and what you are doing here alone in these woods," he said. Kamal had planned numerous stories as cover in case he was detected but all left him in his moment of panic.
"Kamal Redzic, ah, from Potocari and ah, I'm ah, just lost in the woods."
"Regular joker we've got here," said the man to an unseen colleague who had also seemed to materialize soundlessly. "Ask him if he's a Bosniak or a Serb," said the second man.
"You heard him," said the first man; "what are you?"
Kamal was shaking uncontrollably and sweating profusely. If he said he was a Bosniak and these men were Serbs, he

would be shot right there. If he said he was a Serb and the men were Bosnian, the same thing could happen. He made no reply.

"Do you have papers, perhaps an I.D. card?" said the first man. Kamal struggled and eventually pulled out some grubby documents from a small pouch. They didn't state his ethnic origin but they did confirm his name to be the one he had given the men. The first man perused the papers quickly while the second man stood guard.

"OK, we can all relax I think," said the first man. "Papers say his name is definitely Kamal Redzic; that's a Bosniak name if I've ever heard one."

He put down his rifle and offered the man his hand.

"My name is Raif, Bosnian armed forces, pleased to meet you. This is my colleague Hamdi. Why are you here alone?"

The man sat back and gave an enormous sigh of relief.

"I come from Udrc. Two days ago, I was planning on visiting my parents in Potocari but the Serb militias came and rounded up the few Bosniak men who were left in the town. I have no idea where the rest of the people have fled to. I never made contact with my parents. I don't know if they are even still alive. I was scared to death as these militias just rounded up the men and put them into trucks. I have heard that in other towns and villages, they just round people up to bring them away to be shot. I managed to avoid capture by moving about until I could make a run for the woods. Since then, I have just wandered and have tried to avoid contact with anyone. I swear you are the only living souls I've seen in three days."

The men could have questioned Kamal more thoroughly but they seemed weary and accepted his word. By then, a

larger group of people, all looking tired and many of them shell shocked, had gathered in the clearing. Raif introduced Kamal to his leader and another man and his story was quickly related to the group.
"Tell us: what is the situation in Potocari?" said the leader of the group, Hasan.
"It is two days since I have been there but I think it is completely overrun by Serb militias. I wouldn't go back there. And there are lots of Serb civilians on alert also. I tried to steal a few vegetables two nights ago and I was almost killed by a Serb farmer. Even if you get to Potocari, where can you go afterwards? As far as I know, all the roads are now blocked unless the Serbs have considered the place no danger any more but I can tell you, I'm not going back there until the war is over."

Hasan looked at Raif, Hamdi and Drazen and sighed. He waved them to one side.
"I guess this is hopeless. If what the man says is true, we may just be leading our people into a trap."
"But we will be in the vanguard, if something is amiss, we will detect it and halt the column," Raif said.
"My dear Raif," Hasan said, "I know you would give your last drop of blood to protect our little group but we need you alive and with us. I fear that were we to proceed to Potocari, our numbers would be reduced still further."
"I agree," Drazen said. "Look, the woods are thickest here. We are safe from everything except aerial bombardment and I doubt the Serbs think our little band is now big enough or important enough to call out their air force. I know our options are becoming more and more limited but we are all exhausted as well as traumatized. We need to eat

and we need to rest. Remember, we marched all last night and only rested for an hour this morning."

"Our friend is wise," Hasan replied. "We all badly need to rest. We have been moving through heavy woods all day. It is now just after five p.m. I propose we post sentries and sleep in shifts as before. We will meet again at eleven o'clock tonight and plan where we go from here. Our options are poor but we need to think clearly. Let us all rest and then we will plan when we are refreshed."

"If I may make a comment, I think your leader is correct," Kamal interjected. "I for one will be recommending that you don't go anywhere near Potocari whether you are tired or not. I need rest myself but I will gladly help you."

Hasan nodded and thanked the man. He told Kamal that he was welcome to enjoy his rest. Given the way Raif had sneaked up on him unnoticed, watch duty would not be an option. The group began settling down and some food was prepared. Hasan wearily went through the task of assigning sentries. Even though most were exhausted, none shirked the responsibility. Hasan himself insisted on taking one of the first watches but his men eventually talked him out of it. They needed their leader to be fresh and rested; all of their futures might depend on him.

On the journey to Potocari, Milanovic pondered the plight of the remaining Bosniak fugitives. He was aware that they were the remnants of a column whose primary purpose had been to escort Bosnian civilians to safety. Although the column had contained a large number of Bosnian military, the group had no heavy weapons and had no intention of attacking Serb positions or indeed of attempting any hostile act. This was merely a mercy mission to escape the worst excesses of the butchering militias. The fact that the column had almost been decimated already by Serb militia strikes was nothing short of a human tragedy but he couldn't worry about that now. He had already reported as much to Belgrade and they had not wanted to know. He couldn't carry the responsibility for all the atrocities on his own back. But he was determined that this group, if captured, would be escorted safely to Bosnian territory. This of course was contingent on them not acting aggressively. It would be difficult as no doubt they had already witnessed a number of Serbian deceits, not least the pretence of being United Nations troops sent to protect them. He figured that there were very few left of the original column, perhaps a hundred but not many more. In theory they should be easy to apprehend but on the other hand, they would be the survivors from a column of over five thousand so they could be the toughest and wiliest of the lot. His suggestion that they be detained for questioning had been a ploy. Oh he would question them alright but he figured that he knew more about Bosnian military strength and movements at this stage than they did, given that most of them had been wandering around the country for over a week.

He took out his reading glasses and a map of the area, tracing the presumed progress of the column over the previous few days. The assumption was that they were attempting to reach Tuzla. Had they made it past Kamenica hill undetected, they might have stood a reasonable chance. The mountains were high and the countryside tough but the Serb militias didn't wander that high; certainly not where they were unable to bring their heavy weapons. What were the alternatives? Precious few he felt. The only options were to try to make it undetected through the woods and from there perhaps circle Potocari at night and make it overland to Tuzla. But this plan was fraught with danger. Even if they moved under cover of darkness, where would they hide during the day? Even assuming they knew the area, which he doubted, the country was awash with Bosnian Serbs who would surely betray their position. If he were a logically thinking Bosniak, he would consider the situation hopeless. On the other hand, what did the people in the column know of what had happened in Potocari? Most likely nothing, but they were sure to have their suspicions and to be on high alert. What would he do in the situation? He tried to put himself in their position but it was difficult. He had the luxury of armaments not to mention food, drink and transport. He looked at it again. Realistically there was only one way to get to Tuzla and that was through the mountains. But to do that, the column would have to retrace their steps and take on the Serbs guarding the pass. They would have no idea how many men the Serbs would have assigned or whether they had had time to lay mines as they had done at the higher pass. But everything led to this; they could try hiding out in the woods but they would surely starve or die of dehydration quickly. It was summertime and the weather was inhospitable. No, were he the Bosnian commander and if he had a reasonable amount of his men left, he would eventually figure out the only option; try to surprise the Serbs and make a last stand at the pass at Udrc.

Turning to his driver, he ordered him to stop the vehicle. He got out and signalled the vehicle of General Svero

which was running close behind. The General rolled his window down and questioned him:
"Is there a problem Colonel?"
"Not at all General; I just think it unlikely that our Bosniak group will attempt to exit the woods at Potocari."
General Svero shrugged and looked puzzled.
"But where else can they go to Colonel? They are effectively trapped. They cannot go back or to either side."
"Yes, I agree, but don't you think that they will eventually figure that out too and make alternative plans?"
"Perhaps Colonel, but I doubt it. These people have been travelling for days. They are probably tired, hungry, thirsty, disoriented. I think they will be easily captured. I concur with your suggestion by the way. I think these people may be more valuable to us alive than dead but I think, given the number of troops we can deploy, they won't present a problem."
"You are probably correct General, and no doubt you wish to proceed. But, with your permission, I will return to Srebrenica to report to my superiors in Belgrade."
"Of course Colonel; but you are an officer of the Serbian military. You know you do not need my permission. I will contact you when the operation is concluded so you can add it to your report. I wish you a good evening."
He then indicated to his driver to proceed.

With that, the Serb armored division rumbled forward. Milanovic climbed aboard his jeep and instructed his driver to return to base. General Svero, he thought; General? He shook his head in disbelief. Jesus, the man wouldn't make Sergeant rank in a regular army. But the militias were a law unto themselves; they largely determined their own ranks and usually the biggest bully or the one who shouted loudest or was the most blood thirsty became the leader. The General knew little about soldiering but what was going on here wasn't war, it was more akin to a turkey shoot. The man knew his own limitations though, Milanovic granted him that. He would defer to anyone from Belgrade regardless of their rank. He would agree with everything they said but probably do the exact opposite when their backs were turned. He was sure the General, clever as he was, had figured that Sefer didn't want any hand, act or part in the slaughter of the remaining Bosniaks which he had ordered to be captured. The man was now probably delighted to be given a free hand; he would 'clean up' this little mess that the Lieutenant had left and claim the credit for the entire operation. He had promised to send a report to Milanovic when the operation was complete and he would; but it would most likely say that the Bosniaks had offered fierce resistance and they had no option but to engage. It would then report that all of the 'enemy' forces were unfortunately killed in the battle. Although no intelligence would have been gained, the issue of the remaining rebellious Bosnian soldiers would have been finally resolved. But Sefer had his doubts. The Bosnians might be tired, hungry, disorganized and disoriented but unless he was very much mistaken, they were not stupid. They had managed to survive up to now under almost impossible circumstances, albeit after suffering appalling losses. The remaining few must be teak tough to last this long. But he reckoned they weren't finished yet. He very much doubted that he'd be receiving any report that evening from General Svero and he had a feeling that this particular episode wasn't over yet.

Chapter 21

Kamal was initially reluctant to accompany the group and Drazen didn't blame him. He hadn't mentioned it but he had thought himself many times that he might be safer alone. The militias were unlikely to bother deploying resources to catch a few stragglers, but they would almost certainly pursue the column as they might have assumed it was still a large group. Drazen felt that he would be able to evade a checkpoint alone but fifty people together wouldn't stand a chance. Yet he felt a loyalty to the group. He might well have been captured already were it not for them. But he knew there would have to come a time when they would go their separate ways.

Kamal had felt safe in the woods before he had been discovered; he wasn't so sure now. If the Bosniaks could detect him so easily and stealthily, so could the Serbs. Now that the group had passed this way, there would be Serb patrols so he guessed he was safest to stay with the main group. No more than Drazen, he was not a soldier so he brought no military skills; neither did he know the area but they did acknowledge that his information about Potocari had been critical. In fact, when they had reflected and spoken about it, Hasan had acknowledged the mistake; that it had been nothing short of blind panic to head in that direction. They had had little option only to seek the safety of the woods but they should have reorganized when they got there. If the Serbs had followed, so be it; they could have made a stand there and then as it would have been largely hand-to-hand fighting; heavy armaments could not be brought in here.

If it had been heavy going in the woods in day time, it was ten times more difficult at night, even given they had come this way earlier in the day. They were lined up in the usual format with the two best scouts a kilometre in front of the main group, moving with the utmost stealth. Because it was nighttime, they needed other men at two hundred and fifty, five hundred and seven fifty metres, in case they hit a problem and the column had to be halted quickly. Despite having had six hours rest, the majority of people were still weary; many stumbled and fell in the dense undergrowth. Vision was almost non existent so people tripped over endless briars and bushes, acquiring many more scrapes, scratches and nettle stings to add to those they already possessed. Drazen could see this whole thing coming apart and ending in disaster. People were at the end of their tether; exhaustion was beginning to set in and soon, some might become delusional and wouldn't care whether or not they were captured. Some people have extraordinary powers of resilience but most do not and these folks had been stretched beyond their limits. He could see it in the soldiers as much as the civilians. This made for an even more dangerous situation as most of these men possessed powerful automatic weapons. He had witnessed the meltdown of the rest of the group that morning when influenced by the hallucinatory gas but he was now beginning to wonder whether the remainder of the group had, as they believed, been lucky not to inhale much of the poison or if it had been the state of physical and mental exhaustion of the main group that had made *them* more susceptible.

Tonight, he was in the rear guard with three of the remaining soldiers. He decided he needed to act. He asked them to cover for him while he consulted with Hasan and they waved him off. He immediately expressed his concerns to the leader. They needed more rest, food and water. If they encountered the Serbs tonight, it would be no contest. His men were too exhausted to fight. Whatever chance they might have, they needed to be at their strongest, their most alert. In his view, they were currently at the other end of that scale. It only took Hasan moments to consider and agree.

"You are quite correct Drazen; I think I have been leading this column for too long; perhaps the strain is beginning to tell and is clouding my judgment."
"No, I disagree," Drazen responded. "You are only doing what you think is best for your people and you are their best hope. It is absolutely essential that you stay in command. I think the only problem is that perhaps most of your men and all of the civilians are not as strong and as resilient as you are."
"Or you my friend," he said. Word had been passed along to stand down and although it brought quizzical looks from some of the stronger members of the group, the majority breathed a sigh of relief and once more sat down to rest. Sentries were again posted and Hasan said:
"You know, while we are still in great danger, this may be a blessing in disguise. I'm not suggesting the Serbs will stop looking for us but I very much doubt they'll think we

would stay here. Perhaps it is wishful thinking but they expect us to keep moving so when we don't appear, they will be baffled. They will speculate as to where we have got to: we may have evaded their patrols at Potocari; we may have made it through the pass to Udrc; we may even have returned to the mountains above Srebrenica although that is unlikely. I think the one place they won't look for us is here. I'm not suggesting we spend the rest of our lives in these woods as they will figure it out eventually but I think we are safe for now. The one thing we have done every night is to keep moving. They won't expect us to set up camp and they won't venture in here after us either."
Raif said:
"There is also the fact that they don't know how many of us there are. They may have forgotten about us or decided to leave us be."
No one spoke but no one believed it either.

It was late when Milanovic entered the bar. He wasn't in the habit of frequenting it anyway since he had tired of the xenophobic blood thirsty rhetoric after the first evening. So why did he go there tonight? To gloat? Who knew? He had heard nothing from any of the Serb commanders since his return to base but then he hadn't expected to. He had sent off his report to Belgrade, detailing the 'engagement' of that morning and estimating the casualties but omitting the fact that poison gas had been used or that most of the enemy had probably been civilians. He kept detailed notes for himself nonetheless. While it annoyed him greatly to have to send incomplete or inaccurate reports, Sefer Milanovic was not stupid. He knew he would already face a very tricky political situation when he returned to duty in Belgrade and he had no intention of making it any worse. Having finished his report, he decided on a whim to visit the bar. Most of the senior commanders were still present and most appeared to be drunk. What a way to fight a war. He wouldn't blame the front-line troops for over indulging but these were supposed to be the elite command. God help us all he thought.

His previous nemesis, the Lieutenant, was at a corner of the bar, seemingly drinking alone. Ah yes, but then he may have been sulking as he had been left behind when the main division pursued the Bosniaks; or he may have offended someone with a remark about their assumed failure to apprehend or dispose of the remainder. Sefer knew from the man's demeanour that he had a lot of drink taken so he decided that a friendly, conciliatory approach was the best way to gain some information.
"Good evening Lieutenant, a tough day for you but a successful one eh?"
"And why would a Serbian Colonel give a shit about what sort of day I've had?"
The response was more quizzical than hostile. Clearly, the Lieutenant was isolated at the moment and didn't wish to make matters worse. Sefer shrugged:
"Oh I suppose I was being polite to you Lieutenant but if you'd prefer to be alone, that's fine."
"No, no, I know we don't see eye-to-eye on most things, particularly these fucking Bosniak scum but that doesn't mean I won't drink with a fellow Serb."
Milanovic had ordered two shots of slivovitz. Both men now clicked glasses and downed them. He signalled the barman for two more with two beers.

"Well," the Lieutenant started:
"I suppose I have had a successful day but when you view it through the bottom of a glass, it doesn't feel as good as I had imagined. This is just between us Co, Co, Colonel but today was the first day I actually had to encounter the bastards face-to-face. I mean, I've been here all through the war but most of the time I was giving orders to my men. Today, do you, do you know what I had to do, do you?"
The Lieutenant was very drunk, slurring every second word and getting louder by the minute but Sefer let him continue.
"D'ya know, I had to actually kill some of the bastards, actually lots of them. I thought the gas had killed the fuckers but some of them were only dazed. They got up and they fucking attacked me, do you hear that Colonel, and I had to shoot the bastards."
Milanovic noticed now that the man actually had a bandage on his head. It was almost obscured by his cap and he had failed to detect it earlier.
"Were you wounded Lieutenant?" he asked.
"Wounded? Wounded? Ah, this little scratch here," Vladkovic said, removing his cap to reveal quite a significant blood stained bandage. The reasons for his drunkenness and change of demeanour were now becoming apparent. If Sefer was not mistaken, the Lieutenant had had a brush with death this afternoon.
"No, it's just a scratch but I tell you Colonel, I mean, one of these scum actually shot at me, actually winged me, fucking tried to kill me, can you believe that?"
Sefer could well believe it. Was the man so shocked that he didn't realize he was in a war and that his side had been responsible for the slaughter of tens of thousands of his

attacker's people? Or was it vanity? The man seemed affronted by a Bosniak's presumably honest attempt to defend himself. The arrogance of this man knew no bounds, but Sefer would humour him, for now.

He took the two shots of slivovitz from the bartender and they drank them down. Vladkovic then took a long drink of beer, slammed down the glass and belched loudly. Sefer noticed he was getting inquiring glances from the others. He decided to press on:
"But what happened Lieutenant?" he said. "I thought you had an entire division with you in the forest?"
"No, I hadn't. I had fuck all except a few of my men and some useless idiots with a digger to bury those scum. I mean, do you know how many of them there were, there were hundreds if not thousands of the fuckers. All the rest fucked off to Poto, Potocari, with, with you and that fucking cunt Svero over there, fuckin glory hunter."
Milanovic quickly put it together. Svero had ordered the Lieutenant to stay put and rather than be humiliated in front of his own men, he had probably ordered them to proceed to Potocari on the assumption that he would follow. Then he had found himself alone with ghosts, one or more of which had seemingly come back to life and almost killed him. The man was badly spooked but Sefer might be able to use this to his advantage. Right now, he was barely tolerated by the militias and he knew he hadn't a friend in the room. The Lieutenant was an unlikely ally but as he too appeared to be isolated, they might form a temporary alliance. He seemed to have a particular set on the General. Hard to blame him in one sense, Sefer thought, taking a quick glance at the grossly over weight

pug headed man who was currently laughing lustily at a joke told by one of the other officers.

It was difficult to know where to start. He wanted to appeal to the man's better nature but at this rate, he'd have extreme difficulty finding it. He decided on a different approach.
"You know, Lieutenant," he said, calling for two more shots from the bar man. "We haven't always seen eye to eye but you must try to understand, this war is very difficult for all of us. Hopefully it will be over soon and we can get back to our families. Do you have family Lieutenant?"
"What? Ah, family, no, no family. Well, parents yes, in Sarajevo. Hopefully they're safer now, that I hear we've driven out most of the Bosniak scum."
Sefer tried to ignore the heavy racism and continued the conversation.
"When did you see them last; your parents I mean?" he said, in response to the blank look from the ever more inebriated Lieutenant.
"Shee, see them last, ah, three years I suppose, but we keep in touch. They're good people, my parents, the best. Always, always gave me the best."
Milanovic thought he could detect a tear developing at the corner of Vladkovic's eye. Was it the thought of his parents or was it something deeper. The man presumably hadn't got his hatred of Bosniaks from the wind.
"Always gave me the best, the best clothes, toys, sweets, always had me looking my best, not like those fucking Bosniak scum that…."
Vladkovic halted in mid sentence and Sefer could see the man was crying now. He stole a quick glance around the

rest of the bar but most of the officers had gone to bed and the few that were left were drunk and hadn't noticed them. He placed a comforting hand on Vladkovic's arm.
"I know how difficult it is to be separated from family too, particularly when the country is at war."
"But, but, no, you don't understand," Vladkovic mumbled. "My parents, good people but didn't understand. I wouldn't have given him the best toys, not the new toys; just, there was no one else to play with so I thought it would be ok but no, Papa, Papa knew best. I didn't, didn't know you see, I didn't know, you must believe me."
"I believe you Ivan," Milanovic said. "It must have been hard for you."
Vladkovic pushed ever closer.
"No, no, you don't understand. My Papa, he did it for me, only for me. He wouldn't hurt, he was the best."

The man had tears streaming down his cheeks and Sefer noticed General Svero wandering in their direction. He decided to take a chance; Vladkovic was so drunk that it might backfire but he grabbed the man anyway and commenced to laugh uproariously. Vladkovic initially recoiled, then saw the General and laughed himself.
"A private joke gentlemen," the General queried, eyebrows raised.
"Not at all," Milanovic said, "would you care to join us General?"
"Perhaps another time; I think I have heard enough jokes for tonight."
The man gave them both a stern look, obviously confused by what he saw as unlikely drinking companions, and then departed. Lieutenant Ivan Vladkovic gathered himself and said:

"Thanks for that Colonel; I don't know what came over me."
Sefer clapped him on the back:
"For nothing Lieutenant; it was nothing."
The man had gathered himself again and the moment had passed but the mask had slipped. Vladkovic would either hate him or be grateful to him in the morning he felt, if the man remembered anything at all. The Lieutenant had dark secrets in his past but if he managed to eke them out and manipulated them cleverly, they could be very useful to the Colonel.

Chapter 22

The briefing was quieter than usual, with the majority nursing hangovers of varying degrees of severity. Milanovic had been up since 06.00 am and was already on his sixth cigarette of the morning. Lieutenant Vladkovic seemed to possess stronger powers of recovery than most as he looked fresh, showered, shaved and in a pressed uniform. Perhaps he felt the need to save face with his superior officers, Sefer thought, after his blowout of the previous night. As the assembled took their coffee, he noted that the Lieutenant was avoiding eye contact with him; this was good as it indicated either guilt or embarrassment or both. General Svero was looking the worse for wear as he took his coffee silently and slumped into a chair at the end of the table.

Mistakovic took the chair and called the meeting to order.

"Gentlemen, I am pleased to announce that we have been directed to advance to the region around Zepa, which is understood to still be held by Bosniak military forces who are protecting dangerous criminals and fugitives from this and other regions. We are more or less finished here anyway, eh Lieutenant," he said, nodding at Vladkovic. The Lieutenant then confidently recounted the events of the previous morning, describing the 'engagement' with the Bosniaks as another great military victory. He had personally overseen the operation and could vouch for the fact that the entire area had now been 'cleansed' of all Bosniaks. Sefer, seated closer to Vladkovic this morning, nodded silently and made no comment. It was after all, the truth, even if the manner of the cleansing had been highly questionable if not against all the principles of international law.

"Indeed, well done Lieutenant," Mistakovic said as Vladkovic resumed his seat. "You have done well these past few days. But is it not true that a small number of the Bosniak column escaped towards Potocari? Were they subsequently apprehended or liquidated?"

"Comrade Sir," Vladkovic responded. "With great respect sir, I cannot say. I was requested by a superior officer to stay at the site of the initial engagement so I was not involved in the secondary operation".

Sefer smiled inwardly. He could see what was going on here. Mistakovic knew well what had happened even though he hadn't been among the officers gathered in the bar the previous evening. This was an attempt to make General Svero and his Drina Corps look like idiots. Even though the General was technically the most senior officer here, his rank may have been dubiously acquired as he led a largely independent militia group, far less disciplined or organised than the regular Bosnian Serb forces. Although all had basically the same aims, there was fierce rivalry, with each group often attempting to out do the other in their levels of savagery. He had already heard some divisions described as 'soft' because of their habit of only shooting men and boys but allowing women and children to escape. Others were less merciful, some slaughtering all before them and some even systematically imprisoning and raping the women.

"General Svero, I understand that the Drina Corps were involved in that operation. I realise of course that you report separately to central command but I believe you are currently assigned to stay with our group. Would you care to let us know how the operation progressed in Potocari?" Svero gave the assembled officers a look that would chill molten steel.
"With the very greatest of respect to you and your officers and men Colonel," he began, with heavy emphasis on the word Colonel, "The Drina Corps was not involved in what your Lieutenant refers to as the 'initial engagement'. Had they been, we would have properly engaged with the Bosniaks. The correct and obvious course of action would have been to surround them, not to speculatively release a cloud of gas over them, thus allowing many to escape. Between your men and mine, we had enough firepower to finish off all of them."
Sefer noticed the Lieutenant seething but the man did not take the bait.
"Would you care to comment Lieutenant?" Colonel Mistakovic said. Vladkovic took a deep breath and slowly got to his feet.

"Colonel Sir, we did not launch a direct attack on the Bosniaks for the simple reason that we did not have their precise position. With the greatest of respect to our esteemed colleague, it is not possible to engage a foe if you do not know where he is. The enemy was detected the on the previous night by the Drina Corps, who informed us of their presence. However, the Drina Corps did not engage the Bosniaks at that time for reasons best known to them. By the time we had moved into position, the Bosniaks had fled. To pursue them into the woods would have endangered our forces and could have resulted in a disaster for us. May I remind you that these are not refugees? Most of them are heavily armed Bosniak militia and they are reportedly accompanied by violent criminal elements. Had we pursued them, my troops would no doubt have been ambushed. The gassing operation eliminated over nine hundred Bosniak troops and other elements. Had we not taken that option, our own forces would certainly have incurred losses and might have been massacred."

"General?" Mistakovic queried. The man was enjoying this immensely, Sefer noticed. Svero still wore a surly look but he persisted:

"So, what I think the Lieutenant is saying is that he had no idea where the enemy was hiding so he just released his gas and got a lucky break," he said, smugly. "I did not suggest pursuing the enemy into the woods. I said you should have surrounded them, pushing them into an ever tighter area where they would have been forced to defend themselves on our terms, not theirs."

 Vladkovic, unable to contain himself, jumped up and blurted:

"Colonel, Sir, I beg to question how it is possible to surround three hundred square kilometres of woods with one division without accurate intelligence on the precise position of the enemy within those three hundred square kilometres. Sir, if the Drina Corps had responded and attacked the Bosniaks when they initially detected them instead of informing us hours later, we would not have had this problem and we would not now be having this debate."

Svero responded, also getting to his feet:

"And would you suggest that the Drina Corps attack these people in the middle of the night when we only had a small number of men available and no knowledge of the terrain?"

"Gentlemen, gentlemen," Mistakovic intervened. "We are all on the same side here. Let us not waste time arguing over what was a largely successful operation. I am sure that very few of these infidels managed to escape or General Svero's Drina Corps would have found them in Potocari for sure. Your men are still in position there I assume General?"

"Indeed Colonel, Potocari is locked up tight. I can guarantee you that a mouse would have difficulty getting through there."

"Excellent, excellent," said Mistakovic. "With your agreement General, I suggest that you leave a small squadron of men on observation duty there and move the majority of your troops to join with us for an assault on Zepa. Similarly, Lieutenant, you shall leave twenty men to guard the pass to Udrc, just in case the Bosniaks decide to retrace their steps, eh? And I would respectfully suggest that both of you keep your men well hidden. There is no point in advertising our presence to the enemy. If no one is

detected after, say, three days, then your men can join us at Zepa. Is all this clear?"
"Certainly sir," Vladkovic said and saluted.
"Excellent idea Colonel," Svero said, but in a voice dripping with sarcasm. Sefer thought the score was about two all but the Lieutenant might have shaded it.

"They might have forgotten about you and moved on, eh?" Kamal said but the looks he received in return did not reflect his optimism. "I mean, I know I'm only one man but they never searched for me and I'm a free man for five days now."
"Yes, and were it not for the food Hasan gave you, you would be a starving free man," Drazen said. "Don't under estimate these Serbs. I'm sure they know there are plenty of us still hiding in the woods and forests. So what? The berry season is almost over and what's left on the trees and bushes is rotten. We can find spring water to drink but we cannot live on that indefinitely. So we have to come out in the open eventually or we will starve to death. Oh sure, we can organise night-time raids on potato and vegetable plots and maybe even nab the occasional chicken but in the longer term, that is not sustainable. Have you thought of what we will do when the cold winds of autumn blow through here? This is high country Kamal, the winds are unforgiving up here, and I haven't even spoken of winter. Let's say that we did wait it out and we eventually emerge, what are we likely to find? By then, our country will have been ethnically cleansed; it will be a Serb republic with citizens that are more likely to kill us or turn us in to the militias than to help us."

"Your analysis is indeed stark but I think accurate," said Hasan. "But don't be hard on Kamal here. He too has had his own personal struggle."

It was now mid morning. Drazen couldn't remember how many days it had been since he had been snatched from his farm yard. It had probably been less than a week but it felt like months, even at times years. His beloved wife and children were at once both at the forefront of his mind and at the same time a distant memory. It seemed to him that he had been searching for them for a very long time yet he knew that he hadn't even started. The first task was to get out of this hell hole. He looked at his colleagues preparing for another day. The group still had a modicum of food due in part to the fact that the women had been carrying most of the food packs and they had survived the previous day's attack. But it would not last indefinitely they knew. They had to reach some outpost that was still held by Bosniaks; somewhere they would find refuge. It was frustrating that they could not even determine if they were headed in the right direction by trying to reach Tuzla but it was their only option.

Hasan called the group together and explained to them that they needed to move. Everyone had had plenty of rest and although still fatigued, there appeared to be more energy in the group this morning. He explained that they would proceed with even greater caution than before. It wasn't a question of whether the enemy was waiting for them; more when they would encounter them. He told them that they would do all they could to get thru to Udrc undetected but that it was more likely that they would have to stand and fight. For this reason, even though they now numbered only fifty, it was thought safer to spread out even further than before, to give as many as possible the chance to flee if they had to. Most of the soldiers were assigned duty in either the vanguard or as scouts. Only one soldier was asked to guard the rear and Hasan asked Drazen if he would accompany the man. The implication was clear if unspoken; Hasan's family was towards the back so if anything happened to him, he wanted someone he could trust to do his best to guard them. There was almost a pleading in his look when he asked Drazen but the other man nodded immediately and took up his position.

So at exactly midday, when they felt the Serbs would least expect them to be on the move, they headed back in the direction of the pass which would bring them to Udrc and eventually across the high mountains to Tuzla. If they could only have cleared that pass two nights ago, Drazen thought, they might now be on the outskirts of the city. The Serbs would not attack them in the high mountains as they could not bring their heavy guns up there. Cover was also rare but probably easier for a local than a heavily armed militia man who didn't know where he was going. No, the Serbs would leave them be in the mountain range but they would lie in wait for them on the outskirts of Tuzla. So be it he thought; if they managed to get that far, they would take their chances.

Private Radoslav Petrovic was bored. He was chatting with his friend Milan, each boasting to the other of how many they had killed, the levels of danger encountered and the bravery displayed. Yet each man knew deep down that they had never really been endangered. Yes, many Bosnian

Serb soldiers had lost their lives in the war but none in their corps. To date, any opposition they had encountered had been facile and usually delivered with spades or shovels or ancient firearms that either jammed or were long since unusable. Both men yearned for a real war or at least boasted to each other that they did; whether they would be as brave or as successful as they had been up to now was highly debatable. Both had been asked to join the militia in 1992, when the offensive had begun to finally get the accursed Bosniaks out of this territory and to create a Serb homeland in Bosnia. They had been handed a uniform and had received some basic training, supervised by a senior Bosnian Serb Sergeant and an adviser from Belgrade. Both felt they were highly trained and ready for any situation and the way that the Bosniaks had fled from them reinforced their self image.

Both men were among the twenty left by Lieutenant Vladkovic to guard the mountain pass which led to Udrc, the small town which was still largely held by Bosniaks. Over the next few days, this would change, they knew, because the rumour was that when the Serbs captured Zepa, they were going to encircle Udrc in a pincer movement, quickly take control, then mount one final push towards Tuzla. The word was that although there were still pockets of resistance in Sarajevo, all the key installations were now in Serb hands. Neither Radoslav nor Milan had borne any great enmity towards the Bosniaks; in fact both had known many in their schools and in the districts where they had grown up. But all that had changed when Yugoslavia began to break up and these people demanded self determination and their own independent republic. Now it was fine having them as part of the community but no way were Serbs going to be subject to Bosniak rule. The Serbs were the majority; everyone knew that, so it was only logical that they should be the ruling class. The Slovenians and the Croats had already gotten their own independent states and the word was that Serb minorities were being treated badly there. Croat and Bosniak minorities had always been treated well in Yugoslavia and continued to be in Serbia so why should Serbs have to bend the knee here? No, Bosnia would be where they made a stand. This was what their parents had told them; it was what their commanders said and it was what all their colleagues believed so it had to be correct. They had also heard of horrendous atrocities visited on Serb minorities in Croatia during that war and in Bosnia during the early part of this one. Eliminating Bosniaks from this region was only avenging their slain brethren and while it was unpleasant, it was ultimately the only way to finally resolve the situation. A Serb republic populated by Serbs, ruled by Serbs for the benefit of Serbs. A Bosniak minority would only complicate the issue.

Having agreed that they were doing righteous work and would in the end be justified, they resumed talk of their experiences in action to date. The afternoon wore on as they began to speculate on what was happening in Zepa and what they were missing, having been left to guard this God forsaken pass which the Bosniaks had fled from two nights previously.
"How long did Vladkovic say we had to stay guarding this place?" Milan said.
"Careful now," Radoslav replied, "Lieutenant Vladkovic to you. The answer is that he didn't. He was too anxious to

get away to Zepa to join the action. I expect he will contact us later."

"Fuck this heat," said Milan. "Cover me while I go take a piss."

"Sure brother, hey, get me some water when you are down there, will you? This is thirsty work."

Both men laughed. It really was a bum detail they'd been given. The pass was narrow enough that it could be guarded by half a dozen troops provided some had heavy machine guns. By all accounts, the number of Bosniaks who had survived the attack the previous day was tiny. They had a fine view back towards the Srebrenica valley to the north and on both trails leading up to the pass, from the east and the south. There was another approach from where the Bosniaks had fled into the woods to the west, but if they returned, they would have to emerge from there or else circle round and take one of the other uphill paths. Either way, the Serbs literally held the higher ground and were impregnable. Radoslav again checked the two main machine gun positions immediately beneath him for the umpteenth time that day. Milan had just passed them and was heading down to where most of the troops were encamped. He lit a cigarette, lifted his binoculars and scanned the trails again for anything out of the ordinary. There was nothing. He was virtually certain that the small number of Bosniaks who had escaped had either dispersed or had given the Drina Corps the slip in Potocari the previous day. He had heard Lieutenant Vladkovic state that General Svero was not a real General and that he was really a bumbling idiot in a General's uniform. There was no doubt then that Bosniaks could outwit him. But Radoslav Petrovic was a soldier and he wasn't taking chances. He would do his duty, however boring it was or however pointless it seemed. He took a last drag from the Marlboro and crushed it underfoot. He was thirsty; where was Milan with his drink? He glanced down towards the camp but couldn't see him. He couldn't see any of his comrades either; lazy bastards he thought, probably sleeping in the shade.

He cleared his throat to shout down to Milan not to forget his bottle of water but the words froze in his throat as a big hand was placed across his mouth and a knife was inserted expertly between his ribs. On the lower level, behind a bush, Milan finished his call of nature and zipped up his trousers. He marched into camp; where were all these bastards; sheltering from the hot afternoon sun probably. Then he saw the boots of one of his colleagues lying at a curious angle and the awful realization hit him. He reached for his pistol but he never got there as Raif had emerged silently from the undergrowth, grabbed him from behind and severed his carotid artery in one fluid movement.

Chapter 23

The fatal mistake that the Serb squadron had made was to concentrate all of their energies on what was facing them, leaving their rear flank completely exposed. Having detected the group guarding the pass at about two o'clock that afternoon, Hasan and Hamdi had climbed high trees and spent a considerable amount of time assessing the strength of the opposition. They did separate recces and then compared notes. They estimated a maximum of twenty five troops, none of whom seemed particularly alert. In fact, half of them were in camp playing cards and smoking. All appeared to be junior personnel with only a ranking Sergeant left to command the group. Yet the Serbs were in a very strong position. They had mounted two heavy machine gun positions on either side of the pass, both of which were well covered and had an excellent view of all approaches. Anyone trying to storm the pass would be cut to ribbons in a matter of seconds. The only positive was that there did not appear to be any land mines planted. Perhaps they had not had the time or more likely, they didn't fancy blowing any of their own men to bits.

The Achilles heel was the rear. As far as both men could tell, there was no rearguard. Why should there be, no one was going to come back across the mountains even if they had managed to make it through that pass. The only way an approach could be made from the rear was to scale one of the peaks either side of the pass and it appeared that one would need the skills and the balance of a mountain goat to achieve this. They worked their way back to the remainder of their colleagues and delivered the bad news.
"Even though they haven't left many to guard the pass, it would be suicide to attempt to storm it," Hasan said. "We cannot go to Potocari so the only option seems to be to return to Srebrenica and hope the militias have vacated it. It is not a good plan so if anyone has any other ideas? Drazen, with your local knowledge, what do you think?" Drazen was silent for a while and then said:

"There might be another way but it has nothing to do with my local knowledge." He paused and those around him waited in rapt attention.

"What about the other pass? Remember the one on higher ground which they mined? They may not have left a group to guard it. There's probably no reason why they should."

Hamdi protested:

"But Drazen, it is mined. Half of us could be blown to pieces. We can't ask the women and children to risk that."

Hasan immediately saw where Drazen was going and nodded.

"It just might work but we would be taking a huge risk."

There were confused looks all round but the men still listened intently.

"I need ten volunteers come with me," Hasan said.

Immediately, all of the remaining soldiers and a good few of the civilians indicated their willingness.

"OK, thank you my friends. But I need most of you to stay here with the main group and stand guard. I will select ten men to go with me. Our plan will be to track around to the other pass. There will only be ten of us so we should make it there in an hour and a half. If the pass is guarded, we will have to abandon the plan and return. If it isn't, we may be able to track through the minefield by avoiding any of the ground that has recently been disturbed. But I have to warn you friends, this is a difficult and dangerous mission. There may be other patrols; we may not make it through the minefield; we may set off a mine and alert Serb militia. You have to consider that we may not return. If God is on our side and we make it through, it should take less than a half hour to track back around to the lower pass. There, we would hope to surprise the troops who are

guarding it. I propose to leave immediately. If we do not return in four hours, Hamdi here is your new leader."
"But Hasan, I must come with you," Hamdi said, open mouthed.
"No, it is too risky. If we fail, then all may be lost unless someone is here to lead the main group."
The other man nodded and they embraced. No further words were said and the little group silently exited the camp.

The tension among the remaining refugees was palpable. Everyone seemed to realize that this was their last chance; their only chance. Of the soldiers who were left, all took up watchful positions on the perimeter, careful to stay well out of view of the guard detail on the higher ground. Drazen was at a loose end. Even though he had volunteered to go with Hasan, he was inwardly glad not to have been chosen. Had he tripped a land mine, all would have been lost. He found himself again wondering whether he would be safer alone but immediately banished the thought. The others were risking their lives for him, for all of them. He could not sit still so he moved around, chatting in whispers, keeping spirits up, reassuring people. Hasan would make it; he hadn't failed yet; soon they would be heading through the pass to safety. By now he knew everyone by name and was accepted as someone they could depend on. He could see they trusted him and looked to him for encouragement. He was mentally checking on each person when he suddenly stopped dead in his tracks. If he felt he might be safer alone, surely the same thought may have occurred to some of the others? But they had all come so far together, or had they? He realized he hadn't seen Kamal. He ran furiously around the group but the

man was nowhere to be seen. Hamdi was closest to the clearing and he raced towards his position. Hamdi saw the concern in his eyes.
"What's up my friend?"
"The guy you found in the woods," he whispered, "what's his name? Kamal; have you seen him? He's not back in the camp."
"No, I haven't seen him for ages, Jesus no, you don't think?"
Drazen grabbed the binoculars and started scanning the ground in front of the trees which led towards the pass. He could see nothing untoward. Hamdi took the glasses and climbed the first two limbs of the tree he had been leaning against. He instantly jumped down, animated.
"Jesus, I've seen him. He's about two hundred metres forward, just on the edge of the woods, heading towards the Serb position. Is the fucking idiot mad? He'll get himself killed and he'll give all of us away; stay here."
Drazen placed a hand on the other man's chest.
"No, I'll go. You have to stay with the group. Hasan is right. They need you. I'll try to make it. If I'm spotted, try to cover me."
"OK, here, take my knife. Hurry my friend."
Kamal had obviously slipped through the cordon, perhaps when they had been in conclave; Drazen hadn't seen him for some time. He must have crawled through the undergrowth. If he figured he'd be safer on his own, that was fine but not when he was heading right for the centre of the Serb forces. Was he one of the infiltrators they had heard about? Surely not, given what he had told them? But he might be a good actor. Did he think the Serbs would reward him if he betrayed their position? Was he trying to help them by getting closer to the enemy's position? Or

was he just an idiot who had lost it? All of these thoughts ran through Drazen's mind as he raced across the two hundred metres of trees and brush towards the clearing. He couldn't afford to crawl as Hasan had done; there was no time. Unless he rushed, the man would soon be too far away and out of reach.

As he reached the clearing, he dived into the long grass, rapidly crawling on his hands and knees towards the position Hamdi had pin pointed. Nettles stung him; briars clawed and tore at his face and hands, his arms and legs but he felt nothing. He kept moving, blindly. The tall grass was flattened in places where they had traversed the day before. He crawled further, looking left and right. Had he overtaken the man? Had the idiot turned back? Had he already reached the Serbs? He forced back panic and tried to concentrate. He took a quick look up. He could see the Serb machine gun positions and the two soldiers standing at the mouth of the pass. They were talking to each other and one suddenly turned and headed down the track. Had he seen something? Drazen realized he was too far to the left and he had lost valuable time. He contemplated going back but he couldn't. Now they were depending on *him*, and he had to persist. He crawled diagonally towards the right and entered another patch of heavy cover. The briars were thinner here, the grass stronger and taller. He suddenly caught sight of what he thought was a shadow just at the edge of the clearing. He kept going and almost bumped into Kamal. The rustling in the grass alerted the other man who turned his head rapidly. In a split second, Drazen saw what he thought was a combination of surprise, guilt and terror on the other man's face but the crucial thing was that Kamal seemed to open his mouth to cry out. Whether it was in alarm or to alert the enemy, he didn't know but Drazen couldn't take the chance; one sound and they were all doomed. He launched himself on to the other man and grabbed him by the throat. Kamal fought back viciously and elbowed Drazen in the stomach. He then made a guttural sound almost like an animal and tried to bite his hand but Drazen kept it clamped firmly across Kamal's mouth. He had given him every chance and he hadn't taken it. Had the man lost his mind? Kamal wriggled his foot free and kicked backwards, catching Drazen viciously in the groin. He almost collapsed from the pain but still he held on. Holding the man's head with his left hand, he whipped Hamdi's knife from his belt and plunged it into his throat. There was a gurgling sound and instantly there was blood everywhere. The man still kicked viciously but Drazen pushed him down harder into the earth and eventually he was still.

Chapter 24

The ancient taxi wound its way slowly and reluctantly through the dimly lit devastated streets. Barely one street light in a hundred was still working and most of the buildings were in darkness. Many appeared to have been abandoned, shelled, bombed or mortar fired into eventual submission. Some appeared to be standing precariously having been destabilized from continuous pounding. In daytime, they would appear as ugly blackened shells but at night there was an eeriness about them, almost as if they were like giant skeletons, bearing silent witness to a city that had been torn apart but was stubbornly refusing to die. The car was an ancient Yugo which was held together by a combination of battered panels, rust and fibreglass filler. As a precaution, the car was travelling without lights. The thought of what might happen if the vehicle impacted against anything stronger than cardboard made the occupants shudder. Yet the vehicle was moving and the driver had been willing to run the gauntlet of shells, bombs, anti-aircraft missiles and sniper fire to transport them to this remote outpost of the city.

The further progress they made, the more extreme the devastation became.
"This is the worst part of the city now," the taxi driver said. "It is closest to the hills where those bastards have set up their batteries of armaments so apart from being constantly pounded, if a piece of ammunition falls short, it lands here. I don't know why you want to come here anyway; no one lives in this district any longer; it would be suicidal."
"Thank you for bringing us," said the man in the front seat. "You are indeed brave to risk coming here, especially at night."
"You are most welcome," the man said. "You were good enough to trust me and to pay in advance and anything I can do to help a fellow Bosniak is a bonus."
The man directed the taxi driver to stop at the next corner. The three occupants alighted and the car struggled away

into the night. It was almost full dark but there was a half moon which provided enough light to walk by.

"Come, follow me, we must hurry," said the man from the front seat. He led them through a labyrinthine network of back streets and alleys and within moments, both had totally lost their sense of direction and would have had no idea how to return.

"Do not be frightened," the man said. "We have to take this route. It is not safe anywhere now. It would be a disaster if our leader's base were to be discovered."

After walking for twenty minutes, they arrived at another burnt out shell of a building. It might have been an office block or a school or a shopping centre but it had suffered so much damage that it was anyone's guess what purpose it had served in a previous existence. The man led them down a set of concrete steps into a basement type area which might once have been an underground car park or a storage area. It was empty apart from two burnt out shells of cars and piles of rubble. They walked about fifty metres to the far corner of the basement where a door materialized out of the gloom. The man located a button that had been hidden and spoke briefly through an intercom. After a brief pause the door buzzed and opened outwardly towards them. The man waved them through into a long corridor. It was dimly lit but after the blackness of the outside, it appeared to be almost bright. Midway down the corridor, another door opened silently. Another man directed them inside. Two of the visitors were asked to sit in an ante room while the man whom they had travelled with knocked briefly on another door and then went through. A number of men were seated at a round conference table. A man in his late fifties looked up and nodded a greeting.

"General, your visitors have arrived," the man at the door said.
"Thank you Sadik," said the middle aged man, "gentlemen, I think we are finished for now, can you excuse me for half an hour?"
The men rose as one and filed out of the room, some casting brief glances at the visitors. The first man nodded to them:
"The General will see you now."
He opened the door for them and closed it silently, leaving them in privacy. The man rose from the table and although he knew whom he was expecting, gazed in disbelief. The young woman who was the first visitor burst into tears, ran to him and threw her arms around him helplessly, crying, "Papa, Papa."

That Zepa hadn't turned into another bloodbath, Sefer considered a minor miracle. The Serbs showed no sign of slackening in their bloodthirsty quest; most of them anyway. Perhaps his insistence that morning that the Bosniaks finally be treated with some humanity might have been a factor but it was more likely the presence of a relatively large group of journalists and some T.V. crews. The Bosnian Serb leaders had given a press conference afterwards asserting their right to annexe the city as part of the Srpska Republic and stating that any Bosniak who did not wish to remain under Serb rule would be humanely treated and relocated to a safe haven. Hadn't the reporters and T.V. crews seen the buses? Talk of massacres and ethnic cleansing were only rumour they said. While there had been some civilian casualties in the war, hadn't there been in all wars?

There had been loss of life in the taking of Zepa of course. The pathetically few Bosniaks who had put up some resistance had been relentlessly mown down. The remainder of the population was then expelled from all key installations. The town was already sparsely populated; most of the Bosniaks, including practically all the women and children had already fled, fearing a repeat of what had happened elsewhere. Any who were left were put on buses and moved north. Milanovic had been assured they were being transported to Bosniak refugee enclaves but he had no way of verifying this. Tonight in the Zepa bar, the beer and slivovitz were flowing freely; there were even some bottles of champagne in evidence; well, sparkling wine. Celebration was the order of the evening. The big push over the previous few weeks had been very effective. While the military commanders were congratulating each other on their brilliant strategies and sweeping manoeuvres, Sefer felt the reality was that a combination of the military might of the Bosnian Serbs, funded by Belgrade; their willingness to either ignore or bully the supposedly peacekeeping U.N. troops and the sheer savagery of the militias had probably been the decisive factors. After Srebrenica had fallen, other Bosnian towns had quickly followed. Potocari succumbed the next day, followed by Foca, Bratunac and Zvornik. Zepa had been taken this afternoon and tonight, word had been received that Gorazde, further upstream, was also in Serb hands. All of eastern Bosnia was now Serb controlled. Tuzla was still holding out and Bosniak refugees had fled there but with all the Serb militia units now able to concentrate on one target, it was only a matter of time before it fell also.

For the second night in succession, Milanovic found himself drinking with Lieutenant Vladkovic although the younger man was far less talkative this evening. He seemed reserved, withdrawn into himself. The conversation was very general and mainly consisted of queries from Vladkovic about what life was like in Belgrade, particularly nightlife. There was no mention of family or friends, in fact no personal discussion at all. Sefer was happy enough to let the conversation drift; he felt sure that the other man would get drunk more quickly than he would so he would bide his time. A very drunk General Svero, who's Drina Corps had had a successful day, returned just then from the toilet. He paused beside the two men and Sefer waited for the barb. He was wrong.
"Gentlemen, I'd be pleased if you'd let me buy you a drink." Svero said.
"Certainly General, it would be a pleasure," Vladkovic answered. The General ordered three shots which were delivered instantly. He raised his glass.
"Ah, we may differ from time to time about small things but when all is said and done, we are all Serbs, eh? All united in the one cause; to rid our country of this filth, eh?" Sefer or Vladkovic said nothing, merely nodded and clicked glasses.
"Your good health gentlemen and to our victory," Svero said.
"To our victory," the others repeated and all three downed their drinks.
"Ah yes," said Svero. "Soon we can call this our country and live as we want to. Lieutenant, your troops have done

well these past days. I've already mentioned it to the Colonel. When this is all over, I'd be delighted to recommend you for promotion."
"Thank you General," said Vladkovic, "perhaps another toast?"
He signalled the barman to refresh their glasses. He isn't falling for it that easily, is he, thought Sefer. If he's that drunk or stupid, I should have tried to get him to talk earlier. The drinks arrived and more toasts were proposed. There was a loud pop from behind them as another bottle of champagne was opened. Colonel Mistakovic, who was making an appearance tonight, came over with three glasses and insisted the men drink some champagne. The Lieutenant asked if he could propose the toast and the others readily agreed.
"Firstly, I must propose a toast to our great victory but this would not have been achieved without our wise and clever leaders, Colonel Mistakovic, General Svero and our brother from Belgrade, Colonel Milanovic."
Christ, he really is drunk, Sefer thought. Vladkovic continued:
"Gentlemen, to your good health and to the health of your families."
Before they could drink, Mistakovic cut in:
"That is indeed an excellent toast Lieutenant but I feel it merits something stronger than champagne. Bartender, Milos, get us four shots."
The glasses of spirit were again delivered instantly.
"Gentlemen," Mistakovic said, "for the Lieutenant's excellent toast, I propose it be bottoms up."
All four glasses of champagne and slivovitz were downed instantly. Sefer drank the spirit first so he could salve his burning throat with the champagne. He felt the hit instantly

as the combination of champagne and hard liquor hit his system. The Lieutenant had been drinking a lot longer than he so the man would surely be the worse for wear. He was now laughing heartily with the General and with Mistakovic as if they were his lifelong pals. But just as the man was most relaxed, in came the barb that Sefer had been expecting.

"So Lieutenant, any news yet from your men about recapturing those Bosniaks you mislaid the day before yesterday?" Svero said.

Vladkovic was obviously drunk as he replied:

"You mean the Bosniaks we flushed out and your men let slip by you in Potocari?"

Mistakovic laughed loudly:

"Now, now, gentlemen, why spoil an evening worrying about a few missing Bosniaks eh? I mean, these are now a rare breed in this country; difficult to spot, an endangered species for sure."

The other two men hesitated only momentarily and then also exploded with laughter. The Lieutenant ordered four more shots and announced loudly:

"The Colonel is correct. We have cleared most of these Bosniaks out of the country. Who gives a fuck if there are a few living in the trees? When winter comes, it will take care of them. But, to answer the General's question, no I haven't heard from my men. They are still on station but I expect that by now most of them are so bored that they are climbing trees looking for Bosniaks."

He took another loud fit of laughter and was joined by Svero and Mistakovic. While the General had his arm around Vladkovic and was openly toasting him, Sefer could still note the look of grim satisfaction in the man's eyes when he heard that the Bosniaks had still not been apprehended. His initial plan to befriend the Lieutenant again and get some more information from him had now been thwarted, for the moment anyway as it seemed that Svero & Mistakovic had settled in for a long session. The General had started to tell the joke about the Bosnian whore and as he had already heard it three times, he eased away to the veranda and lit a cigarette.

In fact, unknown to Milanovic, the Lieutenant had other reasons to make the Colonel and the General his new best friends. He had tried to contact his Sergeant many times that evening but had failed to do so. The patrol had excellent mobile communications so he couldn't understand why they hadn't replied. He was beginning to fear the worst but did not want to reveal his thoughts. He decided it might just be a communications foul-up. He left word with the communications officer that when his Sergeant called in, he was to be contacted immediately; he then headed to the bar. That had been four hours ago and there had been no messenger.

The Sergeant could not be contacted or would never be contactable again because at that moment, he and his colleagues were lying at the bottom of a ravine with their throats cut. Hasan's little squad had cut them down with ruthless efficiency. The Serbs had all been young men and they had taken no pleasure from the killings but it had long since become a case of them or us and they had to kill to survive. Hasan had not known how close Kamal had been to giving away their position. Had he been able to signal the Serbs, the attack group wouldn't have stood a chance as they were outnumbered and their plan was based on the element of surprise and the unprepared state of the patrol. The column had subsequently made good progress across the mountains although having to move with extreme caution. Supplies had almost run out and as food had to be rationed, people were hungry as well as tired. The patrol they attacked had carried very little food, obviously not intending to remain there for very long. Some of the column had been walking for almost a month now and most were mentally if not physically exhausted. It was only fifty kilometres to Tuzla but it would be a long dangerous journey and there was no guarantee that all fifty of them would make it, Drazen thought.

"The way this city has been treated is beyond belief. The only parallel in history is what the Nazi's did to the Jews. But that was fifty years ago. We are told that civilization has moved on but take a look around you. This is 1995 and these militias want to put us back in the Stone Age. My father fought against the Nazis and I felt I had to stand up for our people again in their time of need. People were fleeing the city so someone had to make a stand."
"But what about the U.N.," said the second visitor? "We heard they had promised to protect Sarajevo."
The man gave a harsh sniff.
"Don't make me laugh girl, he said. Toothless, spineless, they do nothing. Oh I'm sorry, they hold press conferences, haven't you heard? They've told the world on many occasions that they are protecting Bosnia, they're protecting Sarajevo. Look around; do you see anything protected? I will admit that they have kept the airport freed

up, well most of the time, and it has allowed some food shipments to get through. Oh and they also declared a number of safe havens. Did you know that one of them was Srebrenica? Yes, and Tuzla and Zepa but everyone knows it's a joke. The Serbs can bully them any time they like. And as for N.A.T.O.; well let me see, they also threaten the Serbs every now and then. They tell them that unless they stop their bombardment from the hills, N.A.T.O. will target air strikes against them. They have even followed up on the threat once or twice and have destroyed a few Serb gun emplacements but as soon as the offensive stops, the Serbs move back into position again. It is another standing joke really."
The man paused and lit a cigarette. He offered them to his guests but they declined.

"Where was I? Ah yes, N.A.T.O. As for protecting us, the citizens of this city, forget it. In a way I don't blame them; they are on what is called a hiding to nothing. What American or British Mother wants their son or their daughter to die in some foreign field protecting people they don't know and will never meet? No, the world has changed you see. The U.N. commanders on the ground have tried but no matter what they do or how they plead, the Serbs will ignore them, and why? Because the Serbs know they will do nothing because they are afraid. Unless the U.S. or N.A.T.O. acts decisively, it will only get worse. But they are also afraid to act because the Serbs are allied with Russia. The Russians have a power of veto at the U.N. Security Council so they are powerless to do anything through that channel. In the meantime Sarajevo and Bosnia descend further into chaos but we will not leave; if the Serbs want to succeed in ethnically cleansing all of Bosnia, they will not find it easy, because we are now organized and we will fight back. Granted, their weapons are far superior to ours but we will fight nonetheless. But I am sorry, I've forgotten my manners. You have been through a huge trauma and you need to be protected from all this and indeed you will be."

The man who was speaking was the leader of the Bosnian underground resistance in Sarajevo and he was also Drazen's father, Danvor Itsakovic. He now poured coffee for his guests, his daughter-in-law Sonja and her friend Aida.
"I am so sorry you were frightened when you visited our apartment Sonja my dear. We vacated there months ago. The area is very dangerous with many deaths from snipers apart from the Serb bombardment. Here, we are safe for now but we have to ensure the Serbs don't discover us so we move regularly. That is why it took you so long to locate us. Drazen's Mother is with me also and you will meet her shortly. Tell me again what happened in the village, my poor child."

Sonja had only given him a hurried account of that dreadful day at their farm as she became too emotional. Danvor now poured a shot of slivovitz into their coffees and it steadier her somewhat; she told him everything again from the beginning. Although Danvor was listening to an account of the death of his father and his only son, he sat calm and impassive, steeling himself and keeping his emotions in check until later. Sonja brought him right up to date, reassuring him that little Diana was safe and with the three teenagers at an aunt of Fadil's in the north of the city. It was this lady who had heard the rumour that Drazen's

father was organizing the resistance and it was she who had arranged the meeting this evening. Danvor listened in silence, never once interrupting. When Sonja had finished, tears again slipping down her beautiful cheeks, he rose and embraced her.
"I may be leader of the Bosnian resistance but my first duty is to my family. I would ask you to come here but if the place were to be discovered and you were in the company of the resistance, it would be very dangerous. Instead, there is a woman I know who lives in a relatively safe area. It is beyond the range of most of the Serb guns so they tend to leave it alone. I think you and Diana will be safe there and you can bring your friends also of course."
"But what about you and Mama, will you be safe here, when will we see you?"

Danvor sighed and shrugged his shoulders:
"We will be fine but what is safety? In those hills up there, they have artillery, mortars, tanks, anti-aircraft guns, heavy machine guns and rocket launchers. That doesn't include the many snipers who cowardly hide on the roofs of our buildings and cut us down in the street. No Sarajevan citizen is fully safe Sonja, not at home, not at their place of work, not in their schools, not in their shops or marketplaces, not even in hospital, not even in church; there is no refuge, no respite from these pigs. They hound and harass us from dawn until dusk but we will not relent. This is our city; this is our country; if they wish to share it with us, we will be glad to accommodate them but we will not allow them to exterminate our people and our culture. We hate hiding down here like rats but we will do it until we are strong enough to fight back."

The older man realized that his voice had been raised and he softened it once again.

"Thank you so much Papa," Sonja said, "you are a very brave man but…"

Danvor placed his hands on her shoulders:

"I know child, I know. You have more immediate worries. Tonight I will activate all of our contacts throughout Bosnia to look for dear Zoran. My men respect me and I know they will try their hardest to locate him. Don't fear Sonja, he is a strong intelligent boy and if there is anyone who could have escaped, it is Zoran, I am sure of it."

He looked her straight in the eyes as he said it and she nodded eagerly. Danvor had said it with such conviction, he almost believed it himself. He wanted to believe it, with every fibre of his being, but he had seen and heard too much, too many atrocities, too many tales of devastation. Still, he had vowed to try and he would use every resource he had to try to find the boy.

"And Grandmother, I mean, your Mother also."

"Of course, of course my dear but I feel sure that my old Mother is fine. She's the tough side of our family; don't worry about Mama, she'll make it; you'll see. But hurry, you must return now and bring Diana and the other girls here. You will be safe for tonight. I know your friend's aunt is a fine woman and a loyal Bosniak but I know the area where she lives is not safe in day time. We will get you another driver now and you must return with the girls before dawn. Tomorrow we will move you to the safe house. If things get any worse, we can always move you to one of the villages but for now, you are probably better off here. No one trusts anyone in the villages any more. Don't worry Sonja; we just have to work to get your family back together."

She hugged him once again and felt a huge weight slip off her shoulders. She was still desperately distraught but she had always known that when she located Papa Itsakovic, he would know what to do.

Chapter 25

Sarajevo might have been under siege for almost three years. Most of its infrastructure might be utterly devastated, yet amazingly, transport links were still running. Buses were infrequent and unreliable but drivers were still stubbornly making an effort to operate their routes despite the ever present danger of being shelled or shot at. People had adapted, adjusted, done whatever it took to ensure life went on as normal or what passed for normality in Sarajevo. An old trolley bus, long past its useful life cycle, trundled past them as they waited for the driver to take them to their new safe house. All six were travelling together now. Papa had warned them to be careful but he *had* reassured them that to see groups of women and girls travelling together was commonplace as the men were either away fighting, in hiding or had been killed by the Serbs.

Their new driver arrived in a modern people-carrier vehicle. Sonja was initially suspicious as she was sure the man was not a Bosnian. When he introduced himself as Prikan, she knew instantly he was Croatian. It was not that she didn't trust people but Bosnians had had trouble with Croats also and she could not afford to take a chance. The man could see the fear in her eyes and those of Aida.
"Ladies," he said, "let me put your mind at ease. I know I am not one of your people but believe me, we have common cause. My entire family was killed by the Serb militias in the war to free my homeland. I am sure your Grandfather told you that Bosniaks have allied with many Croatians to fight this evil."
"Yes he did," Sonja said, "please forgive us for our distrust and may we offer our condolences to you on your terrible loss."
"Thank you," Prikan replied. "Rest assured we will protect you, all of you, with our lives. Danvor Itsakovic is our beloved commander and a hero of this city. We will not let him down."
Sonja breathed another sigh of relief. Papa **had** said that they had joined forces with Croatians, many of whom also lived in Bosnia and had been badly treated. This man appeared genuine and surely Papa would not have sent him unless he was completely trustworthy. She realized she was becoming hyper cautious. When they reached the safe house, she would try to relax and pray that Papa's network would locate her boy and bring him back to her. Dawn was breaking on the edge of the horizon, a brilliant fireball signaling another scorching day. As with the previous morning, there was no one about this early so they sped through the deserted streets. She was sitting in the back

and she hugged Diana, allowing herself a small smile and a moment to relax.

"Not long now," said Prikan, "only half a kilometre." Sonja noticed that the buildings were noticeably less damaged in this area but it was still no luxury suburb. Everything was still dull and dark and grey. Prikan slowed the vehicle at a red light, one of the very few still functioning in the city and Sonja casually glanced out of the car window. The building on the right was a low squat brick-built one storey, with a number of older militia vehicles parked outside. The roof of the building was festooned with aerials and loose wires were slung downwards and fed into the station, some neatly, some through windows and some hung at crazy angles that seemed to serve no purpose. It was a police station, Sonja presumed and it was probably occupied by Bosnian Serb forces by now. She made a mental note to avoid going in this direction, if indeed it was safe to move around at all.

Just as the light changed, Sonja's heart almost stopped in her chest. She had been daydreaming and almost hadn't seen it but there in the window, clear as day, was her own image and under it, the statement:

Wanted for Capital Murder - Bosniak murderess - Sonja Itsakovic - this person is a highly dangerous criminal. Substantial reward offered.

She said nothing; she used all of her will power to stare straight ahead. This changed everything. It wasn't as if she expected Aida or the driver Prikan to betray her but money changed everything. She knew she would not be making any trips out of the safe house in day time and probably none at night either. Because their journey to Sarajevo had gone so smoothly, she had almost forgotten her night of terror at the camp and she had begun to believe Aida and Nasser and the others who told her the Serbs wouldn't bother looking for her. They had been wrong. The Serbs had gone to a lot of trouble too; where had they gotten the photograph? The women hadn't been documented or photographed at any point. Had it really been her at all? Had she dreamed the entire thing? Had it been someone else? Of course it had been her; who else had murdered a Serb Colonel or was it a General? Jesus, she didn't know. Diana noticed her unrest and enquired as to what was wrong but Sonja merely told her she was tired and the constant journeys were uncomfortable. Diana rolled her eyes and shrugged – the people carrier was extremely comfortable. Sonja thought again and suddenly it hit her; the photograph was a blown-up version of her most recent internal passport picture; she had had her pass renewed last year. She hoped and prayed that the woman who owned this safe house could be trusted and was not tempted to turn her in. How many more people had seen her? Dozens, maybe more; no, she was exaggerating, it was surely no more than a handful. Would the photograph only be in police stations or was it on general release, posted throughout the city? Maybe it was just this station? She closed her eyes and started to pray again as the car pulled up to the kerb and the lady of the house came out to greet her visitors. Sonja stayed in the rear until all the others had alighted, but she couldn't stay there for ever so she eventually took a deep breath and, with a scarf wrapped tightly around her throat, hair and face, she emerged into the early morning sunshine.

The house was located in what had been a relatively affluent part of the city and it was quite large; certainly big enough to accommodate her little group. The lady, who introduced herself as Melita, showed them to their rooms. Sonja was given a spacious room which she would share with Diana; the three teenagers were billeted together and Aida was given a small box room. As they had all left their previous abodes in a hurry, they had few personal belongings other than the clothes they stood up in but Melita discreetly advised them that they could choose fresh clothing from a stock she had in the basement. They all hurried there; the girls were delighted and after all had chosen pretty summer dresses, their mood brightened. They were told that breakfast would be ready in twenty minutes so all then went and had showers. The last time Sonja had stood under a shower had been in the camp commander's bathroom. She involuntarily shivered as the thought occurred to her; still, she had escaped and she thanked God she had managed to protect her little girl. She hadn't mentioned the photograph to anyone and she was wondering if she would confide in Aida. How stupid of me, she thought, after all we have been through together. Yet, there might be a danger; Aida wouldn't betray her but the other woman would be aware that they were in far greater danger harbouring a wanted criminal than an ordinary Bosniak. She might worry and in an emergency, she might not stay with them; no, she decided to say nothing to anyone, for now anyway.

Melita served them a meal of eggs, cheese, vegetables and fruit, with hot coffee. It was simple but delicious. When they were finished, she asked the younger girls to clear away the dishes in the kitchen and she invited Sonja and Aida to take coffee with her in the living room. She was a few years older than both women but not more than in her late thirties. Unlike them, she had blonde hair, blue eyes and fair skin. Sonja felt the woman's hair might well be coloured but her pale skin could not be faked and did not mark her as a Bosniak. Seemingly reading their thoughts, Melita said:

"You are probably worried about my ethnicity; don't be embarrassed, it is natural these days as nobody trusts anyone any more. My Mother was Bosnian and my father was Russian. He was stationed here for many years."

Sonja and Aida nodded. Melita did not say where her Mother or her Father were now and they were too polite to ask.

"This is and always has been my home. It has been in my family for generations. I will provide you with food and shelter but I will ask you to be most careful when going outside and to avoid the streets during daylight hours if at all possible. This is a big house and you are not my only guests. As it is early, the others are still asleep but you will meet them later. All are like yourselves; Bosniaks who have suffered losses or who have been separated from their families. Many people pass through this house and you will be encouraged to know that we occasionally do reunite families and parts of families through our networks. When I started welcoming people three years ago, I thought it would only be for a few months but it has almost become a way of life for me now. I don't welcome everyone into my home even though I try to do what I can for my people. I mainly accommodate refugees recommended by Danvor. He has been a friend of my family for many years and if he recommends someone, it gives me peace of mind. I will leave for work soon so I ask you to be careful in and to respect my home. A lady called Jasmina will come at around ten o'clock to do the cleaning. She has her own key and will let herself in. Don't be alarmed; she is a Bosniak and is completely trustworthy. In fact Jasmina has shown incredible bravery in the siege and has helped many people to flee the city. However, she is steadfastly loyal to me and will not leave herself. Her family has worked with my family for many years so there is a very strong bond between us. There is a pantry off the kitchen which I will show you and the refrigerator is reasonably well stocked with food, despite the siege. Papa Itsakovic is very good to us. Please feel free to help yourselves and to prepare food for the children. You are a guest in my home so what I have is yours. Although my home is large, I am not a wealthy woman but I am prepared to share what I have. If you can pay me some small amount, I will appreciate it but if you cannot, I will fully understand as so many people have lost everything in this damn war; there are so many people worse off than I am."

She paused and Sonja and Aida both began to speak at once, but then hesitated. Eventually, Aida said:

"Melita, we cannot tell you how much we appreciate this and we cannot thank you enough. We both have money and we will be glad to pay you for the food and for the accommodation."

Melita immediately raised a hand to stop her.

"No, no, no, ladies, I am sorry if I gave you the wrong impression. I will not take a dinar from you for the accommodation; my house is yours. All I meant was if you could share in the cost of the food as it is difficult to get and expensive because of the siege. I thank you both for offering."

Both women expressed their deep appreciation for what she was doing but Melita waved them away. She showed them the rest of the house and went to prepare herself for work. As she was leaving, she discreetly called Sonja into the hallway and when they were out of earshot, said:
"Sonja, Danvor has told me what you've been through and it must have been awful for you, you have my deepest sympathy."
Sonja immediately played down her plight:
"Thank you Melita, but I am only one of thousands to whom this has happened. Aida and Fadil and the other girls have also lost their families or been separated from them and they have all been through horrendous abuse in that camp so my suffering has been mild by comparison."
"I know my dear but I heard what you had to do to escape that terrible place. You were very, very brave but you must be aware of something. Do not worry as we will protect you but the Serbs are trying to hunt you down specifically. It is an unusual move for them so whomever you killed must have been important."
Sonja had coloured considerably and was as tense as a coiled spring.
"Sorry if I alarmed you my dear, don't be frightened. I have no problem with you killing that bastard; he got what he deserved. But I need you to be extra careful, even more so than the others. The Serbs have put up wanted posters of you in their police stations so it is probably best not to

leave the house at all. I know this will be difficult but I think it will be safer."

So the woman knew exactly who she was and she also knew about the posters. Sonja knew this meant she would again have to trust a number of people whom she had never met before with her life and the life of her daughter. She suddenly felt small and afraid and vulnerable; how much more of this could she take before she cracked? The other woman could see she was close to tears so she hugged her tightly and assured her that she would be fine. "It will be OK Sonja. This house has been used as a refuge for almost three years now and it has never been breached. You are safe here."

Sonja suddenly felt guilty as she realized that Melita was actually risking her own life in order to protect Sonja and the others. Of course she was; if the Serbs discovered Sonja or any escaped prisoners hiding here, they would surely execute everyone in the house and everyone associated with it. They would probably shoot everyone in the entire street. She felt selfish then so she gathered herself, embraced Melita and thanked her again.

The lady left to try to catch one of the few remaining trams to work and at around nine o'clock, the other occupants of the house appeared. There was a lady called Tamara, with her two children, Nadja, who was six and Omar who was ten. There were three single teenage Bosnian girls, Hana, Majda and Serifa, all of whom had fled in terror from villages where women and young girls were being systematically raped. Finally, there was a young couple, Kazim and Refika. It was such a rare sight now that Sonja was beginning to wonder if they were the last Bosnian couple left alive in the entire country. All of the other women had the same tragic tales to tell; fathers and brothers taken away and murdered; families sundered, none knowing where the remainder of their family were or even if they were alive. All were shy at first but eventually introductions were made and even some conversation ensued. Diana befriended Nadja and they hit it off immediately, Diana delighted that she was no longer the youngest in the group and she set about protecting Nadja as she had seen her Mother and Aida do to her and the other girls. She learns and adapts so quickly, Sonja thought. Kazim told them how he had been in Sarajevo on business at the start of the siege and had become trapped in the city. It was lucky for him as the Serb militia had come to his village a few weeks later and taken away all of the men. Refika had heard rumours of what they did to the women when the villages were unprotected so she fled before they had the chance to come back. She had spent months hiding in various villages before she got an opportunity to enter Sarajevo. Then she had had to set about locating her husband who had been hiding out in another part of the city. Kazim told Sonja he was a part of the Bosnian resistance and that he greatly admired Papa Itsakovic. There were many such houses all over Sarajevo where citizens were given refuge. He assured them there was no reason to worry as no Bosniak would betray one of their own people.

The day was again hot and it was difficult to ask the children to stay inside. Melita had an enclosed garden but it was overlooked so none of them was prepared to take the risk of using it. While it was unlikely that neighbours would report children playing in a yard, in this war, you took no chances and trusted no one. The day passed slowly but Melita had an extensive and interesting library so everyone had plenty to read. The women took turns preparing food and drinks. Kazim had to go out at one stage but he left by a side entrance which was not overlooked and led on to an alley where it could not be seen from which house he had emerged. He had to meet with Papa Itsakovic to discuss plans for an upcoming operation. Sonja offered him money and asked him to bring back some food if he could obtain it. He assured her he would try but the problem was that there was a blockade and foodstuffs were almost impossible to find. Some food was getting through but it was being handled by black marketeers demanding enormous prices. A lot of food was being brought in through the tunnel and Kazim told them that was where Melita got most of her food. He would ask Papa Itsakovic who had access but it wasn't urgent as Melita had sufficient supplies to feed them for another few days. Nevertheless, Kazim assured them that if he had time and if he could get any reasonably priced food for their dollars, he would bring it back. He was in luck; although he didn't return until after ten that night, he arrived laden down with sausages, tomatoes and wild mushrooms. He had encountered a market trader who had brought in fresh supplies that morning, God alone knew how, but the man was prepared to offer them at a fair price to Kazim. Melita had returned at seven in the evening and all of them had eaten but the food was most welcome and was saved for the following days. The only small problem was that Kazim had paid with U.S. dollars; crisp notes that had been stolen from a camp commander's stash by a woman whom half the Bosnian Serbs in the country were looking for.

Sonja went to bed at 11.30, happy that she was safe for now but she knew that sleep would be slow in coming. In fact, she could not imagine ever having an untroubled night's sleep again until she found her beloved Zoran and discovered what had happened to the rest of her family. Diana was already fast asleep and she smiled lovingly at her; at least her little one was happy for now. The day had been punctuated by sporadic bouts of mortar and shell fire and occasional bursts of gunfire. Most had been distant with none close enough to cause concern. This neighbourhood seemed to escape the worst of the violence. The guns and artillery had quieted as night fell with now only a very isolated whoosh when some weapon was fired in the distance. Sonja tossed and turned and stared at the ceiling. There was light from the moon and the swaying of the trees outside her window drew crazy patterns in shadow on the walls of the room. Her night vision had long since kicked in and she had a clear view of everything in the room. The house was very still apart from the occasional click from a water pipe or a groan from a floorboard as the house settled down for the night. She suddenly heard a sound that seemed slightly louder; was it a creaking floorboard? She listened intently and yes, she heard it again, seemingly coming from outside her door. She told herself to stop worrying; there were now fifteen people living in this house and any one of them could have gone to get a glass of water.

The sound was not repeated and the house again grew still. About a minute later, Sonja thought she heard a slight metallic click, different from the earlier noises. She glanced at the door to her room. Had the handle moved a fraction? She stared at it, transfixed – it began to move downwards, ever so slowly. She almost screamed but held herself at the last moment. She still had one of the pistols she had taken from the camp and it was by her bedside table. She swiftly and silently eased out of bed, grabbed the gun, slipped off the safety and pointed it squarely at the door just as the handle reached the bottom. The door began to open inwards very slowly; Sonja concentrated like never before and didn't even dare to breathe.

Chapter 26

We are all affected by our experiences; in fact, all of us *are* the sum total of those experiences. Drazen wondered if the events of the previous days had already affected him so deeply that he would never be the same person? Was all hope lost? Was that why he saw people so disoriented that they killed themselves rather than live another moment in this hell? But no, those people had been gassed, or had they? Was the gas just the final straw that pushed them off the edge? Was it a fear of being captured and tortured or was it that they sought a release from this mind torturing nightmare; this living hell on earth? Was it something similar which had affected Kamal he wondered? He had seemed genuine, a refugee like themselves and they had accepted him into their group. Was he really a Serb infiltrator who just waited until he identified some Bosniaks, then when he got within sight of a group of Serbs, ran for it? No, the man was definitely a Bosniak. He may have been tired and possibly not thinking straight. Did he think the Serbs would reward him for betraying the Bosniak column? Kamal had told them that he knew of the

Serb massacres all over Bosnia and Herzegovina; he was no fool; he had fled Potocari when he had a chance. Why then did he think that giving up his colleagues would even save him, not to speak of rewarding him. Drazen knew that if Kamal had gotten through, the Serbs would have thanked the man. Then they would have rounded up the column, shot all of them and rewarded Kamal with a bullet to the head. Surely he knew that? Surely he knew what he was doing was suicidal? Or was there another explanation? Drazen couldn't afford to wait for one; he had had to act decisively and he did. The others had been extremely grateful to him but Drazen was troubled. He had regretted having to kill his Serbian neighbour on the first night of his flight but he hadn't had a choice; the man was about to betray him. Now he had also killed a fellow Bosniak. He knew the man was also about to betray them but he still couldn't figure it. Whatever else happened in this war, he was now absolutely certain that he would never be the same person again.

The remnants of the column were making slow progress at this altitude. It wasn't that they slowed for the women and children; everyone was exhausted. They were out of food now and had very little fresh water left although they felt they were bound to find some in the high peaks. The going was horrendous; there were no paths, other than occasional sheep tracks which ran in uncertain, criss-cross patterns. They had to climb over rocks and mounds of earth. They tried to take the easiest path but often it just led them into areas that were impassable and they had to retrace their steps. They navigated partially by taking a bearing from the sun but mainly by a sense of direction; by guessing that Tuzla was over there; over that next rise; just a few more mountain peaks away. They climbed incredibly steep ascents only to find even more dangerous descents on the other side. On another day, the mountains would have been seen as beautiful but today they were incredibly cruel and unforgiving. Even though it was now evening, the temperature, even at this level, was relentless – the sun still burning down from cloudless skies. An ideal day to harvest his corn, Drazen thought sadly. While they had expended an incredible amount of energy, he reckoned they hadn't progressed any more than ten kilometres and possibly less. At this rate, they'd all be dead before they reached Tuzla. The only consolation was that the Serbs would not follow them up here. Progress at night was out of the question so all were glad when Hasan called on them to rest underneath a rocky outcrop.

Smoking wasn't prohibited in the bar so when everyone else lit up, Sefer decided to follow suit. The French champagne which someone had managed to locate had long since been consigned to memory but the celebrations were still in full swing. Although it was close to three in the morning, no one had gone to bed yet. Sefer imagined the hangovers in the morning would be ruinous; in fact, he chuckled inwardly, it might be a good thing for the Bosniaks. None of the commanders in this room looked like they'd be taking charge of much in the morning. But no one cared; the war was effectively over and the Serbs had won. Oh there were a few small pockets of resistance but they would be swatted like irritating flies in the coming days. They had heard from the journalists, or at least those brave enough to have a drink with them, that the consensus everywhere was that the Serbs were the victors. Everyone loves a winner – after all, isn't it winners that write the history books, they said. But there was a fly in the ointment; there had been an outcry after Srebrenica. An Italian journalist, Guido Sciera, was still standing at this late hour and regaling the Serb commanders with stories. Sciera obviously knew his audience and was complimentary to the Serbs. As a result, he was getting plenty of exclusive information denied to his colleagues who were either too drunk or too scared to stay drinking. Sciera knocked back yet another slivovitz with a beer chaser and continued with his tale of Srebrenica, even though Sefer was sure the Serb leaders were uncomfortable with this. The journalist's version of events was as follows:

"The rest of the free world was outraged that this could happen in Europe in the 1990's. President Clinton had been in serious trouble in the U.S. He was being seen as a weak leader. The American Government was on strike and he was under severe attack from the Republicans in the houses of Congress. The country was being brought to its knees in a battle about the size of Government. At the same time, Clinton's foreign policy was seen as feeble. Oh he had had some success in Ireland but that conflict seemed to have run its course anyway. Both sides were sick after thirty years of war and a settlement seemed imminent. But Clinton had been afraid to take on the Serbs; well, his N.A.T.O. partners were unwilling for one and most of those were European and it was happening in their back yard. There had been appeals to the Americans to intervene unilaterally but Clinton hadn't wanted to go there. But Srebrenica had changed all that," Sciera said.

"Even though he conceded to the commanders that it had probably been a 'necessary military operation', whatever news emerged had galvanized the west into action. Clinton was now threatening unilateral action against the Bosnian Serbs with or without his N.A.T.O. colleagues support. He had gotten a huge boost in the polls from this and as he was due to stand for re-election in four months, he needed all the help he could get."

"Fuck the Americans," said Svero. "We'll show them what real fighters are made of. Anyway, why should they interfere in our war? This is our land, our people; they should fuck off and mind their own business. Let them come and we'll make them regret it."

"I'm not sure that's quite what they intend," Sciera replied, a bit more nervously now. "They are talking about selected air strikes. I doubt you will see American troops fighting on the ground in Europe again. Clinton is scared of another Vietnam. No, what he needs to do is to get his own house in order first, then a short successful war, preferably conducted from a long distance away and with no American casualties. You know the Americans have smart bombs now; they worked in Iraq. They can start a war from a thousand kilometres away. They never even need to set foot on Serbian soil."

"Cowardly bastards," said Svero. "Perhaps," said Sciera, "but don't underestimate the power of the American military. You'd do best to clean up the few remaining pockets of Bosniak resistance and then to keep a low profile for a while."

Sefer listened intently but said nothing. He was not the type to say I told you so but he knew from the dark glances he was getting from the Serb commanders that they knew that was what he was thinking. He **had** told them, many days ago. There had been massacres all across Bosnia since 1992; indiscriminate bombings and shellings and lootings and rape and pillage but Srebrenica had been different; this had been systematically organized cold blooded murder. He knew that if word got out, the west would have to act and it appeared that they finally would. But still, Svero had a point. The Serbs had effectively won; they had succeeded in evicting the Bosnians from their **own** country. They had set up the Bosnian Serb Republic led by Karadzic and while it wasn't as yet universally recognised, hadn't no less a person than the former U.S President Jimmy Carter referred to him as President Karadzic? Yes, despite everything, the Serbs had something to celebrate. He lit another cigarette and checked his watch.

"You know Guido," Svero said. "You were asking earlier on what we did with all the women and children and old folks. Well, any of them that survived, we've sent them to the poorest regions, what we would call the arsehole of Bosnia." He paused to laugh loudly joined by most of the company. "But of course, we have kept a choice few. You know, not all the Bosniak women are ugly, know what I mean?" He winked broadly. "We have a place near here where we can go for some, as you would say, recreation. You are more than welcome to join us tonight, what do you say eh?" The Italian hesitated. "Come on," said Svero, "you only live once eh, what do **you** say Milanovic, are you gonna join us tonight?"

Sefer said nothing but there was something approaching disgust in his eyes which the Italian, drunk as he was, read clearly. "Ah, you go ahead General," he said, "I've had so much of this fucking slivovitz, I wouldn't be able tonight." and he laughed loudly. "Ah, maybe you're right." said Svero. "In fact, none of us are probably able to perform, let's have another drink," and he ordered another round for everyone.

Lieutenant Vladkovic sat off to the side, chain smoking and downing drink at an even greater rate than the rest. Milanovic, good at reading the signs, knew something was eating at him and decided to try to find out what it was. The Lieutenant had left the bar on two occasions to make phone calls but he hadn't told anyone what his business was. As the night had dragged on, he had thought that the signals officer had either forgotten about him or had left him to drink. But on checking, he dicovered that the man was still on full alert; there had been no communication from Vladkovic's men. He had summoned his next-in-command, a trusted colleague from his own village and ordered him to take four men and proceed to the pass at first light. He was to try to locate the patrol and was to communicate only with the Lieutenant, who would be standing by. After that, there was nothing for it but to get pissed. He gave no thought to sleep because he knew that it would not come easily anyway.

"So Ivan," Sefer said. "How goes it tonight? Any word from your men searching in the trees, eh?" He kept his eyes locked on the Lieutenant who immediately looked away. Ah, so that was it. "No, no reports Colonel but I expect that idiot Svero let those Bosniaks slip away that day in Potocari so I wasn't expecting to hear anything." Sefer nodded and touched his glass to Vladkovic's. The Lieutenant immediately attempted to change the subject. "Isn't, isn't it amazing Colonel, how some stupid dispute in America over what, was it their budget the Italian said, could fuck up all our good work? I mean, I mean, it's none of their business. I mean, take the Russians. They support us, in theory anyway, but they don't start bombing the Bosniaks. I mean, why should those fucking Yanks start bombing *us*? What di, did, we ever do on them?"

Sefer drank deeply and shrugged. "Who knows Ivan, the way the world works any more? Everyone is allied to everyone else yet countries change sides all the time. Then we are living in an age of global communications. If something happens here, it is on news networks all round the world in hours. The media have huge power; they can put their own spin on any story; tell it their own way. They can almost force a Government to start or for that matter, stop a war. We are only small players in the game. That is why we are best to avoid 'conflicts' like the one we had this week because it just gives our enemies ammunition to use against us." The Lieutenant then launched into another long diatribe about what could they do; Bosnian scum; oppressed Serbs; their rights etc etc. He seemed to want to speak about anything except his men and was far more talkative then usual; a sure sign he had something to hide. This was somewhat worrying.

Sefer was prepared to acknowledge Svero's earlier comment; the Serbs had won, of that there was no doubt. The Americans might slow the final advance but only briefly. Anyway, that wasn't his worry. He noted that the

Lieutenant hadn't said that he had definitely received word from his men. Surely they would have reported in regardless of whether they encountered opposition? That could only mean one thing; a Bosnian military unit had survived and had successfully engaged the small Serb patrol. The Bosnians were poorly armed so if they had overcome Vladkovic's twenty odd men, then there might well still be a large contingent of them. He wondered what the Lieutenant would say at the morning briefing. He suspected the man would try to save face and say nothing or pass the issue off. Were it during an earlier part of the war, he would have felt it was his duty to question him and to dig deeper as by withholding information, he might well undermine Serb military action in the Tuzla area. The plan for the following day was to leave a skeleton crew here in Zepa to guard the key installations and for all units to make a final push to Tuzla. The Serb militias were looking on it as a lap-of-honour as little resistance was expected. He decided to leave well enough alone for now; he might need an ally later and the Lieutenant was a possibility. He didn't seem close to any of the others and despite the outward bravado, he displayed vulnerability at times. Sefer wanted to get him talking about his family again but the place was still too noisy, too boisterous to start a deep personal conversation. Glancing over to where Mistakovic, tunic discarded, shirt open to the chest and tie askew, was regaling the company with a Serbian fighting song, Sefer wondered if there would even *be* a morning briefing.

Sonja gripped the pistol tightly and although she was trembling with fear, her hand was steady. Her daughter lay sleeping peacefully in the bed she had just left and anyone who came through that door would die before they got near her. The door opened in almost miniscule movements. Whoever the intruder was, they were taking extreme care not to make a sound. Rivers of sweat ran down Sonja's back and chest. She blinked as a bead of perspiration dripped into her right eye. Her finger tightened on the trigger. Just a gentle squeeze, like Aida had shown her and the intruder was history. The door opened fully and Sonja blinked. There was no one there. But the door handle was still pressed all the way down so there had to be someone. It only took a micro second but it seemed like far longer. Her eyes traced the doorway all the way down, her trigger finger now extended as far as it could go without actually firing the pistol and then she saw – little Nadja, barely tall enough to reach the door handle. Several things happened at once; Nadja saw the gun and screamed. Sonja's adrenalin spiked and she was so afraid she'd squeeze the trigger that she dropped the pistol. Whether it was the child's scream or the clatter of the gun hitting the floor, she wasn't sure, but suddenly the whole house seemed to be awake with people running out of doors and through corridors. Sonja regained a measure of control, picked up the pistol, replaced the safety and put it in the bedside locker. She then ran to the room which Nadja was sharing with her Mother. The little girl was hysterical and Tamara was trying to comfort her. Three pairs of eyes immediately regarded Sonja with suspicion. She tried to explain what had happened but Tamara simply nodded and continued comforting Nadja, motioning Sonja with her eyes to leave. Sonja had already decided she'd better go as the little girl looked absolutely terrified. She explained to the others what had happened and they made light of the incident, advising her to go back to sleep. Thankfully Diana had slept soundly through all the commotion and Sonja slipped back into bed and hugged her. She again lay awake staring at the ceiling, knowing that it was now unlikely sleep would come at all. What has this war done to me, to all of us, she thought. A week ago, I was just a Mother caring for her family; now I've killed in cold blood and I've just scared a little girl half to death. When will the nightmare end?

Chapter 27

Tuzla – three days later:

There were journalists and T.V. crews to witness the arrival of the column in the Bosnian-held territory of Tuzla. Bosnia was now round-the-clock news on all networks. There had been international media interest throughout the conflict but this had waned as the war had dragged on and the reaction from western forces had been one of inertia. But since its escalation and the plundering of the so called 'safe haven' of Srebrenica, attention was focused on the country 24/7. There was initial confusion at how the refugees had made it. Had they been allowed safe passage by the Serb militias as had been promised? The reporters were hungry for stories and scant respect was paid to the dignity of those who had suffered so much. Most of the questions were just ignored or met by blank, vacant stares. These were people who had seen hell and walked through it.

There were a pitiful number who had made it. The T.V. reporters estimated no more than a hundred. Where were their colleagues? What had happened in the mountains? Where were the five thousand or more who had set out?

Had they been massacred? What had these people seen? There were dozens of questions but no answers. The press described them as 'an army of ghosts': men clad in rags, totally exhausted and emaciated by hunger. Some were wearing no more than underwear, some were walking on bleeding feet wrapped in rags or plastic, and some were being carried on makeshift stretchers. There were a few women and some men walking hand in hand with children; all were still visibly shocked and frightened. Some seemed to have lost their minds and were delirious and hallucinating as a result of the immense stress they had endured. A story went round of a soldier who had become so delirious on arrival that he had mistaken his own people for Serb forces and had begun firing until he was killed to prevent further bloodshed. A medical station which had been set up by the Army of Bosnia and Herzegovina confirmed that apart from tending to the wounded, their biggest task had been to hand out large quantities of tranquillisers.

The few people who did speak to reporters through interpreters exuded bitterness. Their ire was directed towards the UN because it had not been able to protect the so called 'Safe Area.' When the refugees realised that large numbers of the Bosnian Army had made it safely to Tuzla through other routes, bitterness and resentment was also directed towards their own forces for their failure to protect them. There were claims that some of the Bosnian soldiers had ditched their uniforms and all military insignia in order to be identified as civilians and allowed safe passage. There was even some fighting and a number of incidents but these were sporadic and ultimately harmless. There was no point. These people had lost the will to fight.

When asked who was the leader of their column, people shook their heads and refused to comment. There didn't appear to be a leader; no one came forward in any position of responsibility.

No one spoke a word; there was no energy in the room. If there was such a state as beyond exhaustion, these men had reached it. Drazen silently cursed his luck. Gazing at his fellow prisoners, some of whom were weeping silently, he knew this was the end; it was only a matter of time. But they wouldn't be killed quickly; no, the Serbs would have their fun. God alone knew what form of agony awaited them when the Serb torturers arrived. Crammed into the small cell with him were Hasan, Raif, Hamdi, Mehmet and five more of their men. They had spent three days trekking over the most difficult terrain Bosnia possessed; they had had no food; they had only found one source of water and that had been two days ago. The only positive aspect of their journey had come when they had stumbled among some other wanderers who had fled from the Serbs from the hamlets of Parlog and Resnik. Other Bosniaks had been hiding out there so the little column was swelled to over a hundred as they neared Tuzla. The discipline which had seen them use point men and scouts in the woods and lowlands had had to be abandoned up here. The ground was treacherous and they needed every able bodied man to assist the weaker members of the group. Some people had collapsed from exhaustion and were being carried. Still, it wasn't an issue as they crossed the peaks and gazed down upon Tuzla without encountering a single enemy.

Perhaps it had been the euphoria of being so close to freedom but they hadn't seen the troops ringing the city as they descended to the valley, probably because they had been forewarned and were out of sight. Suddenly, Serb militia materialized on all sides; they seemed to appear from nowhere, from grass, from trees, from behind rocks. The column must have been sighted from a long way off, Drazen thought, and the Serbs had been primed and ready. They had at least four heavily armed militia men for each of the little group of one hundred people so any resistance was futile. It would have been suicidal. Surprisingly, they were not all shot dead on the spot as Drazen had expected. What he didn't know was that the hillside at Baljkovica where they had reached actually formed the last line separating the column from Bosnian-held territory. There were any number of UN observers and international diplomatic personnel not to speak of media located here and the Serbs were anxious to show that rumours of massacres and heavy handed treatment was 'nonsense'. They were anxious to show that they obeyed the Geneva Convention and allowed safe passage to all civilians.

But for Drazen and Hasan and the other men, it wasn't that simple. While Drazen was a civilian, he was clearly identified as a person of influence and was detained along with the others. What none of them knew was that during the previous evening, a heavy hailstorm had forced the Serbs to take cover. They had assumed the Bosniaks holding Tuzla would do the same but as they were expecting a major offensive the following day, some of the Bosniak troops broke out and attacked the rear of the Serb column, which had become isolated in the hailstorm. Over a hundred Serbian militia had been captured and were being detained in Tuzla. The Bosniaks had also seized a large amount of expensive arms and ammunition including anti-aircraft guns. It had been a serious setback for the Serbs and practically guaranteed that Tuzla would not fall any time soon. Negotiations had taken place during the morning without success but around lunchtime, a Serbian lookout had spied the column descending from the high peaks and they suddenly had been given a massive bargaining chip. It was subsequently agreed that the Serbs would open the Baljkovica corridor to allow the remnants of the column of captured Bosniaks safe passage into Tuzla provided the captured Serbian soldiers were allowed march in the opposite direction simultaneously. But what the Serbs didn't mention was their intention to detain the leaders of the column for what they described as 'questioning about serious war crimes'. Hasan had kissed his wife and child and told them not to worry, he'd be along later; the Serbs wouldn't risk killing them up here; he could see that Tatjana didn't believe him but she proudly took their son's hand and marched with rest of the group down the hill. Drazen had seen courage in the face of adversity many times during the previous week, yet he was stunned at the sheer stoicism displayed by Tatjana, who refused to show emotion to the Serbs as she left her husband to face almost certain death.

It had commenced with the heavy drinking bout of three nights earlier, Milanovic knew, but would any of these idiot militia listen to him? They had almost won the war but had they celebrated too soon? There had, as he guessed, been no briefing the following morning. In fact, no one had appeared apart from himself and Vladkovic. They had ended up sharing coffee and cigarettes and polite conversation. Surprisingly, the Lieutenant had confided in him that his men had been found, all of them, dead, by other soldiers from his division. They had presumably been surprised by the Bosniaks who had fled to the woods. Sefer could imagine the scene: militia lazing about in the sun, not paying attention. Vladkovic had been, as far as Sefer could tell, truthful. The man was clearly worried about the consequences when he reported the loss of twenty men to Mistakovic and he was looking for allies. The small arms that his men had carried had been taken but the heavy machine gun emplacements were intact suggesting that the patrol had not been engaged by a Bosnian army unit with transport but a group of refugees or survivors of the refugee column.

Milanovic had retired to bed at around four that morning and he had been the first to leave. Vladkovic confided that he had left shortly after but that when he had been taking breakfast at eight thirty, most of the commanders were still drinking and by that time, were drunk beyond belief. All had retired to bed shortly afterwards and intended to spend the day sleeping, which they duly did. Sefer was used to their indiscipline but this was a new low. For the commanders of an army to spend an entire day in bed, effectively abandoning their men or leaving them to their own devices was a court martial offence in any disciplined regular army. To do it in the middle of a war was unthinkable. He reported this in full to Belgrade. If they wanted to doctor his report, let them be the ones to do it. He was sick of them. Vladkovic, although possessed of such blinding prejudice, seemed to have the courage of his convictions and at least he showed up each morning looking neat, in Milanovic's eyes, the way a soldier should appear. Mistakovic had eventually surfaced at around four in the afternoon. Vladkovic immediately sought a meeting to report to him on the killing of his men. The Lieutenant asked Milanovic to accompany him, for 'technical advice'. Sefer was bemused but decided to play along. Mistakovic was surprisingly gregarious and forgiving of Vladkovic. He produced a bottle of slivovitz and three glasses and proposed a toast to the memory of their brave dead colleagues. As was the tradition, glasses were raised but not clinked and the liquor was drunk straight down. Mistakovic put it down to 'an unfortunate incident' which there would be 'no need to tell Svero about.' More liquor was poured, presumably to clear the Colonel's hangover and the Lieutenant was dismissed.

Not surprisingly, the Serb forces made no progress at all that day. The men sat about smoking and chatting and probably, Sefer thought, drinking. Alcohol was one of the oldest and most potent weapons of war he knew but there was a difference between allowing the troops a few drinks to fortify their courage and allowing them free rein to get totally pissed. Were there to be a Bosnian counter offensive now, they would all be sitting ducks. The chances were of course that there were scarcely enough armed Bosnian soldiers to set up an ambush, never mind a counter offensive.

The following morning, all of the commanders were present and correct at the briefing and plans for the move on Tuzla were discussed. But there was a casualness and arrogance to the meeting which even surpassed the superior attitude that he had already witnessed on a daily basis for the previous twelve months.

The sloppiness had continued, partially due to the fact that no resistance was encountered on the way to Tuzla. The Serb trucks and tanks and A.P.C.'s roared through the countryside, masters of all they surveyed. The villages and hamlets had been vacated, their occupants either fled to Tuzla, hiding in the woods or dead. At least there had been no more massacres. Perhaps the Serbian blood lust had finally been slaked or perhaps it was because there were no more Bosniaks to slaughter. When they reached the outskirts of Tuzla, the advance units relayed the news that quickly brought them back to earth. The Bosniaks **hadn't** given up and were mounting a last stand. Estimates of the number of Bosnian Armed Forces in the city varied but something between three and five thousand was agreed. Sefer remembered Mistakovic shrugging his shoulders. His Bosnian Serb group rendezvoused with their counterparts in other militias who had the entire city surrounded. The Colonel estimated they had at least ten thousand men and far superior weaponry. There was no need to panic; no need to risk the lives of his men; they would just set up their heavy guns and blast the whole bloody place to kingdom come. It might take a few days, maybe a few weeks, whatever; the outcome was not in doubt.

Sefer would have agreed that the might of the Serbs would, given normal conditions, eventually prevail. But things were changing rapidly. He was constantly receiving requests from Belgrade for updates. He was given little information in return but he gathered that Milosevic's Government had come under extreme pressure from the international community, as he had predicted they would.

He was still a loyal Serb officer but while he had always been cynical about those he served in Belgrade, he was now downright wary of them and what idiotic decisions they might take next.

He had heard that the Americans or NATO or whoever had threatened air strikes against the Bosnian Serbs unless they ceased their ethnic cleansing of the Bosniak population and allowed the people safe passage. Mistakovic and the others dismissed this out of hand as more bluster. Hadn't NATO threatened air strikes against them when they began their move on Srebrenica? They had dropped a few token bombs. Then Serb General Ratko Mladić seized fifty UN peace keeping troops as hostages and threatened to kill them and to shell the Muslim population in Srebrenica if NATO air strikes continued. NATO backed down; the air strikes ceased. The UN peacekeepers agreed to withdraw from Srebrenica and Mladić promised he would take care of and allow safe passage to the Muslim population. They sure took care of them alright, laughed Mistakovic. The Americans and their NATO allies in the west were soft, cowardly, willing to take the easy way out; they would never take on the Serbs and if they did, they would live to regret it.

This rhetoric was fine in a bar late at night and to be fair, much of what the Colonel said was true. NATO **had** backed down, mainly because major European powers had always been wary of any sort of involvement in the Balkans. For hundreds of years, it had been known that that entire peninsula was a toxic mix of racial hatred. The fact that Tito had kept the lid on it for nigh on fifty years just meant that when it exploded, fifty years of pent-up rage and hatred were released. But Sefer felt the west couldn't ignore the conflict indefinitely. In the past, maybe they could get away with it but not in an era of instant global news in the last decade of the twentieth century. He was a keen student of international affairs and he felt it would only be a matter of time before the Bosnian Serbs pushed too far and invited a backlash.

The troops were now encamped around Tuzla although shelling had not begun yet. The plan was to start the following day but the sloppy and casual attitude displayed by the leaders and replicated by many of the troops had cost them dearly. The previous evening, a group of infantry, anxious to obtain shelter from a hailstorm, had sheltered too near a Bosnian Army stronghold on the outskirts of the city and left themselves completely exposed to attack. The Serbs might have wanted to shelter from the rain but the Bosniaks had no such cares and surrounded them, killing fifty, wounding another hundred and capturing the remainder, at least a hundred troops. The Bosnian Serb commanders were all now billeted in Krizevici, where suitable accommodation had been found in an abandoned hotel. Whether it had been abandoned or cleared, Sefer wasn't sure but it was clean and well maintained and appeared to have been in regular use. Although the captured men were not Mistakovic's or Svero's but part of the Bratunac Corps, both men were furious. This was seen as a major embarrassment, almost like being attacked and killed by a dying man. Milanovic didn't say it but the incident was due to indiscipline, over confidence, arrogance and the belief that the war was over which permeated the Bosnian Serb forces. This had come from the top so the front line soldiers could not be blamed.

Some of them had paid for their casualness with their lives. Not that this was any great concern of Mistakovic. He was annoyed that the final push would now have to be postponed. Even the Bosnian Serbs wouldn't commence shelling a city where their own men were held prisoner. Thank God for that, Sefer thought. The incident put somewhat of a damper on the evening and for once, no one got drunk and all retired early.

Their luck turned again and they had then had the break at lunchtime the following day. A group of Bosniaks, led by some of the few remaining active Bosnian soldiers outside Tuzla was observed making their way covertly down the hills towards the city. They were viewed through binoculars and word was passed back to command. For once, the information was correctly received and correctly acted upon. These Bosniaks obviously had no idea that Tuzla was surrounded by Serbs and were about to walk straight into a trap. The order was given to detain the group but not to kill them. Both Milanovic and Vladkovic observed the detention and the subsequent opening of the corridor and exchange of prisoners. The Serbs, suitably embarrassed, were welcomed back to the Bratunac Corps, told to acquire new weaponry and report for duty. Mindful of possible harsher measures, all scurried to obey.

Milanovic was having coffee and his umpteenth cigarette in a temporary field canteen before taking the trip back to Krizevici to contact Belgrade. It was still only late afternoon so he was in no hurry. He spied the Lieutenant marching purposefully towards him.
"Tomorrow will be the beginning of the end, eh Colonel?" Vladkovic said.

"Perhaps in a way Ivan," Sefer replied. "But not in the way you may think, if I can make that assumption?"

"What do you mean Colonel?"

"Well, the city looks well fortified to me and rather than waste many lives on another all out attack, I would be recommending a compromise be reached. I mean, look at it this way: the Bosnian Serbs have won the war; you have captured all the key installations in the country. Oh sure, there is still some resistance in Sarajevo but you control it. You've managed to do all this without provoking outside intervention. So why push it? The few remaining Bosniaks have to live somewhere. I've been told that Tuzla is no beautiful city so why not leave it to them. Draw the line here and quit while you are ahead. If you persist and try to drive the Bosniaks into the ground, you will surely see a NATO response."

The Lieutenant smiled:

"I see what you mean Colonel but it won't happen. You just don't understand us. Most of us wouldn't really be happy until every last Bosniak was burned or buried or turned to dust. It is part of us. Even if it costs another thousand Serb lives, we will attack Tuzla and we will not relent until all of Bosnia is ours. It will not be my decision but I can guarantee you that that is what will happen."

"You know, you may well be right Lieutenant," Sefer added sadly.

"Oh I'm sure I'm right Colonel. I appreciate your argument but this goes deeper than strategy, deeper than military tactics; this is about our core beliefs, what makes us what we are. But I digress; I actually came down to invite you to view our prisoners."

Milanovic frowned. "What prisoners Lieutenant? I thought we guaranteed safe passage to the group in exchange for the return of our own men?"

"Oh we did indeed Colonel," Vladkovic smiled again, "but I am certain that these are the bastards that killed my men up at Udrc so we have retained the most likely suspects. The poor idiots whom we released were so glad to get into Tuzla that they probably didn't even mention it. The men we have imprisoned committed what you are so fond of describing as 'cold blooded murder' Colonel and they must be punished. We have some entertainment lined up for them this evening. Perhaps you'd care to watch?"

The Lieutenant was enjoying this, Sefer could see. He was playing with Milanovic to an extent, testing him. Vladkovic turned round and started to walk towards the centre of the encampment. Not wishing to show his discomfort with the situation and curious anyway, Sefer followed.

Chapter 28

The Serbs had appropriated a spacious house on the outskirts of Tuzla. The place dated from the nineteenth century and would have had a certain grandeur in the days of the Ottoman Empire when the Bosnians were held in great esteem by the Turkish Sultans and noblemen. Native Bosnians were seen as a kindred nationality probably due to closer religious and cultural affiliations. Many Turks settled there and built up the country, bequeathing a strong architectural legacy. Whether the Bosniaks felt a similar affection for the Turks is uncertain. The Ottoman Empire ruled Bosnia for over four hundred years but regardless of any kinship, it didn't stop the Bosniaks from mounting several rebellions and insurrections against Turkish rule although none of these were ever successful. The Ottoman Empire was nonetheless in decline and eventually, in 1878, Bosnia was ceded to the Austro-Hungarian Empire. When the Ottoman Empire was at its strongest and expanded into Central Europe, Bosnia experienced a prolonged period of prosperity. A number of cities, such as Sarajevo and Mostar were established and grew into major regional centers of trade and urban culture. Within these cities, various Sultans and Governors financed the construction of many important works of Bosnian Architecture such as the Stari Most or old bridge and Gazi Husrev-beg's Mosque. Furthermore, numerous Bosnians played influential roles in the Ottoman Empire's cultural and political history. Bosnian soldiers formed a large component of the Ottoman ranks in many military victories, while numerous other Bosnians rose through the ranks of the Ottoman military bureaucracy to occupy the highest positions of power in the Empire, including Admirals and Generals. Many Bosnians also made a lasting impression on Ottoman culture, emerging as mystics, scholars, and celebrated poets in the Turkish, Arabic, and Persian languages.

The problem was that nothing lasts forever and when the administration of the country was taken over by Austria-Hungary, many Bosniak Muslims emigrated to Arab lands. Serbs and to a lesser extent Croats were invited by the Austro-Hungarian ruling classes to settle in Bosnia, inadvertently sowing the seeds for the conflict some hundred years later. Although the Austrians were far seeing and encouraged the development of a pluralist society, nationalism took firm root and within a few years the population was polarized into three strong political groupings: Bosniaks, Serbs and Croats. The situation became so bad that in 1908, the Austro-Hungarians decided to formally annex Bosnia. Tensions became even worse and nationalism grew. This culminated in the assassination of the heir to the Austro-Hungarian throne, Arch Duke Ferdinand, during a visit to Sarajevo in 1914, ironically by a Serb nationalist. This was the spark that led to the outbreak of the First World War. In the intervening period, the three ethnic groups had lived in relative peace, assisted to a large extent by President Tito's victory against Nazi Germany and his subsequent formation of the Socialist Yugoslavia. Tito died in 1980 and Yugoslavia hung on for another ten years but it had always been an artificial State so with the winds of change blowing through Eastern Europe in the late 1980's, break-up was inevitable. What no one had envisaged was how savage and bloody that break-up would be.

The mansion looked like it may have been maintained during the Communist era as it was still in reasonable condition. It was unclear as to how long the Bosnian Serbs had been occupying the house or as to who, if anyone, had been evicted from it or indeed, their ethnicity. What Sefer was prepared to bet was that within a week, the militia would have thoroughly wrecked the place. They were well on the way already with hundreds of soldiers traipsing over the fine floor coverings, smoking, drinking and eating everywhere and leaving their rubbish where it fell. Fine drapes had been pulled down and were being trampled on and architectural features had been damaged.

The prisoners had been kept locked in the basement but had now been relocated to a series of rooms on the first floor. These were spacious and there were any amount of them. Each contained stout door locks which ensured there would be no escape as any windows had been boarded up and sealed. It was in one of these rooms that Drazen now sat. His arms were tied tightly behind his back and his legs were tied to the frame of the chair. His face was badly swollen; his right eye was almost closed; his body was a patchwork quilt of welts and bruises, inflicted by Serbian boots and fists and sticks. The General in charge of the Bratunac Corps, embarrassed by the capture of his men on the previous evening, was anxious to restore his political capital so he wanted to obtain as much information from these prisoners as possible. He had ordered the men from the battalion that had been captured the evening before and just released that afternoon to 'soften them up', before the interrogations began. While there were ten prisoners, all of them were weak and exhausted and didn't stand a chance against a hundred pairs of Serbian boots and fists. In fact, the enthusiasm of the Serbs was such that they would have beaten the prisoners to death, had the General not intervened.

Barely conscious, Drazen sat facing his inquisitor, another Bosnian Serb Lieutenant. The man had not laid a hand on Drazen; that was not his job. Instead, a giant of a man, perhaps two metres tall and weighing at least one hundred and thirty kilos, was systematically beating him. Drazen coughed violently and spat out a tooth as another heavy blow landed on the left side of his face. His face was now almost numb but the pain all over his body was excruciating. He had no idea how long he had been in the room; it had seemed like hours. He had yet to utter one word.
"I think he has had enough for now," the Lieutenant said. Go take a break Nikola; I'll call you when you're required. This one isn't going anywhere."
The big man nodded, took his jacket from a chair and left.
"So, Bosniak," the Lieutenant began, "I ask you again; what is your name? Where do you come from? What crimes have you committed? Who have you killed? Are there still Bosnian troops in the mountains above here? What is their strength? Do they have heavy weapons?"
He had paused after each question but Drazen had made no response.

"I hope you realize that you are putting yourself through unnecessary pain Bosniak. Do you know that big Nikola is only the warm-up act? Oh yes, we haven't even started yet. Believe me Bosniak, you will talk eventually; they all do. You will beg us to talk; you will tell us everything we want to hear, several times over. You will beg to tell us more; you will sell your Mother, your entire family. You have no idea what awaits you."
The man laughed.
"Wait until you see the equipment old Slobodan has. He can make anyone talk. He has never failed. When he attaches those electrodes to your balls, you'll talk so much that you'll be telling us things we don't want to hear, believe me. Oh yes, old Slobodan could nearly make dead men talk. I think he may already be with some of your colleagues so if you listen closely, you will soon hear them. The man laughed again uproariously and then he made a show of a large yawn.
"So, don't make it any harder on yourself, eh? Tell me what I want to know and you need never make Slobodan's acquaintance. Believe me, he is not a man you want to meet. So, come on, one last time eh, be sensible. Tell me what I want to know and no one will lay a hand on you. So, what is your name?"
There was no response. The Lieutenant sighed, shook his head, rose, lit a cigarette and walked around the room.
"OK my friend, there is obviously no point. I think if I reintroduce you to Nikola, his enthusiasm might finish you off before old Slob gets here so we'll let you be." He sat down in the chair again, eyed Drazen and sucked deeply on his cigarette. The door behind him opened quietly and, assuming it was the big Private, Nikola, the Lieutenant said:

"Unfortunately not a word from him Nikola, I think we'll leave him to old Slob. He'll get him talking soon enough with his electrodes."

"Perhaps I could have a word with the prisoner in private Lieutenant," said a new voice. "Sometimes a subtle approach works better than brute force."

The Lieutenant wheeled round in alarm, then jumped to his feet when he saw the insignia of his visitor.

"Of course Colonel Sir," he said as he rose and saluted. "I apologise; I did not realise you had an interest in this prisoner. I thought it was my assistant returning."

"That is quite alright Lieutenant," said Milanovic.

The Lieutenant hurried from the room and Sefer took a seat opposite Drazen.

"So we meet again farmer," Sefer began. "You seem to have many lives. You may not remember me but we saw each other briefly in Srebrenica. It was the night of the massacre. I have observed some of your handiwork subsequently; at least what I assume was yours. But that's another matter. Let me introduce myself. Forgive me calling you farmer but I do not know your name and you seem to be unwilling to divulge it. I call you farmer because your hands show that you are clearly a man of the soil. My name is Sefer Milanovic. I am a Colonel with the Serbian Armed Forces. My mission in Bosnia is to observe and advise. The war is effectively over apart from a few skirmishes so this whole set-up is pointless. However, I can only advise these people; I am not at liberty to command them to release you, you understand. But I guarantee that if you speak to me about what you have seen and what has transpired here, I will do my utmost to obtain your release and that of your colleagues."

Drazen still made no response but raised one eyebrow weakly and glanced at Sefer. The Colonel continued: "You are clearly a farmer and not a military man but you do seem to have allied yourself with a Bosnian military unit. I appreciate you would wish to be loyal but I am not asking you to betray them. In fact, given how long you have been in the mountains, I doubt very much if any of the ten of you have any information whatsoever that may be of use to the militias. So, as I say, this whole set-up is farcical. I am not going to ask you about military movements or numbers of soldiers because if there are any Bosniak soldiers in those hills, they are no threat to anyone. All I ask you is this: Did you witness the massacre of Bosniak men in Srebrenica?"

Drazen made no response but now looked up curiously. His right eye was completely closed so he squinted through his left. Sefer continued:

"I ask you this because I can assure you that *I* witnessed it. It was carried out totally contrary to my will and against my advice. I don't expect you to believe that but it is true. I am concerned that the name of Serbia will be blackened for generations by this act but there is little I can do about it as a serving Serbian Army soldier. On the other hand, you could do a lot."

Drazen still made no response. This man was different to the others and Drazen was almost prepared to believe him but then he realized it was probably a trap. The Colonel was the one playing good cop; the bad one would return later. Even if the Colonel was genuine, he had no intention of telling him that he had indeed witnessed the massacre and had even been, as far as he was aware, the only one who had escaped from it. No, this man wanted to protect the good name of Serbia; surely he would put a bullet in

Drazen's head if he thought he could bear witness to what had been done? But he was going to die anyway, wasn't he? Should he use his last few hours to tell the Colonel what had happened and what he had witnessed? No, it would be futile; it would most probably get him killed more quickly. He continued to say nothing but he did make eye contact now with the Colonel. There was silence for a few moments. Then, from a neighbouring room came the sound of a long, piercing, agonizing scream that chilled both men to the marrow.

The Colonel rose purposefully and said: "Please excuse me farmer." He left the room briefly and Drazen could hear the sound of raised voices. The Colonel returned in a few moments; there were no more screams from next door. "For what it's worth farmer, I have ordered that the torture being carried out next door on one of your colleagues be halted immediately. This entire exercise is a waste of time and energy and as far as I can see is merely serving the sadistic tendencies of a few low ranked militia men. So, where were we, yes, I had asked you about Srebrenica. You will have noticed I asked the other officer to leave the room so I am again appealing to your good nature and common sense. I appreciate that you have seen many horrible things recently, most of them perpetrated by Serbs. I feel the only way we can regain our reputation is to admit that mistakes were made, own up to wrongdoing and when the peace comes as it inevitably will, try to repair the incredible damage done to the trust between the two racial groups. Am I crazy to even contemplate this? Perhaps I am but regardless of what will happen, we will eventually have to share this land again. You see, I do understand the claim of the Serbs to their own homeland in

Bosnia but I also understand it should not be at the Bosniaks expense. Forgive me if I sound like a one man peace mission. Indeed I am not; I am merely a gatherer of information and a dispenser of advice. But I do care for the future of this land and for that of my own."

Drazen now nodded but still said nothing. The Colonel rose and added:

"Think about what I have asked. Remember I have requested that the torture of you and your colleagues be stopped and as the senior ranking officer here, although I am not a member of the militia, they have agreed to my request. But were I to leave here and return to my billet, I cannot guarantee any of you safe passage and I cannot be responsible for what the militia might do when I depart. I must go to see some of your colleagues now. I will return shortly."

As he made his way to the door, it opened ahead of him and Vladkovic stood there. "Ah Colonel, so here you are," questioning our prisoners eh? I hope you have had more luck than the idiots in the other rooms; they haven't learned a thing. To be honest, I don't think these fuckers know anything anyway so we are probably wasting our time. I'm sure it was they that killed my men but I don't want to spend hours finding out. Let's away to dinner and leave these scum to the tender mercies of the Bratunac Corps, eh?"

Before the Colonel had a chance to reply, there was a slight shuffling sound behind them as the prisoner moved slightly in the chair. Both men whirled round. The man seemed to be slumped to the side, one eye trained on the two men.

"That one is close to finished; I doubt he'd even live through what the Bratunac boys want to do to them," Vladkovic said, chuckling.

It was only a slight hoarse croak but the Bosnian prisoner then spoke his very first words of the interrogation. Both Milanovic and Vladkovic clearly heard the man say, "Hello Ivan."

Chapter 29

The Serb police, such as they were, came late the next evening. The trader whom Kazim had made his purchases from in U.S. dollars had changed the $100 note the following morning. The police did not have serial numbers but it was known that the camp commander had had a stash of crisp American dollars so exchange bureau had been warned to report movement of high value notes. The woman who had exchanged the note made the report; she knew the trader so it was relatively easy to track him. The police found him at his market stall and threatened to shoot him if he didn't immediately identify from whom he had received the $100 bill. The trader was terrified but he was adamant that he had never seen the man before. The police stationed two men to maintain a continuous watch on the stall and it was Kazim's misfortune to come by later in the day, hoping to pick up more supplies to feed the little group. He was slightly perturbed when the trader rushed him with his purchases and did not seem as grateful or helpful as the previous day. Still, he shrugged; maybe the trader had been shot at or had a family problem. Who knew in this crazy city? In any event, he had again managed to buy some badly needed food so he made his way leisurely back to the safe house. The trader had nodded to the police who followed Kazim at a discreet distance. Their only mistake, when he entered the house, was not to call for back-up and mount a raid on the building, covering all exits and entrances. But these were not real trained policemen; some of them were merely thugs who had been in the militias. They saw an opportunity to make a name and a few bucks for themselves and went for it.

They rapped loudly on the door which put the entire house on full alert. Sonja immediately grabbed Diana and headed for the basement. Melita had shown her a place to hide behind the ancient hot water boiler the previous day. The others all stayed in the sitting room and continued to watch television. The door knocker sounded again, even louder this time.
"Wait please, I'm coming, I'm coming," Melita said. She opened the door and the two men immediately burst in. One of them vaguely flashed some form of identification and said:
"Policija, where is the man who just entered the house with the food?"
Melita tried to be calm and shrugged.

"Ah, but that would be Kazim, my guest, he brought some food for our party. We are having a little party this evening. He is in the sitting room. But what would you two gentlemen want him for?"

The men brushed past Melita and marched into the sitting room. One of them drew a gun and put it to Kazim's head. The other man said:

"Where did you get the $100 bill you used in the market yesterday?"

Kazim, frightened, stuttered:

"I, I, I got it from a friend."

"What friend, who?" said the man. He then produced a picture of a woman; the same one Sonja had seen the morning before and said:

"Would this be your friend eh?"

Kazim shook his head and went to speak but no words came out because he was already dead. The first policeman had seen the recognition in his eyes and had shot him in the head. A fine blood spray rained down on the couch and the coffee table. The girls sat frozen to the spot, terrified. Refika screamed and wailed but the policeman's response was to grab her by the hair and push her down on the sofa. He stuck the gun to her ear and shoved the photograph of Sonja in front of her.

"Do you want to die next? You have two seconds to tell me, where is this bitch?" Refika, absolutely terrified, replied:

"Downstairs, she's downstairs, in the basement," then she immediately collapsed, sobbing. The second policeman told the first to wait and ran towards the stairs to the basement. This would be a major catch for him. There'd be a big bonus in this. This woman was wanted by every militia unit in the country. He dashed down the stairs, hitting the light switches as he went. The basement was large but contained little except some old furniture, stacks of newspapers and magazines and the central heating boiler. He searched every corner thoroughly but there was no one there. He dashed back upstairs, checked to make sure the front and back doors were locked and pocketed the keys. Then he walked calmly back into the sitting room to where his colleague was holding everyone at gunpoint. Refika was crying softly and being comforted by Melita.

"You lied, you bitch," he said, "she's not in the basement." He advanced to the woman again, gun drawn. Refika screamed, positive she was going to die.
"I swear, I swear, I told you the truth, she was there."
"Leave her alone," said Melita, "She spoke the truth."
"Oh did she, old woman," the man said sarcastically. "Well the bitch must have run to some other room because she is not there now. Right, we're gonna have some fun while we search for her. Now this is a big house so I have no intention of spending the evening looking in every corner. You, old woman, go and bring her here to us. If she is not here in five minutes, we will shoot this bitch. After that, someone dies every five minutes until she appears. In the meantime, we will have some fun, come here you."
He pointed at Hana, and when she did not move, he grabbed her roughly and ripped off the lower part of her clothing. He then undid his belt and threw her over an armchair. Melita rushed upstairs frantically.
"You'd better be quick old woman," said the first policeman. "But I'm gonna fuck this little cow anyway while I'm waiting and so is Teodor when I'm finished. After that, we'll fuck the lot of you, including that wanted

bitch; we might even fuck *you* if you're lucky", he said, as he laughed manically.

Melita ran back down the stairs within moments. Teodor was standing casually and the first policeman was having his way with Hana, who was crying softly.
"Please, please, both of you," Melita said, "I beg you to desist. The woman is not here, she's gone. If you wish to catch her, you should go and give chase," and she tugged the first policeman's arm. He shrugged her off and said: "Do you think we're idiots? Bring her here or this bitch dies as soon as I come."
Melita tugged on the man again and he tried to push her away one handed. The other policeman advanced towards Melita and raised his gun to pistol whip her away from his colleague. Instantly, there was the sound of two deafening explosions. Teodor's swipe stopped in mid arc as in a barely perceptible movement, Melita brought the gun from under her apron and shot him in the face. There was another spray of blood as the bullet exited through the top of his head. The other policeman whirled round but he was helpless as Melita also shot him at point blank range. Both men dropped like stones and were dead before they hit the ground. Melita had never shot someone before and knew she had only one chance to get them both when they were close together. She trembled as she felt the pain in her arm from the pistol's recoil. Hana gazed down at the man who had been abusing her, his trousers around his ankles, his private parts laid bare. She kicked him viciously in the groin several times and while the man was past caring, she seemed to derive some satisfaction from it.
"Where did you get the gun," Refika asked. "I thought you said you did not have one in the house?"

Melita was still shaking.
"It's Sonja's. It was on her bedside table. I, I didn't think, I just took it, oh God."

There were now three dead men in the room but there were eight brave women and Aida immediately took charge:
"Refika and Melita, sit down and we will make you some coffee. Don't worry, it will be fine. Melita, you did great to take on those bastards."
To the others, she said:
"Now girls, there's only one thing to do. Let's hope no one spotted those pigs coming to the house. I think they were stupid enough to try to grab all the credit for themselves so with any luck, they won't even have told their H.Q. But we can't take any chances. First, search them; leave their I.D.'s on them but strip them of anything else that looks valuable. They're not gonna need it where they're going. Then grab them by their arms and legs. Two of you take the other end of this one. We bring them to the basement and light the furnace. Pity it isn't winter time, they would have saved us fuel. Refika, we can decide later what to do with poor Kazim but we have to do it quickly. The police may not have reported the house but we can't take the chance; we can't stay here. We have to dispose of the bodies and go. Girls, will the rest of you please start cleaning up that blood?"
Aida did not know where she got the strength or the presence of mind from but it seemed to calm everyone else. Even Hana enthusiastically joined the disposal crew. As they began hauling the first body, Melita suddenly said:
"Girls, I completely forgot, when you go down to the basement, tell Sonja and Diana it's safe now."

Sonja had headed to the basement with Diana when she had heard the door knocker. They had both squeezed into a narrow space that was situated between the boiler and the outer wall. The boiler hadn't been installed flush with the wall and the angle it made left a small crawl space that just about held her and Diana. She was prepared to wait it out but when she heard the raised voices upstairs questioning Kazim about the money, she knew immediately they had come for her. When she heard the shot, she made her decision there and then; she had to get out and fast. The echo of the pistol shot had sounded like thunder down in the narrow confines of the basement and Diana had started trembling. Sonja searched frantically for some means of escape but the only option she could see was to go back up the stairs. That would have been suicidal. She couldn't defend herself down here either; she cursed inwardly as she remembered that she had left her pistol on the bedside locker since the night before when little Nadja had come calling. She had gotten such a fright that she had not gone near the pistol since. She searched around frantically for another exit. Then she spied a small metal door beside the boiler which seemed to open upwards. She hauled at it and it gave with a small creak. She saw that it was the cover of the coal bunker. The bunker was less than half full as the boiler was not in use and fuel was not available anyway. She tried to crawl her way up along the loose coal to where the bunker opened to the back yard. Diana was smaller so she managed it more easily. She reached her little hand downwards to try to help her Mama and Sonja's heart nearly broke. She knew that if she took Diana's hand she

would send both of them crashing to the bottom again. She kept trying to climb the coal but each time as she slid downwards, she displaced more coal, making it more difficult to climb to the top. She had closed the door which had gotten them access to the bunker and it didn't open from this side so they were now trapped. If the police opened the top of the coal bunker, it was all over. She could see the fading strands of daylight through the slits at the top of the bunker but she couldn't reach high enough to grasp one of the vertical bars. It was tantalizingly beyond her reach. She heard a noise behind her in the basement and realized one of the policemen must have come down to search. She placed her finger over her lips and nodded to Diana. Both stayed perfectly still. After a few moments, she heard the man run back upstairs and drew breath again. Diana whispered from above:
"Mama, I can see the thing that opens it, I'd have to reach outside but I think I can get it, shall I?" Sonja breathed deeply. If even Diana escaped it would be good, but what could she do alone? Now wasn't the time to hesitate.
"Yes darling, please try," she said. Diana hooked her little fingers up through the crack in the bars and expertly slid the bolt across. For a moment, nothing happened; then a small section of coal that had been lodged at the top of the bunker gave way and the gate swung downwards. Diana immediately clambered over the top and looked back at her Mum. Sonja saw her chance of freedom at the same time. The gate had swung down and was now barely reachable. She made one last run at the coal and grabbed hold of the hanging gate. Thank God it didn't open upwards, she thought. She hung on tightly and drew her legs up after her, gripping the wall on the opposite side of the bunker. Then she crab walked to the top until she fell out on to the

dry grass that surrounded the opening. She carefully reached down and pulled the gate upwards, closing the bolt again. Both she and Diana were filthy from the coal dust. She had left her pistol. They had no clothes apart from what they were wearing. She still had her money but after what she heard upstairs, she couldn't use it. But she didn't care; the main thing, the only thing was that they were free again, at least for now.

She grabbed Diana's hand and fled through a back entrance into another, neighbouring garden. She heard two more shots and they both froze.
"What was that Mama?" said the little girl.
"Are those bad men shooting more people?"
Sonja prayed that they weren't but her immediate fear was that the policemen would kill everyone in the house until they were handed herself and Diana. Please God, let it not be those little girls, she thought. For the first time, she could not find the strength or the words to reply to Diana. She rushed through the garden and found a grass covered laneway at the other end. It led out on to a quiet road that paralleled the rear of the Melita's house. They walked briskly, all the time straining not to run. About three hundred metres down, she saw an entrance to a park and took it. She considered hiding in the park but it was futile. There were very few people there but even fewer places to hide and she would be trapped if the park were surrounded. Panic began to assail her as she realized that now there was no Aida, no Melita, no one to lean on. She had no idea how to contact Papa Itsakovic and she knew she would never find her way back to the secret location where they had met. She contemplated going back to Melita's house and waiting until the woman came out, if she ever did. But

the woman could already be dead and even if she wasn't, Sonja showing up would only get her killed. Also, the Serbs would now be watching that house. No, it wasn't an option. She would have to seek refuge elsewhere. She was alive and so was Diana but she had no food, no water and no money and she knew no one. Even though she still had her most precious possession, for the first time, Sonja felt truly alone.

Chapter 30

Vladkovic had not responded but Sefer could see from his body language that he was clearly shaken. Drazen had sunk back into the chair and appeared to be very weak, almost semi-conscious.
"Do you know this man?" Milanovic asked.
"How could I," replied Vladkovic. "He's a Bosniak; I don't speak to Bosniaks."
Sefer shrugged.

"It appears that he knows you Ivan," he said.
"He's bluffing; these Bosniaks will try anything. I'm a tall blonde Serb and Ivan is a very popular name, that's all."
Sefer shrugged but made no move. The Lieutenant wheeled round and made to exit the room but there was a barely audible sound from the chair:
"Ivan, wait, please. I ask you, give me two minutes."
Vladkovic again ignored the man and turned the door handle to exit but Milanovic urged him to wait.
"Ivan, wait a moment," he said. "This man has not spoken one word in detention until he saw you. He clearly either knows you or knows of you. He is willing to talk. Are you not curious to hear what he has to say? He might provide us with some information."
"I have nothing to say to Bosniaks, now or ever."
Sefer knew something was afoot here so he decided not to push the Lieutenant but he was curious to see how it would play out. He said:
"Lieutenant, if you are unwilling to speak to Bosniaks or to listen to them, why are you participating in the questioning of the suspects? I would have thought you'd be anxious to obtain as much information as possible about the deaths of your own men."
The Lieutenant sighed and glanced over at Drazen, who now seemed to have lost consciousness.
"OK Colonel, a few moments won't make any difference. I suspect this man has probably lost his mind anyway or is trying to play tricks on us."

Sefer took the seat opposite Drazen. Lieutenant Vladkovic continued to stand. The Colonel took a handkerchief from his pocket and dipped it in a glass of water. He then touched it gently to Drazen's cheeks and mouth, wiping

away some specks of blood. Drazen stirred and Sefer gave him the glass of water to drink. He sipped thirstily and seemed to regain some of his strength. He tried to speak but his throat was congested. He coughed noisily and a mixture of blood and phlegm and spittle appeared on his lips. He tried again:
"Ivan, Ivan, do you remember me?"
Sefer looked at the Lieutenant who shook his head.
"I have no idea who this man is Colonel. I think he is wasting our time."
Drazen spoke again, more clearly, strength returning to his voice:
"I'm sorry Ivan, truly I am. I should never have done it. It is my great regret in life. I beg your forgiveness. Ivan, it was not your fault; you were young, you knew no better. I was older; I should have shown restraint."
The Lieutenant was clearly discomfited but said nothing. Sefer decided to stay silent and let it develop. Drazen continued:
"Ivan, surely you remember, we were friends once, before all this madness. If our friendship ever meant anything to you, please accept my apology, however late it is. Ivan, I have lost my wife, my son, my daughter; I don't know if they are dead or alive. My grandfather perished at Srebrenica. I need to search for my family. Do you have a family Ivan, a wife and children? If you have you will surely understand. You are my only hope. Please release us; we are no threat to you; we are just simple Bosniaks trying to survive. Ivan, I am appealing to you as a friend; I need your help but first I need your forgiveness."
"I have nothing to say to you Bosniak," Vladkovic said. He turned and walked to the door, opened it and left without looking back. Drazen slumped forward, and would

have fallen out of the chair but for the fact that he was tied to it. Sefer poured him another glass of water and handed it to him.

"So you do speak, farmer," he said. "I have told you my name is Sefer Milanovic. You spoke to my colleague. Can you at least do me the courtesy of telling me your own name?"

"I apologise Colonel," Drazen said. "You are correct; it is pointless to remain silent. I don't have any information which would be of use to you but I will gladly tell you my name is Drazen Itsakovic."

"And what is your connection to my colleague, Lieutenant Vladkovic?"

"I'm afraid that is personal Colonel. I could not tell you unless Ivan agreed."

"As you wish Drazen," Sefer replied.

There was the sound of a commotion and loud argument outside.

"Please excuse me," Sefer said. He went into the corridor where the General in charge of the Bratunac Corps was screaming at a staff Sergeant who was red faced and shaking. Both men continued walking, with the General loudly cursing and berating his subordinate. Suddenly, men started emerging from rooms all along the corridor. There was much cursing and shaking of heads and even some laughter. Milanovic sought out his erstwhile colleague to attempt to find out what was going on. He found Vladkovic in a large adjacent dining room which gave on to a garden that was probably at one time filled with every flower that would grow in this region. Practically every type of tree that was native to Bosnia could be seen from the floor to ceiling French doors which

were ajar. Ivan had found a bottle of expensive looking liquor and a shot glass and was already a few shots into it. "French cognac Colonel," he shouted. "The last bottle in the cabinet; come and join me." Sefer took a small shot glass from the already open cabinet and offered it to Vladkovic, who filled it to the brim.
"What's all the commotion Lieutenant? What's happening?" he said.
Vladkovic laughed uproariously.
"Do you know what these fuckers in the Bratunac Corps can't do Colonel? They can't fucking count, that's what. The idiots who were taken prisoner told their commanding officer that they had all been released but someone's done a body count on the men who were killed last night, added the hundred men who were released today and guess what? They're twenty men short; can you believe that? Now, either twenty men have deserted, which I doubt, or those fucking Bosniaks did not release all the prisoners."
Sefer smiled.
"Indeed Lieutenant, no more then we did. I think that would be touché, what?"
The Lieutenant almost smiled.
"Perhaps Colonel, perhaps, all's fair in love and war, eh? Anyway, they are trying to make contact with the Bosniak leadership in Tuzla to arrange a further transfer. To be honest, I'm surprised they didn't leave them there to rot but I suppose these people we are holding are of little use to us anyway."
Even though Vladkovic was still speaking about the prisoners with contempt, Milanovic was sure that he was secretly glad they were being released.

Some hours later, the door of the detention room opened again and Lieutenant Vladkovic entered, quietly closing it behind him. He withdrew a flick-knife from his belt and released the blade. Drazen sat passively in the chair and eyed him curiously. Vladkovic stepped round the back of the chair and sliced through the bonds which were holding Drazen's hands and feet. For a moment, he still sat there, unable to take it all in. Then he stood and unwound the heavy ties that were still on both of his wrists. Vladkovic could not make eye contact but he said:
"You are free to go; all of your colleagues are being released also. Go to the front hall where you will be escorted to the safe corridor into Tuzla."
Drazen could barely speak:
"Thank you Ivan, I knew you were a good man and would see reason."
"This is not of my doing," the Lieutenant replied coldly.
"Nevertheless, I thank you my friend but before I go, I must ask you again; do you forgive me? It is very important to me."
The Lieutenant said nothing for what seemed like a long time. Then, he walked to the door, opened it and said:
"If you don't hurry, you will miss your colleagues and I'm sure you don't want to spend another night with the Bratunac boys."
Drazen stumbled towards the doorway, eyes still firmly fixed on Vladkovic. As he was about to step into the corridor, the Lieutenant finally said:
"There is nothing to forgive."
Drazen smiled and stuck out his hand and Ivan took it briefly and nodded.
"Thank you Ivan," he said and he hurried to join the others.

The exchange was brief and only necessitated opening the corridor for a few minutes. The twenty Serb soldiers, who all looked mightily relieved, filed past the ten Bosniaks, all of whom seemed in need of urgent medical attention. Some of them could barely walk and were supported by their colleagues. To be fair, some of the Serbs looked like they hadn't been to a picnic either, with many sporting black eyes and facial cuts. When the little band of Bosniaks finally reached the safety of Tuzla, most of the men virtually collapsed and were immediately brought for whatever basic medical aid was available. Drazen refused help and said all he needed was some food, drink and a bed. He was warmly welcomed by a Bosniak family who had no hesitation in offering him a hot meal, some wine and their largest bedroom. He thanked them profusely and asked to be excused as he was badly in need of rest. He didn't bother to undress, just collapsed on the bed and closed his eyes. He had escaped to safety again, but for how long this time; until the Serbs started shelling the town tomorrow? He would assist his new found friends whom he had soldiered with in the mountains when he regained his strength but his priority was still to get to Sarajevo. At the moment, he knew it was impossible; even if he did manage to get there, he only had a vague idea that his wife and family might have fled there. But he could sure try; he had hope again; he had beaten the odds again; he had survived; but this time he had been lucky. How much longer could he continue to defy the odds? How much longer would this dreadful conflict last? He didn't have time to ponder his thoughts as within seconds of laying down his head, he fell into a deep sleep.

Chapter 31

The house seemed completely still as he slowly came awake. There was no sound. The windows had been hung with dark drapes but the morning sun was peeping round the edges reminding everyone that it was still summer and the day would be hot again. Drazen couldn't remember when he had slept so well. For a very brief moment as he went from a sleeping to a conscious state, he was back in the bedroom he had shared with Sonja in his little farmhouse in his village. But reality soon intruded and as he rubbed the sleep from his eyes, some of the enormity of the task that awaited him intruded on his thoughts. He felt a little bruised and sore but the overall feeling was relief. He was not badly hurt; he didn't think the Serbs had damaged any of his vital organs so in a day or two, the superficial stuff would heal and he would be fit to move on again. But to where? It suddenly struck him that the city was too quiet; wasn't there a war on and weren't the defenders of Tuzla expecting another Serb onslaught? He couldn't hear shelling or mortar fire or indeed any sort of gunfire and his room sure as hell wasn't that well insulated. Only then did he think to check his watch. He was astonished to discover that it was after eleven o'clock in the morning. He had slept for over twelve hours; no wonder he felt so refreshed. The lady of the house had left a basin of water, some soap and a towel beside his bed so he undressed and tried to scrub off some of the dirt that had accumulated on his body in the forests during the past week. He washed quickly; he noticed he had grown quite a beard by now but shaving would have to wait. He finished his ablutions, dressed and went to the kitchen.

Already seated at the table were Hasan, his wife Tatjana and son Salim. They were drinking coffee. Tatjana rose and hugged Drazen and thanked him for helping her husband to safety. Drazen looked bemused and adopted an 'I didn't do anything to save anyone' type of look. The woman-of-the-house, a friendly middle aged woman called Sabina, dressed from head to toe in traditional garb, guided

Drazen to a seat at the table and immediately poured him a cup of strong coffee from an oversized pot which was seated on a nearby stove. The coffee was delicious and of course it tasted extra special after their privations of the previous week. Sabina fussed about and started taking the tops off several large pots and pans. She produced oversized plates and started heaping food onto Drazen's, Hasan's and Salim's. Neither man nor the boy refused as the hunger they had experienced over the previous few days was still with them. Tatjana had already eaten and indicated she couldn't have any more just now. Hasan and Drazen tucked into huge plates of Musaka, a baked dish made of layers of potatoes and minced beef, accompanied by Sataras, a dish made from eggplants, peppers, onions and tomatoes. It was all washed down by large mugs of coffee. Sabina offered wine but the men declined. Both declared it the best breakfast they had ever eaten and insisted on paying the woman. Sabina placed here hands on her hips, frowned at them and stood firm:
"No one pays for food in this house. You are our guests; our friends. You are fellow Bosniaks. You would do the same for us; please eat your fill as our guests but you would insult us by offering to pay."
They thanked the woman profusely as they finished up their plates. Yet more coffee was poured and the conversation turned to what their next move would be.

Drazen's previously bright mood turned to depression when he contemplated his situation. Although he did not say it, he felt Hasan was in an infinitely better place, having his family with him. Still, they were in a war zone. As if reading his thoughts, Hasan said:

"It appears the Serbs have decided to leave us be for now. They haven't fired a single shot today. Either they feel Tuzla is not worth fighting for or else they still haven't counted their men correctly and think we are holding some of them prisoner." He laughed as he said this. "I have also heard stories, brought here by the many journalists that are in Tuzla, that the Serbs have been put under severe pressure by the western powers to cease their bloody campaign."

"I think we have heard those stories before though," Tatjana said.

"It's true, she's right," Hasan replied. "The Serbs have thumbed their noses at every previous threat or warning to have come from the U.N. or the U.S. or N.A.T.O. and they have gotten away with it. The western powers either didn't have the political will or the political backing to carry out their threats. But the word now is that Srebrenica changed all that. The journalists are saying it was the worst atrocity committed in Europe since the Nazis. Apparently, huge pressure is being put on the western powers to act so the Serbs may think twice about the warnings this time around. Indeed, perhaps that is why they haven't attacked Tuzla."

"I don't know," Drazen replied. "The city looked fairly well defended last night. Could it be that they don't want to risk getting a large number of their men killed here for what is not really a strategic capture?" Hasan shrugged.

"You could well be right my friend but Tuzla is a strategic location. It's our third largest city. There's not much of it left intact after the three years of war but nevertheless. What are your own immediate plans?"

Drazen shrugged and his shoulders slumped.

"I don't know Hasan. I need to find my family. I need to start looking, first in Sarajevo. But I have wasted the last eight days wandering around the country and I am now in Tuzla. I am farther away from Sarajevo than I was when I started out. I feel I am making no progress; my family need me; they might be in great danger even now and here am I, drinking coffee and eating and not doing anything to help them." He realised his voice had risen and he apologized to Sabina but she dismissed it:

"We understand your situation Drazen," she said. "It must be terrible for you but please don't give up. Sarajevo is only eighty kilometres away and this war won't last forever."

"But it might as well be eight hundred kilometres for all the chances I have of getting through to it now," he pleaded and Sabina nodded.

"Drazen, my friend," Hasan said. "Please don't blame yourself. You have not spent the last eight days wandering around the countryside. You have spent the last eight days trying to stay alive. You have shown outstanding bravery and courage; none of us would be here if you hadn't stopped that mad man Redzic from betraying us to the Serbs. It's true Drazen, believe me; we would all now be in that ravine where the Bosnian Serb patrol lies. So you haven't done a single thing in the past week except try as best you could to survive so that you might continue in your quest for your family. You need to realise this in order to gain the strength to continue the search. I agree that it is pointless to try to get through Serb lines at the moment; it would be suicidal. But things will change and as soon as they do, I will give you some of my best men to accompany you as you try to reach Sarajevo."

Drazen nodded his thanks to Hasan and the others.
"Yes, I suppose you are correct. I have been trying to stay alive. But I should thank you and your men also. Without the protection from the men in your column, I fear I would not have made it. One other thing Hasan: Your men have been brave far beyond the call of duty. They should rest now; they have been through a lot to reach here. What's more, they are Bosnian Army regulars. It would not be fair to ask them to accompany me on a mission. I really appreciate the offer but when I go to Sarajevo, I will go alone. I will never forget your bravery or your kindness but I honestly cannot ask you for more or allow you to risk the lives of your men. They all have families too Hasan and it is with their families they belong."

On the other side of the line, they had no problem accounting for their men but they were having a tough time keeping them happy. Regardless of the strength of the defences of Tuzla, the Bosnian Serbs had envisaged a big push come sun-up that morning. Pound the place with shells; obliterate it off the face of the earth if necessary; then attack with ground forces to clean up; kill any men that were left and take the women prisoner to keep the growing numbers of soldiers gathered around Tuzla amused.

At the morning briefing, the commanders of both the Bratunac and the Drina Corps joined Mistakovic, Milanovic and their regular group. They did not defer to his authority but there was a view that Mistakovic was the only one of them who had a decent clue about military strategy so while they would command their own divisions, they would attend the meeting in a 'consultative' capacity. The General in charge of the Bratunac Corps was quiet, obviously deeply embarrassed by the failure of his men to correctly account for their numbers which resulted in the loss of the remaining Bosniak prisoners. No mention was made of the issue but when overall military strength was being assessed in the light of the day's plans, there were a few sniggers around the table when the General reported on his division.

Sefer sat quietly, listening to the various reports and then Mistakovic's suggested plans for the day. It was basically a clean-up operation, the man was saying. The common theme was 'the war is over.' They just needed to finish off the few remaining Bosnian Army defenders. The Colonel made no mention of the civilians in Tuzla or what their fate might be but if you read between the lines, there was no doubt that it would be as before. There was the added complication that as far as could be ascertained, no one had ordered any buses or civilian transport. The issue wasn't even mentioned so clean-up was taken to mean extinction, not even ethnic cleansing, which, despicable as it was, allowed some people to live by transporting them to an alternative location. When Mistakovic outlined the battle plans, he asked if there were any questions. Some technical issues of a minor nature were raised and resolved but there was general agreement on the strategy. As everyone was about to leave, Sefer raised a hand.

"Yes Colonel," said Mistakovic, "you have a query?"
"I have Colonel, Generals, Gentlemen: the military assessment, as outlined by Colonel Mistakovic, suggests

that there are approximately five thousand Bosnian soldiers or armed defenders in Tuzla. I have heard no estimate of the number of civilians in the city."

"But we cannot estimate those numbers, no one can," Mistakovic said.

"I understand that Colonel," Sefer said calmly. "But if I might finish the point? Intelligence reports say the city's population before the war was one hundred and thirty thousand. We understand, by we I mean Serbian Army Intelligence, that maybe twenty thousand either died from starvation or were killed by other means during the 1994 siege. We further understand that maybe thirty thousand fled the city. Whether any have returned, we cannot say but it is unlikely as we believe most moved to western Bosnia. That still leaves eighty thousand, but it is estimated that only half of these are Bosniaks. There are approximately twenty thousand Serbs and twenty thousand between Croats and other races. Now, a large number of Bosniaks have fled from all areas of the eastern part of the country. Many have been killed but our sources estimate that there could be as many as fifty thousand refugees in the city. I stress that all these numbers are estimates but what is not in doubt is that there are considerable numbers of civilians. Is that agreed?"

Heads were nodding all round the table and it was obvious even the hawks amongst the group knew where Milanovic was going with this. He continued:

"Now gentlemen, we have fifteen thousand Bosnian Serb militia surrounding the city. We have superior weaponry of course but are we not a little stretched? I realise there is a natural tendency to want to take Tuzla but as the Bosniaks who have been driven out of other parts of eastern Bosnia have gathered here, would it be logical to assume they may try to make a last stand?"

"Let them," said Svero, "our shells and mortars will blow them to bits."

"And if they also have shells and mortars and heavy guns General, what would your proposal be in that case?"

There was an embarrassed silence. Even though Sefer was used to them at this stage, he always marvelled at how these idiots had ever won any sort of a battle, let alone a war. The answer had to be the sophisticated weapons supplied by *his* Government. Lieutenant Vladkovic spoke up:

"Colonel Milanovic is correct. It would be unwise to attack the city today in what you might call a 'gung ho' way. The war is practically over everywhere else anyway. With your approval, I propose we hold off attacking and send for reinforcements from our brothers in the other divisions. We can double our numbers within two days; then we can launch an attack with the certainty of victory."

It wasn't exactly what Sefer wanted to hear but it bought him time. He dreaded what might happen if the Serbs broke through the defences easily. What had happened at Srebrenica might be mild by comparison. There were shrugs from most of the commanders but the general atmosphere was one of anti-climax. Mistakovic got to his feet and blustered:

"OK, I see your point Lieutenant."

Sefer noted that he was keen to give the credit to his own man but that was fine by him. He didn't need credit; all he wanted to do was prevent another bloodbath. Mistakovic continued:

"I will send messages immediately to General Mladic in central command and we will reassess the situation when we see what back-up support we can muster. For now gentlemen, I'm sure you will all find something to amuse yourselves."

The men filed out and went their separate ways. Sefer thanked Vladkovic for his support but the Lieutenant shrugged it off.
"To be honest Colonel, I often think most of our leaders are idiots but they've won the battles and got us to here so I don't usually disagree with them. Your assessment of Tuzla was irrefutable though. Had we gone in there today, all of us could have looked like idiots."
Milanovic didn't fully agree with the assessment but said nothing.
"So, Colonel," Vladkovic said, "a free day; maybe we should start early, what? Get pissed and then have an early night. Would you care to join me?"
"It's a little early for me Lieutenant," Sefer said. "I also have reports to do for Belgrade but I would be delighted to join you for an early dinner. I found there is an excellent restaurant just down the street from our hotel in Krizevici. I'd be delighted for you to be my guest this evening; shall we say at six thirty?"
"Why not Colonel; I'll meet you in the lobby at twenty five past."

It was a beautiful evening; the temperature had abated a little today and it was a pleasant eighteen degrees as they strolled to the restaurant. This part of Bosnia had apparently been spared the worst ravages of war and was now firmly in Serb hands. The streets were clean and large pots of flowers adorned many street corners. The trees gave off a sweet scent and the branches swayed gently in the breeze. You could have been anywhere; it was hard to believe that ten kilometres down the road, a bitter conflict was being played out. Sefer had showered, shaved and put on a freshly laundered uniform for dinner. Vladkovic, on the other hand, seemed to be still in the same clothes he had worn that morning. He appeared to have been drinking heavily but the man obviously had the capacity for it as it was not affecting his speech or his movements, at least not yet. The restaurant was Serbian cuisine but there is great commonality between all food habits of the former nations of Yugoslavia. Milanovic ordered bottles of red and white wine and a bottle of slivovitz, which Vladkovic immediately appropriated, much to Sefer's relief. Both men ordered fisherman's soup. Sefer ordered the lamb for main course while his dining partner chose the roasted pork. They were given a wide choice of vegetables and salads to accompany their meals. Both men declined dessert even though the restaurant's menu boasted a vast array of Serbian pies and other sweet confections. Vladkovic drank most of the slivovitz and very little of the wine. Milanovic probably drank most of both bottles and was feeling slightly drunk himself.

He raised his glass in a toast.
"Ivan my friend, I hope you won't be offended but I drink to your good health. You were obviously under great personal strain yesterday with that Bosniak prisoner but your behaviour was exemplary, if I may say so."
Vladkovic seemed non-plussed but shrugged and clicked glasses.
"Thank you Colonel," he said. His voice had thickened considerably so Sefer decided to try to get him to open up.

"It was a hell of a coincidence, that fellow knowing you like that," he said.

"Oh, the Bosniak; it was just pure chance Colonel; from another time. He was lucky to gain his freedom."

"Yes indeed Ivan, but he begged you to release him. I could see it was difficult for you, and didn't he apologize to you also? What was that about?"

"Oh nothing important Colonel, happened a long time ago."

Sefer felt the Lieutenant wasn't going to open up if he kept badgering him with questions. Instead, he filled the man's glass and his own and drank. He said nothing and decided he would let Vladkovic fill the silence. After a considerable length of time, the Lieutenant, now very unsteady and eyes bloodshot, said:

"He's the one I told you about, remember?"

"No, I don't," Sefer said.

"Surely you remember, I told you, the first night we got pissed. Ah, maybe you were pissed at the time too. Anyway, it's ancient history, no, ah, no use now."

"Tell me anyway," Sefer said gently. "I'd like to know."

Ivan shrugged:

"I knew him growing up in Belgrade. I played with him; we played together, quite a lot in fact. I was young, well younger than him; maybe two years but at that age it seems a lot. We played together for a few years. I think I was ten and he was twelve when, when…."

The Lieutenant hesitated, then began talking freely again: "Do you know Colonel, we were actually best mates. I didn't know he was a Bosniak; I didn't know what a fucking Bosniak was. I was just a young boy who wanted to play games and so was he and I played with him, that was it."

"And you were correct but what happened, something must have?" Sefer said.

Ivan looked down into his glass, mellow now, his eyes misting over slightly.

"You can probably guess; my father found out. He was annoyed with me and banned me from ever seeing the boy again but he didn't say why. I stayed away for a few days but there were very few boys of my age in our block so we met again and I played with him. This time when my father found out, he went berserk and beat me badly. He told me the boy was not of my kind; he was a stinking Bosniak and I was never to see him again. A few days later, we met on the street. He wanted to play but I said no. I called him a stinking Bosniak and told him to fuck off. He reacted angrily and beat the shit out of me. He was older and I didn't have a chance but it wasn't his fault either; he didn't know why I had reacted like that. When my father saw that I was hurt, he demanded to know who had beaten me but I told him it was a different boy, someone I knew was a Serb so he let me be. I never saw Drazen again until yesterday."

The Lieutenant took another drink and Sefer left him alone with his thoughts. Was it this incident that had given him the chip on his shoulder that allowed him to bear the grudge, exacerbated over the years by his father's bitterness and racial hatred? Or was it something else entirely? There was an abundance of racism in former Yugoslavia so perhaps the man was just playing to type or the way he imagined he should. He spoke again, slurring his words this time:

"You know, it wasn't his fault; he was actually a good friend; protected me a few times; we did everything together, but it was a long time ago."

"I grew up myself with Bosniaks and Croats and Montenegrin's," Sefer said. "I think we all got along in my district although there must have been tensions there too. It's a great pity when you have two nationalities living in an area competing for the same land; when it's three, it makes it impossible. I think this is the curse that has been visited on our land by previous generations. It is easy to say people should live in peace with each other but it is not that simple. People are by their nature nationalistic and chauvinistic. Fine when the entire nation is composed of the same people but when it's not, it naturally leads to injustice or perceived injustice, even if it is not intentional. When this is suppressed, it will eventually boil over. I wish someone could put the cork or the genie back in the bottle in Bosnia Lieutenant but I fear it is way too late."

They sat in silence for a time, both sipping their drinks. Sefer said:

"Oh by the way Ivan, your friend said his name was what, Drazen Itsakovic?"

"That's correct yes, why?"

"Ah, no reason, I'm just curious. I think it's a common name. He said he had lost or was searching for his wife and children, didn't he? Do you know his wife's name by any chance?"

Ivan shrugged and thought.

"He used to go to the country every summer, to his grandparents. So did I, I think most families had a place in the country. He was always talking about this girl he played with, I think he eventually married her, can't remember her name though."

"It wouldn't have been Sonja, would it?"

"Yes, that was it, Sonja, why Colonel?" Ivan said suspiciously.

"Oh just that I knew someone of that name, that's all," Sefer waved him off. He decided though that he'd have another look at that wanted poster that had landed on his desk this afternoon. It might be best to keep Ivan out of it; the man had enough problems.

Chapter 32

Three days later, Tuzla.

Another glorious day had dawned over Bosnia's third city and still the attack did not come; some of the defenders were now beginning to think it never would. Perhaps the Serbs had had enough; were they running scared? Had they lost their nerve? Drazen doubted this very much and thought it was only a matter of time. He was still staying in the house with Sabina and the others but was getting increasingly frustrated. With the few communications that were still open, he had tried to reach his father in Sarajevo but either the line to his apartment was out of order or the phone lines had failed in the area. For all he knew, his father might not even live there any more; the building might not even exist. He had heard of the siege of Sarajevo and the constant Serb shelling of the city so maybe his Father and Mother weren't even alive still. The tremendous uncertainty of not knowing began to gnaw at him like a living thing until he could stand it no longer. He was with Hasan and his men, who, now fully recovered from the beatings they had endured from the Bratunac soldiers, had been assigned roles in guarding the city's defences.

"Please don't consider me disloyal," Drazen said, "but I have to try to get to Sarajevo. Not knowing the whereabouts of my family is eating me up inside. I have to take the chance; I have to know one way or the other."
"But it would surely be foolish to try to get through Serb lines," Hasan said. "It would be difficult for an armed division; for a man alone, it would be suicidal."
"I realise that, but I've got to find a way. Maybe I'll disguise myself as a Serb; maybe I'll try to get some transport which would be allowed safe passage. I don't know; all I do know is I have to try something and soon."
"I wouldn't advise passing yourself off as a Serb my friend. There are strong similarities between our races but I would know you for a Bosniak at fifty metres. I do understand your feelings; your priority has to be to find your family. Here, we may be attacked tomorrow but on the other hand, the Serbs might just lay siege to the city and we could be here for months. They've done it before you know. I wish I could help you in some way and I would offer you some of my men if there was any reasonable chance of getting through. Right now, to send my men with you would be madness."
"I know and I do not ask for their support but I may stand a better chance alone. If nothing happens in a day or two, I think I will risk it."
"But Drazen," Raif said. "You are a brave man but you are no use to your family as a dead man. You survived alone until you met us by using your wits and intelligence. Use them again my friend; heading towards Sarajevo at the

moment with no transport, little food and drink, through countryside overrun with Serbs is not sensible or logical. Try to think of an alternative or be patient."

Drazen sighed and shook his head; the man was right.

The Bosnian Serb forces surrounding the city had now swelled to over thirty thousand. Serbs had secured practically all key parts of eastern Bosnia and men were free to be reassigned. Reinforcements had been arriving from everywhere. With the commanders of other units joining the morning briefing, space was at a premium. Even though the standing army had more than doubled in size over the few days, there seemed to be more caution in the air. The previous bloodthirsty zeal had been diluted somewhat and Sefer felt the ground had definitely shifted. Either because of his logical critique of their previous plans or possibly because none of the Bosnian Serb leaders wanted to take responsibility, he now found he was being consulted far more frequently. Mistakovic was still in the chair despite the presence of some high ranking officers from the support ranks.

"So gentlemen," he began. "I think it is now time to make the final push and fully occupy Tuzla. We have gun emplacements on all of the hills surrounding the city; all routes in and out are secured. The Bosniaks have set up some reasonable defences so I suggest rather than a full-on attack, we initially soften them up with a strong artillery barrage. We should be in no hurry, perhaps a full day of shelling their positions and then we go for the jugular tomorrow at sun-up."

There were eager nods and murmurs of agreement from around the table. These were fighting men and they had had much success these past few weeks. They wanted nothing more than to press on and finish the job. Of course, the fact that all of them would be observing the battle from their command posts and would not be in the front line was also a consideration. None of them intended dying to take Tuzla, unless there was an unfortunate accident.

"What say you Colonel?" Mistakovic asked Sefer. Milanovic didn't reply immediately but made a point of running his hands through his hair and leaning back from the table.
"May I pose a question?" Sefer said.
Heads nodded around the table including that of Mistakovic. Sefer continued:
"What have we to gain by taking Tuzla? We already control ninety per cent of eastern Bosnia. The Republic of Srpska is flourishing. Karadzic is President. He hasn't been officially acknowledged everywhere but that will come, either for him or his successor. People now acknowledge the right of Bosnian Serbs to have a homeland. What has Tuzla got to offer us? There are twenty thousand Serbs in the city who already control a lot of its key infrastructure. Do you all not agree that to launch yet another attack now would be overkill? I use the word advisedly my friends. We made a grave mistake at Srebrenica and we have lost much sympathy as a result. I fear to think what might happen here if the Bosniak defences are easily breached."

General Svero, who had been quiet at recent briefings, now spoke up. The man was either angry or anxious to show the other commanders his strength.

"I too would like to ask a question," he said. "Why has our friend from Belgrade acquired such pre-eminence in our decision making strategy? He says we have lost support or international sympathy but we don't need sympathy to win this war; we've never had support; we've fought a lone battle all through this conflict but look at what we achieved. Is the Colonel going to take it away from us because he fears a lack of support from cowardly leaders sitting safely in offices somewhere?"

Sefer nodded and cleared his throat.

"General," he began, "there is no doubt that much has been achieved and for that I congratulate you. But the situation has changed. Now, the eyes of the world are on Bosnia, believe me. Half the world's press and media outlets have T.V. cameras and reporters in Tuzla. We even have them here in Krizevici. You ignore these people at your peril. Individually they may not look much but collectively they wield an enormous amount of influence. You see General, you may not have needed the support of the press or the public or the international leaders to win the war but if you don't have them now, you'll stand a very poor chance of winning the peace. Do you all understand?"

There was silence in the room. Hesitation seemed to be the collective feeling. No one said a word because none of them wished to sound foolish.

After a pause, Sefer continued:

"I appreciate all of you are fighting men and I fully respect that. But eventually and in my opinion, very soon, there will be peace. You will not be allowed to keep all the lands you have conquered; of that I am certain."

There were head shakes and strong rumblings of dissent now coming from a number of the commanders. Support arrived for Sefer from an unlikely source.

"Gentlemen, we may not like it but it is true," Lieutenant Vladkovic said. "We have all been caught up in this war and we have been very successful at it. But we need to be clever enough to win the peace also. Personally, I would love to smash the remaining Bosniak resistance to pieces and march into Tuzla but there is a very high likelihood of what people call 'collateral damage'. Oh, wait, I know this hasn't bothered us up to now but apparently people in the west have got all upset by this and have forced N.A.T.O. to turn their guns on us. I understand that even now, there are cruise missiles aimed at our positions around Tuzla ready to launch air-strikes if we advance. Am I correct Colonel?"

Sefer shrugged.

"You may well be Lieutenant. We cannot of course be sure where the missiles are targeted but yes, there is no question that there will be a reaction soon."

General Svero got to his feet.

"But this is an outrage; how fucking dare they? This is our war; this is our country; it's none of their goddamn business," he fumed.

"That's a matter of opinion of course," Sefer said "and while personally I would agree with the General, it may be prudent for us to assume otherwise. I have also heard from intelligence sources in Belgrade that a big issue is being made by the media of an incident in the Markale district of Sarajevo just two months ago on Marshal Tito's birthday."

"That's bullshit," said a new voice. A General Dukic, one of the commanders from the reinforcements sent by Mladic, spoke up.

"I was there at the time. We had the city surrounded. We were on in the mountains to the west of the city. Yes, we fired several artillery shells, but all were aimed at military positions. One of the Bosniaks' own shells was either misdirected or was deliberately sent into a market. They blamed us just because a few of their peasant traders were killed."

"I think the number was seventy one dead and over two hundred wounded," Sefer said. "A relatively small number compared to subsequent events but one that was witnessed and recorded by the media so it received international exposure."

"So what does the Colonel recommend we do now?" Dukic thundered. "Surely we should at least attack the Bosniak military defences? Does he suggest we sit here on our arses indefinitely?"

Sefer smiled.

"Certainly not General, and as I say, I appreciate your frustration, you are a fighter and you wish to get on with the fight. But can I say that it is now the expressed wish of my superiors in Belgrade that we hold our fire for the moment to see how things develop."

Everyone began talking at once but Sefer knew he had them; he had sown enough seeds of doubt for there to be disagreement and uncertainty. What he hadn't told them was that Belgrade had said, foolishly in his view, to hold fire until the media got tired and pissed off somewhere else and then to let them attack full-on. Mistakovic expertly gauged the mood and said.

"Gentlemen, gentlemen, there is much merit in what everyone has said but perhaps we will wait; give the men some time off; let them enjoy themselves. Ah, I understand there are plenty of places where that can be done. Take a break yourselves commanders, you have done well; enjoy the fruits of your labours. Let us say we'll skip the briefing tomorrow so all meet here again in two days time. If there are any developments in the meantime or if I hear from our commander-in-chief, I will let you all know immediately."
"Just before we go Colonel," Dukic said cynically. "Do we know what General Mladic's view on the situation is?"
"He has asked us to make our own judgment locally General," Mistakovic replied.
"Very well," Dukic said, "so, we meet in two days time gentlemen".
He gathered his papers, nodded to his subordinate and they both left the room, followed soon after by the remainder of the attendance.

"So you've won a reprieve of two days Colonel," Vladkovic whispered as he and Milanovic left the room. "How much longer do you think you can hold them off?"
Sefer shook his head. "Who knows Lieutenant? But situations change very quickly, particularly in modern warfare and in two days we may be looking at a totally different set of circumstances." Vladkovic sniffed.
"Perhaps," he said, "I'll defer to your greater experience in these matters. But now, to a more pleasant topic, how about dinner tonight, my treat this time?"
"I'd be delighted Lieutenant, see you at seven."
Sefer smiled inwardly. Ivan had seemingly shed his hostility and was turning into a regular ally and up to now,

a valuable one. He hoped it would continue. He would need all the help he could get over the next few weeks.

A youth, probably no more than nineteen, nodded at Drazen as he left his colleagues and made his way back to Sabina's house for another evening without his beloved family. After a short walk, Drazen noticed the boy was following him. He was not armed so there was no apparent danger. Drazen watched him out of the corner of his eye and slowed his pace to a saunter. When he reached Sabina's house, the boy was still following him but was about fifty yards distant. Drazen shrugged and entered the house where Sabina immediately offered him coffee. The woman was an avid reader and had a large stock of books, stacked on shelves, on tables and in corners at all sorts of angles. Many volumes could also be found in the bedrooms and Drazen had already dipped into some of the classics, although he found he couldn't concentrate enough to actually finish anything. He now took up a volume by Charles Dickens; it would pass an hour; he had nothing else to do so he had to try something to occupy his mind.

After about half an hour, there was a knock on the door. Sabina answered and Drazen heard her in conversation with a man. He heard the sound of feet shuffling behind him and Sabina's voice saying: "I think you have a visitor Drazen."
He wheeled round in shock, worried. No one knew him in Tuzla except Hasan and his men; Sabina wouldn't call them visitors. What was this? The boy who had followed him home stood there impassively and nodded at him. He

was tall and thin and he had huge blue eyes, set in a pale thin face with long pointed features. On closer inspection, he was more seventeen than nineteen as there were only the faintest beginnings of stubble on his pale cheeks. With him was an older man with similar features but slightly smaller in stature. The boy spoke first:

"Forgive me sir; I followed you home this afternoon because I thought maybe I could help you. You see, pardon my eavesdropping but I overheard your conversation today with your colleagues and your desperate wish to get to Sarajevo. This is my father and he might be able to help. His name is Muhamad and my name is Nezir."

Drazen stood up and said:

"Please sit down. Thank you; I'd be delighted to talk to you."

Sabina brought more coffee and cups for the two visitors. Muhamad spoke:

"I have heard your sad story and you have my sympathy. I appreciate that it must be very difficult for you being unable to act. You must get to Sarajevo but it is pointless to take unnecessary risks. It would be madness to take to the roads right now. It is too far to cross the mountains and you wouldn't survive up there but you know that anyway having come from there."

Drazen sighed and nodded. This wasn't getting anywhere. Muhamad continued:

"But as they say, there is more than one way to skin a cat, eh? You are approaching the problem the wrong way. Do you know that the northern side of Tuzla, where I originally come from, is only forty kilometres from the Croatian border? The Croats are our allies now so you stand an infinitely better chance with them."

"But what do I do in Croatia?" Drazen said.

"Oh sorry, I didn't say; that's the best bit. Do you know that people say the U.N. has been useless in Sarajevo? They say they've let the Serbs lay siege to the city for over two years and haven't protected the citizens at all."

Drazen was getting irritated. What was this man talking about? Did his story have a point to it? Croatia? the United Nations? He looked frustrated as the man continued speaking.

"But the one thing the U.N. has managed to do in Sarajevo is to keep the airport open. Without it, I believe many people would have starved. But do you see what I mean? If I can get you across the border with Croatia, you can be in Zagreb in two hours. Then it would be a matter of waiting to catch a suitable flight. There are many humanitarian missions I understand so my associates should be able to get you on to one of them. After that, you can be in Sarajevo in an hour."

Chapter 33

The area around the doorway was barely passable; it was strewn with pieces of shattered brick and concrete, broken glass, dog faeces and all manner of discarded domestic refuse. It had obviously been a long time since the rubbish had been collected in this town. The door itself actually still closed although it hung precariously from two of its original three hinges. It was covered in filth and grime and other matter of dubious origin. There was a small hallway with a hatch to where there had presumably once been a concierge, now long since fled. The few pieces of furniture that had formed the concierge's domain were smashed to pieces and covered in the same dirt and grime. The hallway was filthy and looked as if it hadn't been cleaned in years. Needless to say, the one lift the building had boasted was long since out of order, the elevator car firmly stuck midway between the ground floor and the basement. This could be viewed through the steel mesh which had covered the lift in happier days and which was still more or less intact. It didn't get any better on the stairs or indeed the walls of the building. Everywhere was strewn with the detritus of neglect. There was a dirty liquid of some sort, presumably water, seeping down the stairs discolouring the steps to a rust type hue.

He rushed up numerous flights of stairs to the address he'd been given. He passed numerous other flats on the way. Most seemed abandoned but a few contained makeshift locks possibly placed there by squatters or whoever had been brave enough to occupy the place. It was a one room flat. At first glance, he thought there must be some mistake; surely this couldn't be a dwelling? The room had at one time been painted blue or it might have been turquoise but whatever sheen there had been on the walls had long since been dulled. There was just enough space for a single bed, one chair, a piece of furniture that might at one time have been a dressing table or a chest of drawers but no longer fulfilled either function. There was also an ancient oil-filled radiator which looked like a serious fire risk. There were no curtains or drapes on the windows; no carpets or any sort of coverings on the floor. There was an overpowering smell which was a mixture of dampness, stale or rotten food and urine. There was a pile of clothes in the middle of the floor which just appeared to have been dropped there. He wasn't going to examine them too closely as he suspected that they added to the stench. But the state of the room nor the fire risk nor the smell did not concern him. His greatest worry was that the room was empty; devoid of life. Moreover, it appeared that no one had inhabited this space for some time. Even the clothes did not appear to be those which his Sonja or Diana would have worn; no, they were the attire of an old woman. Had he called to the wrong address? Had he tried the wrong block? But no, he had checked and double checked the address and it was correct. He could not bear to stay in the miserable room now that his hopes had been dashed again so he withdrew into the corridor, then sat on the filthy stone stairs and wept.

He had been in Sarajevo now for five days. Muhamad, his Croatian friend had been as good as his word and had gotten him into Croatia easily. They had left Tuzla in the middle of the night in a cattle truck. Muhamad drove while Drazen shared the accommodation with the livestock. They had gotten through relatively easily, having only been stopped at one checkpoint where the sentry had no wish to examine Muhamad's cargo of cattle. Once inside Croatia, a friend of Muhamad had driven him to Zagreb airport where he had been accommodated on one of the many humanitarian flights between the two capitals. Through old contacts, he had managed to discover that his father was involved in the resistance and he was eventually brought to meet him. Drazen was overjoyed to learn that Sonja and Diana had actually made it safely to Sarajevo and that they had located his father. But his joy turned to panic when his father related the story of the wanted poster and the visit by the police to the safe house. Even though police reinforcements had not come to the house, it was decided it was unsafe and all the occupants had been evacuated and given refuge elsewhere in the city. But there had been no word from Sonja since the day she had fled from the basement. Danvor had put the word out amongst his men to be on the look out for her but no one had seen either her or the child. It was eating Drazen up. He had come so far and been through hell to get here and now it seemed as if his prize had been taken from him just as it was within his grasp.

Sarajevo is not a huge city but it had contained almost half a million people before the siege so it would not be easy to find someone unless you had an idea of where to start looking. Drazen had brought a picture of Sonja from his home but Danvor had warned him to be ultra careful about who he showed this to. With the Serbs looking for Sonja, he would be picked up himself if someone reported him. He longed to ask everyone if they had seen his beloved but he had to contain his eagerness and learn to be patient. Sonja had done very well to get this far; she had had to flee the safe house but had obviously managed to conceal herself and her daughter so the last thing he needed to do was to give either them or himself away. Nonetheless, he had been wandering the streets now for two days. He had spoken to a woman in a café this afternoon whom he was sure was a loyal Bosniak. He had known her family growing up in the city many years previously. She had not seen Sonja or Diana but she had promised to ask a number of people in the district whom she trusted. Meanwhile Drazen had spent a listless afternoon drinking coffee and wringing his hands. At around six o'clock, the woman had returned, excitement in her eyes. An old Bosniak man had observed a woman answering Sonja's description accompanied by a small child surreptitiously entering an apartment block a short distance away a week beforehand. He had subsequently seen them leave and re-enter the building a number of times. Judging by the lights in the block, the old man was adamant the woman and child were in the south facing flat on the seventh floor. The building had been largely abandoned due to a combination of Serb shelling and people fleeing the city.

While there was no visible evidence of Sonja or Diana ever having been in the building, Drazen knew that Sonja would have been careful enough to leave none lest the Serb police come calling. She was a resourceful woman and the fact that she had made it this far meant she would be taking every possible precaution to protect her child and herself. If the police couldn't locate her, what hope had he? Then suddenly the awful thought hit him; something he had up to now refused to consider or even let enter his mind. What if the police had already caught up with her? His head spun as he tried to blot out the awful possibilities while still trying to think. He had to consider it a realistic possibility but the thought was too horrible to contemplate. His wife had killed a Serbian camp commander; what they would do to her if she was captured didn't bear thinking about. Then there was the fear that because she had outwitted them once, they might not be prepared to take the chance and would have summarily executed her. One thought was worse than the other. After he had reluctantly left the abandoned apartment which the old man had said was occupied by a woman and child, he had very quickly checked every other flat in the building but he drew a complete blank. This block was almost completely uninhabited, similar to the building where his father had lived. Of course Danvor had already had that flat checked out many times lest Sonja find her way back there. He doubted she would though; if the Serbs were serious about apprehending her and it appeared that they were, she would be clever enough to stay away from any known addresses with which she was connected.

Drazen was tired now. After his fruitless search, he had checked and double checked the address. He had dashed about like a mad man searching empty apartments, disturbing squatters, slipping and sliding and stumbling through the debris of war and strife but to no avail. When he eventually calmed down, he had sat on the filthy steps of the stairs for a long time, just staring into space, wishing Sonja and Diana to appear; praying they would walk in the front door; Diana would shout 'Papa' and all would be right with their world again. But he waited in vain. It was dark now and no one came; the building was deserted. He looked at his watch; it was now nine in the evening; he'd give it another hour; they may have been out for the day. But he knew in his heart that Sonja would remain indoors as much as she could in daytime. If she found a safe place, she would only go out for food and if she had to move, she would do so under cover of darkness. His father had told him that he had advised Sonja to do this but she would have known in any case. At eleven, he decided to call it a day. He wearily descended the steps to the street and with shoulders slumped and head down, he trudged back towards the café.

"I cannot see why we must continue to dally and delay; we have the finest force of fighting men in the Balkans here and they are armed to the teeth. I say we move today or at the latest tomorrow at sun-up regardless of any advice from Belgrade or even from central command". The speaker was General Dudic who had again dismissed Milanovic's arguments about relative strengths of the

opposing forces as over cautious. Here was a man who wanted blood, Sefer thought. As it was highly unlikely that any of his own or his fellow senior officers' would be spilled, there was a strong possibility that the man would get his way. This morning's briefing was being held in a building barely five hundred metres from the Serb lines, presumably arranged by Mistakovic in anticipation of an attack that day. Sefer again urged caution:
"Gentlemen, I beg of you to use your reason and intelligence. The most important weapon of war is not the strength of your armaments or the bravery of your men. No, the most vital weapon is intelligence. You are all aware of the latest developments in this war. The Croatians have now joined forces with the Bosniaks. These people may not be as beaten as we think. I have heard they are fighting back in Sarajevo. We are under severe international pressure; they are not. They are seen as freedom fighters whereas we are seen as the oppressor. But apart from all that, we do not know if the Croats have boosted the Tuzla defences. Despite what we were told here last week, it appears that we do not have all of Tuzla surrounded in a ring of steel as some of your units incorrectly pointed out. I understand there is a corridor; in fact some say several corridors on the other side of the city in the direction of the Croatian border. We could be walking into a trap; it could turn out to be a disaster".
Mistakovic considered the statement and now responded coolly:
"I hear everything you say Colonel and I take it on board. But with great respect, I think you are overstating the danger. The Croatians have only just thrown in their lot with the Bosniaks. Surely they can't have had time to move divisions to Tuzla and if they had, our scouts would

have detected them. I say the longer we wait *without* attacking, the greater the chances are that the defences *will* be boosted so I recommend we take the city before they have time to mobilize. The longer we stay here, the more we will lose momentum".

There was a buzz in the room as everyone began talking at once. Mistakovic had made a valid point and Sefer could see there was widespread support for it. He needed to respond or he would lose this.

"Gentlemen", he began. "I will be straight with you. General Mistakovic makes a valid point even if we are still not quite sure of the current level of the defences. The simple truth is that for the sake of the good name of Serbs everywhere, we cannot risk another massacre; there cannot be another Srebrenica and I fear that is what may happen if we unleash our troops on Tuzla"

There was uproar in the room; righteous indignation abound. Oaths and racist rhetoric was thrown around with abandon. Sefer had to raise his voice to try to be heard. Suddenly the entire room shook and all grew quiet. Then it shook again and they heard the sound of the exploding shells. As it would have been suicidal for the Bosniaks to launch a counter attack, Sefer had to assume that the Serb softening up process had commenced. He also doubted that it was any maverick squadron leader deciding to take things into his own hands. No, someone in this room had gotten tired of waiting and had given the order. No one spoke but he thought he saw a few knowing glances exchanged. The noise grew louder as the shelling intensified. The men rushed to the window; great plumes of smoke and dust could be seen rising in the direction of Tuzla city centre. Sefer shook his head in frustration. He knew the pattern. They would pound the place with shells and mortars and anything else they possessed; then the infantry would be sent in to finish it off.

There was a loud knocking on the door which could be heard between the shell launches. Mistakovic shouted: "Come in". A young private entered the room looking extremely nervous and made his way to the General.
"Sir, an urgent message just received".
Mistakovic just nodded and dismissed the young man. He opened the flimsy piece of paper, donned his reading glasses and visibly paled as he read and re-read the message. Eventually he cleared his throat and asked all to be re-seated.
"Gentlemen", he said. "Whichever one of you gave the order to commence firing, I would suggest you rescind it immediately. I am not proposing to take any action against anyone but I strongly advise you to comply with General Mladic's orders".
There was a collective intake of breath as Mistakovic continued:
"The order states that Tuzla is not worth laying siege to; the war has taken an unexpected turn with the entry of the Croats so all available units are ordered to head for Sarajevo to boost our forces there for one final push. It seems the siege is holding but is being breached in some areas. I propose gentlemen that we order our men to pack up and head for the capital".
The commanders nodded, muttered some words that were unintelligible. Svero and Dukic were first on their feet suggesting to Milanovic that it was one of them who gave the order to commence shelling Tuzla. He was pleased; the order from Mladic had saved the day. What would happen in Sarajevo was another thing but not a worry for now. He

was just getting to his feet himself when there was a blinding flash and then the whole room went dark.

Chapter 34

It was a beautiful day in the centre of Sarajevo. The sun shone from a cloudless sky and the air, so pungent and acrid with gun smoke for so long, had almost returned to normal. The continuous shelling had stopped and the word was the Serb guns had been pushed back farther into the hills. It was also said that the sniping had ceased as Bosniak fighters identified a growing number of the snipers and silenced them. Today, people were on the streets again in their summer attire; markets were operating; food had been brought into the city; people were smiling as they went about their business. But Drazen was not smiling. After three days of a fruitless search, he was growing increasingly desperate. He had returned to where his father was masterminding the Bosniak resistance, now given a new lease of life by the alliance with Croatia and the promise of N.A.T.O. air strikes if the Serb shelling of the city did not fully cease. Fighting had escalated on the ground as joint Bosnian and Croatian forces went on the offensive and some notable victories had been achieved. The Serbs were being slowly driven back and this had already allowed a partial restoration of the city's electricity and water supplies, which for almost three years had been sporadic or non-existent.

Danvor and Emir were concerned for their son and his search for his family but Danvor couldn't allocate men to assist in the search. Every man he had was deployed in a key function of the defence of the city and although it was heart breaking to refuse, he couldn't accede to his son's request. Drazen understood – he had his family to think of but his father was fighting for every family in the city and trying to ensure the very survival of the Bosniak people and culture. Drazen promised he too would assist in the fight but pleaded for one more week to be allowed search for Sonja and Diana.

Sarajevo was historically famous for its traditional cultural and religious diversity, with adherents of Islam, Christian Orthodoxy, Catholicism and Judaism coexisting there for centuries. Due to this long and rich history of religious and cultural variety, the city was often called the 'Jerusalem of Europe'. It was the only major European city to have a

Mosque, a Catholic Church, an Orthodox Church and a Synagogue located within the same neighborhood. In fact, the city abound with churches and places of worship. Many had been damaged during the war but were still attempting to function. It was rumored that many churches had given refuge to displaced or persecuted persons, regardless of religious conviction and it was true that some church property had been made available to the homeless. But if a person needed to be kept from public view, how was Drazen supposed to discover them? He wasn't particularly religious and was aware that there was much bigotry and rivalry between faiths and religions. To ask the wrong question of the wrong person could be dangerous but he had to start somewhere; now that he had come through such perils to be in the same city as his wife and child, it burned like a fire within him that he could not reach them. He was a Muslim although not a practicing one in the true sense but he knew of the customs and practices of many religions. He walked through the city centre yet again today, watching, looking, seeking, seeing Sonja's image in every dark haired woman he cast his eye on. At times his hopes soared as he thought he detected her in the distance but after this had happened a number of times, he realised it was just a trick of the mind; when you are concentrating so strongly and hoping to see a familiar face, the mind momentarily distorts the images so as to make you think you are actually seeing the person. Even acknowledging this, there were times when he almost ran up to striking looking Bosniak women, some of whom had their faces partially covered but at the last moment he would have to stop himself as some detail he would remember about Sonja would be absent; the nose wouldn't be right, or the ears or the eyes or the cheeks or the shape of her body. It was driving him crazy. He walked once more over the famous Latin Bridge and past the famous Sebilj, the pseudo-Ottoman style wooden fountain in the centre of Bascarsija square. He sat for a while on a bench, and then bought a coffee from the one kiosk that was still working. He had no idea what he would say but he had to try. He took a walk around the district pondering where to start. He crossed the Miljacka River and headed for the main Jewish Synagogue, the Ashkenazi. He tried the door but it was closed. A sign said it was still operative but only on the Sabbath. Drazen was not surprised really as the Jewish population of the Balkans had been devastated during Hitler's war and many Jews had subsequently emigrated to Israel, leaving a relatively small number. He next tried the Emperor's Mosque; he felt more comfortable here as it was his own faith; he knelt, bowed his head and said a prayer. He then waited but no Imam appeared; there didn't appear to be anyone around. He contemplated going around the back and knocking but at the last moment lost his nerve. He resolved to return when it was darker or perhaps on Friday, the Islamic day of worship. He hurried away and paused briefly by the Serbian Orthodox Cathedral; he admired the magnificent building but he did not enter. He was sure the priests there were good, holy men, but they were, after all, Serbs and he could not afford to take the chance that he would be reported or that the cathedral might be infiltrated.

He felt he was going round in circles when he arrived at the Roman Catholic Cathedral of Jesus' Heart. He tried the door and it gave inwards with a loud creak which echoed through the cavernous building. He looked at the statues which adorned almost every surface, the magnificent

painted ceiling and the fine stained glasswork over the altar. Strangely, the building was completely undamaged; perhaps God looks after his own, he thought. He spied the ornate box with three doors in a dark corner and saw an old woman exiting from one of them. He then remembered the Catholic sacrament of Confession. There were two more old women in a queue. He quickly entered a pew and again fell to his knees in prayer. The second woman had now entered the confessional. He waited a few moments until another woman exited the other side of the box and the last woman entered. He then moved to where the women had been queueing, knelt down, placed his face in his hands and waited. One of the women now exited the box and took no notice of him whatsoever. She moved to a pew a few seats away and recommenced praying. Drazen entered the box. He had never been in this position before and knew nothing of the custom. It was quite dark inside which suited him just fine; there didn't appear to be a bench or a chair but there was a kneeler which was softer than the ones in the main body of the church so he knelt. After only about a minute, a small hatch was pushed across which threw some shafts of light into his previously pitch black section. There was a thick wire mesh between him and the middle section which he presumed was occupied by the priest. All he could make out was a dark shadow. The person seemed to be facing away from him. These Catholics really kept the thing confidential he thought. Neither he nor the priest had spoken a word. After a moment, the priest cleared his throat noisily. Not wanting to cause offence, Drazen remained silent.
"Can I help you?" said the priest. An old voice; Drazen took a deep breath.

"I hope so father. Forgive my intrusion. I am not of your faith but I come to ask your advice if that is acceptable?"
"Indeed it is my son; all are welcome here. Tell me, what is on your mind?"
"Father, I know little of your faith but is it true that what we speak of here cannot be repeated to anyone?"
"Indeed it is; you may speak freely. We are all bound by the secrecy and the sanctity of the confessional".
"Thank you father, it is comforting to know it. You may not be able to help me at all but I have heard rumours, stories, that the church has given protection to certain people who were homeless or may have been persecuted or unjustly treated by the authorities. You see father, I seek to find my wife and daughter. I am a simple Bosniak farmer who has survived great strife but I was separated from my family. My wife and daughter had to flee Serb oppression too. I have been told with absolute certainty that they are in Sarajevo but they have disappeared. I have searched everywhere father but to no avail. I have heard that there are many who are being protected by the church?"
"Hmm, a common enough tale my son; you have my sympathies; many Bosnian families have been torn apart and many people tragically killed. But why do you come to *this* church? Why would you think your family would have sought refuge here?"
"I didn't father; I mean, I'm not sure; Father, to be honest, I didn't trust the Orthodox Cathedral and the others were closed and your church seemed to be the only one where I could talk in privacy". The priest chuckled.
"Indeed, but how do I know that you are genuine, eh? You could be a member of the secret police; you do know they know they are active in the city?" Drazen hesitated. The

priest seemed to be a pleasant old man so he decided he'd take the chance.

"Father, have you heard of Danvor Itsakovic, the leader of the Bosniak resistance in Sarajevo?"

"Hmm, let me think; yes, the name might be familiar".

"Father, I am his son, my name is Drazen. I can show you identification if we can go somewhere with a bit more light".

"Ah, that won't be necessary son; I'll take your word. But the short answer to your question is that I cannot help you. I am aware that people have been given refuge by the churches and by that I mean, all the churches. Oh yes, we may practice different faiths but we all love God and we try to spread his message of compassion. I do not know of a Mother and Daughter who are currently being protected but I can certainly check for you. Can you give me their names and I will speak to my fellow ministers who may be able to help. Oh, don't think we have a vast network or anything like that; we don't, in fact, you could torture me and I wouldn't be able to give you the location of anyone so it would be futile. But I do have my contacts so if you can come back later; hmm, can you give me four hours and call back? I have some other work to do and I celebrate the evening mass at five, so if you come back at four, I may have some news for you. Now, please don't get your hopes up because it is unlikely I will be able to help but I will certainly try".

"Thank you father", Drazen said, "I will pray for you but may I ask your name?"

"Of course, I am Father Gregor".

Drazen thanked the priest profusely and gave him the full details of Sonja and Diana. He then left the confessional hurriedly and made for the door. At the last moment he hesitated, took a pew and said a prayer that the priest and his God could help him. There were no more people queueing for confession so after a few minutes, the middle door opened and the priest left the box. He was an old man, definitely well into his seventies with a dark, weather beaten face. Unusual for a priest, Drazen thought, if he spent so much time in the dark, how did he acquire the weather beaten look? Perhaps he had ministered in a rural parish all his life. He was short and somewhat stooped but he proceeded briskly towards the altar, genuflected briefly, and then disappeared through a side door. He had not looked in Drazen's direction and he appeared to move with a definite purpose. Drazen said one final prayer, crossed himself in the Christian fashion, then returned to the square to drink coffee and wait.

Chapter 35

Milanovic awoke to the sound of moaning, coughing and spluttering. He immediately checked to see that all his limbs were functioning. His head felt fuzzy but apart from that, he seemed to be fine. He couldn't see very well because his eyes were filled with dust. In fact, visibility in the room was severely limited and several men seemed to have their throats choked with debris. All around him, the commanders and their deputies lay at crazy angles. Most were gathering themselves together, seemingly unhurt and merely stunned. All of the windows in the room had been shattered and blown inward. Some of the commanders had been cut by flying glass. The room was still intact but definitely structurally damaged. The windows and doors seemed to hang at oblique angles. Sefer didn't think it was wise to hang around here for long as the entire structure was likely to give way at any moment. General Svero was bleeding from a head wound but it had seemingly been caused by a collision with a mahogany cabinet when he was thrown to the floor like the others. It seemed to take several minutes before any of them realized they had been attacked and moved to protect themselves. One by one, they struggled to their feet.

"We are under attack", Dukic shouted. "This is an outrage; we must give the order to recommence firing at once. How dare they, stinking Bosniaks. And where are the fucking sentries? This place is supposed to be guarded. Where are they?" He stumbled towards the door, red in the face with rage, intent on all manner of revenge against someone.

"General Dukic", Sefer shouted, now almost fully recovered. Dukic paused momentarily and swing round.

"I realise you have been hit in the blast the same as the rest of us but surely you haven't lost the power of your ears?"

"What are you saying Colonel?" Dukic snarled in response.
"Listen, open your ears General. Do you hear any shell fire? Do you hear any gun fire? Mortars? Rifles? No you don't because I fear the explosion we have just experienced and were almost unwittingly part of, did not come from the Bosniak side. They are not capable of an attack a tenth of this size".
"Don't talk in riddles Colonel; what are you saying?"
"Isn't it obvious General? You've just witnessed your first N.A.T.O. air strike. They spy on us by satellite, decide where best to bomb us so as to cause the maximum possible amount of military damage but the minimum amount of casualties. Then their AWACS aircraft, twenty kilometres up in the sky where it can't be seen, locks on to the target, gives the coordinates to a ship off shore and they launch a cruise missile. So, the very best of luck to you in your return fire General but I hope your guns have a long range because the guy who launched that missile is probably sitting having coffee about five hundred kilometres away".

Despite their fear and shock or perhaps because of it, some of the commanders started laughing. It became infectious and after a moment, they were nearly all at it. Even Milanovic gave a wry smile, amused that his earlier prediction that none of their blood would be spilled was inaccurate, at least for today. Dukic was furious, almost turning puce with rage, when Mistakovic said:
"Relax General, the Colonel was not poking fun at you. Settle down now gentlemen please, this is a serious situation".

"General Mistakovic", Sefer said. "Sorry to interrupt sir but with the greatest respect, I suggest we suspend the meeting and vacate the building before it falls in on top of us?"

The laughter briefly reappeared but quickly faded back to shock and near panic as they tried to grab whatever papers and personal effects they could find and scarpered from the room in an undignified fashion.

When they entered the hallway, it resembled a pile of rubble. They had been lucky that their meeting room was located on the other side from where the main blast had hit. The hallway and lobby of the building were empty. All of the men had seemingly abandoned their posts. When they emerged into the courtyard, Sefer saw for the first time the devastation that a thousand pound bomb can wreak. The building was located on a small rise overlooking the front line which was less than half a kilometre away. However, in a secure compound midway between it and the line, was where the bulk of the Bosnian Serb armaments had been located. All that remained of it now was an enormous crater, at least thirty meters across and over ten metres deep. One of the first things that hit them was the searing heat. Directly below them in the midst of the crater, a fire burned with such ferocity that it was impossible to go within two hundred metres of it. All around in every direction, smaller fires burned. The blast had uprooted trees, earth, grass, concrete, brick and stone. It had rained down on the surrounding area in the form of rubble with devastating consequences. Anyone within fifty metres of the epicenter of the explosion would surely have been vaporized. Sefer looked back at the building from which they had just emerged and realized they had indeed been lucky that it had not collapsed in on them. Had the Americans known the leaders were in conference here and tried to take out two birds with one stone? Highly unlikely he felt as the meetings were moved around regularly and this was their first morning to meet here. No, it had just been a coincidence.

A junior officer came running up the path just then and made towards Mistakovic.
"Sir, we have at least twenty men killed sir and many wounded. The blast hit our main ammunition dump and I fear obliterated it sir. I can't estimate the full extent of our losses and won't be able to for some time. Sir, I request permission to rejoin the rescue effort at ground level?"
Mistakovic nodded:
"Of course son, you've done well; go ahead and help your colleagues".
The General was clearly shaken by the blast and its consequences. Sefer reckoned none of the commanders had ever seen such destruction on such a scale but he had, many times. The General took out a pack of cigarettes, offered one to Milanovic and lit both.
"It seems as if you were correct Colonel", he began. "Perhaps we have been a little too ambitious or over zealous. It appears that the Americans want to make a statement, to as they say, 'put the frighteners on us", eh?"
The Serbian Colonel did not immediately reply but sucked deeply on his cigarette. "Indeed General, but I fear it is only a warning. The young man said twenty dead and while it is tragic, I fear they could have killed very many more, had they wanted to. No, this is what they call a shot across our bows. The problem now is what to do. General Mladic had ordered you to abandon Tuzla anyway and

make for Sarajevo. It seems the sensible course of action as your colleagues there appear to be losing their grip and the capital is of far more strategic importance. But I'm sure some of the commanders will look upon this attack as an affront and will wish to continue their attack here to make a statement. From my viewpoint, I would strongly advise against it".

"Would you indeed?" said a sarcastic voice from behind him. It was General Dukic, now seemingly calmed down but sipping from a beer bottle. He ignored Sefer and addressed himself to Mistakovic.

"General, forgive me, I am merely trying to wash away some of the filth that is in my throat after this attack. I can assure you though, it is nothing compared to the bile in my stomach and the thirst for revenge that is in my soul".

Mistakovic shrugged:
"You have my sympathies General Dukic but as our friend says, who are you going to attack? Take a look around you. Look at the devastation. This was caused by one, note I said one – smart bomb. The Americans have thousands of them, an endless supply. We can't fight them; we can't see them; we don't even know where they are. They don't wish to kill us, just to damage our weaponry. Take a look; go on, take a look around. What do you see? Jeeps, A.P.C.'s, Rocket launchers, even our tanks, tossed into the air like children's toys and blown to pieces. This is modern warfare. We can continue to Sarajevo and use conventional methods of warfare but I predict there will be no more outright attacks on cities or towns or on civilian populations, unless we all have a death wish".

"General Mistakovic, I venture to disagree", Dukic said. "You can call us Serbs whatever you like but no one will ever call us cowards. We stand and fight whereas the Americans drop their bombs and run. This strategy could silence our few tanks and heavy guns, but it will have much less effect on our militias' main strength, which is our easily concealed light mortars and irregular infantry. I'll bet none of our equipment on the front line was damaged. So what if we lost a few tanks and ammunition; there's plenty more where that came from. They can have their air power but if we fight cleverly, take and then occupy the towns and cities, where will they launch their air strikes? At civilian targets? I very much doubt it. Don't be despondent General; we have a lot more cards to play and this war is far from over yet. If the Bosniaks want to fight back, let them, but by God they will do it on our terms". Mistakovic shrugged and seemed to take heart. "You may be right General", he said, "but I fear our options are becoming more limited".

Drazen was back in the church by three thirty and entered the confessional box at ten to four. Four o'clock came and went and there was no sign of Fr Gregor. Five past four, ten past; he risked opening the door slightly; there was no queue for the confessional, just a couple of old women praying before a side altar and another lighting some candles. He closed the door again and tried to calm himself. Four fifteen went by and four thirty. Was the delay a good sign? Was the priest on to something? Or would he ever return? Was Drazen being set up? Was he stupid and foolish to believe the old man? Should he flee before it was too late? But if he was being set up, the police would be waiting for him outside. Hope turned to panic to despair and back again. At ten to five, he heard a shuffling noise. He again risked cracking the door slightly. He released an enormous sigh of relief as he saw the priest approach the box, alone. The man entered and Drazen immediately returned to his kneeling position. The partition slid back noisily.

"Are you there my son?" said Fr Gregor.

"Yes father".

"I must apologise for the delay. It took longer than I anticipated. I had many calls to make but young man, God smiles on you today. I think I may have good news for you".

The priest squeezed a thin piece of paper beneath the grille and said:

"There is a woman and child who answer the description you gave me at this address. It is a nunnery. The sisters there do not mix with outsiders so when you go, please pay them due respect. Ask for a Sister Alina; she may well be the one who answers you anyway. But please don't get your hopes too high. The woman who is being sheltered by the sisters says her husband is dead. Now this may well be because of what you told me but prepare yourself; it may not be your beloved but I pray to God that it is and that you find happiness my son".

Drazen was overcome with emotion and could barely speak.

"Father Gregor, I don't know, I can't say, how can I thank you?"

"You can thank me by going in God's name son and saying a prayer for me. Go now quickly; you must reach the convent by seven this evening and I must go to say evening mass".

"Thank you again Father", Drazen said. "I will never forget you".

He hurried from the box, ran across the church, nodded towards the altar and fled to the street. He could just make out the address in the priest's spidery hand writing. The convent was on the other side of town but he knew the area. It was only five o'clock. If he could find a bus or a taxi, he could be there in ten minutes. If not, he'd surely walk it in an hour. He was in luck again. He had barely gone a hundred metres when a vacant taxi hove into view. It was an old Opel but still serviceable. He told the driver the address and he agreed to take him for two German marks or one American dollar. Because of the war, the local currency, the Dinara, was practically worthless. Inflation was running at millions of per cent per month so local paper money was worthless. Drazen had managed to keep much of the money he had 'acquired' from Goran on that first night in July so he was able to pay his way.

The taxi wound its way through little back streets occasionally emerging into wide avenues. The driver seemingly chose the safest route and Drazen did not disagree. He was so overjoyed he heard not one word of what the taxi driver was talking about; it was probably comments about the war anyway so he got away with an occasional nod or a yes or a grunt. He was as excited as a child on Christmas morning. Despite what the priest had said, he had already convinced himself that it was his Sonja and Diana who were at the convent. Who else could it *be* seeking refuge? This was his lucky day, he was convinced of it. He thanked God for bringing him through the horrendous experiences of the previous weeks unscathed and also for keeping Sonja safe. Even though it was early evening, there was little traffic and the taxi moved relatively quickly but not half quick enough for him. When after ten minutes, they finally arrived at the convent, he jumped out of the taxi and paid the man, thanking him profusely and leaving him an over sized tip. It was only when the car disappeared around the corner that he realised he should have asked the man to wait but in his excitement it didn't matter; they could get another taxi.

The convent was a massive old building with long narrow stained glass windows at the upper levels. It was surrounded by a wall which was at least three metres high and appeared to be a metre thick. Certainly seems a safe place to hide he thought. He raced to the door and pulled the large old fashioned bell which was suspended from an overhead pulley. He heard a low chime echo somewhere in the building. After a few moments, the door opened a fraction and a voice said:
"Yes, can we help you?"
"I, I'm, I wish to speak to Sister Alina", he said, momentarily forgetting what Fr Gregor had said to him.
"I am Sister Alina", the voice behind the door said. "Who sent you?"
"Oh, sorry Sister, I should have said, it was Fr Gregor. My name is Drazen Itsakovic and I seek my family". The voice now turned pleasant.
"You must come in". The door was opened and a pretty young nun stood before him, dressed in full white habit with a blue cowl. She led him through a small courtyard, scrubbed spotlessly clean, into a room with a number of hard benches.

"Please wait here a moment", she said. Drazen could hardly contain himself. He was so excited; he thought his heart would burst out of his chest. He prayed constantly that he had reached the end of his search. After a few moments, the nun returned alone. His heart sank.

"I must ask you a question", she said. "The woman we have here is very sceptical. Do you have a photograph of her or of yourself with her that I can show her".

Drazen nearly stumbled in his efforts to take out the photos and give them to the nun. "Yes, yes, of course I have. Look, here and here, take them, take all of them".

The nun disappeared again through the door and Drazen heard muffled voices. Then he heard a shriek and the door opened and his beautiful wife burst through and ran the last few steps and fell into his arms, sobbing uncontrollably. They held each other like they never had before, both too numb to speak. Eventually, Sonja managed to mutter: "But how, I thought, I was sure, oh God forgive me, I was sure you were dead".

"Not now my darling, I will tell you all later; but Sonja, where is our little daughter?"

"It's OK; she's safe; she's with the sisters. I couldn't bring her with me. I feared it could not be you and didn't want to disappoint her but you will see her soon my love; oh, she will be so excited".

Sonja was still overcome with emotion, her body trembling, huge tears pouring down her beautiful cheeks. Drazen was smiling and crying at the same time. He was so incredibly happy and he hated to break the moment but he had to ask:

"And our boy, Zoran, what of him Sonja?"

She stopped shaking momentarily and froze. She looked deep into his eyes and saw the pleading, the hope against hope, the expectation. He returned her gaze and in that moment, he saw incredible pain, pain beyond what he could imagine. She could not speak but shook her head almost imperceptibly. It was almost like a shiver. Then she closed her eyes and buried her head in his chest for she had never before known such a bittersweet experience of pleasure and pain and she could not bear to look at him any longer.

Chapter 36

Dawn was breaking; watery grey and yellow tints streaked the darkness. They turned into increasingly clear, shadowy shapes; these in turn materialized into the familiar sights of buildings, trees, houses, parks and surrounding landscape. Then suddenly the shadows disappeared and the shapes became irrelevant; a small thin band of orange crept over the horizon. Drazen watched from the high window of the convent, mesmerized, as the band gradually increased in size and began to take shape. Within minutes, a complete orange disk was visible, changing colour even as he viewed it to a pale yellow. Then came the first hints of warmth, radiating on to his body, coming slowly at first, then building to a glorious heat. It was going to be another scorching day, he thought. He glanced around; the wetness of the night on the branches of the trees and the grass and the paths had already vanished, evaporated in the first rays of sunshine. It was already a glorious day and he was glad to be alive; glad that he had found his beloved Sonja and Diana. He could live again; he now had reason to hope and embrace life again. But just as his excitement reached fever pitch, the realization hit him like a hammer blow to his chest and it was as if the sun had not risen at all and he was still cloaked in darkness. For despite his search, he still had not found his beloved Zoran. He vowed there and then to search every corner of this land and others if necessary to find the one missing piece, the part that would put his world back together. He glanced over at the sleeping forms of his wife and daughter and he thanked God that at least three quarters of his little family were safe for now.

His thoughts were interrupted by a discreet knock at the door. Careful not to disturb Sonja or Diana, he tiptoed quickly and cracked the door a fraction. It was Sister Alina, who greeted him with a smile. It had been the nun who had suggested he stay the night at the convent. They had not seen any suspicious activity in its environs but in Drazen's haste to get there, he could not say for certain if he had been followed. The nuns were aware of the 'crime' for which Sonja was sought and they were serious about her protection and conscious that danger could lurk in any corner. In fact, Drazen had been in such ecstasy at discovering his family that he had been momentarily careless. He later scolded himself for being less aware than the sisters were. Sr. Alina now discreetly invited them to come for breakfast. A messenger was being sent to his father early that morning and his advice would be sought about the best way to exit the convent. Despite all of the barbarity that had taken place over the previous three years, they were fairly certain that the Serbs would not storm a Catholic convent. Even if they did, Drazen thought, they would need some serious artillery to breach these walls.

General Mistakovic and the other Bosnian Serb leaders had taken Sefer's advice and their own leader's orders and withdrawn from Tuzla. The triumphalism and celebration of the previous weeks was now replaced by a fear that the prize was going to be taken from them just as they reached the summit. Some of the leaders blamed the Americans and their N.A.T.O. allies but most, including Vladkovic, admitted to Milanovic that the massacres of civilians had probably played as big a part in inviting an attack as their swift and ruthless takeover of all key installations. But while there was a feeling that the ultimate victory that they sought was slipping away from them, most were intelligent enough to realise that they were probably never going to get away with evicting the Bosniaks from their own land and taking it over, lock, stock and barrel. No, only the Russians or perhaps the Americans got away with that one, the more cynical amongst them said. The more astute realised that they had made huge progress and won many important battles. Whatever the final outcome would be, Bosnian Serbs and the Republic of Srpska would be a key part of it. Oh, they'd be rapped on the knuckles for their brutality but there were now far fewer Bosniaks to raise a voice in protest and ultimately, the aggressors would be listened to. Spirits were lifting again as they neared Sarajevo. They controlled all of east Bosnia and a good part of the remainder of the country as well. Sarajevo had been under siege for three years and while the Bosniaks were still fighting back, one final concentrated push and it would be over. The Americans wouldn't dare to drop any smart bombs here; the civilian casualty rates could be horrendous. Yes, taking Sarajevo would leave them nicely poised, if and when the U.N. peacekeepers or the interfering foreigners ever came up with a plan.

Drazen first woke Diana, who rubbed her eyes, tried to force them open, then stretched and realizing where she was, jumped into her father's arms and held on for dear life. The little girl had been so overcome with excitement the previous evening that it had been well into the night before she got to sleep. She had insisted that her father hold her while she settled down to sleep and that he be there when she woke up. Drazen was as good as his word. He lifted Diana into his arms and carried her over to where Sonja was sleeping. If it had been after midnight before Diana had gotten to sleep, it was surely five in the morning before Sonja had managed to close her eyes. After the awful task of telling her husband that she had become separated from their son, she had calmed and together they had rekindled their hopes. Although Drazen had been told of her ordeal by his father, he listened while Sonja recounted her story. She had assumed that her husband was dead, buried in that mass grave in Srebrenica with his friends, his neighbours and of course his Grandfather. She had gone through her travails of the previous weeks on the assumption that she was alone, another widow of the conflict. Drazen hadn't wished to hurry her but he wanted to hear about Zoran and he wanted forensic detail. She eventually told him that things had been desperately confusing. All the men had been taken away and all the buses crowded with Bosnian women, children and the elderly. They had first made their way from Srebrenica to Potocari; they had been told nothing but rumour spread like wildfire and people believed they were headed for Sarajevo. Why this was, no one knew as Sarajevo was under siege. The awful truth about where some of them were headed was soon revealed. The buses had stopped in Potočari and yet more people had been crowded on board. They had then headed in the direction of Kladanj. The convoy of buses was stopped at Tišća village; all occupants were ordered out and the vehicles were searched again. Some Bosnian men and older boys were found on board and were removed from the bus. It was Zoran's misfortune that he looked a little older than his thirteen years and he actually looked of similar age to some of the older boys discovered in hiding. The senior Bosnian Serb officer had then ordered the women and children to get back on board the bus and had told them they were all lucky not to have been shot, given their harbouring of fugitives. As they were boarding, the officer had selected Zoran and ordered him to go with the fugitives. Sonja had clung to her son and had shrieked that he was only a young boy; the Serb officer had calmly put his pistol to Sonja's head and told her that she would either release the boy or they would all be shot. Zoran stood tall, kissed his Mother and told her he would be fine and joined the men being held at gunpoint.

Drazen had hung his head at that point as his father had told him that he had heard intelligence reports that Tisca had been one of the key filtering points for Bosniak refugees being ethnically cleansed. It was here that the Serbs had routed all transport convoys; they had operated a strict women and small children only policy and enforced it rigidly. The operation was well-organised; prisoners taken from convoys were informed that they were merely being detained and all were initially transported by truck to a local school which had been fortified for the purpose. But when the school was filled, the prisoners were told that they were being transferred to more permanent accommodation. They were loaded on board other trucks and brought deep into the forest, usually at night and shot dead. Mass graves had been prepared and the whole operation had been carried out in secret. Drazen's only hope was that the story was only rumour; there were no eye witness reports; on the other hand, no witnesses suggested a well organised operation; it also suggested no one had ever escaped. Sonja had held him then, cradling his head in her arms while he wept as the awful realisation sunk in. But she refused to abandon hope; their son was resourceful beyond his years; after all, she had believed, she had been absolutely certain that her husband was dead but here he was in her arms. Believing that her son might have survived was entirely feasible.

He stood over her, watching her now and she instinctively opened her eyes. All three of them held each other tightly for what seemed like a long time. Eventually, Drazen had to tell them Sr. Alina wanted them to come for breakfast. They would be leaving the convent today and although her husband had been miraculously returned to her, Sonja knew that the day would still hold many dangers. Drazen wanted to evacuate his wife and daughter from Sarajevo as soon as possible. His idea was to fly them to safety in Croatia, using the same route he had come in on, until the war ended; Sonja was wanted by the Serbs for a serious crime and it was too dangerous for her to remain in the city, never mind the country. Drazen had promised his father he would join the resistance as soon as he could and would fight to free the city. But Sonja wouldn't hear of leaving. She was staying with her husband and that was that. She wasn't going to be ethnically cleansed; driven out of her own country by thugs. They had argued long into the night about it but had not reached a resolution. They had eventually fallen asleep, exhausted. This morning, he decided he would not mention it, lest there be any noticeable tension evident to little Diana. She had just gotten her father back, Sonja had argued; the last thing she needed was for him to disappear again. Resistance or not, surely he had suffered enough; done enough for the war effort with his struggles over the previous weeks. Drazen reflected that he hadn't even told her half of what had happened him. There had been no mention of their Serbian neighbour or of his killing of the traitor in the forest. She had been through enough herself he thought; better keep his own stories for another time.

Sr. Alina served them their breakfast. It was basic fare; coffee, black bread and eggs with some juice for Diana. Although there were reputedly over a dozen nuns in the convent, they were a closed order and Drazen had seen no one apart from Alina. He thanked her profusely again and offered to pay for the food and shelter but she refused. If he wished to make a donation to the convent, he could do so at a later date, she said. For now, best to keep his meagre resources for what awaited them in the outside world, she advised. Although he was deliriously happy to have been reunited with his family, he had this overriding feeling that he shouldn't be there. He needed to be up and out and away. He needed to search this country from top to bottom all over again to try to find his son. Even if his search was fruitless, he had to do it; he needed to do something to allay the pain. He was restless, anxious to move and Sonja sensed it in him and understood.

The convent bell chimed once, causing all of them to jump briefly. Sr. Alina went to the outer doorway and returned a few moments later with two men who were known to Drazen as two of his father's best lieutenants. Transport had been organised and three other men were waiting. Danvor was taking no chances. Sonja went to collect their few belongings and rushed back. Both she and Diana hugged Alina and thanked her profusely. Tearful goodbyes were said. They made their way through the doorway where two more men, heavily armed, stood watching the surrounding area. One of the men passed a set of documents to Drazen. His father had followed his advice and had had documents prepared to allow Sonja and Diana leave Sarajevo that morning. They would stay with trusted friends of his in Zagreb until it was safe to return. Drazen anticipated protests from his wife so he just nodded his thanks to the man and said nothing. They all climbed on board the minivan which was equipped with blacked out windows in the back. All five armed men, including the driver, came with them.

The bright early morning sun had surprisingly given way to more unseasonal cooler weather and there was almost an autumnal feel to the air. Dark clouds blocked out the sun and a breeze was coming in from the east. Before long, the first drops of rain appeared on the windshield and as they made progress through the city, it grew to a steady downpour. The windows began to mist up but if anything, it provided more cover and they were unworried as they transited the pock marked and devastated metropolis. The driver had been told which route to take and was staying to back streets where there was little traffic and no official vehicles. It was Sonja's first venture back into the outside world since her sojourn in the convent and while she was not nervous, there was always a tension in the air and there would be until she was either safe or the conflict was over. The drive took them close to the city's outskirts and they even caught occasional glimpses of the Bosnian Serb gun emplacements in the hills. The driver assured them that they were quite safe though; the Serbs were only interested in shelling the centre or the parts they hadn't as yet driven the citizens out of. The area they were driving in seemed devoid of any form of life. Empty blackened apartment blocks bearing silent witness to a terrorised population, for whom clinging to life was more important than continuing to live in an area where they would be systematically picked off or eliminated by the ceaseless pounding of enemy artillery.

The American smart bomb caught all of them by complete surprise. The last thing they had expected was to be derailed by friendly fire. The bomb scored a direct hit on a Serbian stronghold immediately above their position but the blast devastated the entire area. The shockwave lifted the minivan clean off the road and tossed it like a toy into a small hollow that ran alongside. Then a mountain of debris which had been thrown hundreds of feet into the air, rained down upon them. When it eventually subsided, the overwhelming sensation was the silence. There was no return fire; this was not a battle in the conventional sense. The Serbian guns on the hillside had no target to attack; no enemy to zoom in on; no way to defend themselves against this type of attack.

The minivan lay on its side at the bottom of the hollow. It was partially covered by the debris that had come from the hillside. Drazen was the first to regain consciousness. Sonja was trapped between the rear seats and he immediately started towards her to try to set her free. She recovered consciousness quickly. She had some cuts and bruises but was physically fine apart from being badly shaken. Diana had been thrown forward and was lying across the divide between the front seats. Drazen noticed that the driver's head appeared to have caved in and he seemed to be dead, having taken the brunt of the force when the minivan had landed on its side. Diana was completely unmarked but was she hurt? They struggled through the wrecked vehicle to free her. She was unconscious but they thanked God she was still breathing. Two of the men had been thrown free of the vehicle and Drazen noticed them gingerly getting to their feet. Another soldier, who had been sitting directly behind the driver also seemed to be dead. He quickly checked both men for a pulse but found none. Would this nightmare ever end, he thought. All of the doors had been jammed shut but as all of the glass had been shattered, they easily exited the vehicle. Diana was still unconscious and he gently lifted her from the vehicle lest it catch fire and delicately laid her on a patch of grass. She seemed to be breathing normally and to be merely concusssed but they couldn't aford to take chances. Their escorts had fared far worse than they had and Sonja again felt guilty. These men had risked their lives to escort them to safety and now two of them were dead, killed ironically not by the enemy but by well meaning foreigners who were trying to free the Bosniaks by breaking the stranglehold on Sarajevo. But it was her and her family's fault, she thought; it was her they had been escorting. The fifth soldier lay unconscious where he had been thrown from the vehicle. He had head injuries and needed urgent medical attention. One of the others had a broken arm and his colleague was limping badly, also in need of attention.

Although Sonja's first instinct was to run to safeguard her child, she found she could not abandon these men. She also didn't want to move Diana lest she had suffered internal injuries. The district they were in seemed deserted; devoid of life; a complete absence of people or vehicles.

Contact with Danvor was out of the question; they would just have to take their chances. Sonja left Drazen to take care of Diana and she ran; through the empty streets; across long abandoned junctions with non-functioning traffic lights. She ran to where she thought the city was still functioning, hoping, praying she would see someone, anyone who could help them. She passed shops, schools, public buildings, parks, playgrounds, all abandoned, all part of some ghostly world but none of them occupied by the living. She thought she saw a church in the distance, one that hadn't been hit, one that still looked in good condition. She ran in that direction. In the distance, she heard a sound, a vehicle, could it be? She stopped, breathless, her chest heaving. The sound grew louder; it was coming her way. Then it entered the other end of the street she was standing on. It was a taxi; she sighed with relief and wandered into the roadway, her right arm raised to signal the vehicle to stop. The car was an old Lada, rusted through but still functioning. It slowed as it approached and made its way to the kerb. There were two men in the vehicle. Sonja made her way to the nearside window as the passenger rolled it down.

"Please", she said, "can you come? My family are hurt; they've been in a car accident"
The passenger eyed her curiously and the driver immediately stepped out of his side of the vehicle.
"Well well Mihail", said the driver, "it looks like our lucky day".
Sonja blinked, confused, then took in the two men again and looked at the vehicle. She had just made a dreadful mistake. It wasn't a taxi, it was an old police car, with the roof sign battered and weather beaten. Too late she

realised her mistake; the passenger was already out of the car and grabbed her; his colleague quickly coming to his aid and they bundled the struggling woman into the rear seat.

"So this is the little bitch half the country is looking for", the driver said.

"Yep, sure looks like it", said the passenger. "I can see a serious promotion coming up for you and me Filip".

"Indeed Mihail, but first we have a little fun with her, eh?"

"Lots of places around here where we can do that, why not? It'll be nothing to what will happen to her when she gets taken into custody, so we might as well take our share now".

The man called Filip took the wheel and his colleague sat into the back with Sonja. He grabbed her roughly, twisted her hands behind her back and slapped a pair of steel handcuffs on her wrists, tight enough to almost cut into her skin.

"That'll keep the bitch quiet for now", he said. "Drive on Filip".

Sonja wanted to scream, to fight, to rage against her bonds, against her hard luck, against herself for being so stupid but no sound came from her lips. She knew it was over; this was the end. She sank down into the seat and plumbed the absolute depths of despair.

Chapter 37

The policeman was correct; there were hundreds of abandoned buildings which would have suited their purpose but Filip knew a perfect place. He drove just a few hundred metres and pulled into the parking lot of a derelict apartment block. He parked the car under an awning around the back where it was completely hidden from view. His colleague Mihail bundled Sonja out of the car and roughly forced her across the cracked and rubbish strewn concrete path. They entered the block and climbed four flights to the second floor. The all pervasive smell of dampness, urine and decay invaded every crevice here also. It was a depressing place. Filip pushed the door into a flat that looked somewhat better maintained than the norm. He looked around briefly, checking that the area had not been disturbed.

"All clear Mihail", he said, "bring the bitch in here".

On closer inspection, the apartment was like a thousand others, seemingly abandoned in haste, with the floor strewn with old clothes and bric-a-brac that the former occupants had presumably deemed worthless or at least not valuable enough to go to the bother of taking with them in their haste to reach safety. There was still some furniture in the apartment including a table and chairs and what appeared to be a serviceable bed.

"So this is your little love room you've told me about", Mihail said, with a laugh.

"Oh yes buddy, no one will disturb us here and as the windows seem to have miraculously survived, no one will hear the little lady either".

"Windows or not, I think she could scream for Bosnia if she likes but no one will hear her in this district. Even if they did, they'd be too cowardly to come near us".

Sonja was pushed into the bedroom and thrown down on the bed and Filip went and locked the outer door of the apartment, pocketing the key.

"Let's relax a while buddy", he said, extracting a flask of slivovitz from his tunic. "This will add to our enjoyment".

Both men drank deeply from the flask and then had a mock argument about who would go first.

"But it was I who recognised her", said Mihail.

"Right, but I'm more senior and anyway, I found the flat", Filip retorted.

Both men laughed loudly and lustily and took another swig from the flask.

"Here, finish it off my friend and let's get started, I'm as horny as fuck", said Mihail, unbuckling his belt.

Sonja had rolled herself into a ball on the bed, trying to make herself invisible. But there was no door between the living room and the bedroom and the men watched her closely. She blamed herself for her plight; how could she have been so careless, so stupid. A thousand thoughts flooded her brain; her poor Diana, was she badly hurt? Did she need medical attention? Would she survive? Would Sonja ever know? She tried to calm herself and to think straight. The break while the two men drank gave her some hope. Damn it, she had come this far, was she going to let two rookie policemen beat her? Disgusted as she felt, she steeled herself and resolved to try. She would never defeat two grown men physically so she would have to use guile and possibly every other method she could think of to escape this. Even if it involved having sex with both of them, she'd suffer it, if she could just hang on that bit longer. She was convinced they would not kill her; she was a wanted fugitive and every senior Bosnian Serb commander in the country wanted to get his hands on her. No, these were junior policemen and their bosses would want them to keep her alive for her show trial. This at least gave her some peace of mind. Even if she failed, they couldn't kill her. She hardened her resolve.

Both men came into the bedroom. They had both removed their uniform trousers and underwear and both were fully erect. Sonja immediately felt deep fear and loathing and disgust as the leers of the men made it quite certain what was about to happen to her. Filip grabbed her roughly and tried to tear off her top, but she rolled away from him and he stumbled over the edge of the bed, laughing hysterically. Mihail pulled at her then and slapped her roughly across the face. Sonja's initial impulse was to spit in his face and scream curses at him; she had no idea where she found the strength from or where the words came from but she suddenly heard a voice which sounded like her own saying:

"Look, if I have to do this, let's make it easy on all of us. You don't want to go back to your wives or girlfriends with bites or scratches and I don't want to get beaten up. You'll never get all my clothes off with these handcuffs anyway so if you use your heads and take them off, maybe we can all be civil to each other?"

"Ah ha", said Mihail, "the bitch wants to be fucked, where are those keys?"

"They're on the kitchen table", Filip said, "but be careful, remember this bitch has killed before, she's a wanted murderess".

"Ah, she killed with a knife buddy, but she has no knife today. And we won't lie down and let her massage us like that idiot in the camp. We'll also make damn sure she's not concealing anything too"

Mihail went to get the keys and quickly released Sonja's wrists.

"Thank you", she said and she stretched her arms to restore her circulation. She then began to undress slowly as the two men watched in fascination. She placed her clothes in a neat pile and then sat forward on the bed. Mihail, true to his word, checked to ensure she wasn't concealing a knife or any other weapon.

"OK", he said, "let's see how good she is when she has no knife and there's two strong Serbs fucking her".

Sonja again fought an urge which was screaming from her senses to lash out in rage. But she overcame it and just sat there quietly, seemingly defeated by superior forces. She shook her head and shrugged.

"OK buddy, you're first, go for it", Mihail said.

Filip was closest to Sonja anyway and he immediately pushed his penis into her face. She touched his manhood and began to caress his balls and lower groin area. The man moaned with pleasure.

"Oh yes, maybe she's not a bad bitch after all. Oh yes, ah lovely, this is gonna be the best ever", he said.

Sonja looked to where Mihail was standing, breathing heavily.

"Come here", she said, forcing a smile. "You don't want to be left out. Why don't both of you take me at the same time? I'll just kneel up on the bed and you come around behind me".

Mihail looked to his colleague for approval and the other man nodded eagerly. They couldn't believe their luck. Sonja continued massaging Filip and she felt rather than saw Mihail roughly approaching her from behind, fumbling to separate her legs. She knew she would only have one chance at this and she tried to free her mind of all other thoughts, desperately trying to ignore the vile acts that these perverts were trying to inflict on her. She could not see the man behind her so she tried to picture where precisely he was, judging from his fumbling movements.

As he was just about to penetrate her, she reacted. With her right foot, she lashed out viciously at the man behind her, catching him square in the groin. Simultaneously, she squeezed Filip's testicles with every ounce of strength she could muster until she was sure she had mashed them to a pulp. The man screamed so loudly, it sounded like a banshee's wail and he collapsed against the wall of the apartment in utter agony. She heard Mihail, the man behind her, grunt in pain but she didn't wait to see him doubled over either. Both men had been taken totally by surprise. They had made the fatal mistake of under estimating a woman alone against two men. They had also failed to spot that when Sonja had taken off her clothing, she had kept her stout shoes on. She was instantly on her feet and away to the living room, where she had previously noticed both men had left their guns in their holsters. She had imagined having to grasp one of the pistols and trying to figure out how to fire it while being chased but no one followed her to the living room. She had obviously scored two direct hits as both men still lay gasping on the floor of the bedroom.

She grabbed the first pistol, released the safety catch and dashed back to the bedroom, where Mihail was just struggling to his feet. Filip was still lying against the wall and he had gone deathly pale. She pointed the gun at Mihail who looked like he was about to charge at her. "Don't move a fucking muscle, you sick bastard, or I'll blow your balls all the fucking way to Belgrade", she said. The man cowered and placed his hands on his head. "Don't think I won't shoot because I fucking will, and don't even think about trying to attack me or about following me. Count yourselves lucky that I don't shoot you down like the filthy dogs that you are. If you leave this building within the next two hours, I'll make sure there is someone waiting outside to gun you down. Now, take off the rest of your clothes and I mean everything"

Mihail quickly pulled off his shirt and threw it in her direction. Filip had made no move so she fired the gun into the partition above his head. The noise in the small room was deafening. The man jumped and immediately obeyed. Sonja was still naked but she did not allow it to interfere with her concentration. She next ordered Mihail to place the handcuffs he had removed from her on to his colleagues wrists. Without ever taking her eyes off him, she then backed into the sitting room where she took the other handcuffs from Filip's belt. She returned to the bedroom, stuck the pistol into Mihail's ear and ordered him to place his hands behind his back. He did so without question, shaking violently as he pleaded with her not to shoot. With both men handcuffed, she then kicked Mihail in the kidneys, sending him sprawling across the bed where he landed on top of his colleague.

She then calmly laid the gun on a chair and dressed herself quickly. She took both sets of men's clothes and bundled them together on the kitchen table. She tied them together with one of the belts and jammed the spare pistol into the middle of the bundle. She found the car keys in one of the pockets and took them together with the policemen's wallets and identity cards. She gave a wry smile when she momentarily saw a picture of what would happen to these two once their superior officer learned of their fate; handcuffed naked in an abandoned building; weapons and uniforms and identities stolen and best of all, vehicle missing. She doubted they'd be having long careers in the

Bosnian Serb police force. Before she left, she ventured back into the bedroom. Some of the colour had returned to Filip's cheeks but he began to pale again as she approached. She selected him first, placing one pistol to his temple and the other to his balls:
"So this is your little love room, is it?" she said. No response. She pushed the pistol viciously into his groin and the man again shrieked in pain.
"Yes, yes, but it's just an empty flat, I don't own it", he said.
"And have you defiled other girls in here? Be careful with your answer".
"No, no, I swear it, no, it's just a room I use to bring girlfriends. They come here voluntarily, on my Mother's life I swear it".
She next moved to Mihail and repeated the procedure:
"And how about you, you sick prick", she said, viciously.
"No, no, not me, I swear. I've never even been in this room until today".
"OK", she said. "I'm leaving now. Count yourselves lucky to be still alive. If my husband was here, he would have shot you down like dogs. Remember what I said about the two hours. Remember also that I have both of your I.D.'s. I also have your passports. I know your addresses. I know where you both live. If I ever hear of either of you being involved in any type of an assault on a woman, ever again, I will visit you when you least expect it and I'll cut your balls off. Do you understand?"
Both men assured her profusely and repeatedly that they did.

She then unlocked the apartment and left with the large bundle under her arm. She even took their shoes and socks and underwear. She locked the door as she left but the lock was not a strong one so she figured the men would beat it open eventually. It might take them an hour. She didn't for an instant think they would wait for the two hours she had specified. Once she had left, one would spark off the other. Anger would replace fear. Next would come false courage or bravado and they would outdo each other vowing to get out of the place and get after the bitch. They would surely know that she wasn't going to hang around waiting for them downstairs. Quite how they were going to chase after her stark naked and handcuffed, she didn't even bother to speculate but as the image formed in her mind, she almost smiled. She reached the car and dumped all of her booty on to the rear seat. She quickly unlocked the vehicle, sat in and started it up. Both men had left their radios sitting in chargers on the dash and there was a constant squawking from them. An insistent voice kept asking them to respond and confirm their location. If the man requesting the information was annoyed right now, he would be furious later, she thought.

She started the car and spun it round, back in the direction she had come. It only took her a few minutes to make it back to where the little group was huddled together. She could read the initial looks of confusion and panic on the faces as they saw the police car, then the relief when they realised it was Sonja at the wheel. She screeched to a halt and jumped out. Drazen came round and said:
"What took so long? Where did you get the car? Are you OK?"
"It's a long story my darling", she said as she sighed with relief and once more collapsed into his arms. Over his shoulder, she saw that Diana was sitting up and chatting to

one of the injured men. All of them looked pale but seemed to be over the initial shock of the explosion and crash. All had received or carried out some sort of makeshift attention to their injuries. One man had his arm in a sling and another had made a crutch from a plank of wood. Diana lay where they had left her but she had recovered consciousness. Drazen held Sonja tightly. He knew she must have been involved in some sort of incident as she was shaking a lot more than she had been following the explosion. He decided now was the time. He sat her down on the front bonnet of the car and looked into her eyes:

"Sonya, don't be upset but I think Diana has a broken femur. There is no way I am entrusting her care to a hospital in Sarajevo. The hospitals are as likely to be shelled as anywhere else. Also, these men urgently need medical attention. One has a broken leg and another has a broken arm. I think my father will be able to get them a Doctor but Diana needs a specialist. We have to take her to Croatia. If we hurry, we might still make that flight that my father arranged for us. I will have to travel with you because Diana will need to be carried lest she be further injured".

"It's OK my love", Sonja said. "No arguments. Forget what I said before. I'm leaving this country with my daughter and I'm not coming back until this madness is over".

Even though they had once again been placed in danger, Drazen was surprised at how easily Sonja had agreed to leave. When he would hear what she had had to go through to get here, he'd understand.

"OK", Sonja said, "Drazen and I think Rufad, you two look like those uniforms on the back seat will fit you best. Can you put on yours with your injured arm Rufad?" The man assured her he could. Sonja immediately took charge. "Right, Drazen, you drive. Rufad, you take the passenger's seat. The rest of us can squeeze into the rear and place Diana across our laps. It's not an ambulance and it's not perfect but I vote we go for it. Don't worry about the former occupants of the car. They won't need it any time soon. Let's first get to the airport and try to catch that flight. After that, one of the others can take the uniform and rendezvous with Danvor's people".

All of the men nodded eagerly and together they climbed on board and gently placed Diana in the rear. Even though the little girl was in pain, she bravely shrugged it off and was quiet. The poor girl had learned a lot in the past few weeks, Drazen thought. He started up the Lada and they continued on their journey, with Rufad guiding him on the best route. Sitting in the middle of the rear seat, Sonja said, "I think it's best if we take the main roads. After all, this is a police car. You are both dressed as policemen and you have guns and ID's. You are Serbian policemen escorting some citizens who were injured in that cowardly American air strike this morning to a hospital. If you encounter any trouble, step on it and use the siren".

Chapter 38

Sefer thought it ironic that as the Bosnian Serb momentum began to slow and the euphoria of the earlier victories began to fade, his stock rose ever higher, particularly with the middle and lower ranks. Gone were the suspicion, mistrust and even hostility of the previous weeks. He was now seen as the wise head from Belgrade, trying to curb the excesses of leaders who time had proven to have been more lucky than skilled and who were really men of straw, or in some cases, outright idiots. Lieutenant Vladkovic, who had initially been his bitter adversary, was now his constant companion and confidante. It was as if Ivan was trying to distance himself from his own senior officers, whom he now openly questioned and criticized and sometimes disdained. It may have also been delayed shock at the enormity of what they had done, the sheer savagery and bloodletting. Perhaps people like Ivan did have a conscience and were now having pangs of remorse. Sefer had seen similar reactions before. He had been a keen student of warfare and military tactics and of course he also knew his history. There was a strong parallel with Nazi Germany here; the, 'we were only carrying out orders' excuse. It may well have been true in many cases, Sefer couldn't say for definite, yet he had seen sheer naked hatred in the eyes of the officers and the men as they went about their bloody task. Then again, even that could be explained away also. He had seen at first hand the horrendous bestiality of the Croatian war and he was aware that Bosniaks had also carried out some appalling atrocities against Serbs and Croats. Revenge killings followed more revenge killings in a never ending cycle. Was this was just a pause or maybe all sides were tired of the bloodletting and massacre that had become a daily feature of life in this corner of Europe? He certainly hoped so.

They had been camped on the outskirts of Sarajevo now for three days and contrary to the initial belief that one major push would see them take the city, it seemed that they would either have to totally reconsider their strategy or else dig in for a longer campaign. Autumn was in the air and he was not looking forward to a winter up here in the hills. The basic problem was that the Americans or N.A.T.O. or whoever were watching their every move. Whenever they tried to launch an attack or mount an offensive, the Americans launched air strikes. Most of these were precisely targeted and dropped from aircraft very high above the Serb positions. They did have air defences and surface-to-air missiles but reconnaissance was poor and by the time they got to fire their S.A.M. missiles, the bombers had usually turned and were out of range. They had succeeded in shooting down an American jet but the pilot had bailed out and had been rescued by Bosniaks. There was a rumour that a French jet had been shot down the day before but it was unconfirmed. They had some of their own aircraft but in terms of an air war, there was just no point in the Serbs even trying to take on the might of N.A.T.O.

His lodgings weren't half as comfortable as he had been used to previously but it didn't bother him. The commanders were based in an appropriated house set five kilometres back from the entrenched Serb positions in the hills above Sarajevo.
"What's your accommodation like?" said Ivan, as they downed their second beer of the evening. They had managed to find a comfortable bar run by Serbs which was in a secure area and safe from attack so all of the senior officers had repaired there this evening.
"Oh it's basic but fine for me, I don't need much", Sefer replied
"Mine is pure shit, filthy and smelly", Ivan replied and then laughed, "I suppose it's a lot better than what those

poor fuckers on the front line have got, not to speak of the ones they're dropping shells on".
"Why the sudden concern for your enemies?"
"Oh no, I'm not concerned; war is war but don't you sometimes wonder at the pointlessness of it; the suffering and the bloodshed?
Perhaps he *was* developing a conscience, Sefer thought.
"I have seen a lot of wars and a lot of different armed conflicts Ivan and I have never seen one which ultimately was worth a fraction of the suffering it caused or the death and destruction it wreaked, so yes, to answer your question, I do wonder about it all the time".
"But you are a military strategist, you advise on the best course of action to be taken in a war situation. How can you think like that?"
Sefer smiled. "Just because I am a military strategist, it doesn't mean that I always recommend military intervention. Most times I don't. In this conflict, it was already under way for many months when I was assigned here. If a war is already on, the best you can do is advise your allies of the best way to win it. To recommend a cease fire would be beyond my remit in that instance".
"I see, yet you strongly recommended leniency in our campaign to get rid of the Bosniaks; is that not a recommendation to cease fire?"
"Not at all; Ivan, my friend, let me tell you a few things. First of all, I am a peace loving man. I am sure that you are too; perhaps deep down, all of us are. I am also a rational person. I realize some conflicts are unavoidable and I realize countries and peoples need to be strong and able to defend themselves. This usually involves violence of some form or another but violence should never be used gratuitously or in a pointless way. If you wanted to

relocate the Bosniaks to another part of the country, there was no reason why it could not be done. Oh, they would hate it and they would resist but by killing large numbers of them, you just make the remainder hate you more and far, far worse, you put the international community in a position where they are forced to intervene against you".

"But there were killings and murders of civilians on both sides", Ivan said.

"I am quite sure you are correct but not on the scale of Srebrenica. You see, if this was fifty years ago, you might have gotten away with it but not today. There are reporters and T.V. cameras everywhere. There are also satellites all around us, monitoring our every move. I don't doubt that many of your colleagues have shown bravery in this war and many have given their lives for the cause but I feel your leadership has not been wise and has gotten you into a situation which will be damn difficult to get out of".

Vladkovic drank deeply and thirstily from his beer and said:

"You know, I think you are correct Colonel. The more I've seen of our senior commanders, the more I think they are fucking idiots. Pumped up little war lords commanding their own little armies, the only thing they have in common a hatred of Bosniaks. Most of all, I blame that idiot Mladic. You know it was he who gave the order to liquidate Srebrenica?"

Sefer nodded and Ivan continued:

"I was caught up in the glory of it; we were all pumped up. We were told the only good Bosniak is a dead Bosniak. They had to be eliminated in order for us to assert ourselves. But you are correct Colonel; we could never ever kill all of them. And the surviving ones and their children and their children's children will hate us forever. How many Jews did the Nazis kill? Six million? It was supposed to be the final solution; yet Israel is stronger than ever today and the Jews are still everywhere and still powerful".

"Indeed", Sefer spoke gently, "only last year, the Hutus in Rwanda set out to finally eradicate the minority Tutsi tribe. They slaughtered almost a million before the international community intervened. Then most of the participants had to flee the country as refugees for fear of reprisals. I am afraid my friend that we repeat the mistakes of history over and over again. These days and this time specifically, we do it in the full glare of the international press".

Their evening was interrupted by several loud explosions. Even though they were five kilometres from the front, the entire building shook and the blasts were loud even at this distance. Vladkovic eyed the Colonel in alarm.
"More air strikes?"
"I would guess so. I think we are now in a stalemate situation. Every time our forces launch an attack, the Americans launch an air strike from wherever that attack originated from. We must have tried a few night-time launches to see if we could get away with them. Obviously the Americans were paying attention".
"Why wouldn't they with their fucking satellites and air support?"
"Yes, but do you appreciate where we are in this? They don't want to fight us or outright defeat us. They just want to stop us from advancing any further. For that, perhaps we should be thankful. Shall we finish our beers and go see if any of our colleagues need our assistance?"

Vladkovic initially looked startled but readily agreed. It wasn't that he was a coward, far from it but he would have felt it beneath a senior officer to assist the wounded in a battle situation. Sefer had no such qualms. He had seen too much suffering; a wounded soldier was a wounded soldier and by the sound of things, there might be a fair few hurt this evening. He reckoned that was the fiftieth air strike on the Bosnian Serb positions around Sarajevo since they had arrived. There had been many hundreds more on Serb positions elsewhere in the country too. Surprisingly, there had been relatively little loss of life. Obviously the satellites were doing their work efficiently and pinpointing where the arms dumps and artillery positions were. Nonetheless, they had lost over two hundred men here alone and that figure would rise. Field hospitals were poor and many had died from lack of expert medical attention. They sat in the jeep now, the Lieutenant driving slowly towards the front, with his lights off.
"I think you can use the lights Ivan", Milanovic said. "There are no Bosniaks up here and the Americans are not interested in a lone jeep".
The younger man was slightly embarrassed; he flicked the light switch and the twin beams lit up the gravel path ahead of them. He paused momentarily as they hit the asphalt road but there was no traffic. In the distance they could see fires in every direction but they appeared in the main to be small; the fires backlit the vista of the night-time Sarajevo below them.

"I'm sure it must be a wonderful view in peace time", Sefer said. Vladkovic shrugged:

"Too bad for us Colonel. But, you were saying back in the bar that we were being forced into a corner. So where do we go from here?"

Sefer took out his pack of cigarettes and lit two, giving one to the Lieutenant. He inhaled deeply and looked at the younger man but said nothing. He could see the Lieutenant working it out for himself.

"So are you saying they are forcing us into a cease fire?"

"With any luck, yes. I think that's the best outcome we can hope for right now, don't you Lieutenant? I mean, you don't get to take over the entire country but surely you never expected that anyway? As you said yourself, no matter how many Bosniaks you kill or displace, there will always be many more who will still want to live here and will fight you for it. I think that on balance, you are in a very good position. They won't let you keep it all of course but for now, the fact that you control most of the country gives you strength. Better to have it and cease fire now than to lose some of it as the Bosniaks get stronger and remember they now have the Americans to take us out as they please".

"You make a convincing argument Colonel", Vladkovic replied. "But I fear many of our leaders are so caught up in the success we have had so far that they see the few setbacks as just a blip; they will want to press forward, first chance we get. I mean, you have heard their rhetoric and bullshit each morning about the glory of our cause and the justness of our victory".

"Yes, I appreciate that many of them do Ivan but with the greatest respect, I would suggest that if they wish to fight on against a combination of the Bosniaks, Croats and half of N.A.T.O., then they are stupid beyond belief. What's

the phrase Lieutenant, better to quit while you are ahead, eh?"
"I agree Colonel, you are definitely correct, but how will we convince the others?" "I intend to make the argument I just made to you at the briefing meeting tomorrow morning. I have already communicated my intentions to Belgrade and they are one hundred per cent behind me. They have come under enormous pressure over the past few weeks, both from our allies and our enemies".

They arrived at the site of the first air strike. It was at one of the strongest positions they had held, commanding a view over at least half of the city. The Bosnian Serbs had been happily lobbing shells from here down into the city for the best part of three years. The gun emplacements were unapproachable from the front as it was a sheer cliff face and the defences were virtually impregnable from the rear. The artillery was actually mounted on a small rise which sat atop the hill and was easily protected, from ground forces that is. The scene of devastation that greeted the two men was far worse than they had imagined and many times stronger than previous attacks. At first glance, Sefer thought the Americans must have used several bombs but the more he viewed the area, there appeared to have only been one explosion, albeit massive. The entire area was still lit up by fires which were burning in every direction, some fiercely and some steadily dying away. The entire rise or hill where the armed position had stood had disappeared; the topography of the area had been totally rearranged. Trees and shrubs had been pounded into matchwood. Rocks had been mashed into gravel or vaporized. The few soldiers that were present just stood there, staring in awe. Milanovic enquired as to casualties but the officer he had addressed just shook his head and told him there was nothing left. Anyone within half a kilometre of the area had been blown to pieces. The guns had not been active so there had just been a skeleton crew of four men on the hill. Whether there had been any more in the vicinity, he could not say. There certainly were no wounded or dying men. There was just silence.

"It appears as if the enemy's bombs are getting ever larger", Ivan said. Sefer raised his eyebrows.
"Yes Lieutenant, I must admit I have never seen devastation on such a scale. I have heard they have new Maverick missiles but this appears to be one of their Tomahawk Cruise. It certainly seems as if they want to send us a message because as far as I know, these things cost about five million dollars each".
The officer Milanovic had spoken to told them that there had been five smaller missiles targeted at key positions to the south and west of where they stood. The bombs had been smaller but the damage they had caused had again been very serious. Sefer lit another cigarette and surveyed the scene.
"I think Ivan, the best place to hold the strategy meeting in the morning is right here". The Lieutenant nodded.
"It would certainly bolster your argument Colonel. God alone knows what this place will look like in the light of day".
"If this doesn't convince them to stop, nothing will but nonetheless it will be difficult to convince some of the hawks to stand down. Then if they agree to a cease fire here, we have to persuade them to talk to their colleagues elsewhere and convince them it is pointless to continue". The Lieutenant smiled and touched Sefer on the shoulder.

"You know Colonel, I think you may get your chance to convince them all by yourself. I heard a rumour this evening that General Mladic himself will attend our meeting in the morning".

Chapter 39

The tension ahead of the meeting was palpable. Word had come through over night that the death toll from the multiple air strikes had exceeded one hundred men but Milanovic very much doubted if this was the reason why the commanders were so exercised this morning. Most of the Bosnian Serb Generals and Colonels and Lieutenants were present and additional chairs had to be obtained to accommodate everyone. General Mistakovic was trying to calm the group and maintain some discipline. But speculation was rife and the officers kept breaking into little caucuses and sub-groups. Although the meeting wasn't due to start until eight thirty, Sefer had arrived with cup of coffee in hand at eight. He was shocked to discover most of the chairs already occupied. Vladkovic was already seated and they nodded to each other. Any hope they had held of having the meeting out doors near the main bomb site had evaporated with the rumour of Mladic's attendance. Even at this high level, the military leader's whereabouts could not be confirmed nor could the time of his arrival nor could it even be confirmed that he would attend. It seemed overly fussy and cautious to Milanovic. Granted, there was a war on but there was no possibility that the Bosnian Serbs had been infiltrated; given what they had been through, the very idea was preposterous. No, Sefer was convinced that it was due to Mladic' need to make an impression; a grand entrance to show everyone how important he was. Sefer had seen his like before in the Croatian war and in other skirmishes where he had been involved. The real leader will inspire his men, entering and exiting quietly and without fuss; he will lead by example and will earn his respect from his expertise and his reputation, not from his title. The Mladic's of this world were the opposite. He had only met the man once but had been struck by the man's vanity and giant ego.

The room was now crammed as everyone seemed to want to either see the great leader or, perhaps more aptly, to be seen. Commanders were still entering and there was no more space for chairs. Mistakovic called for order. "Gentlemen, gentlemen, can we have some attention please. We need to concentrate and to be businesslike for our esteemed visitor. I am sorry but can I ask that everyone below the rank of Colonel withdraw? We really cannot accommodate everyone. I assure you, everyone will be briefed immediately afterwards".
The meeting again descended into chaos. Sefer raised his eyebrows and whispered something into Ivan's ear. The Lieutenant stood.
"General Mistakovic, sir", he said: "I understand your need for decorum but at this crucial stage of the war, I believe it is imperative we are all aware of what is happening, not to speak of our wish to hear our military commander. May I respectfully suggest that you move the meeting to the gymnasium across the road? There is ample room there for all of us and there is a stage where our visitor can address us from which I am sure will suit him better than this crowded place".
Mistakovic frowned and looked irritated in a 'why didn't I think of that' sort of way. There was widespread support

from the floor for moving the meeting so he reluctantly agreed.

They re-convened five minutes later. The gym was huge and it was well appointed. Orderlies rushed over with extra coffee and water. Fresh trays of pastries materialized. Mistakovic called for quiet and opened the meeting. A discussion started which almost immediately morphed into an argument about the type of missiles the Americans or N.A.T.O. had used the previous evening and where they had been fired from. That could not be resolved so it spread to an argument about which militia group had been better positioned and camouflaged against the air strikes. At this point, the discussion became heated and Mistakovic called for order and asked what plans those divisions which were still intact had for making progress. This time, argument became uproar with everyone blaming everyone else for what had gone wrong. Neither Milanovic nor Vladkovic had uttered one word.

"I'm beginning to regret insisting I stayed at the meeting now", Ivan said as an aside. "I was correct; these people are idiots. They argue about things that are past or things that make no difference or things over which they have no control, like the air strikes. Not one of them has shown the slightest sign of leadership. Come on, let's sneak down the back and get a coffee. No one will notice".

Milanovic shrugged and smiled briefly.

"I suppose you're right. Yes, let's get more coffee".

They moved towards the back of the gym where an orderly poured the coffee for them and offered a pastry. Both men declined. Out of the corner of his eye, Sefer saw a commotion outside. Several armoured cars and jeeps had arrived and one of them had just disgorged their visitor.

Milanovic looked to the top of the room and cleared his throat loudly. Mistakovic caught his eye and Sefer nodded. A hush quickly descended on proceedings. The small squat, barrel chested man with the hooded eyes and grey hair marched through the rear door surrounded by functionaries and acolytes, who watched his every move. He wore simple camouflage fatigues and stout army boots. He wore no medals or insignia. He was effectively in battle dress whereas the commanders were all in their best uniforms. Milanovic and Vladkovic stayed where they stood and were therefore first to be greeted. Both men still held cups of coffee in their hands so Mladic frowned deeply and turned away. Mistakovic almost burst a gut in his mad sprint to reach the leader and apologized profusely for not being on hand to greet his visitor personally at the door. This was frankly ridiculous as they had not been told at what time he was arriving or even if he would come at all. In fairness, Mladic shrugged and waved away the man's apologies. Mistakovic led him to the plinth at the top of the stage and invited him to address the gathering.
"We were just discussing our plans for the next phase of the war, my General, Mistakovic said but I am sure you will have your own thoughts on that".
Mladic shrugged.
"Perhaps; what were your own plans General?"
Mistakovic reddened deeply. There were no plans of course and he suspected that Mladic knew just that. Nonetheless, he stuttered on:
"We had not yet reached agreement my General but there have been proposals for a swift pincer movement from the south and east, to be carried out under cover of darkness. There was also a proposal that we cease all shelling during

daylight hours so as not to invite air strikes from the western powers".

Milanovic could scarcely believe what he was hearing. These were proposals which had been made days ago and both had failed utterly. He hoped for the man's own sake that Mladic didn't know this. On reflection, he assumed he didn't but as he hardly seemed to be listening and was totally absorbed in his own self, he supposed it did not matter anyway.

Mladic nodded and Mistakovic sat down.

"Good proposals General, thank you but I think we need a little more at this stage. I heard about your misfortune last night and let me start by offering my condolences to the various commanders on the loss of your brave men".

There was a murmur of thanks and nodding of heads.

"I am sure you and your men are just bursting to hit back and to show the enemy what brave Serb soldiers are made of".

Again, there was the murmur of agreement and even a smattering of sporadic applause. He might be a rank amateur, Sefer thought, but he's good enough to convince this lot. Within two minutes, he had their rapt attention. From now on, he could say almost anything and they would believe him. To be fair, he did have an imposing presence, allowing for the fact that he was standing on a stage about a metre higher than everyone else, but he did radiate an aura nonetheless. Mladic continued:

"You and your men have done exceptionally well. You have won many hard battles and we now control most of the country. Thanks to your efforts, Radovan Karadzic is recognised internationally as President of the Bosnian Serb

Republic." There was louder applause this time but Mladic waved for them to be silent.

"You have also succeeded in removing the curse, the plague on our lives these past centuries, our natural enemy, the Bosniaks. For that I thank you from the bottom of my heart. Oh yes, they have gone running to those stinking cowards, the Croats but even if they all fight together they will be no match for us".

This time the applause grew into cheering but Mladic waved them down again.

"Gentlemen, I am not a fool. I am aware that there is now another player in the game but they are a rather reluctant player. The type who doesn't like to get their hands dirty or their blood spilled; the type who like to drop bombs on innocent men and then run away to safety; the type who if you push them will be too squeamish to stay involved, believe me".

The men could not contain themselves and this time the applause was rapturous and grew to a standing ovation. It was as if Mladic was winning the war for them right there on the stage. He was somewhat inspirational, Sefer thought, at least to a rabble rousing crowd in a bar but he had not made a single valid military point as yet and he had been speaking for fifteen minutes. Lieutenant Vladkovic had not joined in the initial applause but he did get to his feet for the ovation. Whether he was inspired or if it was peer pressure, Milanovic couldn't tell. He alone of the attendance remained seated throughout. Mladic then went on to recount the three year history of the war, describing brave Serb deeds in battle after battle. Military victories were gloried in; massacres became brave actions. By the time he was finished, the man had re-energized and invigorated the Bosnian Serb leaders and convinced them they were unbeatable. It was all rhetoric but they swallowed it whole. Was Karadzic like this also, Sefer wondered? Was that where Mladic had learned it from or was he a natural orator himself? He never made eye contact with the man but he was aware that Mladic had noticed he had not joined enthusiastically in the applause or the esteem given to him. The man seemed mildly irritated by it but made no mention of the fact. Did he know who Sefer was? Most probably he did and had he made any mention of the Colonel's silence, he risked Milanovic questioning his rhetoric and possibly undermining him. Yet there was no way he could lose; he held everyone there in the palm of his hand. The reason probably was that deep down, the man was just a simple school yard bully and bullies are drastically lacking in confidence, hating to hear any dissent or questioning. Mladic was raising his voice again and building to a climax:

"Comrades, what is the one thing that our western enemies cannot stomach? I will tell you – blood. They will not spill their own. They bomb our positions but say the bombs are 'surgical strikes', yet they spill brave Serb blood. But of course these bastards are not around to see the blood of our brave men. No, but the only reason they came into this war in the first place was because we spilled a little Bosniak blood in Srebrenica and their accursed media told them about it. They were afraid they would be unpopular with their electorates unless they acted. How many did we kill then? Five thousand; eight thousand? A fraction my friends, a fraction of the number we will kill unless they agree to cease their pointless, unfair and one-sided action. If they want blood, we will give them oceans of it. How many are left in Sarajevo? Four hundred thousand? Let's say we attack in earnest and kill fifty thousand? What can they do? Nothing, because we will then be in the city and they wouldn't dare to bomb so called civilian targets. What's more, it will be their actions in killing Serb soldiers which will have prompted this backlash so they will have to stand down. They will look silly because we will be braver than them and we will call their bluff. Then my friends, we will ascend to our rightful place and we will rule over all this country and be rid of our enemies forever. There is no one on this earth tougher than a Serb and it's time we showed them that a Bosnian Serb is even tougher".

The audience rose as one and cheered Mladic to the echo. They congratulated each other and patted each other on the back and some were almost in tears. The General stood down from the podium and was seen out to his vehicle by Mistakovic. The room was in uproar. You could almost smell the testosterone. Milanovic sensed that these men were almost willing to go out and fight for their leader with their bare hands, but not quite. Mistakovic came back in and ascended the steps to the podium. Some of the men were still cheering wildly and cheered their own General. Mistakovic smiled broadly.
"Calm down gentlemen, calm down", he said. "We have serious business to attend to. We have a war to win here". There was another cheer.
"General Mladic sends his apologies. He would love to have met all of you in person but unfortunately he had to dash to another meeting, with the President I think so he could not stay."

That was clever, Sefer thought. Get in, say your piece and get out again quickly. Leave them wanting more and maintain the mystique. All the men had seen him, they had been in his presence, they had been inspired by him and then he was gone. The whole thing had been perfectly stage managed. Mistakovic continued:

"Gentlemen, we have heard a truly inspirational leader in our midst this morning. To me, it is quite clear. There are now no alternative strategies to be pursued. Our leader has told us what we must do; be swift and decisive and strike at the heart of the Bosnian capital. I would now welcome your proposals as to how best and how efficiently we expedite this order".

There was a flurry of activity and some hushed voices. Then a clear strong voice made itself heard above the din: "General, may I make a proposal?"

"Of course, General Galic, please proceed, we'd be delighted to hear it"

"Well, let me say that I too was inspired by the words of General Mladic and it seems to me as if he is quite correct in his assessment. There is only one way to shock the westerners to their senses and that is to spill more blood. Do any of you remember Markale?"

Several men nodded and Galic continued.

"It's the main Bosniak market in Sarajevo. We lobbed one mortar shell in there last year, early February, around lunchtime. I think we killed about seventy Bosniaks. Oh there was a big outcry and we eased off at the time. It was the wrong decision I felt and it seems now that General Mladic agrees with me".

"What are you proposing General Galic", Mistakovic asked.

"Well it seems clear. We assemble our men on all sides of the city. In the parts we already hold, we will notify our own people. We draw up a list of all strategic buildings we need to capture and we assign one or two to each division. We coordinate the entire operation beforehand and we ensure that all attacks occur simultaneously. Then, just before we launch the attacks, we drop not one but fifty shells into Markale market. With any luck, it will obliterate anyone within a kilometre of it, including nosey journalists. It will throw the city into chaos. Before the N.A.T.O. bastards know what's happening, we will have taken the city".

The men glanced at each other, digesting the proposal, nodding eagerly. There was some sporadic applause. Jesus, Sefer thought, this is becoming like one of those born-again-Christian gatherings. They were all as high as kites on bullshit.

Mistakovic suggested a smaller group of the key Generals get together in the smaller meeting room to refine the plan for the big assault on the city. He invited Milanovic to join them. Vladkovic eyed him and motioned as if to say, why not comment here? Sefer felt the man might be correct. The Generals were so pumped up he had no chance of talking them down once they got over to the General's office. They'd probably be so pumped up that they'd start with a few shots of liquor. He cleared his throat.

"General, colleagues, if I might say a few words before we break up?"

"By all means Colonel", Mistakovic replied, confident now that whatever it was that Milanovic would say would be easily refuted. He too had been utterly convinced by Mladic's theory.

"I am very much aware of the high esteem in which General Mladic is held," Sefer began, "and I have no wish to diminish it in any way. What does concern me, as a military strategist, is the apparent lack of logic of the plan."

There were some gasps and sounds of dissent. Mistakovic decided he'd settle this here and now, with everyone present. If the Serbian Colonel wanted to openly disagree with General Mladic, that would be his problem.

"Go ahead Colonel", he said.

"Well, I am sure General Mladic is an inspirational leader and I am sure he keeps himself informed of everything that is happening but I don't recall him asking for a briefing on last night's events or indeed inquiring as to the current state of your forces. Neither was there any mention of military tactics and how an ambitious plan such as this might be put in train."

Mistakovic laughed softly and was joined by the others.

"That is fine detail and not for General Mladic to worry about Colonel. I am sure he trusts us, his commanders, to be up to speed on military tactics."

This is what worries me, Sefer thought. He shrugged.

"OK General, that is fine. But it is my view and also that of Belgrade that to attack further and have any more bloodshed would only be detrimental to your overall position and would disadvantage you in any forthcoming peace talks."

There was an audible gasp in the room. General Galic took up the point:

"We are aware of your view Colonel but with very great respect, no one is talking about peace talks or cease fires in this group. We are in a war and we will fight until we win this war. That is the decision of General Mladic and I thoroughly agree with him as I'm sure do most of my colleagues."

There were shouts of agreement so Milanovic shrugged. "I was retained as your military adviser so I am here to dispense advice General. If you do not wish to take that advice, that is your prerogative. I wish you well in your assault on Sarajevo but I don't see a role for myself in the planning of it, given that I am totally opposed to it and that it is my view that in the current state of preparedness of your troops, it is bound to fail. I have no further part to play here today so I will retire to my quarters. If you need me for any reason, you know where I am. Good day to you gentlemen."

You could hear a pin drop as Sefer left the room but sadly, no one followed him.

Chapter 40

"How many young men will die because of that idiot's bullshit speech? How many innocent civilians will be slaughtered in the market or in the city itself? How damaging will it be to our future?"

Lieutenant Vladkovic was on his third beer having also downed three shots.

"Careful Ivan, we are not alone here. I feel the same way but I fear there is little we can do about it so best to keep your counsel for now", Sefer said. He felt a responsibility to the young man because there was no doubt that it had been he who had changed the Lieutenant's views.

Another man who had been drinking alone now moved towards them. He wore the uniform and insignia of a Colonel in the Bosnian Serb forces. He was tall and broad shouldered and looked to be very fit. He had a pale complexion and although he wore a cap, the edges of his hair appeared to be a fair colour. He had a square shaped sculpted face which was unlined and ice blue eyes which gave away nothing. He nodded a greeting as he approached them at the bar.

"Good evening gentlemen, do you mind if I join you for a moment?" he said, in slightly accented Serbian. Both men nodded assent. The stranger pulled over a stool and signaled the barman for three beers. He might have been wearing the uniform of a Serbian Colonel but Sefer was willing to bet he was not a Serb; if pushed, he would say the man came from much further east.

"Can we speak frankly?" the man asked?

"It depends on what you wish to talk about but go ahead for now", Sefer said. The man took a swig from his beer and then set it down on the bar counter. He took a paper napkin from a stack on the bar and wiped his mouth delicately. Milanovic had noticed him at the meeting that morning and had assumed he was attached to one of the militia groups. He was now convinced that he was not.

"I noticed you at the meeting today", the stranger began. "My impression was that you were not overly convinced by the great General Mladic".

Neither man said anything but motioned for the man to continue. He took another drink from his glass and repeated his little ritual of wiping his mouth.

"You must forgive my poor manners", the man said. "I have intruded on your company and I have yet to introduce

myself. I am Vladimir Alexandrovich Ignatyev. I am sure you can guess where I come from. So as I say, let us be frank. I thought the General's performance today was a joke and I am sure you feel the same way, yes?"
Milanovic shrugged.
"You saw how I questioned the man's strategy so my opinions on the General are not a secret. In terms of jokes though, I fear that it is most of the Bosnian Serb militias that are a joke".
The new man chuckled and shrugged.
"Well, it was Belgrade who armed them to the teeth brother.''
"Yes, and who armed Belgrade?"
Ignatyev laughed and raised his glass to the other two. All three drank deeply.
"Fair point I suppose. You have obviously guessed that I am Russian. You are also correct in that we provided the arms to your country but at least we got paid for them. I doubt you'll ever see a cent from these idiots". He laughed again.
"Does it really matter?" Sefer asked.
"No, I suppose it doesn't Colonel. You must forgive me; I revert to the custom in my country where we always look to assign the blame when something goes wrong. Do you know one of the most common sayings in Russia is 'who's guilty' or 'who fucked up?"
"Yes, I am aware of this and you are not the only ones; but why are you telling us this Colonel, or may I call you Colonel? I mean, officially I assume you are not here given your choice of a Bosnian Serb uniform?"
Ignatyev smiled.
"You may call me Colonel if you wish but my rank is of no consequence. You are quite correct in that I have

effectively broken cover to speak to you although with my accent, my origins are pretty much an open secret anyway. No, the reason I sought you out Colonel is that you appear to be the only one here with any sense of reality".
Ignatyev paused and Milanovic nodded for him to continue.
"You see, I spoke about a fuck-up; well, if this 'plan' proceeds, we are talking about the biggest fuck-up of the war, possibly of the century. Our strategic interests lie with Serbia of course but how this little skirmish turns out, quite frankly, we don't give a damn provided it doesn't damage us. You see, right now, we are not here. Yes, they have military advisers but they are Serbs, not Russians. If this little party that Mladic encouraged them to throw comes off, there will be hell to pay and there will be no hiding place for any of us".

Milanovic drank deeply from his glass, nodded and looked at the Russian.
"So you seek to avoid embarrassment, and of course bloodshed?"
"Avoiding bloodshed is not my primary concern Colonel unless it results in embarrassment so you are probably correct on both counts".
Sefer was conscious that Lieutenant Vladkovic was rapt with attention but had not spoken a word since the Russian had joined them. Had he known about it in advance; surely not? Yet the Russian had approached them both; he had not sought a private conversation. Most probably he had been observing both men all day or even for some time before that. It wasn't difficult as they were now constant companions. This man was most probably a Colonel in the G.R.U., Russian Military Intelligence, reputed to be far

better skilled not to speak of ruthless than their counterparts in the civilian world, the F.S.B. Ignatyev had more than likely deduced, correctly, that Milanovic and Vladkovic were of one mind.

"So what can a simple Serbian Colonel and a Bosnian Serb Lieutenant do to help you?" Sefer asked.

Ignatyev sighed, took another sip of beer and wiped his mouth again.

"I think it is more what we can both do to help each other Colonel, if I may say so. You see, we strongly suspect there is a plan afoot. I don't believe for a moment that General Mladic is as stupid as he appeared at that meeting today".

Sefer raised his eyebrows as the Russian paused for effect.

"We understand that Karadzic is already involved in secret peace talks with the Americans. He has a line to a former U.S. President and he has, correctly in my view, decided that now is the time to cut his losses. The tide has already turned against the Bosnian Serb militias and if he waits, his negotiating position becomes weaker. But the man is extremely devious. The word we hear is that he says he cannot control Mladic, who wants to mount one final push and that he needs concessions in order to bring his military commander on board. Those concessions are almost ready to be granted".

"So what's the issue?" Ivan said, speaking for the first time.

"The issue, young man", Ignatyev said, "is that Karadzic and Mladic, far from having fallen out, have never been closer. The concessions will be granted and Karadzic will announce that they have officially declared a cease fire. The plan is then to ignore this and to have a serious bloodbath in Sarajevo but to blame it on the Bosniaks or even the Croats. General Galic is strongly suspected to be in charge of the attempted deception. Did you notice it was he who proposed the attack on the market?"

"Yes, but why would that matter?"

"Because he will attempt to make it look like the attack was either self inflicted or came from the Croats or was a mistake. You see Mladic knows he hasn't enough men here for a major offensive; he knows that if they attack they will be repulsed and defeated; the chances are they will be wiped out. But who will then be able to tell who started it? The Bosniaks will be seen as the aggressors and Karadzic will be able to wrest even more concessions from the peace talks".

"But if our forces are wiped out here, it will surely weaken us overall?" Ivan said. The Russian Colonel smiled.

"If Karadzic sues for peace, what need has he of your militias? He no longer needs to fight and if you all get wiped out, he can blame you for Srebrenica and every other massacre that occurred; he can start with a clean slate and say unfortunately the perpetrators of those atrocities were killed in Sarajevo".

Vladkovic looked shocked.

"So, we are being set up?" he asked.

"In a manner of speaking, yes".

"But what's the Russian interest in stopping this?" Milanovic asked. "If the Bosnian Serbs obtain more concessions, so what; it is not contrary to your strategic interests".

"No, it isn't, but we oppose the plan for two reasons. Firstly, while Mladic is not stupid, he or Karadzic are no Einsteins either. In a word, we doubt the plan will work. Quite frankly, we think it will be a bloodbath. God knows how many civilians will be killed. The Bosniak and Croat forces will fight back and your forces will be decimated. If the attack on Markale goes ahead, the Americans will launch so many air strikes that they will flatten every Serb position within ten kilometres of Sarajevo. You have no idea of the fire power they can unleash. What you have seen to date is but a fraction".

The man grew silent so Milanovic filled in the blanks for him:

"So the Bosniaks will win the battle of Sarajevo; the Bosnian Serb forces will be wiped out but because it will signal the end of the war, their attempted deception will be seen through. Being decimated will be seen as their own fault because they were the ones who started it. The concessions already given will be rowed back. The west will come in and go through the city forensically and the Serbs will be blamed. Belgrade will be deeply embarrassed and by extension, so will Moscow, am I correct?"

Colonel Ignatyev nodded.

"More or less, yes".

"And the other reason you wish to stop the plan Colonel?"

Ignatyev smiled.

"Why, the oldest reason my friend, self preservation. I am assigned here until the war ends as indeed I assume you are. I have no wish to be part of the collateral damage or indeed, part of the inevitable post-mortem".

Milanovic nodded.

"In all honesty, I have to say I share that sentiment. But what can we do at this stage. I am sure our colleagues have already worked out a brilliant plan for the offensive and are ready to go tomorrow morning".

Colonel Ignatyev smiled again.

"You are partially correct; yes, they have prepared a plan, such as it is, but the offensive is not planned to commence until the day after tomorrow".
He glanced at his watch:
"That gives us about thirty six hours, which should be plenty. In fact, we should probably get some sleep and start early in the morning. No point trying now".
Lieutenant Vladkovic looked totally mystified but Milanovic wasn't. He knew exactly what the Russian had in mind. In fact, when he had assumed that it had been he alone that Ignatyev had wanted to speak to, he had been wrong. The Lieutenant had been his real target but he needed Milanovic to get to him. Vladkovic downed the remainder of his beer and asked:
"But what can we do Colonel? All of the Generals have prepared the plan and they will give the orders in the morning".
The Russian Colonel now draped his arm over Ivan's shoulder.
"They will indeed Lieutenant but surely you have seen enough of war to know by now that it is not Generals who fight battles. Neither is it they who carry out orders. Most of that work is done by people at your level Lieutenant. Can I assume that you are in reasonably good standing with your peers?"
Ivan smiled as the realization dawned on him. Clever people, the G.R.U., Sefer thought.

Chapter 41

As planned, the second attack on the Markale market took place two days later on August 28th, just after eleven am. General Galic may have wanted to launch fifty shells but only five hit the target. Where the other forty five went was unclear. Some may have fallen short; others may never have left their launchers but exploded on the spot due to equipment being damaged. Others may not have been fired because the men were either demoralized or had been secretly informed that they were being sacrificed by their leadership. But the overriding suspicion was that the Bosnian Serbs were just running out of ammunition. Practically all of their arms dumps had been hit by air strikes. Artillery was destroyed in vast quantities; some which had seemingly survived intact later proven to be damaged. The N.A.T.O. alliance had after all, done their homework. They had hit the Bosnian Serbs where they were strongest, in their military might on the ground. While the first attack on the market in 1994 had killed sixty eight people with a single shell, the second attack only killed thirty seven. A large number of people were injured nonetheless.

Danvor and his men had been about to launch a military offensive in any event but this new attack only made them accelerate and redouble their efforts. There was initial shock as the shelling had all but ceased over the previous weeks and everyone felt the war was winding down. Rumours spread like wildfire; a major Serb offensive was expected against key Bosniak installations. Danvor's resistance, with help from the regular Bosnian Army and the Croats, were ready for them but the attacks never materialized. Lieutenant Vladkovic was, as the Russian Colonel had deduced, well respected among both his peers and their men. He did not know all of the divisional commanders of course but he knew most of them and where he didn't, he knew people who knew the others. He was aware that what he was undertaking was effectively treasonable and at times he wondered if he had made a terrible mistake by trusting the Russian. If he had been discovered, he doubted that this army would have afforded him the consideration of a court martial. It was more likely he would receive a very swift bullet in the back of the head. But he had put it to the back of his mind; what other reason could the G.R.U. man have for wanting him to halt the action. Confidentiality was crucial yet difficult to achieve given the number of people he had to confide in. But he achieved it; Slavic people were always good at keeping secrets; perhaps they had had much practice. On the other hand, it is surprisingly easy to keep a secret if you believe your leaders have abandoned you to certain death.

When the order came to advance on that autumn morning, all of the divisions took the routes that had been assigned to them to enter the city. All lined up in a precise and disciplined pattern. To the Generals and Colonels, nothing seemed amiss. If the Lieutenants had needed any further confirmation of Ivan's assertion that they were being sent to their doom, they received it in the fact that not one of the senior officers accompanied their men. The Generals, or at least most of them, may not have been aware of Mladic' fiendish plot but they knew enough about the state of their forces and about self preservation to realise that this was an extremely dangerous exercise. In fact, after the initial euphoria of Mladic' visit had worn off, some even voiced mild concern as to whether the plan would work at all. This was quickly ridiculed by General Galic and others. Hadn't General Mladic himself been the author of the plan? Were they going to question his bona fides? The mild outburst of dissent was instantly quelled and the plan was prepared. The excuses offered for not accompanying their men were that this was a precisely targeted exercise using small groups of soldiers; leaders giving orders would only slow them down; in addition, the commanders had to stay to oversee the strategic effects of the offensive and to collate the reports from each division as they advanced. What utter bullshit, Vladkovic thought, as he led his group of three hundred and fifty men down the mountainside. The approach to which he had been assigned precluded the use of vehicles. Obviously he had no intention of trying to lead his men into the city but his mission was doubly dangerous in that they had no transport and if they were surrounded by Bosniak forces, they would be sitting ducks. The Bosniaks would hardly believe them if they told them that they had effectively mutinied and had no intention of attacking the city. Given the enmity and bitterness between both sides, he doubted they would even get close enough to try it. In a show of solidarity, Milanovic accompanied this group, the only one with the rank of Colonel or above to do so.

Vladkovic had warned him the exercise could be dangerous, even accounting for the fact that they were not mounting an all-out assault. Milanovic had laughed loudly, something he rarely did these days.
"I expect it will be Ivan my friend, after all, we are at war", he said. The real plan, worked out between himself,

Colonel Ignatyev and the Lieutenant and which had been agreed with each of the junior divisional commanders, was to proceed to the outskirts of the city. There, they would 'encounter' so called Bosniak resistance. Their advance scouts would be the ones who would find that the city was far better defended than anyone had thought. They would report back to the Lieutenants who would agree that any further progress was deemed to be impossible. It would be difficult to coordinate as versions of the same story would have to be recounted by each commander. Milanovic was unworried though. He had told the others that it was his belief that the city *was* actually well defended in most areas so that even if they had obeyed their original orders, it was highly likely they would meet resistance long before they reached their individual targets. Their orders were to get into position around the city, dig in, then advance on the signal that the shells had begun to be launched at the market and the city centre in general. We will hardly need a signal for that, Ivan thought, the noise will alert everyone. The theory was that the shellfire attacks would cause panic, forcing the Bosniak defenders to abandon their posts and leaving the way open for the Serbs to charge unchallenged to their targets.

The shells were launched on schedule and they did indeed cause panic but only in the area where they scored direct hits. Elsewhere, the defenders of the city held firm. Milanovic and Vladkovic were seated on an old fallen log smoking cigarettes when they heard the boom of the shell launches from overhead. They both looked at each other and shrugged. The whole situation was surreal.
"How long did we agree to wait here for or sorry, I am forgetting myself", the Lieutenant said. "I meant how long

are we going to continue to fight through these strong Bosniak defences?"

Milanovic dragged deeply on his cigarette and considered: "I think Ignatyev suggested late afternoon".

"But you would propose a longer stay, if I read you correctly, eh Colonel?"

"Ivan, my friend, what we have to do is consider the possibilities".

The Lieutenant looked confused.

"What possibilities? Ah, do you mean, how will we explain that we have been fighting to breach the Bosniak defences all day, yet we have no casualties?"

Milanovic threw his head back and laughed.

"No casualties, what do you mean no casualties Ivan? I have seen several men fall already. It will have grown to dozens later if we need it to. Your Generals have no idea of how many men they have left under their command. They don't know how many are wounded and in need of hospitalization. They are unlikely to ask you about it when you come back either and do you know why Lieutenant; because they couldn't care less. All those little warlords and jumped up Generals care about is their own skins and their own little slice of the glory. So no, I am not thinking of casualties or the consequences of our inaction today".

"But you spoke of considering the possibilities before we decide when to return?"

"Yes I did", Sefer said, "and quite frankly, they are worrying. For example, the first possibility is that there may not be a camp to return to".

Ivan's eyes widened.

"Yes indeed", Sefer laughed again. "I was thinking that one of the advantages of us being down here is that we will miss the air strikes when the N.A.T.O. forces retaliate against General Galic's attack this morning".

"So it wasn't entirely bravery on your part that allowed you to accompany us?"

"You could say that Lieutenant but if you have been following the advice I have given at every stage of this war but particularly since the Americans became involved, you would have known that anyway".

The Lieutenant nodded slowly and smiled.

"Yes, you did say that if we had the temerity to launch more shell attacks on the city after being warned repeatedly, N.A.T.O. would bomb twenty seven types of shit out of all our positions".

"I did indeed but I think our Russian friend put it more subtly".

"Where is he by the way? Not at base camp I hope?"

"For his own sake, I hope not but I very much doubt it. No, he mentioned the possibility of continuing with the division he has been assigned to. They have been tasked with discovering and destroying the tunnel the Bosniaks have been using".

Almost as if on cue, the earth shook and the sun was blotted out from the sky. The sound of the explosion was deafening. Although the men were all dug in to safe positions under cover of the forest, the shock wave knocked over everything in its wake including anyone who had been standing. Milanovic and Vladkovic took cover behind the log. Immediately after the shock wave, the sky began raining earth, bits of trees crushed into match sticks and all manner of green foliage. They reckoned the blast had been the closest to them yet, directly impacting the hillside about fifty metres above their position. It was

followed almost immediately by another blast, off slightly to the south. This was followed by a further explosion in the other direction. Although the blasts were further away, the shock waves could be felt and the debris reached them. The sky was still brown from dust and the amount of other matter that had been thrown up by the successive strikes. Ivan tried his radio to contact his men several times before he got a reply. He systematically checked each squadron and confirmed that all were unhurt. He instructed each commander in turn:
"All troops dig in, hold your positions and stand by. It looks like we are best advised to hold here for now".
The blasts continued apace. There were so many now that they lost count. They couldn't see any aircraft but they had to be up there. This number of bombs could not be launched from offshore. The missiles were small to medium sized, probably launched from U.S. F15 jets or F/A-18 fighter bombers. French Mirage jets were also participating and Sefer had even heard a rumour that the German Luftwaffe would see action for the first time since 1945. Yes, the N.A.T.O. forces seemed to want to make a harsh statement once and for all. Whereas up to now, air strikes had been sporadic and specifically targeted, these seemed to be dropping everywhere, albeit on the Bosnian Serb side. What have these idiots done by launching their shells, Sefer thought. They've just brought the entire might of half the world's military aircraft down on our heads.

All through the afternoon, the men stayed in their positions. Most of the blasts were far enough away as to not have much effect but they were not taking any chances. These bombs arrived at their target faster than the speed of sound, in other words, with no warning. If one of them lands anywhere down here, Sefer thought, we will all be dead before we even know we've been hit. All he could do was pray that the Americans stuck to the higher ground and he had never been very good at that. Lieutenant Vladkovic had been sending occasional reports back to General Mistakovic at field head quarters but as the afternoon wore on, communication became sporadic and then ceased altogether. Ivan said that things appeared to be chaotic back at base, with no one apparently in charge or no one with a clue as to what they should do. When they could obtain no reply on the radio, they were unsure if the command post had been hit by a bomb or if the commanders had just upped and deserted their posts. If the bombs had been getting closer, Sefer had no doubt that it was the latter that had happened. At least it relieved Ivan of the need to invent fictitious battlefield reports, not that anyone appeared to be interested in listening to them anyway.

At around 18.00, the explosions ceased. There had been momentary lulls throughout the afternoon but when there had been nothing for about fifteen minutes, they were fairly sure the planes had gone home for now. Ivan gave the order that men could leave their positions but to maintain caution. Everyone stood up, walked around and stretched and then tried to banish the ringing and pounding noises from their ears.
"So, where to now Colonel?" he asked.
Milanovic shrugged.
"I suggest we give it another hour to an hour and a half. Wait until dusk. Then we'll try to find if there is anything at all left up there".

"Sounds good to me", Ivan said and they both lit cigarettes.

"You know, I was think….." The Lieutenant never finished the sentence as he was thrown backwards on to the forest floor. Milanovic heard the report of the weapon a nano second after he saw Vladkovic clutching his chest. He dived for cover, once again employing the stout log. All around him, men were screaming and moaning in pain. Automatic rifle fire seemed to be coming from the south, from the area which they assumed had been held by themselves. Then it changed and they were being attacked from the north, from the direction of the city. Milanovic couldn't see who was shooting or where they were hiding. It was terrifying. He had drawn his service pistol but was powerless as he had nothing to shoot at. Gunfire continued to pour in, most of seemingly precisely targeted. He had no idea how many men had been wounded or killed. He daren't move for fear he would have his head blown off. He wasn't sure if any of the Serbs had managed to return fire. Like him, they probably had no one to aim at. During a brief lull in the firing, he chanced a look towards his fallen friend. Ivan had his hand on his chest and seemed to be bleeding profusely. He had gone a deathly pale. Sefer crawled over to his position and tried to assess the wound. Ivan had been hit in the upper chest area; the bullet had avoided the heart or he would be dead already. Nevertheless, if he did not obtain medical attention soon, he would bleed to death. He looked at Sefer but could not speak and appeared to be in heavy shock.

The firing recommenced and Sefer heard yet more screams of dying men and the moans of the wounded. Then, almost as quickly as it had begun, the firing stopped. All was silent and from somewhere to the north, a man with a loud hailer declared:

"You are surrounded by the forces of the Republic of Bosnia. Lay down your weapons and surrender and you will be treated as prisoners-of-war. If you resist, we will continue firing until you are all killed. Almost immediately, tired and beaten men began emerging from trees and dropped their weapons in a pile in the clearing. He noticed there were pathetically few of them, probably no more than seventy. He noted briefly that over a few short weeks, the morale of these troops had gone from sky high to rock bottom. Had it been poor leadership; had it been the entry of N.A.T.O. to the war, or had it been Srebrenica? This was a study that might be carried out one day he thought. In the meantime, his immediate priority was to stay alive and attend to his friend.

The Bosniak fire had been expertly targeted for sure. He stood up and asked some of the troops to help him to assist their commander. The men rushed over eagerly. One of them had paramedic training and he set about trying to staunch the wound. The Lieutenant was fading in and out of consciousness. Bosniak soldiers emerged from the forest on all sides and checked the surrendered troops for weapons. They were brisk, disciplined and businesslike. Unlike many of our side's militias, Sefer thought. They allowed the Serbs to provide medical attention to the wounded and even assisted with their own paramedics.

Lieutenant Vladkovic had been stabilized but the paramedics were unsure as to whether they could move him. The increasingly dark stain on the forest floor bore testament to the amount of blood he had lost. Sefer bend

down on his haunches and enquired of his friend. Ivan opened his eyes and said:
"It looks like I won't have to invent stories of casualties after all Colonel".
"Indeed Lieutenant, but it looks like it'll be a Bosnian hospital you'll be doing your explaining in anyway".
Ivan shook his head sadly.
"I don't think so Colonel, not today".
He slipped back into unconsciousness. Just then, a man in battle fatigues emerged from the Bosniak group. He was carrying an automatic weapon but he didn't really look like a soldier. He walked over to the little group and said:
"Is it Colonel Milanovic?"
Sefer looked up and, seeing the Bosniak man who had previously been their prisoner, confirmed that he was indeed whom the man thought.
"And how is your friend?" the young man asked with a concerned look.
Sefer looked to the medic who was attending to Vladkovic. The man shook his head sadly. The Bosniak soldier bent down, took the Lieutenant's hand in his own and said:
"I'm sorry I couldn't return the favour to you Ivan. Please forgive me".
But Ivan was gone. Only then did Milanovic realise that he still had his side arm. In his rush to help his friend, he had forgotten to hand it over. He removed it from its holster and passed it over to the man who had just arrived, apologizing for his tardiness. He was a proud Serb but surrender was the only option here and he was basically a practical man.
"It is ok Colonel, the man said. I knew you were not going to use it as I know you are a man of honour"

"Thank you", Sefer said. "I believe you are also. Drazen Itsakovic, isn't it?"

The man nodded in the affirmative.

Chapter 42

Major General Steve Rawlins didn't want to be there; in fact, he didn't want to be anywhere else on the planet except in his small ranch in South Carolina. He had booked this vacation a long time back and he was so looking forward to riding the few horses he kept on his spread and chilling with his wife Carol and their kids. It wasn't a large ranch, just over a hundred acres, very small in fact for the area but that didn't bother him. It was his; it was where he had grown up and as an only child, he had inherited it when his parents passed on. He had long since moved to the city of course and had seen service with the military in lots of places, both within and outside the U.S. He had joined the military cadet school straight from high school and was a career soldier. In fact, he reckoned he had been in almost every trouble spot on the planet this past twenty years, including the Gulf War. It seemed that when there was a problem that needed sorting, the plan was to send for Steve. Not that he ever played a big role in the fighting or the military strategies. No, where General Rawlins came into his own was in cleaning up the mess when the guns finally fell silent. He was an expert negotiator and had brokered deals in many places which had avoided a lot of unnecessary deaths. He was scrupulous about his work. He could often have negotiated peace deals which were more favourable to his own side but he had demurred. Steve's mantra was that it had to be just and fair to both sides and had to be seen to be so. It was simple; if the deal wasn't perceived to be fair, it wouldn't last and war would break out again. He found this concept so simple, yet men ignored it all the time. They always wanted to push for more for their own side; maybe they gained a little extra glory for themselves in the short term but history would not judge them well. For Steve, all you had to do was to know your history and look at what he adjudged to be the greatest evil visited on the twentieth century; Nazi Germany. The conflict started by Hitler and his cronies eventually cost the lives of over forty million people; yet Steve firmly believed that the Second World War would never have happened, because Hitler would never have come to power, if the peace settlement negotiated after the first World War had been fairer.

He stood two inches over six feet in his stockings and was a very fit one hundred kilos in weight. He was two years the wrong side of forty, quite young to have achieved his rank but in today's army, with so much engagement throughout the globe, he wasn't the only high flyer. Yes there had been a downsizing after the cold war ended but the threat had barely been consigned to history when it was replaced by a newer, more sinister and infinitely harder one to detect. Steve Rawlins was one of the new breed, highly educated, spoke three languages including Arabic and was proficient in I.T. He had also seen action in the field and was combat hardened from his various tours of duty, most notably the Gulf conflict. He was a pleasant looking man, with a broad welcoming face, square jaws, bushy sandy hair and blue eyes that gave nothing away but could look right through most people. He was the ideal negotiator. He had never played poker but he had been told many times that he should have. His default expression was impassive and he sometimes appeared disinterested but it would be a grave mistake to think you could hoodwink this man. He had been assigned to N.A.T.O.'s European Headquarters for the previous six months in a monitoring role. When the western powers commenced their air strikes on the Bosnian Serbs in response to international outrage at the treatment of the Bosniaks, his military commanders in the U.S. did not ask Steve for his advice, either militarily or tactically. But when it appeared that the Serb resistance was weakening, he was asked to go in and broker the peace deal. The fact that it was the Thursday before he was due to depart for his long awaited vacation meant that he now knew it was hopeless. There would be no vacation this year for him. This deal would be about as complex as he would ever negotiate; hell, finding peace in the Balkans had been eluding better men than him for centuries. All the big European powers had dabbled there and all had gotten their fingers burnt. This was probably why Clinton had held off getting the Americans involved until he seemingly had no choice. The Russians were tacitly backing the Serbs but they were clever enough not to get involved on the ground or if they did, they were well concealed. Steve was apprehensive about the task he had been given and as yet, it hadn't even started. The war was still on, even if the final outcome was now inevitable.

He had no complaint with the weather or with his quarters. The warm daytime sunshine and cooler evenings could have been a match for the weather in Carolina these days. In fact his daughter had told him on the phone the previous evening that conditions were almost identical. His heart felt heavy when he thought of her. Little Nicola was seven years old and loved the horses at the ranch. Steve junior was nine and was already an experienced horseman and they only visited the place three or four times a year. With a heavy heart he forced himself to push his wife and children to the back of his mind; he had important matters to discuss; disputes to settle. It seemed there would always be some group somewhere that needed a calm voice, a reasoned individual to resolve their problems. His thoughts were interrupted anyway by his desk phone ringing.

"The Bosniak delegation are here General", the orderly told him. "Great, send them in Sergeant", he said. The door opened and Danvor Itsakovic led in a group of three men. Rawlins shook hands and greeted each man warmly in turn, sat them down and offered coffee. All three accepted and they made small talk for a while. The General was surprised to find that all three spoke excellent English and did not require an interpreter. He was also delighted to discover that they were intelligent and very reasonable men. This process might not take that long after all, he mused. Yeah, he thought, they're very reasonable because they're talking to me and want to make a good impression on the Yank. Wait until there are Serbs in the mix and we'll see the hard line stance being adopted. His depression returned as he imagined himself here for months. He was sure Sarajevo was or had been a beautiful city but right now, it had been battered by three years of siege and it was not exactly showing its good side to him. His favoured option was South Carolina but really, anywhere on the planet was a better option than here, wasn't it? He pulled himself back to the present as the leader of the delegation, Itsakovic, made a point:

"You see, right now General, we are facing, what is the expression, an empty chair, yes?"

"Go ahead", Rawlins said.

"Well we are the only ones here apart from yourself and we cannot negotiate with you sir. We need the Bosnian Serbs in the room also".

"I agree, but we are in constant touch with them", the General said.

Danvor Itsakovic smiled.

"Really", he said. "Is that contact through Belgrade or Moscow or is it as far away as London or Washington?"

It was now General Rawlins turn to smile.

"You make a fair point, Mr. Itsakovic. Communication with the other side is not what it might be just yet".

"Please", the man said, "Call me Danvor, and this is Hasan and Yusuf. You see General, we appreciate what you are trying to do for us. Brokering peace is a very tricky business, I think even more so in this part of the world".

He raised his eyebrows and Steve Rawlins nodded for him to continue.

"Well, how shall I put it General; we want peace, yes, we have always wanted peace. We did not start this war even though I know there has been unrest on all sides and I am aware that some Bosniaks have not exactly covered themselves in glory. But yes, we do want peace; we are sick and tired of fighting and defending our people and our city. But it cannot be peace at any price. We have suffered much General and with very great respect, I am not sure if the people in charge in Washington or Moscow are in a position to appreciate this".

The General nodded and then said:

"Danvor, let me be straight and up front with you. I don't want to be here. Right now, I'd prefer to be back in the States at my ranch with my two small kids. I was asked to mediate between the two warring factions here. I was only given the task last Thursday but I have been in the region for six months. I have used the time available to me to study your history. I have looked at every conflict that has ever occurred in this country. I have read every available piece of information on this present conflict. I am aware of the savagery and the butchery that has gone on. I am not some wet-behind-the-ears PR guy who's been sent out by N.A.T.O. to make them look good. I have negotiated peace settlements in Iraq and in Africa. I can assure you I will go to enormous lengths to be absolutely fair to all sides in any dispute in which I mediate. If it can be done, I will certainly do my very best to achieve it".

"Forgive me General", Danvor responded. "Perhaps it is my English. Your own personal bona fides are not being in any way questioned and I apologise most sincerely if I gave that impression. In fact, we are very much aware of your proud record and we are delighted you have been appointed to mediate. No, you see the entire thing comes back to that empty chair I referred to. What I mean is, we don't want to negotiate by proxy with someone in Belgrade or Moscow. We want to negotiate with the Serbs who are still up in those hills and who, despite everything that has been thrown at them, are continuing to bomb and shell us".

General Rawlins nodded.

"You make a good point Danvor but as of now, there appears to be a disconnect between General Mladic's remaining troops and their sponsors and allies. All I can do is to listen to your peace demands and put them to whoever is acting on behalf of the Serbs".
"I am afraid that will not work General and if I know anything about you and your experience, I think you will agree with me".
Danvor smiled showing even teeth and the General laughed briefly.
"Perhaps you are correct", he said, "but we must do what we can. People are still dying and getting injured out there and we must do what we can to stop it".

They were interrupted briefly by the General's phone's insistent buzzing. He excused himself and hit the answer button.
"Yes Sergeant, is it urgent? I see, fine, send him in. It appears that there is a young man outside with a message for you Danvor", he said. The door opened and Drazen stood there. The General waved him in and busied himself fetching a refill for his coffee. Drazen spoke to his father and the other two men in whispers. The conversation became animated and the men seemed to be considering something. Eventually, Danvor spoke:
"General, this man is my son, Drazen. He came to us on another matter but I think he may have inadvertently come up with a possible solution to our problem".
"Great, let's hear it", Steve said: "Drazen, good to meet you, why don't you take a seat and tell us yourself?"
Both men shook hands and Drazen sat down uncertainly.
"General", he began, "We have had an engagement with a detachment of Bosnian Serbs and we captured quite a large

number of them. Among these men is a Colonel in the regular Serbian army; we understand he was their military adviser. This man is highly intelligent and we understand that he is respected by the leadership of the Bosnian Serbs. He is a pragmatic and reasonable man as I can testify to myself, having encountered him more then once in this war".

Hmm, wonder what he means by that, Steve thought. Still, this is good; they're not all blood thirsty freaks.

"What I am proposing", Drazen continued, "is that we request this Colonel Milanovic to intervene with or negotiate with the remaining Serb leadership in the mountains. If they agree to a cease fire, then both they and the Colonel could join our talks here in Sarajevo".

"I think that's an excellent idea Drazen, but will this man co-operate with us?"

"I cannot say for certain that he will but I can say that he is a reasonable man".

"Why don't we all break up for an hour and you go and ask him? Gee, I sure hope you've been treating him well?"

"I can assure you General that all prisoners-of-war have been treated with dignity", Danvor said.

"I'm delighted to hear that my friend", said the General. "So let's all meet back here in an hour, and hopefully you'll be accompanied by this Colonel Milanovic".

Chapter 43

"You want them to do what?" Milanovic said: "Withdraw all their heavy weapons from the hills and cease the siege of Sarajevo".

"Yes", Danvor said, "and also remove all weaponry from the environs of any other safe area currently policed or protected by the United Nations".

Sefer nodded:

"Well, gentlemen, first of all forgive me for my initial shock. You realise I have been indisposed for the past few days but surely there *are* no heavy armaments or even light armaments remaining in the hills? I mean, I saw the destruction on the twenty eighth with my own eyes. No one could have survived those strikes. I'm surprised that the hills themselves are even still there".

There was silence in the room for a few moments, then General Rawlins cleared his throat and said:

"Perhaps you underestimate the resolve or the resourcefulness of your allies Colonel Milanovic but I can assure you that the Bosnian Serbs were up and running again on the morning of the twenty ninth and have continued their attacks, albeit sporadically, in the intervening days".

Milanovic shook his head.

"But that is sheer madness. I mean, I know their military strength. Surely most of their heavy guns have been destroyed in the air strikes".

"Apparently not", Danvor said, "or else they have managed to bring in replacements under cover of darkness. It appears they are intent on making Sarajevo a sort of last stand of sorts".

"But surely N.A.T.O. have kept up their campaign of air strikes as they threatened they would if the Bosnian Serbs did not cease their attacks?"

Steve Rawlins hesitated momentarily and then took up the story:

"Well, you see, it's complicated. Can I be frank with you Colonel Milanovic".

"Please do", Sefer replied.

"Well, look, you probably realise N.A.T.O. don't really wanna be involved in this here war. No one wants to be in the Balkans but our hand was sort of forced, are you with me so far?" Sefer nodded for him to continue.

"You see, the ultimatum was to cease attacks and withdraw all heavy weapons. Now when your allies attacked Markale market on the twenty eighth, there was serious loss of life, hence our boys felt justified in pounding the living hell out of those guys up there in the hills. To be honest, we felt as you do; we thought that's gotta be it; they'll surely get the message this time. But as we say, next morning, the gun emplacements had been restored. Now to be fair, the Serbs have only launched a few token shells and we reckon they've been careful enough to drop them on to buildings or areas that are uninhabited so there's been no loss of life. But at the same time they're saying to us, we're still here guys and we're still capable of fighting. Now if N.A.T.O. launch another bunch of missiles on them, they're gonna shout foul and if there's loss of life, which there damn sure will be, we ain't gonna look good. You could say I suppose that it's a cat and mouse game".

Sefer nodded and thought hard.

"But the heavy armaments are still in position?"

"Yep, far as we know".

"Have you given them a deadline to withdraw them?"
"Yes, midnight on the fourth of September or the air strikes recommence".
"That's two days from now, so why do you need me?"
"Can't you guess", Rawlins said.
Sefer shrugged and raised his eyebrows.
"I could make many guesses General but I think you have the advantage over me; you have obviously been studying the situation for some days".
"I guess that's a fair point Colonel so I should level with you. We hear lots of rumours down here; there's talk of last stands and bloodbaths; very emotive stuff; to my mind, sheer madness. Then, one could argue that much of what has gone on already in this war was sheer madness".
"You won't get any argument from me on that score General", Sefer said. "But I think what you are trying to tell me is that you think the militias in the hills are crazy bastards who will refuse absolutely to cease fire and will insist on going down fighting and will kill many innocent civilians while they are doing so".
"I guess that about sums up our views Colonel".
"Let me tell you General, that I have no wish for this conflict to be prolonged for one more week or day or even one more hour. On that point, I am sure we are in total agreement. But I can tell you that before I was captured, I had advised the senior Bosnian Serb commanders of the hopelessness of their position because of their inability to fight back against air strikes. I urged a cease fire over two weeks ago but I was not heeded. I can also assure you that I had the full backing of Belgrade in this recommendation and I know I had backing from Moscow also. So I am really not sure if I can be of any assistance to you at all".

Danvor interjected at that point:
"We understand your position Colonel and we know you are an honourable man. We know also that you may not be able to influence all of them but if you can even make some of the leaders change their minds, it may shorten the conflict for all of us and may save lives".
Sefer nodded slowly:
"OK, I will certainly try but of one thing I can assure you gentlemen; despite the sheer savagery that has taken place and the horrendous acts that have been perpetrated against Bosniak citizens, most of the soldiers you will find in those hills, that is if there are any left up there, are merely following orders. I know it is a cliché but the longer I spent with them, the more apparent it became to me. Those men are as sick and tired of bloodshed and killing as you are and they want peace. If there is madness or craziness in those people, to my mind, it resides with their leaders. But enough of this; you asked me to assist and I would be glad to. Have you established a telephone link with the Serb camp?"
There was an awkward silence around the table and some confused looks. General Rawlins then smiled and said:
"No indeed we have not Colonel. Frankly, I don't believe in keeping honourable men as prisoners, particularly men who are prepared to assist for the greater good. Our Bosnian friends here are of one mind with me on this so you are a free man. You can go where you wish but we would ask you to make your way back up there and try to convince these people to stop before it's too late".
Sefer glanced at the General and over to the Bosniaks.
"Thank you General and gentlemen, you are most kind and may I also say, most practical. I will do my very best but I

am but a simple military adviser, a strategist. I'm afraid I do not have your experience in the field of negotiations".

"Ah hell, look", General Rawlins said, "we all know the real long term peace negotiations will be done by Izetbegovic and Milosevic, probably Tudjman of Croatia also. But in order to get to that stage, we need a cease fire on the ground first. Sometimes that's more complicated to achieve. There is also another issue you see; Karadzic is the self declared President of the Bosnian Serb Republic. Now until Srebrenica, there was a strong possibility that he too would be involved in any settlement but now calls are growing internationally for him to be treated as a war criminal. Please use this in your attempts to influence those commanders. You know yourself Colonel, even two weeks ago, the Bosnian Serbs were in a stronger position than they are now. Their influence is waning with each passing day. You need to convince them that this war is gonna get settled, with or without them so if they want to be brought to the table, they better leave their guns at home. You understand me?"

"Perfectly General; I've been making the same argument for weeks. Gentlemen", he said, turning to Danvor's people: "Thank you for your accommodation these past few nights. I cannot say it was a pleasure being a P.O.W. but you certainly did not make it unpleasant for me and I thank you for your humanity. I assume I won't be returning to the accommodation and as I am fully dressed, I can leave right away".

Danvor immediately stood up and took Milanovic's hand: "Thank you Colonel. My son and his comrades will escort you to the outskirts of the city; they should be ready to leave in an hour. May I also thank you for your personal kindness to my son in the past".

Steve Rawlins placed two beefy arms around both men and said:

"You know guys, the more of you I meet, the more I'm convinced of the old adages: 'people don't start wars, politicians and generals do' and 'peoples are not evil, only individuals are'. It's been a pleasure to work with both of you. Now if we've got an hour to kill, can I invite you guys to lunch with me?"

Danvor had to rush away to another meeting but Sefer was glad to accept the invitation. The food in the P.O.W. quarters had been OK but haute cuisine it was not so he was ravenous.

It has often been said that wherever American soldiers travel to, regardless of the circumstances or the privation of accommodation, the food is always good. The simple reason for this is probably because they bring it with them. General Rawlins ordered up two prime rib eye steaks with home fries, fresh vegetables and salad. Both he and Colonel Milanovic ate with relish, the Serbian complimenting the American on the quality of the food. The General refused a slice of pecan pie but the Colonel was delighted to accept his. Both men then sat sipping mugs of coffee.

"I've been reading the history of your country and indeed of the whole region Colonel to try to get a handle on what's really going on here", Rawlins said.

Milanovic smiled. "Indeed General, and have you found it interesting?"

"More like fascinating but more than a little confusing".

"Indeed General; they say that to understand any place, you must first know its history, but in the case of the Balkans, it could take one a lifetime to understand it so maybe it is best not to even start. Perhaps that is why we have had such bloody conflicts. When an issue is too complex to understand, it leaves the way open to apply simplistic reasoning, almost always by unintelligent people. Throughout our history, and you can argue that this conflict can be traced as far back as the sixth century, we have had our share of these people. They use people's natural fears and biases to fuel unease and stir up hatred and then use this for their own ends".

"Indeed, I've encountered similar situations in many countries. You know, I read somewhere that although Bosniaks, Croats and Serbs are all supposed to hate each other, you have almost identical cultures?"

"You are quite correct General. We are one but at the same time a divided people. Many things have divided us; religion is the most obvious. The Croats are Catholic, the Bosniaks are Muslim and we are Orthodox Christians. But to the broad minded man, who cares, eh? We all follow God. It should be no basis for division, yet it is. Now there are other reasons to divide us too which I won't deny. Over the centuries, we have formed alliances with different groups; probably the worst and most recent of these was the decision of some of the Croats and Bosniaks and even some of our people to align themselves with the Nazis during the Second World War. That led to a lot of bitterness".

"Yet Tito managed to hold it all together for forty years. Was that a repressive period?"

"Not that I am aware of General, no, but I suppose there was a residue of hatred from the previous conflict. There were many atrocities carried out in that war too. They built up and simmered during that period and came to the surface all too easily in this decade".

"Don't get me wrong Colonel, I'm not into who started what but it appeared to me as if a lot of what's happened has been because the various peoples which made up Yugoslavia wanted to run their own affairs but met resistance from the Serbs?"

"It is true that Serbians have always been the dominant force in the region", Sefer said, "and we've probably gotten used to being top dogs. But having said that, Tito was a Croat and all our peoples were treated equally during his reign. I guess our current leader is not blameless either but then he could argue that the economic strength of the country was being eroded by the secession of first the Slovenians, then the Croats and Bosniaks. But probably the greatest problem of all has come from the fact that over time, all our peoples became integrated with each other; as you say, we have almost identical cultures. But then, when someone whips up the hatred, people realise they don't want to live next to their Bosnian or Croat neighbour any more, even though they have done so for generations".

"Well, much as I abhor this 'ethnic cleansing' that has taken place, maybe when things settle down, it may keep the lid on things for the future. Then again, it is a shame; full integration of different cultures and traditions is the ideal solution when it works and is one of the things that has made my own country great."

"Indeed General, but I fear this is still the old world and we are unlikely to see it again in this region for hundreds of years. It is sad but best left alone at this stage I think. One point I would make to you General, before I leave. I

suspect you are a wise man and will work this out for yourself in any event but don't be influenced by the media coverage. I would be the first to agree that what was perpetrated by Serbs at Srebrenica and many other places were appalling crimes but they were not the only ones. There have been very many other atrocities carried out by all sides beyond the glare of the TV cameras and news crews. These Bosniak men with whom you negotiate are reasonable and rational people and I thank God for that, but be careful General, for there are many who are not."
Don't forget that before the war started, all three sides had agreed to a partition of Bosnia into three inter-dependent republics. It is arguable as to why this did not proceed but the Bosnian Serbs would say that it was because the Bosniaks got greedy and felt they had given away too much territory. They then attacked the Serbs who retaliated. I am only giving you their side because as you will appreciate General, there are always two sides to every story. In Bosnia, sadly, there are three."
Rawlins nodded gravely:
"Thank you Colonel, very interesting and very sound advice, I'll bear it in mind."
"But now." Sefer said, "I have work to do. It was a pleasure to meet you and thank you for a most excellent lunch. I do hope we can meet again."
"Indeed Colonel, the Bosniaks have worked out a way to communicate and a way to get y'all back here when the negotiating starts so I'm sure we're gonna have many hours together."

Chapter 44

The Bosnian Serbs held out for two more weeks, still trying to maintain a brave face and occasionally launching token attacks, which were always answered in merciless fashion by N.A.T.O. air strikes. Milanovic managed to make contact with the leadership, such as it was. Mistakovic had disappeared and no one could tell him whether the man had fled or if he had been killed in one of the massive explosions caused by the air strikes. The attacks had become more frequent and the targeting less remote than heretofore or perhaps the satellites were even better than they thought; perhaps they could ascertain where the leadership was. Of that leadership, General Mladic was nowhere to be seen and it appeared that most of the other Generals or at least any of them with a spark of sense had already fled the area. General Galic and General Svero were the only two remaining commanders that Sefer knew; one was a total Mladic devotee and a fanatic; the other was an idiot. Needless to say, they completely ignored their Serbian ally and the deadline of the fourth of September was ignored. They launched some token shell attacks on populated areas and the response was immediate and devastating. Even though they were now in a bunker some three kilometres from any of the gun emplacements, it was the first time that Sefer genuinely felt in fear of losing his life. Many times he asked himself how it had come to this and what was he doing there but he had been a prisoner-of-war and he had given his word to try. As a man-of-honour, he felt obligated to see it through to the end.

The next deadline communicated by N.A.T.O. of the tenth of September was also ignored but as the air strikes began totally decimating their men and equipment, Sefer eventually persuaded the Generals that they were in a hopeless position. He also appealed to their vanity; it would not be surrender, merely an agreement to cease firing and to negotiate with the U.N., N.A.T.O. and of course the Bosniaks. They would be the men who negotiated on behalf of the Bosnian Serbs; not Mladic or Karadzic whom he presumed were already in hiding, although he did not say as much. History would record that they were the men that had saved face for the Serbs when all had seemed lost. He convinced both Generals to travel down with him to the pre-arranged point where he would rendezvous with Drazen and they would proceed to the negotiations. Sefer was the one to make the call, initially to General Rawlins as Galic and Svero would not allow any direct communication with the Bosniaks. The agreement reached was that a cease fire would commence immediately. The Bosnian Serbs would begin to dismantle their heavy weaponry and withdraw them from Sarajevo and from Tuzla and Mostar and Banja Luka and everywhere else the Generals could communicate with.

For his part, General Rawlins agreed that N.A.T.O. would suspend air strikes provided all heavy weapons were withdrawn within forty eight hours.

Milanovic's plan allowed the Serbs to cease fire with some dignity. The Bosniaks allied with the Croats had been making steady progress across the country and the Serbs had grown tired and demoralized. Sefer felt they were dangerously close to being overrun anyway. But it had been the air strikes that had been their downfall, the final nail in the coffin. He had estimated that when they had advanced on Sarajevo just a few weeks before for 'the final push' as the commanders had termed it, they had had around eighteen thousand men, hundreds of tanks and any amount of mortars and other heavy artillery. He could not be sure but he figured that between deaths and desertions, they had less than a thousand able bodied men left. Their remaining weaponry was a joke, as most had been blown to kingdom come. But he convinced the leadership that the N.A.T.O. commander or the Bosniaks were not aware of this; Galic and Svero could still march proudly into the city and negotiate a peace settlement. Milanovic had made a discreet call to Rawlins and had briefed him in advance; the American General said he understood completely and would pander to their egos. He stated that he could not guarantee that the settlement would be favourable to them but Sefer was quite sure that neither man would have been able to tell the difference; they certainly wouldn't once Steve Rawlins had worked his magic.

It took a little longer than forty eight hours to complete the technicalities which both sides required to allow them to sit down with each other but eventually, on the twentieth of September, N.A.T.O. confirmed that all conditions had been met on their side. They formally stood down all forces and terminated 'Operation Deliberate Force' against the Bosnian Serbs. General Svero and General Galic marched down the mountainside with their aides, accompanied by Colonel Milanovic. They were escorted to N.A.T.O. headquarters by Drazen Itsakovic, where they were greeted by General Rawlins. All four men entered the conference room, which was already occupied by Danvor Itsakovic and his two Lieutenants. The Bosniaks took one side of the table, while the two Bosnian Serb Generals and Colonel Milanovic took the other. General Rawlins took the chair. The war was over.

General Rawlins did a sterling job pandering to his guests. Never one to stand on ceremony or exaggerate his own importance, he dropped hint after hint and allowed the Bosnian Serbs to come up with the solutions, always following up with an, 'why didn't I think of that' type of remark. At times Milanovic was downright embarrassed but the two Serbs seemed to love it. Were they aware that the real negotiations would take place elsewhere and that this was really just a holding operation? Perhaps they were but he didn't think so. The Bosniaks did make some token demands but both sides rapidly agreed a way forward and the cease fire was permanent within a few hours. Both sides then tentatively shook hands and General Rawlins invited all of them to dinner. Not surprisingly, all refused and withdrew to their own separate headquarters. They might agree to a cease fire but it would be some time before they would break bread or raise a glass together.

Chapter 45

Even though they had only been separated this time for a few weeks, the reunion was as emotional and as traumatic as the first one, perhaps even more so. The huge relief Drazen had felt when he had finally been reunited with his wife and daughter in the Catholic convent had been tempered by the realization that they were still not out of danger. Now when Sonja and Diana flew in from Zagreb, he was overcome with emotion. For Sonja, the few weeks she had spent in Croatia were arguably worse. She had found a husband whom she had believed to be dead but her joy was short lived as he had been snatched away from her almost instantly to fight for the resistance. She had had no way of knowing if she would ever see him again or of how long the war would last. When they arrived back at the apartment which had been Drazen's childhood home, now reoccupied again, Emir, Drazen's Mother, took little Diana away to play as the little girl could not figure out why her Father and Mother kept bursting into tears. They had been through such severe trauma over the previous two months but it was the knowledge that the conflict was finally over that seemed to herald an outpouring of emotion. When Drazen had found Sonja in the convent, they had had only one night together and had just clung to one another. Now they made love with a passion and an abandon they never knew they had. Each new morning that they woke up, they thanked God that they still had each other. They were staying with Danvor and Emir and little Diana was never too far away, which was how they wanted it. Neither of them spoke about it but despite their happiness, there was always a shadow which hung over them; as if a part of them was missing; and of course it was.

Drazen had initially wanted to scour the countryside to search for his son but his Father had warned him against it. Cease fires or truces rarely meant what they said and it would be some time yet before all guns would fall silent and the countryside would be safe again. Drazen could not understand this but General Rawlins and the others assured him that his Father was correct; there were probably very many people still out there who wanted to settle old scores and were still willing to do it even though they had agreed to lay down their arms.

"Believe you me Drazen," Steve Rawlins had said, "I've been involved in conflict resolution all over the world and it's never over when they say it's over. If the hate between the Serbs and the Bosniaks and the Croats goes as deep as I believe it does, these people will take every opportunity they can get to put one over on their neighbours. You see, it might be a long time before they get another chance. And I'm not differentiating between sides; as far as I can see, there have been huge injustices perpetrated by each ethnic group. There's no official police or agreed rule-of-law in place yet so you'd need to be careful out there."

He was right up to a point in that several hundred breaches of the cease fire were reported in the first days but these eventually faded to a trickle and a week in, had disappeared entirely. It was Drazen's view that the citizens on all sides were weary and worn out from the conflict and he was probably correct. Hate had dissipated and was replaced with exhaustion. The country was drenched in blood. Later it would emerge that a staggering three hundred and forty five thousand people had lost their lives.

The country would never be the same. Whether they wanted to or not, it was unlikely that the different ethnic groups would ever live with each other or ever trust each other again.

But that was for the peace makers and the diplomats to resolve; Drazen's priority was to search every square metre of the countryside to try to find his son. He had discussed the initial taking and transportation of the people by the Bosnian Serb militias with Sonja and they both agreed there was a strong possibility that Drazen's Grandmother, Edita, might still be alive. She had initially been on the bus with Sonja, Diana and Zoran. The boy had been taken off at Tišća. Sonja and Diana had then been segregated from Edita at the next checkpoint. Sonja wasn't sure of the name of the village but it should be easy to trace. At that point, Edita had still been on the bus; Sonja had thought they had been heading for Sarajevo but in retrospect, that had only been a rumour. She had eventually been hand picked for one of the rape camps; where the bus carrying Edita and the others had gone, she had no idea, but the odds were strongly against Sarajevo; it was more likely destined for Tuzla. If Edita were still alive, would she know anything about Zoran's whereabouts? It was unlikely but Drazen was willing to try. What neither he or Sonja would admit, though both thought it, was that there was probably a much higher possibility of Edita being alive than Zoran. Casting the thought from his mind, Drazen resolved to set out from Sarajevo just ten days after the cease fire had been agreed. Even though Sonja had begged him to let her accompany him, he refused absolutely. He was supported by Danvor and Emir on this. Even though it was heartbreaking to be separated from his loved ones so soon again, he knew he had to try. It could still be dangerous and he would be accompanied by two other Bosniak resistance men who were on a similar quest. They would have a vehicle and they would be armed. Drazen and Danvor stressed to Sonja that it would be madness to bring a woman and a child. She protested and said Diana could stay with Emir and Danvor but still Drazen held firm. Although he never said it, she knew what he was thinking; if anything happened to him, at least his wife and daughter would be safe. If she went with him and something were to go wrong, Diana would end up an orphan. With a heavy heart, she eventually relented.

Next morning, Drazen met with his two fellow travellers. He was delighted to see that one of them was Hasan Munic, his old friend from the forests, who had commanded the ill fated column that he had stumbled upon in the hills. Hasan had come to Sarajevo in the last days of the siege to help the resistance. Miraculously, his wife and child had survived the long trek over the mountains and were now safe with relatives in Tuzla. Hasan was going back there to meet them but he was also attempting to locate the rest of his family including his parents and grandparents, his sister and her husband, none of whom he had heard from in over a year. Both men embraced warmly and Hasan introduced Samir, who was heading to Tuzla to attempt to locate his wife and children. Realising that the man was in a far worse position than himself, as he had not seen his wife and two boys for over a year, Drazen immediately agreed to travel to Tuzla first. All three men resolved to stay together until they were absolutely certain that the danger had passed and they could move freely again. Hasan had managed to get hold of an old jeep which although used during the war, did not have any military markings or insignia. All three men dressed in civilian clothes; the war was over; no point in giving the impression otherwise or drawing attention to themselves. Hasan drove and they very quickly cleared the city limits. Even in the short time that had elapsed, some semblance of normality was beginning to return. The permanent road blocks with their reinforced blast-proof concrete barriers were still there of course, but a path had been cleared around them and traffic was moving normally again. In some cases, heavy lifting equipment had been brought in to clear some of the larger obstacles. When they emerged into the countryside, he was pleased to see that there was even some work going on in the fields. Now that they were no longer in danger of being attacked or worse still, rounded up and shot, some farmers were taking advantage of the still dry sunny weather to bring in a late harvest.

But the country was pock marked with the remnants of war. It wasn't just Sarajevo that lay in ruins. Most small villages were still intact but the evidence of the conflict was everywhere. Roads were damaged; bridges had been broken; great holes caused by shell fire could be seen at regular intervals. What could not be seen was the blood that had been spilled or the bodies of the dead, most no doubt bulldozed into mass graves like the one that had been intended for him. After they had driven over half the journey, Drazen realised he had seen the farm workers because he had looked for them. Sadly, the vast majority of the fields lay untouched; most would not be harvested this year; some might be the following year but probably by different ethnic groups. He shook his head as he viewed the wealth of food lying untouched; it could not be helped; they had enough food for now and he had a far more important task to undertake.

They reached Tuzla in just over two hours. On the way, Hasan had stopped and given some hitch hikers a lift; it transpired that they were on a similar mission. When they reached the country's second city, the extent and the scale of the task they were undertaking became evident. They were not alone; displaced persons were everywhere, shell shocked, disoriented, traumatized, beaten down, defeated. All were seeking family members; wives, children, parents, brothers, sisters, the list was endless. They were told that the same pattern was repeated all over eastern Bosnia. Everywhere, Bosniaks roamed the country looking for their relatives. Unfortunately, the vast majority would be disappointed. Their loved ones were dead and gone; indeed, most of their graves would never be discovered. Families that had been thriving, living, breathing testament to the future were no more; wiped out; the survivors' lives blighted and any hope they held of happiness shattered forever.

Drazen spent the rest of the day combing Tuzla with Hasan and Samir. Hasan's wife had already been searching for their relatives but hadn't been successful in tracing any of them. Neither was there any sign of Samir's wife and two boys although the man was not despondent. His boys had been young he said and would surely not have been taken by the Serbs. Perhaps his wife had taken them into hiding. He resolved to try again the following day. Hasan was similarly upbeat even though his wife had come up empty. As they ate their evening meal, prepared by Tatjana, Hasan assured Drazen that this would be no easy task. Hundreds of thousands of people had been moved around the country and records were sketchy and in some cases didn't exist at all.

"But surely now that the war is over, displaced people will return to their own towns and villages and the issue can be sorted out quickly?" Drazen said.

"Not necessarily", said Hasan. "Very many won't know the war is over. How could they? They are hiding in the mountains and in the forests and in the fields".

"And what will happen to them when the winter comes?"

"Drazen, my friend: The war has lasted three years. I daresay there are people in those mountains who have survived more then one winter already."

Drazen's eyes widened; despite all he had been through, he was still naïve and now he felt stupid. Of course, the war had been on since 1992. He had been so wrapped up in his own world back on his little farm that he had let the outside world pass him by. That had always been his way; he had always eschewed the big city for the simple pleasures of country life.

"Yes of course Hasan." he said. "Forgive me; I'm afraid I still have much to learn about this war."

Hasan smiled, showing white teeth against his almost ebony skin. "Don't be discouraged my friend. This is going to be a long process and yes, I will be the first to acknowledge that thousands, no, hundreds of thousands have been killed. Therefore it is logical to assume that millions of people will not see their family members again and will be disappointed. But there are many people still out there and it is our task to find them and if we can, reunite them with their families. Hopefully some of them will be our own." he added as an afterthought.

Drazen nodded his agreement, then he rose and thanked Tatjana for the excellent meal; but he then excused himself on the pretext that he was tired and they had another busy day tomorrow.

He had always known his search would be difficult if not impossible. People search for loved ones all the time but this was different; this was the aftermath of a bloody war. He fought his rising panic and despair and clung to some hope. He thought of his long quest to find Sonja and Diana and he had succeeded; but no one had tried to kill them, he thought. Then he remembered what Sonja had had to go through and he felt guilty in a confused sort of manner. The more he thought about his position, the more depressed he became until he eventually fell into a troubled sleep.

Chapter 46

Samir suggested a visit to one of the outlying villages where refugee camps had been set up for the displaced, the traumatized, the abused and in many cases, the starving. Hasan warned both men that while the camps were staffed with well meaning agency workers and U.N. personnel, some of them were harrowing to visit, peopled as they often were with those who were beyond hope or help. Bosnia was going to have massive mental health issues in the coming years he assured them. They drove the short distance to Zivinice and turned off the main road to where, in the distance, they could see a vast expanse of tents and temporary dwellings. There was a sentry at the gate but one could come and go as they pleased. The entire place seemed to be totally disorganized and overcrowded. The sentry waved them through when he saw their papers but Hasan asked him where he might find the camp commander, apparently a French man called Jean Baptiste Blanc. Hasan had called ahead and set up an appointment. They were directed to the centre of the camp where they found a series of Nissen huts that had seen better days but were serviceable. In the middle of these was an office, with all manner of people coming and going. They found the French man easily enough, as he was the only one in sight with pale skin and blonde hair. He was surprisingly young and fresh faced; Drazen would have put him in his late twenties but perhaps he was older. He was dressed in blue jeans, a casual jacket and a "Medecins Sans Frontieres' tee shirt and he was surrounded by people making all sorts of enquiries of him.

"Dr Blanc?" Hasan enquired. The Doctor nodded, pointed to the outer office and held up three fingers. He just had to deal with a small issue and he would join them outside. He was as good as his word and came to join them presently. He had a pleasant smile and he offered warm firm hand shakes to all three men.

"Welcome gentlemen," he said. "Please forgive the chaos. We are not as disorganized as we might seem. We have a lot of people and a lot going on here and I am delighted to report, we have had very many reunions here already. Yes, many people come here looking for their relatives and they don't find them so they move on to the next camp but many are successful also so don't be despondent." The Doctor had a very sunny disposition. Drazen appreciated the man's help but it was obvious that he had not been here

for the worst excesses of the war. A pleasant looking dark haired middle aged lady with a slightly harassed look then approached the group and nodded to Dr. Blanc.
"Ah Maria, come and meet our guests."
The Doctor quickly handled the introductions and got down to business.
"Now gentlemen, Maria here is the finest records clerk I have ever come across. Believe it or not, she has managed to obtain the names of all of our inmates here, all seven thousand of them, even those with slightly diminished capacities. Some have official documents and some do not but Maria has catalogued them all. She has even segregated them by age, sex, region and town and of course by family name. Now we realize that not everyone will give us their correct names; even though the war is over, it takes some people longer than others to trust again but we respect that. All are welcome here and may stay for as long as they wish. Now gentlemen, as you can imagine, I have a very full schedule so can I suggest that initially you go with Maria here to look at her records to see if any of your family members are our guests. If you are not successful in finding them, you are more than welcome to take a good look around the camp. As you can see, very many people have taken us up on this offer. That is probably why our camp seems so chaotic."
The three men readily agreed and thanked Dr. Blanc warmly. He promised that he would see them again before they left and hurried away to meet his next visitors.

All three men went with Maria but very quickly established that none of their relatives were in this camp, at least they were not listed in Maria's excellent computerized listings. Hasan saw the look on Drazen's face and smiled.

"Do not be discouraged my friend." he said. "This is but one of hundreds of camps all over the country. We will look in them all if we have to. Then I am sure there are hundreds if not thousands of displaced persons who have not taken refuge in any organised camp."

"You are right of course Hasan." Drazen replied. "Let us go and search through the camp and we may be more fortunate."

They set off in different directions, having agreed they would meet again in two hours. It was still early morning and there was another camp situated in Banovici, to the south west that Hasan wanted to visit in the afternoon. This camp was apparently run by an American and Hasan had also made contact with him.

Despite the size of the camp, Drazen made his way through it fairly quickly. He reckoned that within an hour, he had scanned everyone in the crowd; it was easy enough as he could rule out all women, children and older people. There were a few young boys but there was no one who looked remotely like his son. But Hasan's words had calmed him and he was still upbeat. It could be a long search; he was prepared for that. He saw a canteen serving food and queued with some of the refugees. The food was being served by a combination of U.N. personnel and Bosniak natives. The meal served was substantial and wholesome. He ate heartily and spoke to many of his fellow diners, openly telling them of his quest. Most were in a similar position although some were trying to make their way back to other parts of the country and were just using the camp as a stopping-off point. As they sat sipping coffee after their meal, Drazen produced photographs of his son. The others scanned the photos intensely, genuinely trying to help but none had seen the boy. A man called Milan asked about his own plight and Drazen recounted his experience of surviving the Srebrenica massacre. Milan was from Potocari and Drazen knew that it had been the next town to fall.

"You know," Milan said, "Srebrenica is what changed the war or rather the fact that it was publicised but what many are not aware of is that it was as bad in Potocari the following day. Those bastards got a lust for blood and they were crazed when they reached our town. You know of course that many fled Srebrenica and came to us seeking refuge; also, the Serbs had transported many people the previous day and left them with us."

Drazen was suddenly interested, hoping his son might have been among them.

"Go on, tell me more." he said.

"Well," Milan said, By the evening of 11 July, approximately twenty thousand Bosniak refugees from Srebrenica were gathered in Potočari, seeking protection within the UN compound there. Several thousand had pressed inside the compound itself, while the rest were spread throughout the neighbouring factories and fields. Though the vast majority were women, children, elderly or disabled, all of whom had been brought there in buses by the Serbs, we estimated that there were at least three hundred men inside the perimeter of the UN compound and at least eight hundred men outside. The Dutch refused them entry, claiming their base was full. Conditions in the town were deplorable. There was very little food or water available and the July heat was stifling. The people were panicked, they were scared, and they were pressing against each other and against the UN soldiers that tried to calm them. People that fell were trampled on. It was a chaotic situation. God knows how many were killed in that way alone. They were afraid the Serbs were going to come and kill them all and they felt they had nowhere to go. I don't know how they survived the night but they did. Next day, on 12th July, as the day wore on, the refugees in the compound could see Serb militia men setting houses and haystacks on fire. Throughout the afternoon, Serb soldiers in civilian clothes infiltrated the crowd and many men were killed. I myself saw thirty bodies heaped up behind the transport building, alongside a tractor-like machine. My friend says he saw a soldier slay a child with a knife in the middle of a crowd. He also said that he saw Serb soldiers execute more than a hundred Bosnian Muslim men in the area behind the zinc factory and then load their bodies onto a truck. Soldiers were picking people out of the crowd and taking them away. Another friend told me how three brothers, one merely a child and the others in their teens, were taken out in the night. When the boys' mother went looking for them, she found them with their throats slit. That night, Serb soldiers came into the camp and raped some of the women. This happened in the close vicinity of Dutch U.N. peacekeepers who did nothing to prevent it. My friend says a Serb soldier told a mother to make her child stop crying, and when it continued to cry he took it and slit its throat, after which he laughed. He and his colleagues then raped the woman. Stories about rapes and killings spread through the crowd and the terror in the camp escalated. Several individuals were so terrified that they committed suicide by hanging themselves or cutting their wrists."

Despite everything he had been through and what Sonja had told him, Drazen was shocked and astounded again. The man was recounting the story in a deadpan fashion, clearly making no effort to embellish it. A woman who had been sitting at the table added:

"Have you ever heard of the ultras? I mean the Serbian ultra-nationalists." The men nodded. "They were the ones who really caused it. They acted like programmed robots," she said. "They had no human feelings at all. They murdered, they pillaged, they raped and they burned. Many of them were mercenaries from Russia and Ukraine or criminals Milosevic had released from Serbian prisons. They incited some of the local Serbs. They wanted to spread hatred among us. They might have succeeded for a short time but they won't in the longer term. The Serbs and the Croats and the Bosniaks of Bosnia are one people and one day we'll live together again, as we always have."

Drazen was encouraged by the woman's positivity and he asked: "Will it happen even after all the barbarity and bloodletting?"

"We won't forget, but we will forgive," she said. "The process has already begun. We are not all Bosniaks here you know. There are Serbian families living in this camp on the other side of the corridor from us. We help each other, we go for food together. The war was not their fault but that of bigots like Karadzic and Milosevic. We will recover and live together again. Bosnia has always been like that. But if you want to hear what we are really bitter about, it is the people who promised to protect us and then betrayed many of our people. They had security zones, no-fly zones overhead and the Blue Helmets of the UN in their armored cars but the Serbs kept on murdering us. In the end, we had to defend ourselves."

Emboldened by the open discussion, Drazen asked:

"Were any more of you it Potocari or maybe in Tišća or that region? I am looking for my son, a boy of thirteen, who was taken also."

He stopped, suddenly embarrassed at the sea of sympathetic faces that surrounded him. The crowd had grown as they had listened to the various accounts of the war. Suddenly, it was quiet and then an old man spoke up:

"I am not sure I can help you my friend but I will try. My name is Fikret Vuvojevic and I am from a village close to Tišća. I heard many stories during the war, some relating to boys captured by the Serbs but I have no idea who the boys were or where they had come from, do you see?"

"Yes, yes, of course," Drazen said, anxious for the man to continue. "This would have been around the eleventh or twelfth of July last year."

"Hmm, yes, well I can't be very accurate on dates but it may well have been around the times of the massacres. What I heard was that the Serbs had captured so many men, women and children that they didn't know what to do with them. Confusion reigned as to whether they were to shoot them all or just the men. Then no one was sure as to up to what age they were supposed to dispose of people. It is appalling I know, but these were soldiers trained to obey orders you see and their commanders wanted to get it right so they apparently contacted their headquarters. Well anyway, sadly, word came back to kill all males and to treat the females as they liked. I heard that checkpoints had been set up in the village for all traffic. A bus arrived laden with young boys who had been taken from other buses. The bus was stopped at the checkpoint and an officer directed the driver towards a nearby school where many other prisoners were being held. At the school, there was more confusion and a soldier on a field telephone appeared to be transmitting and receiving orders. Sometime around midnight, the boys were loaded onto a truck with many other men who had their hands tied behind their backs. They did not bother tying up the boys. At one point the truck stopped and a soldier on the scene said: 'No no, not here. Take them up there, where they took people before.' The men and boys became suspicious and when the truck reached another stopping point, some of the boys jumped off and ran away to hide in the forest. Shortly afterwards, they heard continuous shooting which they presumed was the execution of the men who had remained on the lorry."

Drazen was so excited, he could not contain himself:

"But what became of the boys, do you know?"

The old man cleared his throat and chose his words carefully.

"I'm not sure. I know of another story but I don't know if it concerns the same boys you see. Well, as I say, the boys hid in the forest. Now, a few nights later, the RS Army captured a number of Bosniaks. I believe four children aged between eight and fourteen were captured by the Bratunac Brigade and taken to the military barracks in Bratunac. I am afraid I have no knowledge of the fate of the boys. I am sorry. I do know that the next day, an RS soldier was killed trying to recapture some of those in the forest. Thereafter, the Zvornik Brigade was called in and told to clean up the area and execute anyone found but I am not sure if they captured anyone. I'm sorry, that is all I know. I hope this is of some help to you."

Drazen thanked the man profusely. His story was not definitive but it nonetheless offered hope. Boys had escaped; he could only hope Zoran had been one of them. At the last minute, he remembered his manners.

"And what of you Fikret Vuvojevic," he said. "What is your story and whom do you seek?"

The old man's eyes suddenly seemed to sink back into his skull and he looked very old. It was as if someone was draining the life blood from him. He sat quietly and said nothing for a time.

"I am sorry if I intruded," Drazen said.

"No, no, I am sorry, of course I will tell you my story but I am afraid I am living in this camp because I have no home to go to any more. It was burned out by the Serbs two years ago. My son-in-law was shot dead trying to defend it and I was badly beaten. My daughter and my two beautiful grand-daughters were taken away and I have not seen them since."

The old man's eyes misted over and he became very sad.

"Perhaps they were taken to some of the other camps," Drazen said. "They would be free now." Fikret nodded.

"Yes, you speak the truth my friend and bad as those camps were, I now wish they had been taken there because there would be some chance they could come home."

The old man paused again. Even though the canteen was packed, no one made a sound. All listened in awe and respect. Fikret continued:

"But I fear not because you see the rumour around our village was that the local Bosnian Serb militia chief wanted the girls for himself. They were all three very beautiful you see. I believe they were held captive by this chief for over a year. Oh, this was not unusual; I believe it happened all over the country. This man has now disappeared as he is wanted by the UN for war crimes. His house has been searched but there was no sign of my girls.

The UN people fear that he may have panicked when the war ended and ran but that beforehand he disposed of anyone who might be able to testify against him. I am afraid that at this stage, all we are looking for are graves."

The man's voice tailed off. For the second time that morning, Drazen was so upset that he could not speak. He was not alone. He saw harrowed looks all around him. The old man just sat quietly. Drazen went to him and they embraced.

"Thank you so much for the information," he said. "It has given me new hope. I really hope you find your girls."

The old man just nodded silently and they parted.

Chapter 47

March 1996, seven months later:

He is seated in the main square of Srebrenica having coffee; Spring has come and the trees are beginning to turn green; the snow has been melted now for over three weeks and is but a distant memory; the grass has recovered its strength after being beaten down all winter by the heavy snow, but it is now asserting itself again. Small flower buds struggle to survive in the crisp March wind but their very presence offers new hope. But will there be any new hope for him? He has kept a careful account in his head and he is sure that this is his two hundred and thirty fourth day searching. He is due to have another meeting, yet another interview; the relentless and never ending and seemingly hopeless task must continue. Everywhere he has looked has led nowhere. Every avenue he has pursued has been a dead-end. But his journey has not been without hope; there have been times when he imagines that his son is close but each time, his hopes are dashed again as the trail proves false or leads nowhere. He has travelled the length and breadth of the country. He thinks he has been in every camp. His colleagues are spread across the different locations also and they have had as much luck as he. They decided months back that it was best to pursue their own individual searches. Now that the country is peaceful, there is ease of movement for everyone and there is a slow recovery although much of it is still in chaos. He hasn't always been alone; sometimes his father comes with him; sometimes his wife will accompany him. At times, he even brings his little daughter. He likes spending time with her so he will bring her when he thinks the stories won't be too sordid. If he feels they are becoming so, he will ask her to go and play with some of the other children. He is grateful for that; at least a child can play innocently again in Bosnia, not like little seven-year-old Nermin Divovic, who was shot dead by a sniper in Sarajevo in 1994 while innocently playing in the street. Who could have done such a thing, he has pondered a thousand times. What sort of a monster? What form of hatred must one possess to actually line up the cross hairs of a powerful automatic weapon on the little head of an innocent young boy and to then pull the trigger, killing him instantly and leaving him lying in the street in a pool of blood. Each time he recalls the story, it chills him to the marrow when he thinks of his own young child. He thinks of the stories he has heard about the Nazis and about Stalin's Russia; but surely they could not have been as cruel as this? This is just one story he has heard directly from the families involved. He has heard accounts of the war now from at least a thousand people –

all are anxious to have their story told; all anxious that someone hear about the shocking deeds that were perpetrated. He has heard the story of the butcher from Visegrad who had one of his own hooks pushed down his throat. It was tied by rope to the back bumper of a car and they dragged him through the town so people could see him and hear his cries. Then they beheaded him and played football with his head. Finally they threw his remains into the river. He had heard of a man who had had his arms hacked off and was forced to drink his own blood. He was also beheaded and thrown in the river. He had heard of over three hundred people pushed into a Mosque in Gorazde and then burned alive. He had heard of girls throwing themselves out of high windows to avoid being raped and of girls running screaming from houses having been set on fire when their captors had no further use for them. Each story was more harrowing than the next and the chilling thing was that all were true and could be corroborated. He has listened carefully to all these stories and after a few weeks of searching, he decided to write them down. He was sure that better men than he would eventually write the history of the conflict but for now, he was in a unique position to record people's testimony. He had also visited the hospitals and seen horrendously mutilated patients receiving therapy treatment: the one-armed, the lame with or without crutches, a man without arms. In the ward with three seriously wounded men, a Doctor pointed out a hole opened by a shell that passed between two beds and fortunately did no explode. He has seen unbearable images of three recently admitted women: two wounded by mortar bombs, the third hit in the neck by a sniper's bullet when she was walking along laden with containers on a search for water. Each case is a story, each story an atrocity. A Croatian man walks on crutches and sits on the edge of his bed to talk. A grenade exploded right by him as he was walking down the street and he bled for a long time, but because of the bombing nobody could help him in the middle of the street. 'The Chetniks' as he refers to Serb soldiers, also a term for former World War II Serbian Nazi-collaborationists, he says, 'want to sow hatred in our hearts to prevent us from staying together. But look at this ward: the beds are occupied by me, by a Serbian, and by a Bosniak. The three of us live here like brothers'. These occasional shows of unity and reconciliation help keep him sane and provide him with hope for the future and a reason to continue his search.

But after all this, he is still no closer to finding his son. Neither has his Grandmother been found despite his and his father and mother's efforts. He sits sipping his coffee. They all know him at this stage; the man who is looking for his son. Very many people have abandoned the search for their loved ones, realizing that as the people return from the camps to their homes, the chances of finding their loved ones diminish. If the loved one is an adult male, the chances are almost zero. If it is a female and she has not been found by now, chances are close to zero. He knows he will not find his son here and that he should move on from this place but today he cannot summon up the energy. He feels an overwhelming sense of despair. He has returned to his small farm, expanded now to include his neighbour's holding. He knows his neighbour is dead because he was in the same mass grave that he himself escaped from. He will farm it until his neighbour's wife returns, if that ever happens. He is one of the very few who has braved returning to his former home. But he takes the attitude that he never had any problem with his Serbian neighbours before so he is willing to try to live together again. They are initially hesitant as he is the only Bosniak who has returned but they soon accept him. These are gentle people, farming folk. Some may have got caught up in the fervour whipped up by the militias but if they did, they are not saying. All has now returned to a level of normality. His immediate neighbour has faithfully looked after his few cows and gladly returns them to him. His house is untouched; no Serbs have been moved here although he understands they may have occupied other holdings. His home is still his home. It was always a small dwelling but they never found it restrictive. There was enough room for all of them and the house was always full of life, love and laughter. Now it seems large and empty somehow. His wife and daughter are there and he thanks God in his every waking moment for sparing them; but it is still not the same; he misses his Grandmother rising before everyone to prepare breakfast and his Grandfather sitting at the head of the table dispensing advice and wisdom to anyone who was willing to listen, and indeed he often did. But every generation passes; it was the natural order of things and he would recover from it. The one hollow in his life, in his entire being was the absence of his son. No amount of forced good humour or cheer would fill it. Alcohol helped for a time but it was a false help; a fool's paradise and he didn't intend to go down that route. No, he preferred to keep his emotions raw and on edge; he hoped it would give him the courage and the drive to keep on looking even when everyone else had given up their searches and all hope had been abandoned. But not today; today he could just about summon the energy to order a cup of coffee. He knew he was neglecting his farm; his wife was covering for him and some of his Serb neighbours helped out from time to time, perhaps out of guilt. But he knew he would have to come to a decision soon. The planting season would be here in a few weeks and he knew he couldn't face it. They had all received emergency food aid from some of the agencies who had descended on Bosnia after the war. But this had tailed off and it would soon be his responsibility to plant the crops that would feed his family again. The thought of doing this work alone drove him into a deeper abyss than he was already in and he just seemed to stare ahead, at nothing, for a long time.

A man asks him if it is OK to join him at his table. He acquiesces with a wave of his hand. The man is dressed in blue jeans and a white tee shirt with the words 'United Nations' written on it in bright blue. He is accompanied by a dark haired woman. The man seems familiar somehow but he hardly notices him; he is too deep into his depression to bother to wrack his brain to think where he has seen the man before. What difference would it make anyway? He seems destined to travel forever on his lonely fruitless search. The man who has joined him clears his throat and gently says:
"I am sorry to disturb you my friend but can I be of any help to you?"
Drazen blinks, shakes his head and slowly pulls himself into the present.
"Sorry, I was distracted, what did you say?"
"I asked if I could help you."
"With what?"
"With your quest my friend; sorry, you do not appear to recognise me. You are Drazen Itsakovic, yes?"

Drazen blinked again and eyed the man carefully.
"Ah, Colonel, I am sorry. I did not recognise you without your uniform, but what brings you to Srebrenica?"
"First of all, you can drop the Colonel. I am no longer a Serbian Army Officer, for now anyway. I requested a two-year leave-of-absence and they almost tripped over themselves to grant it. I think they were delighted that I wasn't coming home to be honest, as anyone associated with this war is tainted and quite frankly an embarrassment to Belgrade now. But my apologies, I have been very rude. I haven't introduced my friend: Please meet Selma."
Drazen smiled and nodded at the lady who offered her hand. He took it warmly. He noticed for the first time that she was quite tall and very attractive.
"You haven't met Selma before but your wife has. I met Selma by accident in the days immediately following the cease fire when I travelled the country trying to convince the remaining outposts of Bosnian Serbs that it was over. Selma was among a large number of women being held in a Serb prison camp that was in the process of being abandoned when we arrived."
Drazen's mind spun as he recalled Sonja's story. He was immediately overcome with emotion as he realized who the woman was. She looked exactly as Sonja had described. He suddenly felt guilty for his moping and depressed state. Compared to this woman, he had suffered nothing in the war; his privations were inconsequential. He stood, looking sheepish, with tears streaming down his cheeks. Selma smiled and embraced him.
"I am so sorry," he said. "I did not know who you were. I owe you so much."
Selma smiled again, "you owe me nothing; you have suffered also; we have all suffered much. All we can do is

to try to move on and rebuild. Sefer and I are doing our own little bit for Serb-Bosniak relations," she said, as she winked.

Drazen felt even guiltier; this woman was incredible. Her attitude and her sheer courage, despite all she had endured, gave him renewed strength. Sefer said:

"Do not be upset Drazen. We have all been through a desperate trauma. I decided that in all conscience I could not return to Serbia without making some effort to help to repair the damage done to this country."

"But you were just a military adviser; the atrocities were not your fault."

Milanovic shrugged: "I advised the people who carried out most of them. I have seen much. That is part of the reason why I can help. Selma and I are working with the U.N. trying to trace the location of some of the graves."

He noticed Drazen wince and he put his hand on his shoulder:

"Don't worry my friend; we try to trace the living also and we have had some success already so don't be despondent. I have to be honest with you though; almost half a million people lost their lives in this war so very many people who are searching will find no trace at all of their relatives; the lucky ones will find their graves; the very lucky will find their loved ones alive."

Drazen was still overcome with emotion but he nodded silently.

"We are aware of your quest Drazen," Selma said. "We would be willing to help you if you would work with us?"

Drazen immediately jumped up:

"Of course, anything; tell me what to do?"

Sefer then briefed him on their work. They had just begun work on uncovering the mass grave in Srebrenica and they wanted Drazen, as the only eye witness that they knew of, to assist them. They knew where one of the graves was but as Sefer explained, it wasn't that simple.

"To be honest Drazen, I didn't see very much of the actual killing but I am not for a moment suggesting that I wasn't aware of it happening. I was and it sickened me to my stomach. Do you remember that first night when our eyes met in that bar?"

Drazen nodded.

"Well, I knew you were a Bosniak but I tell you I was glad. If only one person had survived, it cheered me. I wished you well and I did not report you."

"Yes, I realize you must have kept quiet," Drazen said, 'and I thank you.'

"But that is not what we came here to discuss," Sefer said. "You know where the main mass grave site is located but there are many others. Drazen, there are hundreds of these graves all across the country. It will take years and even then, I doubt all of them will be found. If it is not too harrowing for you, would you be willing to accompany us to the site?"

"Yes of course, I will, and you will need some DNA from my grandfather I presume, and I should be able to get some from many of my neighbours also."

Sefer and Selma both nodded and thanked him. Drazen waved them away.

"There is no need for thanks. We all need to work together now to build a future where we can live together. Sensible people all over the country have been saying this to me also so it is encouraging. But I am sorry, I have forgotten my manners. Where are you staying?"

"We have a room in a small hotel here in town."

"Well go and cancel it straight away because you are both coming home with me and staying in my house. Sonja would be very upset with me if I didn't persuade you so that is an order Colonel." All three smiled.

Chapter 48

Sonja's initial reaction was one of shock but then she rushed to embrace Selma. Both women clung to each other for a long time. Diana was out playing with her new puppy and Drazen ushered Sefer on to the balcony for a smoke, leaving the women their privacy. He also brought a bottle of slivovitz and two shot glasses. Several cigarettes and shots of liquor later, they staggered back into the house. Sonja and Selma were still weeping freely, sitting together holding hands. But their tears were now joyful and both women were laughing.

"I think my wife has found a new sister," Drazen said and Sefer nodded. He went to get a drink for the women but he noticed Sonja had opened a bottle of local wine and both of them had filled glasses. Sonja insisted on preparing a full dinner and Selma said she would not stay unless she was allowed to help. The men offered to assist but were dismissed. Both women disappeared into the kitchen and Drazen poured more slivovitz.

"May I be so bold as to raise a toast to your son and to your quest to locate him," Sefer said.

"Of course my friend; do you know, I think you came along at just the right time. I was feeling very depressed today and I didn't even go to meet the man I had arranged to speak to."

"I'm sorry, that was probably because we approached you."

"No, no, no, not at all, I was already two hours late, but it is OK. I can see the man again. I know where he lives. No, I just could not summon the energy today. I was actually about to abandon my search completely and come back here to plant some crops and take care of my animals."

"I don't believe that and I don't think you do either Drazen. From what I know of you and what you have been through, I know you will never abandon your search. You may have bad days but you will have good ones too."

"Perhaps you're right Sefer, but you and Selma really gave me a boost today."

"I'm glad, and you gave us a boost also."

The men then left the war to one side for a while and chatted about football which led to many uproarious tales both of participation in and attendance at previous matches and their aftermath. The men formed an easy relationship. It was so frustrating, Sefer thought, how a few bigots could stir up such inter-necine hatred between peoples who were essentially similar. He had always found all of the peoples of the Balkans to be more or less the same; they shared the same culture and the same interests; in fact, judging from the delicious aroma coming from the kitchen, they shared the same cuisine also.

About an hour later, Sonja and Selma emerged with delicious Cevapi, with fried potatoes and vegetables. Diana was called and ate quickly. Drazen opened another bottle of wine and poured glasses for all of them. After the initial emotion, they all sensed a growing bond between them. They talked easily right through the meal. Sonja produced Sutlijas for dessert and also served coffee at a later stage. They drank more wine and slivovitz and talked long into the night.

The atmosphere was wonderful and Sefer did not want to spoil the moment but at one stage during the night, he decided he should mention it:

"Have you heard about wanderers?"

"Do you mean people who are still in hiding or wandering through the forests or mountains?' Sonja said.

"Yes, I do. You know, some people estimate that there may be thousands still up there but our estimates in the UN are closer to hundreds. The problem with most of them is that they have no communication with the outside world so they don't know that the war is over."

"Yes, that is the tragedy," Drazen said.

"We have interviewed a lot of them," Selma said, "and most are deeply traumatized; far more so than people who lived through the war in camps or as soldiers. They are terrified of being discovered and fret all the time, moving from place to place. It is a very difficult existence."

"You would think," Sonja said, "that they would realize that hostilities have ceased now that the guns have stopped."

"Some of them did," said Sefer "and they came down; others that we spoke to just assumed that the war had moved to another part of the country and thanked God that they were safe."

"How did you eventually get them to come in or get the word to them that the war was over," said Drazen.

"Well, as you know, there is not a lot to eat in the mountains and often not even enough water. To feed themselves, the men used come down at night and take potatoes and other vegetables from the fields around the Serbian villages as all they had to eat in the mountains or the forest was leaves and slugs. The local Serb population got annoyed with losing their crops so they began to mount patrols around their villages but we persuaded them to let the UN move in and have no armed force nearby. We mounted loud speakers in strategic locations which repeatedly announced that the war was over; the guns had stopped and everyone was welcome to come down and return to normal life. The Bosniaks would generally sleep by day and wait for the cover of darkness before moving on. The fact that the messages were given at night was probably a mistake because due to previous impersonation of the UN by Serb militias, they just didn't trust us. This continued for a long time. The wanderers were clever too; they sometimes managed to take more than vegetables. The people of Milici, a village on the route to Tuzla, discovered the disappearance of livestock last November and formed an armed group to search for the thieves.

Again, we persuaded them to lay down their arms and we compensated them. Eventually most of the stragglers in that region came down from the mountain. Some of the Bosniak men were those that had fled from the Srebrenica region, similar to yourself; They returned to the area when the guns fell silent since this was familiar territory and they knew where to find food. From here, they would once again set out across the hills towards Žepa or they attempted to reach Tuzla. Some arrived in Tuzla after many months, having been wandering around the area between Srebrenica and Udrc with absolutely no sense of direction. Most were in a bad way physically and mentally. Many were emaciated and all were ravenous with hunger. The overwhelming emotion from all of them upon hearing the war was over was just relief."

"A bit like our column when we got there I guess," Drazen said.

No one voiced the thought that was in all of their heads; the hope that Zoran might be up in the hills somewhere. No one wanted to say it because in truth, all four deemed it unlikely. Eventually, Sefer averred to it in a subtle way. "You know, some people we meet have abandoned all hope but we find that the stronger individuals never give up and will keep searching until they have definite proof, in other words DNA evidence."

They all clicked their glasses and agreed that the search would continue. It was very late into the night when they eventually retired to bed. Sonja had so much to discuss with Selma that, as she said herself, they would have needed a week to catch up. The men also chatted easily and eventually finished with more cigarettes and a final shot each to finish the bottle.

On the following day, they commenced the painstaking work of excavating the mass graves of the hundreds and thousands of poor souls who had perished so cruelly in what essentially had been a pointless conflict. Although Srebrenica had only occurred eight months previously, the heat had accelerated decomposition and the only definitive way to positively identify victims was DNA. This would be a long and complex process but in the meantime, relatives could take some comfort from other indicators. A tin of cream, a cigarette lighter, prayer beads, metal tobacco cases, combs, a personal document in a pocket, a shard of bone, a tooth. Each of these objects represented a person, officially missing, now presumed dead. When later confirmed by DNA, at least it gave closure to the person's family, that was where there was any family left to mourn. Although it was gruesome work, Sefer, Selma, Drazen and Sonja undertook it willingly and took their reward from the solace which was provided to the families. Drazen was invaluable in identifying dozens of victims from scraps of clothing and other personal effects. They were later easily verified by DNA. After they had unearthed all they could in Srebrenica, they moved on to Potocari. Experts had been searching the area for months with detection equipment for identifying human remains. They had discovered even more graves than had been found in Srebrenica spread over a wider area although thankfully with not as many victims. None of them had known anyone in Potocari so they enlisted the help of local people. Drazen sought out the old man Fikret Vuvojevic, who was now living in his partially reconstructed dwelling in Tisca. Fikret knew many from Potocari. Sadly, he had not located his daughter or granddaughters. He readily agreed to assist the team in identifying the bodies. Even though he was a broken man, Drazen felt the work, gruesome as it was, was in a way therapeutic and helped Fikret to cope with his grief.

He had continued with his search for Zoran, painstakingly following up on each lead regardless of how small. These were becoming less frequent now as the country slowly returned to normal and people settled back into their homes. The country had effectively split into three separate states but all needed to co-operate with each other to survive. Ethnic cleansing had left its ugly mark and there were large tracts of the country in the east now where there were no Bosniaks. In the west, there were large areas where there were no Serbs. As far as anyone knew, most of the wanderers had come down from the hills. There were probably a few diehards still holding out but no one knew for sure. As the weeks and months passed and he became busier and busier with the exhumations and he saw the dreadful burdens many people had to bear, the pain eased and he slowly began to accept that maybe it wasn't meant to be. He never said this to Sonja and he placed it in God's hands. Part of him wanted to still believe but he had been disappointed so often that he barely dared to hope any more. Still, he was grateful; he had a beautiful daughter and a lovely wife; his parents were still alive in Sarajevo; that was more than what fifty per cent of the country could lay claim to; that was the deep scar that the war had left.

One evening as he was finishing up for the day on one of the sites in Potocari, an old man came in seeking news of his son. Drazen was about to ask him if he could come back in the morning but at the last minute he caught himself; who knew what this man had gone through to have the courage to come here? He sat and smoked a cigarette with the man and listened to his fascinating story. The man told him that he was over eighty years old. When the Serbs had come to his farm, they had taken his two sons and his grandson. He had long since assumed that all three had been shot and was resigned to the fact. Then the strangest thing happened. One evening his door had opened and his younger son and grandson had walked in. The man had almost suffered a heart attack and died on the spot. When he recovered his composure, he had embraced his loved ones and reunited them with his daughter-in-law, the boy's mother, who had moved to the city. They all now lived together again as a big happy family. None of them had any idea of what had happened to his eldest son. While they had been taken together, they had been separated in detention centres. His younger son and grandson had managed to escape in a mass break-out from Manjaca camp and had hid in the hills ever since, constantly moving and staying on higher ground apart from at night, when they risked raids to obtain food. Drazen was fascinated; he smoked cigarette after cigarette, listening to the man's story. The man told him that he eventually felt strong enough to try to trace his eldest son. He assumed the man had been executed and was willing to provide DNA or whatever the search group needed to assist in the search. He had gotten most of his life back and he wanted to lay his other son to rest. Drazen promised him he would do his best for him but asked the man to stay a while. He explained his own situation and asked:

"Where did your son and grandson stay when they were in the mountains and did they ever meet other groups?"

"Well, you'd be better off asking them but yes, they did tell me they met other groups occasionally but it was when they met the three young men that it eventually led to them coming home."

"What young men," Drazen asked, "tell me."

"Well, you see there were about ten of them together but one day they got spooked and had to split up. My son and grandson and another man got left behind. The group were headed to Tuzla as they had heard these loud speakers saying the war was over. They wanted to believe it so they decided if they could get to Tuzla, they'd be able to tell for sure as it was a Bosniak stronghold. But then they lost contact with the other seven. They couldn't get to Tuzla without crossing the main Konjević Polje to Nova Kasaba road but were unsuccessful every time they tried. There were too many people around."

"But I crossed that road also, it's so close to my home village."

"Yes, well apparently there is an easier way to cross it undetected but they didn't know this until one day they met with three boys, just teenagers who apparently lived locally but were also in hiding. These boys escorted groups across the road all the time as they knew the easier way around. My son and grandson crossed and managed to reach Tuzla a few weeks ago. They confirmed that the war was over and then made their way back here."

"Yes, yes, I know about the secretive way too. But these boys who escorted them, where is their camp, how do you reach them?"

"I can't say; I think it is well concealed as my son only stumbled upon it by accident. But I promise you I'll bring my grandson tomorrow when I come with my son's DNA. He might know."

Drazen did not sleep a wink; he told himself he was foolish to get his hopes up again. It could be anyone up in those hills; what's more, whoever it was could be hundreds of kilometres away by now. No, the man said they were based there. He didn't mention a word to Sonja; he couldn't do it to her. If his hopes were dashed once again, they would be his alone. She had suffered enough. At six am, he eventually abandoned all hope of sleep. It was July again and the sun was already high in the sky. It would be another scorching day. The old man had said he would be there by nine. He was as good as his word. His grandson was called Allen; the boy was eighteen; he said he had a good idea as to where his erstwhile guides were hiding out but he felt it would be dangerous to approach other than from a distance. He and his father had been held at gunpoint when they had wandered into the boys hideout. Allen was willing to leave straight away to try to find it. Drazen borrowed Sefer's car but said nothing about his destination. They drove in virtual silence for an hour. The only description Allen could give was that all three boys were tall and blonde; not much use, so was half the country. When they reached Drazen's village of Konjević Polje, they took the road to Nova Kasaba and parked about three kilometres north of the town. From there, Allen led him into the heavy scrubland that was the foothills of the mountains. The boy paused several times to check his position and gauge his sense of direction. Eventually they emerged into a relatively flat but slightly sloped plateau. The surface was smooth rock. Despite living relatively close by, Drazen was not familiar with this approach to the mountains. He would have made his approach from the more sheltered northern side. They made steady progress now that the land was relatively without obstacles. Then

Allen stoppped again and looked through a pair of binoculars he had brought.

"Over there," he shouted, "I think the hide is over there." He immediately let out a long low whsitle, followed by a series of short blasts, followed by two more long whistles. "This was the signal they told us to use if we ever needed help again," he said. After a few moments, someone emerged from behind a rocky outcrop about a half a kilometre away. Allen immediately showed himself and waved at the boy who had emerged. He immediately began shouting:

"The war is over guys, has been for months. It's time to come home. I have someone here, a Bosniak who wants to meet you. He's fascinated with your story and wants to record it. Look, neither of us are armed and we have come alone. Check if you like, look around."

After a few moments, two more bodies emerged from the hide. All three began walking, slowly but steadily, towards Allen. Not wanting to scare them away, Drazen emerged slowly and followed about fifty metres behind. The boys were too far away to see yet but he didn't recognise the gait of any of the three. More cautious now, he slowed his pace. The doubts that had assailed him were back again. Why had he got his hopes up? Was he to be forever going off on wild goose chases? Allen had now reached the group; he had embraced all three and was chatting animatedly to them. Drazen had fallen at least a hundred metres behind now but as he had come this far, he decided he should meet the boys and listen to their story anyway. He quickened his pace. As he was about seventy metres out, the boy on the left said something to his friends and began to sprint towards him. The distance narrowed; sixty metres, fifty. But no, this boy was much taller and broader.

Still, it had been a year. The distance was closing rapidly now; forty metres, thirty, twenty. Drazen stopped but the boy kept coming, a worried look on his face. But he need not have worried. Drazen had only stopped to fall to his knees to give thanks. Now he stood, opened his arms and finally embraced his son.

Printed in Great Britain
by Amazon